THE

Ending

I WANT

SAMANTHA TOWLE

Jodi Marie Maliszewski, this one is yours.
And so is Liam.

My seat belt is fastened. Window shutter is down.

I have a window seat. I *hate* window seats. Because I hate flying. No, actually, that's wrong. I don't hate flying. I'm afraid of flying. So, sitting by the window with the view of clouds and sky for the next six and a half hours, reminding me that I'm thirty thousand feet off the ground, is going to be torture for me—not that I don't deserve torture. I deserve everything I have coming to me. And in the grand scheme of things, flying on this plane really doesn't matter.

But in my defense—yes, I'm defending myself against myself—fear is not rational. It doesn't give you a choice. It just is. So, yeah, I'm afraid.

Still, I know what matters is the reason that I'm on the plane. I'm going to London—the place I have always wanted to go. I'm going to see where my mother was born and grew up, where my parents met and fell in love. And, while I'm there, I'm going to complete my list.

The list.

I pull the piece of paper titled Things to Do If I Live from my bag. It's the list I wrote when I was sixteen years old, and I had a life-threatening brain tumor.

I have one of those again—a brain tumor, I mean. Well, I'm almost ninety-nine percent sure. The symptoms are here again—the severe headaches, vomiting, and fatigue. I just haven't actually gone to my doctor to have it confirmed. Because, if I do, Dr. Hart, my doctor, she will want me to have surgery and radiation therapy and take endless amounts of medication.

She'll want me to fight to live.

And I don't want that.

I just want to complete my list while on the trip I was supposed to take with my family before they died, and then…

I don't know what's at the end of that sentence. Actually, yes, I do know. *Death* is what's at the end of that sentence.

Death and relief. Relief because I'll get to be with my family again.

I plug my headphones into my cell and put the buds in my ears. I select the Music app on the screen, find the song I want, and hit play.

The sound of Coldplay's "Paradise" starts to bleed into my ears.

This song was played at my family's funeral. I listen to it regularly, not to only torture myself—because I deserve to be tortured—but also to remind myself of what I did, what I stole from my family—their lives. It's not that I need the song to remember because what I did is always there. The knowledge that my mother, father, brother, and sister all died because of me is with me every single second of each day.

But what this song does remind me of is that I will get to see my family again, and when I do see them, I'll be able to tell them how very sorry I am. I'll be able to beg them for their forgiveness.

I'll be with them again. Hear their voices and the sounds of their laughter, touch them…hold them.

It's all I want.

And, now, thanks to the tumor growing in my head, that day will be sooner rather than later.

I'm going to die. And it's a relief.

Maybe I should rename my list to Things to Do Before I Die.

Grabbing a pen from my bag, I pull the Hunter Airways brochure from the storage pocket on the seat in front of me. I put my foot up on the back of the seat and rest the brochure on my thigh. Then, I sit the paper against the brochure. I correct the title at the top of my list.

Things to Do ~~If I Live~~ Before I Die

There. That looks better. More appropriate.

Okay, so let's see if anything else on here needs to be updated.

Go to London, England.

Kiss a boy.

Kiss a boy definitely needs updating. I've kissed a boy since I wrote that.

I draw a line through it.

~~Kiss a boy.~~

Okay, what should I put there instead? What haven't I done that I want to do?

I've never kissed a stranger. That sounds like it could be fun and daring.

Perfect. I'll put that.

~~Kiss a boy.~~ *Kiss a stranger.*

Okay, what next?

Have sex.

Done that, too.

Benjamin Harley in the backseat of his dad's Toyota. It happened a month before my family died. I've not had much sex since. Benjamin and I did it a few more times after that first time.

But, when my family died, it changed things. It changed everything.

I have had the occasional meaningless one-night stand here and there over the years when I had too much to drink or the pain and loneliness was just too much to bear, but getting close to anyone wasn't something I was looking for. I'm still not. But I figure I'm dying, so I might as well go out with a bang—literally.

I draw a line through that and write…

> ~~Have sex.~~ *Have <u>LOTS</u> of sex. Have sex with a stranger. Have sex with a stranger outdoors.*

Okay, what is it with me and strangers? Kiss one. Have sex with one.

The one-night stands I had weren't complete strangers. I spent some time with them—drinking with them and learning a little about them, like what their names were—before I jumped into bed with them.

I want no-names-wild-monkey-sex-within-minutes-of-meeting-a-stranger sex.

I guess it just seems hot—the thought of having sex with a total stranger. Someone who doesn't know me. I wouldn't be Taylor, the girl who killed her entire family. Or

Taylor, the brain tumor girl. I'd just be the no-name chick, the girl to have sex with.

And the good thing is, everyone in England is going to be a stranger to me. Not that I'm going to have sex with the whole of England. Just a few guys will do.

Maybe I should add more sex things to the list.

What haven't I done?

I've never received oral sex.

Sad but true.

Every time Benjamin and I had sex, he was too busy trying to put the condom on and put his dick in the right place to worry about giving me oral sex. And the one-night stands I had were for one reason only—for me to get off as fast as humanly possible. And I wasn't exactly caring about how I got off, so long as I wouldn't have to think or feel anything for that short period of time.

But I should at least have oral sex before I die. Even if it's only one time. I don't want to die an oral sex virgin.

Next to *Have sex with a stranger outdoors*, I write…

> *Receive oral sex.*

There. That'll do it. Next…

> *Dye my hair pink. Or purple. Or any cool color.*

> *Go to a rock concert.*

> *Get drunk.*

I've done that one—hence the reason I ended up losing my virginity in the backseat of Benjamin Harley's dad's Toyota.

I put a line through that one and write next to it…

> ~~Get drunk.~~ *Get totally wasted until I vomit and pass out.*

Perfect.

Get a tattoo.

Have something pierced.

Sing in public.

Dance in the rain.

Experience a true moment of romance, like they do in the movies.

Okay, that's just plain cheesy. But, in my defense, when I wrote that, I was sixteen and thought I was going to die.

You're twenty-two and going to die.

Romantic moment stays then. Not that it's going to happen. Romance only happens between couples and people in love—and I'm not down for either of those things.

Do something that scares me.

Flying on this plane scares me. Does that count?

No, that sucks. I cross that out and write…

~~Do something that scares me.~~ Do something that terrifies me to the point of pissing my pants.

There. Perfect.

That's the end of my list.

Is there anything else I want to add? I press the tip of my pen to my lips.

A shadow falls over me. I pull the buds from my ears as I flick a glance to my left, and my eyes meet with a suit. A very nice black suit covering a really broad chest.

I drop my phone in my bag. Then, I remember my list, which is still visible on my lap. I turn the paper facedown and then place my hand on top of it.

In my peripheral, I see Suit Guy remove his jacket and stow it in the overhead compartment.

Hello, biceps. I can see them clearly through the shirt hugging them tightly.

Lucky shirt.

The guy clearly works out from the looks of it.

Suit Guy takes the seat beside me and turns to me with a smile on his face. I take in that face for the first time and—

Holy effing shit!

Hotness incarnate is sitting next to me.

Actual pure male hotness. All men should have been made to look like this. Seriously.

He looks like Clark Kent without the glasses, which would mean he looks like Superman—the Henry Cavill version.

Superman in a suit.

Lord, help me.

Dark brown hair with a natural wave to it. His nose has a slight bump, like it was once broken. Gorgeous eyes with the kind of long dark lashes that girls envy, perfect full lips, and tan skin.

He's just…hot. I can't think of another word to say—sexy, gorgeous, beautiful. Yep, he's all of those.

I'm totally unprepared for this level of hotness—well, any kind of hotness, to be honest. I'm dressed in yoga pants and a T-shirt. I wanted to be comfortable for traveling, and now, I want to slap myself.

I am not dressed to meet a man of his caliber, especially not now while I'm going to be seated next to said man for the next six and a half hours.

Honestly, I can't even remember if I put on deodorant.

Oh God, please let me have put on deodorant.

I'm trying to covertly sniff my armpits when he says, "Hello," in the most delicious British accent I've ever heard.

I hear a whooshing sound in my ears. I'm pretty sure it's the sound of a hundred panties dropping on this airplane—my own included.

Not that I haven't heard a British accent in real life before because I have. My mother was English. I've just never heard a male English accent before, except for on television.

And I've never heard *his* English accent.

Sex toy manufacturers should record his voice saying dirty things and put it into vibrators. They'd sell out in seconds.

"Hi." My word comes out strangled.

He smiles again—*God, he has a beautiful smile*—and then he glances past me to the window.

I take advantage of the moment to eye-grope him. I mean, who wouldn't? You don't see many men like this every day.

He's built and tall. His long legs barely fit in the space in front of him.

God, I want to climb him like a tree.

When I bring my eyes back to his face, he's staring at me, and he's smiling—an amused kind of smile because he knows I was totally checking him out.

I should be embarrassed, but I'm not. Because I don't care. It was totally worth getting caught just to be able to stare at him.

How the hell am I going to cope with sitting next to him for the next six hours?

My sex hormones are off the charts just from being in close proximity to him. I might need to go to the restroom and put my hand to good use just for some relief.

Or…he could be my stranger.

Now, wouldn't that be something?

"You have to have the window shutter open on takeoff," he tells me, nodding in the direction of the window, pulling me from my reverie.

I think I'm supposed to move to open the shutter, but I can't seem to function like a normal human being right now because I've had the normal knocked out of me by this English Hottie here.

And then he goes and shows me that beautiful smile again, sending my body into overdrive.

He moves forward, leaning over me—I'm guessing to open the window shutter—and I don't know what comes over me.

Maybe it's because he smells like heaven with his rich cologne and something totally masculine. Or because I haven't stopped thinking about sex since he sat next to me—well, actually, I was thinking about sex a fair bit before that also. Or maybe it's because his delicious, kissable lips are so close to mine. Or because he's just *that* hot.

But I kiss him.

I totally plant my lips on his, and I kiss him.

chapter 2

Guess my sex hormones got the better of me. Because I'm kissing a stranger.

Holy fuck! I'm kissing a stranger! What the hell am I doing?

When I wrote *Kiss a stranger* on my list, this wasn't exactly what I had in mind. Said stranger kind of had to want to kiss me, too. Not just have me plant my lips on his without his permission.

Oh God, I've just kiss-assaulted him. I'm so going to jail.

Abort mission! Abort mission!

But, oh my God, his lips feel so good and firm, like a man's should, but plump enough that I want to bite them...and he just tastes so phenomenally good. Like cinnamon and coffee and just something uniquely him.

I can't seem to part myself from him.

So, we're here, my lips stuck on his, and he's frozen in place.

All in all, this has probably lasted seconds, but it feels like hours.

Hours of his delicious lips against mine. *God, wouldn't that be something?*

This moment is *so* going in the spank bank. Even if it proves to be the most embarrassing thing I have ever done, I don't care. I'm totally revisiting it in my head later when I'm alone.

Okay, Taylor, time to move your lips off the nice, hot stranger.

I'm just readying to pull away when the craziest thing happens. English Hottie moves his mouth. His lips part on a whisper of a moan, and he starts to kiss me back.

Holy shit.

His hand touches my face. His fingers push back into my hair, getting all tangled up in it, and then he tips my head back and starts to kiss me. I mean, really kiss me.

Now, I'm the frozen one.

What do I do?

Kiss him back, you idiot! You have the hottest guy you've ever seen with his tongue in your mouth—oh God, his tongue is in my mouth…

My hand finds its way to that awesome chest of his, my fingers curling into his shirt. His chest is as hard as I thought it would be. I can feel the ridges of muscle beneath my palm.

Needing to feel more of him, I slide my other hand up his chest, feeling those awesome muscles, and over to his shoulder. I curl my hand around the back of his neck.

He groans in my mouth, and it's *the* sexiest sound I have ever heard.

Then, he starts to kiss me harder, like he's hungry and I'm the food source.

Jesus Christ. This is the hottest kiss of my life.

English Hottie's other hand comes around my waist. He unclips my seat belt without even looking, and he tugs me closer.

Of course, I go willingly.

His hand moves from my waist and lands on my thigh. He lifts my leg, putting it over his, and then he slides his hand up my leg. High.

Oh my God!

I feel close to combustion. And my vagina is getting ready to start a party all on her own.

God, this guy is good. If he can do this while we're both fully clothed, then I wonder what he could do if he had me naked in bed.

And, right now, I wouldn't be opposed to that.

Do they have beds on airplanes?

Then, the moment is suddenly broken when the intercom announcement comes on with the captain telling us there's a slight delay while we wait for another plane to take off before ours.

Our mouths part. Both of us are breathing heavy, staring into each other's eyes.

God, his eyes are amazing, really unique—a mixture of green and hazel, like a greenish gold. They remind me of autumn when the leaves are turning from green to brown.

Autumn just officially became my favorite season.

I can't remember ever feeling as turned on as I do right now.

The instant my lips connected with his, my body felt like it was doused with gasoline, and a match was struck between my legs.

And I don't think I'm alone in this. I can see the heated glare of lust in his stunning eyes.

Then, the realization of what I just did hits me.

I just mauled a complete stranger with my mouth. *Oh my God!*

I don't know whether to laugh maniacally or crawl under my seat in embarrassment.

Yanking my gaze and my leg from him, I turn in my seat and stare at the window, which I can't see out of because the shutter is still closed.

He never did get to open it because I stopped him with my kiss-crazy mouth.

I quickly slide the shutter open and stare out at the open airfield.

I can't believe I just did that. I kissed him. Holy shit!

I kissed a total stranger. A hot stranger but a stranger nonetheless.

Guess I can cross that one off my list.

A bubble of laughter climbs up my throat, but I manage to hold it in.

Really not the time to laugh, Taylor.

You just kissed the guy. You don't want him to think you're crazy.

He already thinks you're crazy. You just kiss-attacked him, moron!

And kissing a stranger who I have to sit next to for the next six hours probably wasn't the best idea.

Nice going, Taylor.

Oh, shit! What if he's married? I could have just violated a sacred bond. Forced the guy to cheat.

Turning my face a little, I surreptitiously check out his left hand, which is resting on his thigh—*he has really nice thighs*—and there's no ring.

Thank God.

But what if he has a girlfriend?

Well, he did kiss me back, so I would hope the hell not.

Still, I should probably say something. Like, *Sorry for kissing you.*

But I can still taste him in my mouth.

I touch my fingers to my lips, and I can't help but smile. At the memory of his kiss and the way he felt under my hands, a quiver happens in my belly.

It's really hard to be sorry for kissing him when he's made me feel this amazing. But I should say it anyway even if I don't mean it. It's just good manners to apologize when you've kissed a guy you don't know without any warning even if he did kiss you back.

"Um…I'm not exactly sure why I just did that." I bite my lip, unable to look him directly in the face. "I'm really sorry."

He's silent for so long that I have to look. And he looks like he's…almost offended by my words. Or maybe he's just offended by me planting my lips on his. I mean, I would be offended if a random person kissed me out of the blue. Well, maybe not if they looked like him. I would pretend to be offended, but inside, I'd totally be doing cartwheels.

His eyes meet mine, and his look sears through me. "Don't be sorry. I'm not." His hot English voice sounds all rough and sexy, making me shiver even more.

And…he's not sorry that I kissed him. Interesting.

"But you lied when you said you didn't know why you kissed me," he adds.

That gets my attention. My brows lift. "I lied?"

"Mmhmm. You know why you kissed me."

"I do?"

"It's because I'm irresistible." A smile flickers in his eyes, lighting up his whole face.

Goddamn, he's handsome.

I fight to keep the smile from mine. "Oh, is that so?"

"Yep. Strange women kiss me all the time."

"God, it must suck to be you."

"Yeah, it's hard going." He gives a dramatic sigh, that damn smile still on his face.

I stare down at my hands as a beat of silence passes between us.

"Actually," I say, "it wasn't that—not that you're not irresistible—but I kissed you because I wanted to kiss a stranger."

I lift my eyes back to him. He's still looking at me.

"Interesting thing to want to do."

"I have a whole list of things I want to do."

Why did I tell him that?

My eyes seek out my list, which is on the floor along with my pen and the Hunter Airways brochure. They must've fallen when I was busy sticking my tongue down his throat.

Leaning down, I pick them up and set them on my lap—list facedown, of course.

He stretches out in his seat and then nudges my leg with his. Heat travels from the spot he just touched, heading straight to my happy place.

"Well, I'm glad I could be of service to help you cross that off your list," he says. "If you have anything else on that list—you know, like sex in an airplane bathroom—then I will definitely be down for helping you out with that, too."

I can't help but smile. "Good to know. Thanks."

And, now, I can't stop staring at the restroom sign.

Fuck.

Well, that's exactly what I'm thinking about—or more like, him doing it to me in that restroom right there.

"You're thinking about it right now, aren't you?" he says, his voice low, like he's just read my mind.

I slide my eyes to his. My breath catches at the look in them. Lust, total lust.

I force myself to focus on anything but that lust. "Of course I'm thinking about it. You can't say something like to a person and not expect them to think about it. But thinking and doing aren't the same thing."

"No, they're not." A pause and then he says, "So, you and me in the bathroom?"

"No."

"It's off the list?"

Grinning, I shake my head. *This guy is funny. And hot. Dangerous combination.* "It was never on it," I tell him.

"Shame." He chuckles. "Damn fucking shame."

A stewardess appears beside us. She's looking down at English Hottie. "Sir, the captain asked me to come and check on you. Are you absolutely sure you don't want to be in first-class? We can make adjustments."

He stares up at her, a firm smile on his lips. "No, I'm fine here." He flickers a glance at me, which instantly heats me up on the inside, and then he looks back to her.

He's turning first-class down? Who does that?

She shifts her stance, her eyes flickering over the cabin. "Well, if you're absolutely sure. But if you change your mind, I can move you straight away. If you need anything, just call me, and I'll get it."

"I will"—I watch his eyes go to her name badge— "Sarah. Thank you."

She lingers, just staring at him, and then seems to come to. "Okay, well, I'll be back to check on you soon, sir."

Wow, the power of good looks. I don't think she even realized I was here.

"So, I guess I should formally introduce myself—you know, seeing as though we've already shared saliva. I'm Liam." He holds his hand out to shake mine.

My eyes go to his large hand. Seems weird to shake his hand after I've just had his tongue in my mouth, but what the hell?

I slip my hand into his. His hand his smooth and strong, and it dwarfs mine. He curls his long fingers around my hand and squeezes. My mouth goes dry, and my panties get wet.

"Taylor," I say, my voice sounding incredibly husky. Almost sexy. Very unlike me.

"Taylor," he repeats softly. "Beautiful name for a beautiful woman."

I laugh softly, rolling my eyes. "Smooth."

"I can be rough when I need to be."

Holy…

I actually gulp because…well, him saying those words in that English accent—hot as fuck.

"So, Taylor, with the list from Boston—"

"I never told you I was from Boston."

"You're on a flight from Boston. Call it a wild guess."

"Well, you're on a flight from Boston, but you're not from Boston." I don't know why I'm being so obtuse. But being this way with him is kinda fun.

"My English accent gave it away, huh?" He smirks. "Okay, so, Taylor, with the list, who isn't from Boston—where are you from?"

"Boston." I grin.

He lets out a deep laugh. It resounds in my chest, leaving me with a warm glowy feeling.

"You make me laugh," he tells me.

"You say that like not many people do."

His eyes pin mine. "They don't. I'm a hard man to please."

I can imagine.

"So, is that the list?" He taps a finger to the paper in my lap.

"It is." I curl my fingers around the edge of it.

"Can I see it?"

"No, you can't see it," I say, offended that he thinks he can.

"Why not? What's on there?" He's leaning closer, curiosity written all over his face.

I lean away. "Nothing. It's just private."

"I think you and I are past private. You just had your tongue in my mouth."

"So? Y-you had your tongue in my mouth." And I'm five years old.

A smile slides onto those awesome lips of his. "And I am more than willing to put my tongue back in there. Just say the word."

I roll my eyes. "You're not kissing me again"—*why did I say that? I would totally kiss him again. Sometimes, I could really slap myself*—"and you're not reading my list either."

"Okay. Whatever you say." He leans back in his chair, stretching his legs out the best he can with the limited room he has.

And I relax in the knowledge that we're past this conversation.

Until the bastard snatches my list from my lap.

"Hey!"

Liam turns away, so all I'm getting is his back as I try to grab my list.

"Give me that back!"

"*Go to England. Kiss a stranger. Have* lots *of sex*," his deep voice rumbles out the words I wrote.

He glances at me over his shoulder, a shit-eating grin on his face.

I don't even bother with trying to get the list back now. What's the point? He's already seen it.

Bastard.

I fall back into my seat, my face feeling like a blowtorch went at it. "You're an asshole," I mutter.

He turns to face me, my list in his hand but still held out of my reach. "Aw, don't be like that, Taylor, from Boston. I was just curious to read it."

I'm pretty sure he's going for contrite, but he's failing miserably.

I glare at him. I'm going for death-by-laser stare.

It doesn't work because he gives me a panty-dropping smile. I'd like to say I'm unaffected, but I'm not; however, I don't let him know that.

"Curious? I don't think so. An effing thief? Yes."

He laughs. "I'm sorry. But you don't need to be embarrassed. It's a good list." He looks back to my list. "*Have sex with a stranger*," he continues on reading. "*Have sex with a stranger outdoors.* You do know I can help you with all of these, right?" He lifts a brow at me.

I give him the middle finger.

He laughs again and looks back to the list. Then, he stops laughing and stares at me with what can only be described as complete horror. "You've never had oral sex?"

Fuck.

Why the hell did I put that on my list?

Because I wasn't expecting someone else to read it.

Mortification fills every part of me, and my face starts to burn.

Fighting against my discomfort, I fold my arms over my chest and lift my chin. "So what if I haven't had oral sex? It's not like it's the law, you know."

"Well, it fucking should be. I just…" He scratches his head. "How in the hell has someone who looks like you not had a guy go down on her before? I'd think men would be queuing up, begging to do it."

"Clearly, they haven't been," I mutter, turning my eyes away.

"Well, we need to rectify this immediately," he says, determination in his voice, yanking my eyes straight back to his.

"What?" I squeak.

"I'm going to make you come with my mouth, and tongue."

Holy Mary, Mother of God!

"I'm not going in the airplane restroom with you." My voice is still squeaky, and that burn of embarrassment has turned into a total hot flush.

A deep rumble of a laugh escapes Liam. "Trust me, gorgeous, there would be nothing more uncomfortable than me trying to go down on you in an airplane bathroom. The first time you have oral sex, it should be fucking stupendous, something you'll never forget. So, the moment we land, you and I are going straight to my place, and I'm going to strip you naked and give you the pleasure of my tongue. For hours."

Hours?

My insides wobble. But my voice is clear. "I don't think so."

What?

"Why not?" He frowns.

Yeah, Taylor, why not?

"Because I don't want a pity fuck."

He shifts in his seat, facing me. "One, *not* fucking you would be the pity. And, two, I never said I was going to fuck you. I said I was going to give you oral sex."

"Well, I don't want pity oral sex then."

"Believe me, there'll be nothing pitiful about it. Just mind-blowing fucking pleasure."

A hot rush of heat hits me straight between my legs. I squeeze my thighs together.

He notices and grins.

I put my hands on my lap, covering my lady parts. "I'm not going to your place with you," I tell him. "I don't know you. You're a stranger. You might be a serial killer."

"I might be. But isn't fucking a stranger on your list?"

He's got me there. "It is, but you're not exactly selling me with the serial-killer shit."

"I'm not a serial killer, I promise."

"Said the serial killer before he slit my throat open."

He throws his head back, laughing loudly.

A smile pushes onto my lips. His laugh is incredibly contagious.

Why am I so bothered if he is a serial killer? So I die a little early. At least I'd get to experience cunnilingus before I do.

I'm kidding. Sort of.

"Where do you live?" I ask him.

He stops laughing and cocks a brow. "Chelsea. It's in London."

Chelsea…nice area.

I ponder his offer for a moment. *Can I really do this?*

Well, you don't exactly have much time left to live, and it's not like you have a line of men offering to do this.

"Okay," I say.

"Okay?" he repeats. He sounds a little surprised, which is odd, considering this guy's high level of confidence.

"I'll go back to your place with you, so we can…well, you can"—I gesture a hand to his face and then my crotch—"do *that*."

Seriously, what is wrong with me?

A hot smile spreads across his gorgeous mouth. "Glad to hear it."

He hands me back my list.

Taking it, I fold it up and put it along with my pen back in my bag.

Oh my God. I can't believe I just agreed to go and have sex with him—well, not sex. Oral sex.

Oh, who am I kidding? I'll totally end up having sex with him.

If he's putting out, I'll be taking.

When you have as little time as I do, pondering on the rights and wrongs of sexual etiquette clearly go out the window.

I'm not exactly sure of what to do now. I'm just all kinds of excited and nervous about what's going to happen when we land.

God, six hours of sitting next to him, knowing what he's going to do to me soon…I don't know how I'm going to talk to him or look at his mouth without imagining where it will be in those six hours.

On me—that's where his sexy-as-sin mouth will be.

I have to hold in a squeal of excitement.

Picking up the Hunter Airways brochure, which is still in my lap, I cross my legs and open it up just for the sake of having something to do.

And the first thing I see is Liam.

Literally.

There's a photo of him in the magazine.

"Hey, there's a photo of you…" The words die on my tongue when I actually take in the foreword.

Holy shit.

"You're Liam Hunter?" My own voice is like a dull thud in my head. "As in, the owner of Hunter Airways? And a bazillion other companies."

I'm staring at him. He's staring at me.

Then, his lips lift at the corner. "Well, I don't own a bazillion companies. But, yeah, I am Liam Hunter."

"Oh God," I groan, covering my face with my hands. "I kiss-attacked the guy who owns this plane."

I hear Liam's deep chuckle, and then he tugs my hands from my face, forcing me to look at his face.

"It's not a big deal."

"It's *so* a big deal. I kiss-attacked Liam Hunter," I repeat, groaning again.

"You really need to stop groaning like that because you're turning me the fuck on."

He shifts in his seat, and I follow his stare down to his crotch.

Oh.

Oh, wow.

He totally has a hard-on.

I've given Liam Hunter a hard-on.

"Yes, you have."

My eyes flick to his. "Did I…did I say that out loud?"

"You did."

"Oh fuck," I groan.

"For fuck's sake, groan like that again, and I'll be going down on you right here and now. I don't give a shit who sees," he says in a hushed tone.

My eyes bug out of my head. "You can't do that!" I whisper back, shocked.

He levels me with a look. "I own the plane. I can do whatever the fuck I want."

Okay then.

"And just so you know, you kissing me was the sexiest thing that's ever happened to me."

I'm still wobbly over his prior comment, but I manage to slide him a look. "I guess you don't get out much then."

"Oh, I get out plenty." He gives me a look that tells me that Liam Hunter gets out and about regularly.

Then, something occurs to me.

"Hey, why are you sitting in economy? You own the plane. You should be sitting in first-class. Or on a throne or something. Anyway, don't you have your own plane to fly you all over the world?"

"I do have my own plane, but it's in London. And if I'd sat in first-class, then I wouldn't have sat next to you, and I wouldn't have gotten that awesome kiss. And you and I wouldn't be heading back to my place the moment we land, so I can make you come."

True. But still…

"If I owned this plane, I'd be sitting in first-class."

"First-class doesn't interest me. You, on the other hand…*you* interest me a lot."

He interests me a lot, too. Especially his tongue and hot body.

"And I leave first-class seats to the paying customers. Also, why would I want to move when I have first class sitting right next to me?"

I fight a smile. "Your pick-up lines are terrible. Anyone ever tell you that?"

He gives me a mock-offended look. "I haven't had any complaints before."

"I don't think it was your pick-up lines they were after. And I don't mean your money either."

"You're referring to my big cock?" He deadpans.

I laugh. He's so confident…and honestly, it's a huge turn-on.

"I guess I'll know the answer to that question later," I say softly.

"Yes, you will."

Holy…shivers.

24

Then, something occurs to me.

"How old are you?" I ask him.

I know for sure that he must be older than me, but he doesn't look that old.

"Why?" He eyes me suspiciously.

"Just wondering."

"I'm thirty-two. Your turn."

Wow. He's ten years older than me. How hot is that?

But it might not be hot to him that I'm younger.

"I don't know if I should tell you…" I bite my lower lip. "You might change your mind if I do."

His expression freezes. "You're not seventeen, are you?"

"Fuck no." I laugh. "I'm twenty-two."

"Thank fuck for that." He exhales, his face relaxing.

"You are ten years older than me though. An older man. Like a sexy sugar daddy."

He chokes out a sound. "I'm thirty-two, not fifty-two. And call me a sugar daddy again, and I'll be rescinding the oral invitation."

I laugh. For real. It's loud and happy, and it feels alien. I can't remember the last time I laughed like this.

It was before my family died.

But he did that. He made me laugh, and he's made me smile a ton.

And he's going to do so much more—with his tongue on the most intimate part of me.

Oh God, I can't wait.

I'm going back to Liam Hunter's place to have sex.

Liam Hunter, the gazillionaire businessman, who owns airplanes, credit card and finance companies, hotels—*crap, I'm even staying in one of his hotels*—and so much other stuff that I can't even remember. And he's older than me, which is just so incredibly sexy because he must be all experienced with sex.

This is going to be amazing.

I'm going to be tongue-fucked by Liam Hunter, and I cannot wait.

God bless, England.

chapter 3

It's seven thirty in the evening when we land in London.

I'm in England.

I can't believe I'm actually here.

I pull my carry-on out from underneath the seat in front of me and hang it on my shoulder while I wait for Liam to get his bag and jacket out of the overhead compartment.

Standing in the walkway, he lets me out first.

I can feel him at my back as we exit the plane with other passengers.

When we step off the plane onto the jetway, a guy in a high-vis jacket is waiting there.

He approaches Liam. "Mr. Hunter, if you would come this way, please, I'll take you to passport control."

"You have someone to take you through passport control?" I ask Liam.

"They open a separate one for me." He actually looks a little embarrassed telling me this.

"Well, us mere mortals have to line up." I smile. "So, I'll see you on the other side."

I wonder if I will see him on the other side?

He's made no mention of me going back to his place since he said it at the start of the flight.

"No, you won't because you're coming with me." He takes ahold of my hand and starts to lead me along, following high-vis guy.

We enter passport control and walk straight over to a passport booth.

"Siobhan will take care of you, Mr. Hunter," high-vis guy tells him, stopping by it.

I can see the other passengers, who are starting to filter through, staring at us from across the room. If I were them, I'd be hating on us right now.

"Can I have your passport, please?" Siobhan says with a bright smile, her eyes focused on Liam.

"Ladies first." Liam gestures to me.

Moving forward, I hand Siobhan my passport.

"First time in England?" Siobhan asks me.

"It is." I smile.

"Well, enjoy your stay," she says, handing me my passport back.

Liam hands his over to her, and then I feel his chest pressing against my back.

"Shaw," he says, looking over my shoulder at my passport.

"That's my name." I put my passport away in my bag.

"Welcome home, Mr. Hunter." Siobhan hands Liam his passport, giving him another dazzling smile.

"My luggage?" he asks her.

"Already collected and with your driver."

"Thank you."

He takes my hand again and starts leading me away from passport control and in the opposite direction of baggage claim.

I tug him to a stop. "You might have your luggage, big boss man, but I need to go get mine."

"Already collected and in my car. I told them to get yours as well."

"And how did you know which luggage was mine?"

His brows draw together. "Because I own the airline. Your seat number is in the system—my system—which is connected to your luggage at check-in. I tell my staff to get your luggage, and they do it."

I put my free hand on my hip, my head tilting to the side, eyes assessing. "Does everyone do what you say?"

The look he gives me…I feel it all the way down to my toes, only pausing along the way to pay extra special attention to my vagina.

He steps close, so close that I can feel the heat of his body through my clothes. And, God, he's tall. He towers over me. I have to tip my head back to look at him.

"Yes, everyone does what I say." His tone is low and sexy. "But I have a feeling you're going to be the exception to the rule."

"And you would be right about that."

"Thing is"—he leans his face in close, his warm breath brushing over my lips—"I might like control and really like people doing as I tell them, but I love a challenge more. So, game fucking on." Then, he slaps me on the ass and walks off, leaving me standing there with my mouth wide open.

Cocky son of a bitch. And it's so fucking hot.

"You going to stand there all day, Boston?" he calls over his shoulder. "Or are you coming?"

Coming? Definitely.

And…Boston? Guess I have a new nickname.

I start walking, and picking up speed, I catch up to him.

Liam pushes through the door, walking into the arrivals area.

Grabbing my hand again, he leads me over to a guy who's clearly waiting on him. "Paul, this is Taylor Shaw from Boston. Boston, this is Paul, my driver."

"Nice to meet you." I smile at him.

"Likewise. The car's just outside, sir," he tells Liam.

Liam and I follow Paul outside. The air is cold, and I shiver. Liam wraps his arm around me.

We follow Paul over to a flashy black Mercedes. Paul opens the back door. Liam ushers me in first and then climbs in next to me. I put on my seat belt. Paul gets in and turns on the engine.

"So, where are we going?" I ask as Paul pulls out into airport traffic.

"My place…if you still want to?"

I turn my face to find his closer than I expected.

God, he's gorgeous. I really want to kiss him again.

We haven't kissed since that one time when I surprise kissed him.

"I want to," I say softly.

His eyes darken, and the look in them makes my insides clench. He cups my cheek with his hand, brushing his thumb over my lips.

For a moment, I think he's going to kiss me, but he doesn't. He just sits back and puts his arm around me. I snuggle into his warm, hard body and close my eyes. I should be looking at London as it's the first time I'd be seeing it, but Liam's body is just so inviting.

I must have fallen asleep because Liam is gently shaking me awake.

"We're here," he says.

I blink open my eyes to see his staring back at me.

"Hey." I smile.

"Hey." He smiles back. "We're at my place."

"Oh, right." I sit up. Grabbing my bag, I hang it on my shoulder.

Liam gets out of the car and then holds a hand out for me. I take his hand, and he helps me out of the car.

"I need to get my suitcase." I gesture to the trunk of the car.

"Paul will bring it up for you."

With my hand still in his, Liam leads me into a fancy-looking building.

"Good evening, Mr. Hunter," a guy behind the security desk greets him.

"Evening, John." Liam lifts his hand.

We stop at a bank of elevators, and Liam presses the button. The door opens immediately, and I follow him inside. He presses the button marked Penthouse and then inputs a code into the keypad. The doors close, and we're alone.

And it hits me that I'm here, alone with him, and we're going to quite possibly have sex—or, at the very least, have oral sex.

My body starts to vibrate with nerves and excitement.

I can't believe this is actually happening.

I'm in England, in an elevator with the sexiest guy I've ever met, whom I've known for exactly seven hours, and I'm going up to his place to partake in a round of oral sex.

England is awesome.

"You nervous?" Liam says from beside me, his voice sounding low and deep in the silence.

I glance up at him. "I'm a little nervous," I admit.

"Don't be." He brushes his knuckles over my cheek, sending shivers hurtling through me.

The elevator comes to a stop. We get out, and I follow Liam to his front door. He flips open a keypad and punches in another code, and then I hear a lock click open.

"Don't you have keys in England?"

He grins at me and then swings open the door, letting me through first. I step inside his apartment.

Wow. Big and fancy.

But I don't get a chance to properly look around because Liam shuts the door, and then I'm yanked back and pushed up against it. His mouth is on mine a split second later.

He's kissing me.

And it feels amazing. He's amazing.

My bag slips off my shoulder, but I barely register it hitting the floor because I'm too caught up in him, caught up in his kiss.

His hands are in my hair, his tongue in my mouth. "I've waited seven long fucking hours to taste that mouth again," he rumbles against my lips. "Even better than I remembered."

Then, he's kissing me again.

Harder, more intense.

And it's awesome.

I wind my arms around his neck, my fingers sliding into his hair. It's softer than I expected.

Liam's hands leave my hair and move down my body. Finding my ass, he grabs it and lifts me. My legs come up around his waist.

And, now, his impressive erection is pressed right up against my aching clit. Only our stupid clothes are in the way.

I want more. I want all of him.

There's a solid knock on the door behind me, frightening the shit out of me.

"Jesus Christ!" I jump.

Liam chuckles. His mouth still against mine, his lips brush over mine as he speaks, "It'll be Paul with our luggage."

"I'm guessing he needs to come in?" I stare into his eyes.

"Yeah." That's all he says, but he doesn't move.

I don't want to move either, but we can't leave Paul out there all night.

"Okay, well, you let Paul in, and I'll go freshen up."

With some reluctance, I notice, he lets me down to my feet. "Guest bathroom is down the hall, second door on your left," he tells me.

I slip off my shoes, not wanting to walk across his nice hardwood floors in them, and then I retrieve my bag from the floor. Hanging my bag off my shoulder, I pad barefoot across the living room and down the hallway to the bathroom, my legs shaking the whole time.

I let myself into a plush bathroom and lock the door behind me. I put my bag on the vanity counter and stare at myself in the mirror.

My hair is all mussed up from Liam's hands being in it, and my cheeks are flushed.

Laughter bubbles up inside me, and I have to cover my hands over my mouth to curb the noise.

I can't believe I'm here, doing this.

Crazy but amazing.

Well, I wanted to live before I died. Do those things on my list.

Tonight is the start of that.

I feel the rumble of it coming before it hits. I should have expected it. All that traveling, it was inevitable.

The pain strikes me hard. I clutch my head in my hands, crying out. I have to bite my lip to stop from being too noisy. I don't want Liam to hear.

It feels like my head is splitting open.

Then, the nausea hits.

I make it to the toilet just in time before I throw up the contents of my stomach.

Arm on the edge of the toilet, I rest my head against it, praying for the pain to pass soon.

Please stop. Please stop.

But this is the price I have to pay for all I've done. The price I pay to be able to die.

As soon as I feel able to stand, I get up and get my pain pills from my bag. I shake two out and swallow them down with water from the faucet.

I'm sweaty, and I have vomit breath. *Great.*

I grab my travel toothbrush and toothpaste, and I scrub my teeth clean.

Then, I decide to take a quick shower. Tying my hair back into a ponytail, so not to get it wet, I turn the shower on and wash my body, using the shower gel in there.

Having the shower makes me feel a lot better.

I grab a towel from the rack and dry off. I get out the clothes that I packed in my carry-on—clean panties, bra, leggings and tank top—and dress in them. Not exactly seductive clothing, but it's slightly better than the yoga pants and T-shirt I was wearing.

I decide to leave my hair in a ponytail. I put my dirty clothes away in my bag, hang it on my shoulder and let myself out of the bathroom, heading back to Liam in the living room.

He's not there, but my suitcase is. It's sitting by the front door.

"Liam?" I call out.

"I'm in the kitchen."

Having no clue where the kitchen is, I head in the direction of where I heard his voice coming from.

I easily find the kitchen. It's really nice with glossy black cupboards and work surfaces.

Liam is in there, his back to me, standing at the stove, wearing a T-shirt and running pants. His hair looks damp. He must've had a shower, too.

"I took a shower," I tell him. "I was feeling gross after the flight. Hope that was okay."

He smiles at me from over his shoulder. "No problem at all. I thought you might be hungry, so I made food— chicken stir-fry. You're not a vegetarian, are you?"

He cooked.

"No." I smile. I'm not actually hungry after the headache and vomiting, but he went to the trouble, and I don't want to seem rude.

"Take a seat." He gestures to the breakfast bar.

34

I walk over and sit up on one of the stools. I watch while Liam dishes the stir-fry into two bowls. He brings them over, putting one in front of me. Then, he gets two forks from a drawer and hands one to me.

"This looks really good," I tell him. And it does. Smells good, too. My stomach rumbles in appreciation, which surprises me, as I normally struggle to eat after I've had an episode.

"Do you want something to drink?" Liam asks me.

"Water would be great."

He goes over to the refrigerator and gets two bottles of water. Taking the seat beside me, he hands me one of the bottles.

"Thanks." I unscrew the cap and have a drink. I put the water down and start in on my stir-fry. "This is really good," I tell him around my first mouthful.

"I'm glad you like it." He smiles over at me.

"You like to cook?"

"I do." He nods. "I just don't get a lot of time to do it."

"You should make more time. You're really good."

"Wish I could, but work takes precedence. I find it hard to delegate. So, cooking, like everything else, goes by the wayside."

"But you make time to pick up strange women on airplanes and bring them back to your place?" I raise my brow, smiling.

"Oh, I always find time to do that, especially when those strange women are as hot as you." The heated tone in his voice leaves me squirming in my seat.

We finish up our food, and I help Liam clean up.

I'm just loading up the last dish into the dishwasher when I feel him come up behind me, his hands taking ahold of my hips.

My heart pauses and then jumps, and my pulse starts to race.

I turn and look at him over my shoulder. Our eyes connect, the air suddenly becoming very thick between us.

I straighten up.

Liam moves me around to face him. His hand lifts to my ponytail. He tugs the tie out and runs his fingers through my hair.

"Are we done with the small talk and pleasantries?" he asks, low.

I swipe my tongue over my lower lip, loving the way his eyes flare at the movement. "Yeah, we're done."

"Good because I want you in my bed. Now."

He grabs my ass and lifts me off the floor, and my legs wrap around his waist. He captures my mouth in a hot kiss as he starts to walk through his apartment. He carries me into his darkened bedroom and deposits me onto his extremely large bed.

"This is a big bed," I comment.

"It is, and I'm going to make you come on every inch of it."

Holy shit.

Liam reaches out, hooking his fingers into the waistband of my leggings. He pulls them down my legs, tossing them to the floor. My panties are next to go.

My legs start to tremble, my stomach doing cartwheels, in anticipation of what's about to happen.

Liam's hand goes to his crotch, and he cups his dick through his pants as he stares down at me.

So, so hot.

"Boston, I'm going to lick you so good, and make you come so fucking hard that you're going to be begging me to fuck you."

I'm pretty sure he's right. I'm close to begging already, and he hasn't even touched me yet.

He's going to go down on me.

A man who looks like him is going to take my oral virginity.

I send up a silent prayer. *Thank you, God. I know I don't deserve it, but thank you.*

"Take your top off." His voice is commanding and sends me to attention.

I scramble to take it off, removing my bra as well. I chuck them to the floor.

His eyes are pinned on my breasts when he says, "Spread your legs."

God, he's so dominant, and it's incredibly sexy.

Doing as he says, I part my legs.

"Wider."

I part them wider, and I don't even feel embarrassed. Just ready. So very ready to get this party started.

Liam leans forward. Sliding his hands under my thighs, he pulls me down the bed until my ass is on the edge.

He gets down to his knees. I can't take my eyes off him. *This is really going to happen.*

"You're wet for me." It's not a question.

I'm clearly wet—dripping, in fact.

"You're so fucking hot," he tells me as he runs a finger through my folds, making me tremble.

Then, he puts that finger in his mouth and sucks me off of him.

It's the sexiest thing I've ever seen.

"You ready to have your mind blown, Boston?"

I'm staring at him, dumbstruck. My heart is beating out of my chest.

He's so beautiful. And he's kneeling there, between my legs, wanting to pleasure me.

Finding my voice, I whisper, "Do your worst."

His lips lift at the corners. "Trust me when I say, it'll be the best. The best you will ever have."

Then, he leans forward and puts his mouth on me.

And everything else ceases to exist.

"Oh my God." My head falls back onto the bed, and my fingers grip the duvet covering the bed.

Liam licks a path up my center. My body shudders, and my toes curl.

I've never felt anything like it. There are no words to describe how amazing this feels.

All thoughts and feelings have narrowed down to that one small place on my body and what Liam's skilled tongue is doing to it right now.

The whole world could be on fire, and I wouldn't care.

I just need this…*him*.

The feel of his tongue sweeping over my clit in those teasing, maddening movements…is torturous, but it's the best kind of torture. I want it and more of it.

My body is burning up with a fever. I feel like I'm going to come out of my skin.

Then, he pushes a finger inside me, and I nearly combust.

"Liam!" I cry out, my hands leaving the bed to grab his hair.

He starts fingering me while licking my clit, and it's incredible and intense and just *everything*.

My hips start moving of their own accord, in time with him, and I can feel the orgasm building up to epic proportions.

"That's it, babe. Fuck my mouth," he rumbles against me, the vibration of his voice pushing me further over the edge.

So, I do. I continue to shamelessly rub my pussy against his mouth.

Then, he sucks on my clit, his teeth grazing over it.

I'm pretty sure I levitate off the bed, and then I'm coming.

And I'm coming harder than I ever have in my life.

I scream to God and to Liam and maybe even say that Liam is God.

But he is. He's the god of oral sex.

Seriously, it's pure ecstasy.

Every one of my muscles seize in the most delicious way as a heat spreads throughout my body, and I never want it to end.

But, like all things in life, it has to end.

My body falls lax onto the bed.

I feel Liam kissing his way up my body, but I can't move. I'm too relaxed.

He stops at my breasts, paying special attention to my nipples.

I slide my fingers into his hair, lifting his head so that he's looking at me. "That was…"

"Amazing. Mind-blowing. Out of this world." He grins.

"All those things and more. Thank you."

His brows pull together. "You don't have to thank me."

"I know, but I do. I big, big thank you."

He chuckles.

I bring my head toward his, softly kissing him.

The kiss quickly turns heated.

He's still dressed and between my legs, and I need him naked. Now.

"Tell me I can fuck you," he says, breathing heavily into my mouth.

"I thought that was already a given." I smile against his lips.

Getting to his knees, Liam reaches back and pulls his T-shirt off over his head. We both go for his pants at the same time. Liam wins and takes them off.

He reaches over into his nightstand and gets a condom from the drawer. I watch as he rolls the condom onto his impressive length.

When he's fully sheathed, he lifts his eyes to mine.

I lick my lips.

His expression darkens.

I part my legs.

He's on top of me in seconds with his mouth back on mine, kissing me like his life depends on it. "I've wanted to do this from the moment you kissed me on the plane." Then, he thrusts his cock all the way up inside me.

"Oh my God!" I cry out.

He stills inside me.

My body is adjusting to his size when he presses his nose to mine and stares deep into my eyes. "You feel so fucking good. Even better than I imagined." His breath whispers over my lips.

I can feel his heart beating against mine while his cock is buried deep inside me.

I wrap my legs around him, my hands sliding up into his hair. "Fuck me, Liam. *Now.*"

His eyes flare, and he growls. He captures my mouth in a kiss, and he starts to fuck me.

His movements quickly become intense. He's fucking me so hard that we're moving up the bed with each thrust he gives.

Liam's hand goes under my ass, lifting and tilting me.

He pulls his cock out to the tip and then slams back in. He hits so deep inside me that I scream.

His mouth is on my neck, kissing, and then I feel his tongue sweep over the shell of my ear, driving me crazy.

He kisses his way back to my mouth, and I'm turning my head to meet his lips, needing to kiss him more than I need air right now.

His tongue slides along mine, fucking my mouth as thoroughly as his cock is fucking me.

Liam groans, and it sounds like pure pleasure. It sends thrills racing through me, as I realize that I'm affecting him in this way.

"Tell me you're close, babe, because I can't hold off any longer. I wanted to last, but you're just so fucking hot, and I waited too long to fuck you."

I am close, but knowing how much he needs to come, I decide to aid the process along. I reach a hand between us and start to rub my clit with my fingers.

Liam stares down at my hand. "Fuck yeah. That's it, touch yourself." His eyes come back to mine. They're all dark with lust. "You're so fucking beautiful, Taylor."

He thinks I'm beautiful?

He starts fucking me again with slow, drawn-out movements while I continue to rub my clit.

My second orgasm hits as hard as the first, and I'm coming like a rocket. "Liam!" I cry, my hand gripping his arm, nails digging in, as I ride out my orgasm.

"Jesus! Fuck! I'm…fucking…coming," he groans.

Taking my mouth again, he kisses me through his orgasm, my own body still trembling with aftershocks.

And he keeps kissing me, long after he's come, and I like it a lot.

The sex was out-of-this-world, but I like kissing him just as much. I've never been kissed the way Liam kisses me—so incredibly thorough. Like the kiss isn't just a precursor to sex. He kisses me because he wants to.

"That was fucking amazing," he says, brushing my hair back from my forehead. "If I'd known it would be that good, I wouldn't have waited the last seven hours. I'd have for sure insisted on fucking in the airplane bathroom."

I slap his ass, and he chuckles.

He kisses my lips one last time, and then says, "I'll just get rid of the condom."

He gets up off me, and I feel the loss immediately. It surprises me just how much.

I watch his sexy naked ass go into his bathroom. I hear water running, and then he emerges a few seconds later.

He climbs back onto the bed. Getting a blanket from the bottom of the bed, he covers us with it.

He places a kiss on my chest between my breasts. He cups one in his hand, running his thumb over my nipple, making me shiver.

"You have really great tits."

I laugh.

He looks up at me, dark lashes fanning as he blinks. "What?"

"Nothing." I smile. "You're just different. Not like any guy I've ever met before."

He smiles widely. "And you, Boston, are not like any other woman I've ever met before."

I take that as a compliment, as I bet he's met a lot of women.

Liam lifts up and softly kisses me on the lips. Then, he takes me in his arms.

I lay my head on his chest, listening to the steady beat of his heart.

"I'm really glad my meeting was canceled today."

I glance up at him. "You weren't supposed to be on that flight?"

"No, I was due to fly back tomorrow, but the meeting I was supposed to have today was canceled, so I decided to fly back. And I'm really fucking glad I did."

"I'm glad you did, too. Guess us meeting was meant to be."

Liam stares at me for a long moment, and then he gently presses his lips to my forehead.

I rest my head back down on his chest, running my fingers over his chest hair.

It's not long before I hear his breathing even out, and I realize he's fallen asleep.

I don't want to overstay my welcome, and I want this moment to be what it was supposed to be—a one-time thing with a stranger.

Only Liam doesn't feel so much like a stranger anymore.

I gather up my clothes in the dark. But I can't find my panties.

Not wanting to wake him, I forego my panties, and I quickly dress out in the hall.

Then, I go to the kitchen and get my bag. My shoes are still by the front door, so I put them on, grab my suitcase, and let myself out of his apartment.

I take the elevator down.

The night watchman is still on the desk, so I ask him to call me a cab.

The cab turns up five minutes later. The cabbie puts my suitcase in the trunk.

I take a seat in the back. "Hunter Hotel," I tell him.

I give one last look to Liam's building, touching a hand to my lips. I smile at the memory he's just given me, but feel a twinge of sadness that I won't see him again.

chapter 4

I wake to the sound of a phone ringing. Really fucking loudly. It takes me a moment to realize that it's the hotel room phone. Reaching out a hand, I grab the receiver of the phone on the nightstand beside my head.

"Hello?" My voice sounds rough.

I didn't get much sleep last night. I couldn't stop thinking about Liam. About the sex I had with Liam. And I was wishing that I'd stayed with him. That I was waking up with him and not to this ringing phone.

"Guess what I have in my hand?"

Liam?

"Liam?"

"The one and only."

It's him. A big smile spreads across my face.

"How do you know which hotel I'm staying in?" I ask.

"I have my ways. So, are you going to guess what I have in my hand?"

"No. I'm more concerned with your stalking abilities."

Honestly, I couldn't care less. I'm glad he found me. I just like playing with him.

He sighs. "You flew with my company. You're staying in one of my hotels. I have access to the agents you booked with. It wasn't hard to find out which hotel you were staying at. All it took was one phone call."

"Did you make the call?"

"No, my assistant did," he says, sounding like there's absolutely nothing wrong with that.

I laugh. "Do you do anything yourself, Hunter?"

"Of course I do. I give amazing head. I fuck—hard." That makes me shiver. "And I cook stir-fry for list-making Bostonians who won't stop asking questions."

I laugh again. I love that he makes me laugh.

"You did cook for me. You also gave me amazing head—my first ever—and you fucked me very well."

"Why, thank you, ma'am," he says, his accent thickening. "Now, are you going to answer my question?"

"Which was?"

"What do I have in my hand?"

"I don't know. My ability of foresight was slightly hampered by a phone ringing and waking me at the butt-crack of dawn."

"It's not the butt crack of dawn. It's ten a.m. I've been up and working for hours. Wait, you're in bed?"

"I am." I stretch out in the warmth of the bed.

"What are you wearing?"

I bite down on the smile that I've been wearing since I heard his voice down the line. "I thought you wanted me to guess what you have in your hand."

"I want to know what you're wearing more." His voice has dropped an octave lower and sounds all sexy and seductive.

"Pajama shorts and a top." *Why did I tell him that?* I should have said something sexier than pajamas.

But then his resounding moan tells me that I said the right thing.

"Your knickers," he says, his voice sounding rough.

"I'm knickers?"

"No, you're not knickers. I have your knickers in my hand."

"Do you mean, my panties?" I giggle at the word *knickers*. It sounds so funny.

"Say that again." His voice is raspy.

"What? Panties?"

"Yeah. It sounds sexy as fuck when you say it."

"*Panties*," I say again, elongating the word to tease him.

And it works.

I hear him groan.

"Turned on?" I ask.

"Like you wouldn't fucking believe."

That has me pressing my thighs together.

"So, yeah"—he clears his throat—"I have your *panties*. The panties you left at my place after you snuck out this morning."

"I didn't sneak out this morning. I left after you fell asleep last night."

"Same thing."

He doesn't sound happy that I left. I'm surprised at that.

"Aw, don't you like being snuck out on, Hunter? Or is it usually you doing the sneaking out?"

"I don't sneak out on a woman. I just tell her that I'm leaving after I'm done fucking her."

"What if she's at your place?"

"Then, I pass her, her coat, tell her thank you very much, and show her to the door."

"Nice. So, why didn't you show me to the door?"

"Because I wasn't done with you."

"You weren't done?" I let out a nervous laugh, unsure of where this conversation is heading.

"No. I woke up with a raging hard-on and no you there to fuck. So, I had to come to work, sporting a massive erection. It's raising some eyebrows from my staff."

With that image, I can't stop the grin that covers my face. "You should have jerked off before you left for work. And, hang on, you're at work with a hard-on and my panties in your hand?"

He lets out a laugh. "When you put it like that, it sounds really pervy."

"It is pervy! You've been walking around with my panties in your hand."

"I haven't been walking around with your *panties* in my hand. They were in my pocket. They're in my hand now that I'm in my office, alone, talking to you. God, I can smell you on them, Taylor." His voice drops lower. "I can still taste you in my mouth, and it's making me so hard. I *need* to fuck you again."

He needs to fuck me again.

"Now?" I breathe the word out.

"I've got a meeting in five minutes. I'll be at your hotel room in an hour. I want you naked and ready for me. We're going to fuck, and then I'm taking you out, so we can start making a dent in your list."

Holy God.

"Has anyone ever told you that you are insanely bossy?"

"I'm not bossy. I'm just a man who knows what he wants, and right now, I want you. I want to be between your thighs with my cock deep inside you, fucking you hard. That okay with you?"

Ermahgerd.

"Y-yes."

"Good. I'll see you in an hour."

Then, he hangs up on me.

Holy shit!

I thought last night was a one-time thing. But, now, he's coming here, and we're going to have sex again.

Oh my God.

I call room service for breakfast, and then I go take a shower in preparation for Liam coming.

I dress in my knee-length skirt with red flowers on it and a white strappy top. And, of course, I've put on my best underwear.

Breakfast arrives soon after. I quickly scarf down some toast with marmalade on it. I'm totally trying to be English.

I'm just finishing my coffee when there's a firm knock at the door.

Putting my cup down, I go over to the door and open it.

And there stands Liam. He's wearing a charcoal-gray three-piece suit with a white shirt and gray tie, and he looks hot as hell.

He strides through the door. Hooking his arm around my waist, he brings me up onto my tiptoes, and he takes my mouth in a delicious kiss as he kicks the door shut with his foot. My hands flutter to his chest.

"Hi," he rumbles against my lips.

"Hi." I'm breathy and seriously turned on already, and all he's done is kiss me.

"Don't you ever leave my bed again before I'm done with you."

I blink my eyes open, and stare into his. "Yes, sir."

"So long as we know where we stand."

"God, you're bossy."

"Well, people generally do what I say without complaint."

"Except for me."

"Except for you." He smiles against my mouth, and I love the feeling.

I love it a little bit too much.

"Do you want something to drink?" I ask, tipping my head back so that I can properly look him in the eyes.

"No, I don't want something to drink…and you're dressed." He speculatively eyes me, tugging on a strap with his finger. "I specifically told you that I wanted you naked."

"Well, I thought it would be more fun if you undressed me."

The predatory look in his eyes has me stepping back toward the bed, and it sets off a swarm of butterflies in my belly, which are quickly heading south.

"I want you to undress for me. Strip. Now," he orders, his arms folding over his broad chest.

God, I want to strip him out of that sexy suit of his.

"Bossy," I mutter.

"I didn't hear you complaining last night when my head was between your legs, making you come. Now, take off your fucking clothes."

After that little speech, I have nothing…nothing but wet panties and hard nipples.

My hands go to the zipper on my skirt, and I slowly lower it. I push the fabric down over my hips, letting it pool at my feet. I step out of it. I pull my top off over my head and drop it on top of the skirt, leaving me standing here, in my underwear.

His eyes darken with appreciation. And, in this moment, I've never felt sexier and more powerful.

"Underwear as well." His commanding eyes meet with mine.

I remove my bra first, loving how his eyes go to my breasts and seem to get stuck there. I hook my thumbs in the elastic of my panties and shimmy them down my legs, toeing them off to the side.

The shy part of me wants to cover my body with my hands, but I refuse to be that shy girl.

Especially not with the way that Liam is looking at me right now—with absolute appreciation for my body.

There is nothing more empowering than having a man look at you like Liam is looking at me.

In this moment, I'm not Taylor Shaw, brain tumor girl. I'm Taylor Shaw, sex goddess.

With that bolstering my confidence, I say, "Now that you have me naked, what are you going to do with me?"

Liam unfastens his eyes from my breasts and pins me with a hot stare. "Things that will have you coming for days. Now, get on the fucking bed."

I scramble up onto the bed without hesitation.

Eager? Hell yes, I am. I know how this man fucks—hot and hard and thorough.

Liam toes off his shoes and yanks off his tie. After removing his jacket and vest, he then takes off his cuff links, putting them on the nightstand by the bed.

He unfastens his pants, pulling his shirt free. Unbuttoning the top few buttons on his shirt, he reaches back and pulls it over his head.

I stare unashamedly at his chest. I didn't get to appreciate it in the darkness of his room last night.

But, now, I'm seeing, and holy hell am I appreciating.

He's cut and ripped. All the way down to his V.

He is a man who works out and reaps the rewards for it.

Well, I'm the one currently reaping those rewards.

Liam has a man's body. A real man's body.

There's no waxed chest here. There's hair smattering his chest and a happy trail leading all the way to the promised land.

I've never been a chest-hair-on-a-guy kind of girl. I'm now officially converted.

All I want to do is run my tongue over that chest hair and follow that happy trail down into those pants to what I know awaits me there.

"Like what you see?"

I lift my eyes to his. "Very much so. But some of you is still covered." I gesture to his pants. "Take off your fucking pants, Hunter."

He grins at me. It's a lazy but oh-so sexy grin.

"I want you to take them off for me." His words are very distinct. He steps toward the bed, so he's standing by the edge of it.

Getting up on my knees, I reach for his zipper and lower it. The sound is loud in the silence.

I slip my hands into the back of his pants and push them down, letting them fall to the floor.

Liam kicks them off to the side.

I slide my fingers into the waistband of his boxer shorts and tug them down.

His cock springs free.

And then I'm just too distracted to get his boxers fully off.

I can't take my eyes off his cock.

It's just so hard and big, and...*there*.

Liam removes his boxer shorts the rest of the way. I wrap my hand around his cock. He groans, his stomach muscles tensing.

I got that he was big from the feel of him inside me last night, but looking at his cock right now in the light of day, I'm wondering how the hell it actually fit.

Pre-cum beads on the tip, and my mouth waters to taste him.

I lean my head down and lick the tip, loving the shudder that runs through his body.

His fingers slide into my hair. "Suck it," he rasps out the command.

I glance up at him. The look in his eyes...I've never seen a man look so on the edge of need.

I give him a seductive smile, and then I lower my mouth over his cock, taking him in.

I haven't had a lot of experience with giving head. But I want this to be really good for Liam, so, I give it my all, wanting to make him feel as amazing as he makes me feel.

I wrap my hand around the base, jacking him off, while I suck him.

He seems to like it as his grip on my hair tightens, and he says, "Yeah, fuck, that's it. Suck it harder."

So, I suck harder.

His other hand takes ahold of my hair, and he starts fucking my mouth with his cock, hips pistoning back and forth. "Jesus...your mouth feels so fucking good," he groans.

I rest my hands on his hips, going with what he needs. His cock feels amazing, sliding between my lips.

Without warning, he pulls from my mouth, and then I'm none too gently pushed down onto the bed. He spreads my legs and gets down on his knees. His mouth is on my pussy in seconds, his tongue pushing inside me.

"On my God!" I cry out.

Liam lifts his head and stares at me. "Right now, I am your god, and don't you fucking forget it."

Holy...wow.

He pushes a finger inside me. And another. Fucking me with them, he starts to suck on my clit.

Seconds later, I'm exploding around his mouth.

I didn't realize how worked up I was. Guess that's the power of oral sex. Or just the power of *him*.

"Move up to the head of the bed, and get on your stomach."

I lift my lazy head, still lax from the orgasm, and look at him.

"Now," he says.

I don't argue because I know that whatever he has in mind will mean more pleasure for me.

Face pressed into the pillow, I hear Liam moving around, and then he climbs on the bed. A condom lands on the pillow beside my head.

He takes ahold of one wrist and then the other, bringing them together above my head. He starts to wrap his tie around my wrists.

"Um, you're tying me up?" I glance back at him.

"Looks that way. You have a problem with that?"

Do I have a problem with that?

"No." I shake my head. "So long as you untie me at the end. I don't fancy being on the receiving end of a hotel maid's joke."

He chuckles low and deep, and then he leans in and captures my lips in a hot kiss. I can taste myself on him. It's crazy erotic.

"Don't worry. I have plans for you this afternoon that don't require you being tied to a bed."

He ties my bound wrists to the metal headboard, using the remainder of the tie.

I'm figuring he does this often, as he has me bound and tied in less than a minute.

I feel him press a kiss between my shoulder blades. Then, he starts to kiss his way down my spine.

His hand runs over my ass cheek…and then he slaps it.

"Ouch," I hiss.

I feel his lips press to the offending sting, his tongue running over the area, soothing it.

I haven't been spanked before.

Gotta say, I quite like it. It feels…naughty and incredibly sexy. Especially when I'm tied up and totally at his mercy.

I feel his finger run between my ass cheeks, causing me to tense. "Have you ever been fucked up the arse?" he asks, voice low.

I crane my neck back to look him. "No."

And I don't know if it's something I ever want to do.

But, you're dying, Taylor. So, why the hell not? What do you have to lose?

Swallowing past my natural nerves, my voice shakes as I say, "But...I wouldn't be opposed to trying it out."

Surprise flickers in his eyes, and then, soon after, a big, dirty grin spreads across his lip. "Has anyone ever told you before that you're a man's wet dream?"

A laugh escapes me. "Nope."

"Well, you are. A hot fucking wet dream. I've been dreaming about a woman like you since I hit puberty."

"You don't get to fuck many asses?" I ask.

"Not as many as I'd like." He slaps my ass again. "And I'm going to fuck your hot ass...but not today."

"Why not?" I ask. I actually feel a little disappointed. I was getting all ready to psych myself up for it.

"Because spit alone won't do it, and unless you have some lube, I'm not going near your ass."

"I don't have lube. It's not something I thought to pack." I smirk at him.

"I'll just have to make sure I have some the next time we have sex."

"We'll be having sex again?" I raise a brow.

"We'll definitely be having sex again." He leans down and presses another kiss to my ass cheek, making me shiver.

I let my head fall down onto the pillow as I feel Liam get to his knees.

His hands grab my hips, and he lifts me. I bring my knees up to support myself. God knows how because my body currently feels like jelly.

Sex for me before was never anything like it is with Liam.

With Benjamin, we were just inexperienced kids, and my one-night stands were just fuck-and-goes.

Sex with Liam is so much more. There are so many feelings that come with it...and it's incredibly intense in sensation that I'm halfway between madness and ecstasy while with him.

His finger pushes inside me again, and he starts to fuck me with it.

I'm panting and beyond needing him inside me when he reaches over and picks up the condom.

His finger leaves me. I whimper at the loss.

I hear foil tear.

I glance back to see him rolling the condom on that magnificent cock of his. His dick is straining upward, looking hard and so ready to fuck me.

He catches my eye. The smile he gives me is a dirty one, filled with a hot promise.

Liam holds my stare as he lines his cock up with my opening. Very slowly, he starts to push every delicious inch of him inside me until my eyes are closing with total bliss.

He takes his time, fucking me with measured, languid movements. Pulling all the way out and then pushing back in, inch by delicious inch.

It's the best kind of torture.

"You look so fucking beautiful right now," he says in a rough, low voice.

I can't ever remember being called beautiful by a man I was fucking…except for him.

I look back at him, the bind on my wrists pulling. It stings, but I like the bite of pain.

"So do you," I tell him.

Something flashes through his eyes. Something hot and urgent. Then, his control snaps, and he starts fucking me hard and relentless. One hand on my hip and the other pressed on my lower back, he pumps in and out of me, dominating my body.

I've never handed myself over to another person in this way before, but I love the way it makes me feel.

Liam lifts his hand from my back and puts his thumb in his mouth, wetting it.

The next thing I feel is that wet thumb sliding between my ass cheeks while his hand palms my lower back.

When it touches my puckered hole, I tense. "I thought we weren't doing ass play?"

"I changed my mind. That okay with you?"

Is that okay with me?

Yes…yes, it is.

I look back, meeting with his eyes. "Yes," I whisper.

Heat flares in his eyes.

Holding my stare, he slows his thrusts down and focuses on teasing his thumb over that sacred, untouched part of me.

Even though I told him yes, I still can't help but tense, knowing what he's about to do.

"Relax for me," he whispers.

So, I do. I close my eyes and give myself over to him.

When I feel the tip of his thumb enter me, I moan, partly from the burn but surprisingly in pleasure, too.

"Are you okay?" he asks, his voice sounding rough.

"Yes," I breathe.

"Can you take more?"

I nod my head.

He pushes his thumb in a bit further. The burn increases, but it's not painful, just uncomfortable. There's something else, too…something good. I feel full of him, and a desperate need starts to overtake everything else. Suddenly, the burn doesn't matter because I want more—more him, more of what he's doing to me.

Liam has stilled his movements, his cock seated inside me, his thumb up my ass.

And, now, I'm the one taking control, telling him with my body what I want. I push back against him and start fucking myself on him. Fucking my pussy with his cock and my ass with his thumb.

"Fuck yeah, that's it, babe. God, the moment I laid eyes on you, I knew you'd be a hot fuck."

I want to touch my clit, but I can't because my hands are bound. I'm totally at his mercy.

He seems to sense what I need as his other hand slides from my hip and moves around my front to my clit.

He rubs my clit with his thick finger.

I'm coming seconds later with his finger on my clit, his dick in my pussy, and his thumb up my ass.

And I keep coming. I'm still coming when he pulls his thumb out of my ass and his finger off my clit.

His chest presses to my back, and his hands go around my wrists. His mouth pressed to my shoulder, he starts pumping his cock in and out of me.

"God, you're so fucking hot, Boston. I could fuck you for days."

"So, do it," I whisper. "Fuck me for days."

He growls and starts pumping in and out of me even harder.

Skin slapping skin, his hips pound against my ass.

"I'm…fucking…coming," he growls. Then, he sinks his teeth into my shoulder in the most delicious way as he rides his orgasm out in me.

When he's done, I collapse down onto the bed. Liam comes down with me.

"God, you weigh a ton." I chuckle.

"All muscle, babe." He nips my shoulder with his teeth, and then he gets up off me, pulling out of me.

I decide that's my least favorite part of having sex with Liam—him pulling out of me. I don't like the feeling of losing him from my body.

He unties me from the bed and unwraps the bind around my wrists. I turn over to face him. He takes ahold of my wrists and rubs his thumbs over them, massaging.

It's the sweetest thing.

Then, he leans down and kisses my lips, humming a sound of pleasure over them.

And I change my mind. That's the sweetest thing.

"I'll just get rid of this." He nods down at the condom on his still semi-hard dick.

How is he still hard?

I watch his naked ass leave the room and go into the bathroom.

"You should have a better room than this," he tells me as he comes back out from the bathroom.

"What's wrong with this room? Are you saying your hotel rooms are shitty?"

"No." He climbs onto the bed.

Taking me in his arms, he shimmies us down the bed until we're facing each other, legs tangled, arms holding.

I'm getting the impression that Liam is a cuddler.

"I'm saying that you should be staying in a better room. You should be in a suite."

"I don't need a suite. I'm one person. This is all I need."

"I like suites, and if I'm going to be spending time here, in bed with you, then I want to be doing it in the best of my hotel rooms."

"You'll fly coach, but you won't stay in a simple hotel room."

"What can I say? I'm a complicated guy." He grins. "I'll have you moved to a suite later."

"You will, or your assistant will?"

Another grin. "My assistant will. I'll be busy doing other things."

"Such as?"

"You."

Oh. Well, I can't argue with that. But still…

"I don't want a suite."

"I know. But you're getting one." He presses a soft kiss to my lips.

And, in this moment, I realize that arguing with Liam Hunter is fruitless. He's used to getting what he wants.

"Anyway, you're going to be spending time here?" I question, going back to what he said before.

"We can fuck at my place, too. Either works for me, so long as we're fucking."

I'm still stuck on the spending-more-time-together bit.

"And we have your list to work on," he adds.

"My list?"

"Yeah, I'm going to help you complete it."

"You are?"

"I am." He smiles.

"And what if I don't want you to help me?" Shit, that came out sounding a little sharper than I intended. "I don't mean, I don't like fucking you because I do. I like it a lot…but beyond that, I can't do any more."

He stares at me for a long moment, his eyes darkening. "I don't do more than fucking. But you're alone in this country, and you seem like you could use a friend while you're here. How long are you here for?"

"Two weeks." *Then, I go home to die.*

He runs his fingertip over my lips. "So, we'll keep fucking for the two weeks you're here because, for some unknown reason, my cock likes you a lot. And when we're not fucking, I'll help you complete your list."

"Why would you do that?"

"I'm a charitable kind of guy." He lifts a shoulder, a teasing smile on his lips.

"Don't you have work to do?"

"My PA is always telling me I need a holiday. This can be my holiday."

"Helping me complete my list is a holiday to you?"

"We'll be fucking in that time, too."

"Of course, because the fucking is very important."

"It is very important." He slides a hand down my side, grabbing my thigh. Then, he hitches my leg over his hip and presses himself against me.

He's hard.

"Again?" I question.

A smile lifts his lips. "I've only got two weeks' worth of fucking you. So, yes, again."

He's right about that. We don't have longer than two weeks.

Maybe I don't even have that left.

chapter 5

We're lying side by side after a very active second round of sex with me riding Liam, which contributed to us both coming hard and fast.

"Tell me about the list."

I turn my head on the pillow to look at him. He turns his face toward me, meeting my eyes.

"Tell you what? You've already seen it."

"But why the list? What's the reason for writing it?"

He wants a reason. It's not like I can go with the whole truth, so I go with a half-truth.

I stare up at the ceiling. "When I was sixteen, I had a brain tumor. It was…aggressive. There was a point when I wasn't sure I was going to survive. So, I wrote the list with all the things I'd never done with the hope that I'd survive and be able to do them."

And, now, all I want is to die. Ironic, huh?

"And here you are." His hand touches mine.

I move my eyes back to him. "Yeah," I exhale. But I shouldn't be here. I should have died then. If I had, then they would still be here, living and breathing.

One life for four. I would trade mine in a heartbeat.

"Why wait so long to do the things on the list?"

I look away again. "Some things…happened. There was just never a right time." I lift a shoulder to downplay my words.

But there's nothing to downplay the fact that my family died because of me.

He brushes my hair off my face with his hand, bringing my eyes back to his. "Why is now the right time?"

Because the tumor is back, and I'm ready to die. I'm ready to join my family. I just want to do a few things before I go.

He's staring at me, curious and tender, and I really need him to stop.

My eyes go back to the ceiling. "Because…it's just time."

I know his eyes are still on me. I feel exposed. And I don't like it at all. Liam's a smart man. He'll know there's more to it than what I'm saying. But, right now, I need him to be smart enough to realize that I don't want to talk about me.

So, I fake a smile on my face and go to change the subject, hoping he goes along with it. The art of deflection—I've gotten pretty good at it over the years. "So, Mr. Mega-Rich Businessman, tell me how you became so successful." I slide a glance at him, that forced smile still on my face.

I know what's in the public domain about Liam. I knew a little about him already—he's a name people know—but I wanted to know more, so I Googled him earlier. Call me nosy, but I was curious about the man who was about to come and stick his dick in me for the second time.

Liam Hunter made his money in airplanes after setting up a small private chartered airplane company that flew rich business people all over the world.

Soon after, he expanded, investing in larger airplanes and moving into the travel industry—vacations, long-haul flights, that kind of thing. A few years later, he bought out a failing hotel chain, rebranded it, and turned it around, making it a big success. Those hotels of his are all over the world.

A few years after buying the hotel chain, he went in a different direction and set up Hunter Finance—credit cards, loans, mortgages—and from there, he built a financial empire.

Liam has the *Midas touch in business*—not my words. It was a quote from an article I read about him.

I really don't know how the guy has time to sleep.

His expression doesn't change. He just shrugs and says, "Because I'm awesome. And because I treat business like I treat fucking."

I turn on my side, so I'm facing him, putting my hands under my cheek. "And how's that?"

A smile slides onto his lips. "A mutually beneficial transaction where I make the other party feel good about what they're getting. They leave with a smile on their face, and I still come out on top."

That makes me laugh.

"Why airplanes?" I ask, intrigued. Honestly, if I were to set up a business, that would be the last thing I would think of going into.

"Because I love to fly. There's nothing more freeing than being in the air."

"There's nothing more likely to kill you than plummeting from thirty-thousand feet." *Well, except for a growing tumor in your brain.*

He gives me a disapproving look. "Babe, you're statistically more likely to die in a car crash on the way to the airport than you are in an airplane."

"Still, I'll take my chances in a car. At least I'd be on the ground."

"Crushed and mangled in a car wreck."

Laughter bursts from me. "Quite a picture you paint."

He grins at me. It's such a boyish grin, making him look years younger than the thirty-two I know him to be.

"Boston, I'll have you loving flying before you head back home to Boston."

"That was a lot of Bostons for one sentence. And, as for the flying, I highly doubt it, but thanks." Smiling, I free a hand from under my cheek and run it through his thick hair.

"Is that your family?" He nods at something over my shoulder.

The smile on my face freezes because I know what he's looking at.

I have a framed photo of my family on the nightstand. It's all I have left of them, except for my memories.

I put the picture up last night when I got here after being at his place. It's the only thing I unpacked.

When I put it up, I didn't expect Liam to come over here and start asking questions. I should have taken it down before he arrived. I should have thought about it. But I was too worried about what to wear for his imminent arrival.

I wasn't thinking.

That's my problem though. I never think.

"Yes, it's my family." Turning from him, I get out of bed. I pick the picture up and put it facedown. Moving across the room, I get the hotel-supplied robe from the hook on the back of the door and pull it on.

When I turn back, Liam is sitting up in bed, his back resting against the headboard, sheet pooling around his waist.

"And your family doesn't mind you jetting halfway across the world on your own?"

"They're all dead." The words are out before I can stop them.

I could have said anything. I could've lied. Although lying to Liam just doesn't seem to be something I can do—

well, apart from not telling him that I'm dying. That, I definitely won't be telling him.

I watch as his expression freezes. Then, sympathy and pity fill his eyes.

I hate sympathy and pity. Almost as much as I hate myself.

"Jesus, Taylor, I'm so sorry." His eyes go to the downturned picture and then come back to me. "How—"

"House fire. They all died in a fire at the house I grew up in. Any more questions?" I snap.

I didn't mean to snap. It's not like it's his fault. It's mine.

I just…I don't talk about this. Them. Any of it.

All I want is to see my family again.

I want to bake with my mom. And play catch with my dad. And argue with Parker over the bathroom. I want to tickle Tess just so I can hear her laugh and see her beautiful smile.

But I can't have that. Because they're gone. They're dead.

And all I've got is this goddamn list, which I'm going to complete. I'm going to see this city where my mom grew up, the place where she met my dad and they fell in love. I'm going to do all the stupid things that sixteen-year-old me wanted to do…and then I'm going to let this tumor kill me.

And I'll finally be with them again—where I belong.

Why did I have to stay out that night? Why did I insist on sleeping over at my best friend's house? Why did I have to ask my mother to wash my favorite hoodie so that I could wear it on the flight we were supposed to take the next day? The flight to bring us to England. Why did the dryer have to have a fault and catch fire? Why did I, a few weeks earlier, have my dad take the batteries out of the fire alarm because it kept going off all the time?

Why couldn't I have just stayed home?

Why couldn't I have died at home with them instead of having to die here alone?

Why did any of it have to happen?

The only saving grace I have is that this tumor in my head is soon going to kill me.

"I'm sorry. I didn't mean to pry." Liam's gentle voice brings me back to the now.

My hand is clutching my stomach, and I can feel wetness on my cheeks.

Turning away from him, I brush the tears away. "I'm going to take a shower," I say, walking toward the bathroom.

"Taylor?"

I turn back to him. The pity's gone, and I'm relieved. "What?"

He's staring at me like he wants to say something.

So, I beat him to it. "Look"—I sigh—"I don't talk about my family—ever. And if we're going to be spending time together, you need to know that. Okay?"

He nods. "Okay. But…if you ever change your mind…I'm here. I just want you to know that."

A lump appears in my throat while tears burn my eyes. I nod in response, unable to speak. Averting my eyes, I tighten the robe around my waist.

When I look back up, he's still watching me. Our eyes hold in silent understanding.

Then, a small smile appears on his lips.

"Well, hurry up and get your hot arse in the shower. And don't take all day because we have plans."

"We do?"

"I'm taking you out to start on your list, remember?"

"Yeah, I remember," I say before heading into the bathroom, thankful for Liam's ability to switch moods as easily as I can.

chapter 6

"A hair salon?" I look up at the sign on the shop where Liam's driver, Paul, has just pulled up in front. "This is where you're taking me?"

"Dye your hair pink. Or purple. Or some other cool color."

He remembered it from my list. The list he read once, a day ago on the plane.

I feel oddly touched that he remembered.

"How did you remember that?" I ask, turning to him.

"I remember everything off that list. Especially the, *Have lots of sex*, and *have sex outdoors*." He flashes me a salacious grin.

With my face flaming red, my eyes move to Paul sitting in the driver's seat. "Jesus, Liam," I hiss. "Paul is sitting right there. He can hear you."

"Paul's not embarrassed, are you?" Liam says, with that damn grin still on his face.

"No, sir."

"Paul might not be, but I am!" I smack Liam on the arm.

He laughs at me, and then, he opens the car door and takes my hand, pulling me out with him.

"Wait here," he tells Paul, leaning back in the car.

He shuts the door and leads me toward the hair salon.

"You know, I need an appointment to have my hair colored," I tell him as he pushes the door to the salon open.

"You've got one. I made it for this morning."

"You made the appointment?" I raise a brow. "Or your assistant did?"

He gives me an offended look. "I made the appointment. A friend of mine owns the salon."

"Liam!"

I turn to see a stunning woman moving across the salon, quickly heading for us—well, Liam.

She has black hair with these cool purple streaks in them. She's tall—a lot taller than me, but that isn't hard. She's wearing these skinny jeans that look like they were made especially for her and a really pretty fitted shirt.

She's stunning, and I instantly hate her.

Okay, well, I don't hate her. I'm just jealous of her natural gorgeousness.

I know I'm not ugly, but I am nowhere in her league.

She throws her arms around Liam, kissing his cheek and hugging him.

It's clear they're close.

Maybe as close as Liam and I are.

Liam lets go of my hand, so he can hug her back.

The twinge I feel in my stomach is most definitely not jealousy.

Okay, maybe it's a little bit of jealousy. Stupid, I know.

I watch them and the way she hugs him. She hugs him in an intimate way. Like they've been close before. Like she knows his body the way I know his body.

Jesus, they've had sex.

He's had sex with her.

I can't believe he brought me to the salon of a woman he used to fuck.

Or maybe still fucks.

The twinge in my stomach tightens into knots.

"It's been too long since I last saw you," she tells him. Aside from being gorgeous, she has an awesome English accent.

Her hand is still pressed to his chest, and I have an irrational urge to rip her hand off him.

Down, Taylor.

Jesus, what is going on with me?

I cross my arms over my chest to make sure I don't do something stupid, like break her fingers.

"When did we last see each other?" she asks him.

"Cam's birthday."

"God, yeah, that was six months ago. That was a good night." She smiles at him. It's a dreamy kind of smile.

A we-had-sex kind of smile.

Ugh.

"Yeah, it was a good night," Liam says low. "Megan, this is Taylor," he finally deems to introduce me.

I hold my silly anger in and smile at her. "Hi," I say. "You have a really nice place here.'"

I might be suffering from Jealousy 101 and want to punch Liam in the face for bringing to the salon of the woman whose vagina he has intimate knowledge of, but I can't deny that the salon is nice.

"Thanks." She smiles at me. It's a friendly smile. "So, when he called me earlier to book you in, Liam said that you want to dye your hair. What color are you looking to go?"

I finger my dull dark blonde hair, looking at her beautiful shiny black hair. She's gorgeous, and then I suddenly can't figure out why Liam is interested in having sex with me.

He's had sex with someone like her. She's tall and beautiful and stunning.

And I'm five foot three on a good day. I have a definite ass, but I'm just…mousy.

"Pink," I say, going with the first color on my list.

"Cool." She smiles. "Pink, it is. Are we talking bright pink or light pink? Pastel, like candy-floss pink? That's all the rage at the moment. That, and gray."

"Candy floss?"

"Cotton candy," Liam explains.

"Ah." I nod. Dude talks my language.

"Well, I'm definitely not going gray. Candy-floss pink," I tell her.

"Fabulous." She smiles. "Now, do you want pink highlights or full head?"

"Full head." If I'm doing this, I'm going to do it properly.

"Okay, well, I've got you with Jamie today. He's my best colorist. He'll have your hair transformed in no time. He's a genius with color."

"Jamie," she calls over to an Asian guy with a purple Mohawk.

He smiles at me as he approaches.

"Jamie, this is Taylor. Taylor wants to go pastel pink, full head." Then, she asks me, "Are we just coloring or cutting as well?"

I touch the edges of my hair, which hangs a few inches past my shoulders.

"I could take it up to sit on your shoulders," Jamie says. "Go for a choppy bob. That would really suit you. You have a great jawline and bone structure. God, I would die for cheekbones like yours."

I touch a hand to my cheekbones. I didn't realize there was anything amazing about them. They feel pretty standard to me—you know, as far as cheekbones go.

"You could carry off a choppy bob, no prob. And the cut would look even more fabulous with the color you're going for. It would really show it off. And the blue of your eyes will really stand out against the color."

"That sounds great." I smile.

I would say yes to anything Jamie says. He just sounds so enthusiastic and like he really knows what he's talking about. And he said I have a great jawline and bone structure, so I really like him.

"Okay, well, let's get you seated, and we can get started."

"How long will she be?" Liam asks Megan.

"About three hours, and then she'll be done."

Liam comes over to me. "I've got to go back to the office, but I'll be back to pick you up in three hours."

"Okay."

My expression is stoic. I can't bring myself to smile at him because I'm still annoyed that he brought me here.

He gives me a confused look. Then, he cups my face in his hands and leans down, pressing a soft kiss to my lips.

"See you soon," he whispers.

Then, he's leaving with Megan walking him to the door, and Jamie is ushering me to my seat.

"That man is sex on a stick," Jamie says to me as I sit in the seat. "I hope you don't mind me saying."

"Not at all. He is sex on a stick." I smile at the memory of Liam being inside me just an hour ago and all the dirty things he did to me in bed.

Jamie puts a gown around me and fastens it at the back of my neck. "He's not just hot either. He's a really good guy. He helped Megan buy this place, you know."

Wow. He bought her this salon.

I have this sinking feeling in my stomach. He must really like her.

I can't believe he brought me here. If they had something together and he liked her enough to buy her a salon...then he brings me here, to meet with the woman he's currently fucking...well, it's just poor taste.

I suddenly feel bad for Megan, too.

"Wow. That was kind of him."

"Yeah. Liam is a great guy. Sadly, he's straight though, but you already knew that." He gives me a conspiratorial wink. "Have you met Cam yet?"

"I haven't." I have no clue who Cam is.

"He's Megan's older brother. He and Liam are best friends. Known each other since school. Now, Cam is one fine male specimen. Straight as an arrow as well." He frees my hair from the gown. "How did you meet Liam?"

I meet his eyes in the mirror. "On the flight here."

"So, how long have you known him?"

I flick a glance at the clock. "Um...about...thirty-six hours."

Jamie grins at me, causing a goofy smile to slide onto my lips. "You are my idol, girl." He lifts his fist, fist-bumping me. "Right, I'm just going to mix up your color, and then I'll be back. Then, you can tell me what the inside of Liam's apartment looks like 'cause I've always wondered."

He gives me a wink, and I'm guessing *apartment* is code for something else.

"Do you want a drink?" he asks, his hand on my shoulder.

"Coffee would be great." I smile.

Three hours later, my hair is three inches shorter, and it's pink.

And I have to say, I love it.

It looks really edgy and hot.

Liam hasn't returned yet, and I'm at the counter, ready to pay.

"Taylor's already paid for," Megan tells the girl at the reception counter.

"I am?"

"Liam paid. Didn't he tell you?"

"No. He didn't."

"Sounds like Liam." Megan smiles softly. "Speak of the devil."

I turn to see Liam coming through the door. Instead of feeling happy to see him, I just feel pissed off.

First, he brings me here. Then, he pays for my hair, like I'm his little woman.

I don't know which I'm madder about.

"Wow, look at you…gorgeous." He slips his fingers into my hair.

Ignoring his compliment, I turn abruptly, forcing his hand to fall away.

"Thank you," I say to Megan. "And would you give this to Jamie and tell him thanks?" I push a twenty-pound note into her hand.

"Of course." Megan smiles.

Moving away, I brush past Liam, leaving the salon.

"Hey"—Liam catches my arm as I've just exited the salon—"what's wrong?"

I spin around to face him, a frown on my face. "You paid for my hair." My tone is accusing.

Wariness enters his eyes. "I did."

"And why did you do that?"

"Because I can."

"Because you can." I grit my teeth.

I am mad about the money, but really, I'm pissier about Megan. It's stupid, I know, but it is what it is.

And his superior attitude is annoying me even more.

So, he's going to get it about the money and not about the fact that he took me to his fuck buddy's hair salon.

"I can pay for my own hair, thank you very much. I'm not a fucking charity case."

He frowns, his dark brows drawing together. "I know you're not a charity case. I just thought it would be a nice thing to do."

"Well, I don't want your nice." I turn from him and start walking again.

He stops me and stands in front of me. Refusing to look at him, I stare past him.

"Is there something else going on here?" he asks.

"No." *Yes.*

"So, you're just mad because I paid for your hair?"

I grind my teeth together and bring my eyes to his. "Yes. I don't like people to pay for me. I pay my own way in this world."

"Okay." He blows out a breath, the look in his eyes contrite.

And then, suddenly, I feel like a total bitch.

"I'm sorry I paid for your hair without consulting you first. I wasn't trying to be a dick. I just wanted to treat you. A welcome-to-England kind of thing."

"You welcomed me to England just fine last night with your tongue."

That's my lame way of trying to defuse the situation I just created. It's a crappy attempt. But it makes him laugh, a deep chuckle rumbling in his chest. The sound eases my guilt a little.

"Yeah. That was definitely a good way to welcome you to my country."

I smile, unable not to.

"I'm sorry." His voice is low, and it touches me deep inside.

Liam lifts a hand to my head and wraps a lock of my new pink hair around his finger. "Your hair looks really sexy. I can't wait to see it spread out all over my pillow." He steps close, pressing his chest to mine.

And, just like that, he has me.

I stare up into his eyes. "I think we can arrange that."

He drives his fingers into my hair, gripping it, and tips my head back. "I'm going to wrap your sexy pink hair around my fist and pull it hard while I fuck you from behind."

I swallow down. "I-I...think I can live with that." My voice trembles with a sudden need. A need for him.

He brings his mouth down to mine and kisses me deeply, slowly, his tongue sweeping over mine.

It's a knee-buckling kiss. I have to grip his arms, so I don't fall over.

"So, am I allowed to take you for dinner before I take you back to my place to fuck you?" he murmurs against my lips. "Show that pretty hair off that I got into trouble for paying for."

My eyes flutter. "I could eat," I say, still feeling breathless from his kiss. "But I'm paying for dinner."

He tips his head back. "You are not paying for my dinner." He looks appalled at the idea.

I let out a sigh. "Okay, Caveman, how about we go dutch?"

"How about I pay for it all, and you can just like it?"

"How about I don't? You wanna pull my hair while you fuck me from behind? Then, I'm buying dinner."

He laughs low and deep. "Fine. I won't pull your hair. I'll just fuck you the old-fashioned way and still buy you dinner."

"Ugh," I grumble. "You're impossible."

"I'm not impossible." He chuckles. "I just know what I want. Okay, how about this? I'll buy you dinner, and you can pay me back in sexual favors when we get back to my place."

"Um, you want me to hooker myself out for dinner?" I glare at him.

A salacious look crosses his face, his lips tipping up into a grin. "I have always wanted to fuck a hooker."

"You ass!" I slap his chest with my hand.

Chuckling, he wraps his arms around me and presses his nose to mine, staring into my eyes. "I'm not an ass. I'm hot. And you want me bad."

"That's debatable since you just called me a hooker."

"I didn't call you a hooker." He frowns.

"You asked me to pay for my dinner by giving you sexual favors."

"Ah, now, you're just twisting my words all up. I said I'd always wanted to fuck a hooker—"

"Not making me feel better."

"And I didn't call you a hooker. Babe…" He brushes his nose down the side of mine, kissing my cheek and then the corner of my mouth. "How about you let me buy you dinner, and I'll go down on you in thanks? How does that sound?"

"You want to thank me with oral sex for you buying dinner? How does that make sense?"

"It makes sense because I get to pay for dinner and not have you mad at me." A sexy smile slowly creeps onto his lips.

"You have a really weird idea about what constitutes winning, Hunter."

"And that's why I'm so successful in business, Boston."

"Because you have no clue what winning means?"

"No. Because people would rather be fucked by me than fucked over by me."

Laughing, I shake my head. "You are a strange man, Liam Hunter."

"And aren't you just glad you met me?"

I stare up into his face. "Oddly, yeah, I am."

He kisses me one last time and then releases me.

I follow him over to his waiting car. He opens the door, and I climb into the backseat. Liam gets in next to me.

"Hey," I say to Paul.

"Hi, Taylor." Paul smiles at me through the rearview mirror. "Your hair looks great."

"Thank you." I smile at him.

"Take us to Cam's," Liam tells Paul.

I rest my head on Liam's shoulder, a feeling of contentment around me, as Paul pulls out into the London traffic.

chapter 7

"So…Megan…she's nice," I say, chewing on my thumbnail.

We're still in the car. London traffic is heavy, like all the time. I'm staring out the window, looking at the cars next to us.

I feel Liam look at me, but I keep my eyes on the window.

"She is. Why do I feel like there's something more to that statement than just Megan being nice?"

"Well…she's very pretty."

"She is pretty."

I stop chewing my nail and slide my eyes to him. "And…Jamie was telling me that you helped her buy the salon."

His brows draw together. "Jamie has a big mouth."

"So…did you? Buy it for her, I mean? Because that's a massively kind thing to do for someone—buying them a business."

"I'm a massive guy—in all respects." He flicks a smile in the direction of his crotch.

I'm too frustrated to even laugh, so I just sigh and stare out the window again.

I don't know why it bothers me so much that he bought the salon for Megan. I guess...I just think he must really care about her to have done that for her.

Since I lost my family I haven't had anyone to care about me. I know it was my choice, to keep people away, but that doesn't stop me from feeling envious that Megan had Liam when she needed someone.

For the last four years, I've had no one.

So, what I'm feeling right now, this envy, it's stupid. I know that. But I'm a girl, and I'm dying, so I'm allowed this moment of stupidity.

Liam takes my chin in his hand and turns my face to him. "I didn't buy the salon for Megan. I loaned her the money. She paid me back once the business started making money."

"Oh, okay." I turn my face back to the window.

He sighs. "Is there something else?"

I lift a shoulder.

"Taylor." His tone is firm.

I turn back to him. "Well, I'm just wondering...if you've slept together. I just kind of got the impression that you had. And if you have in fact had sex with Megan, then taking me there, to a place owned by a woman you used to fuck—or still fuck—well...it was just really poor taste."

His mouth tightens. "You're right. It would have been in poor taste. I might have a lot of faults, Boston, but poor judgment is not one of them. I haven't had sex with Megan. Nor do I ever intend on having sex with Megan."

"But you bought her a business. Nothing says *I want to fuck you* like that." *What is wrong with me? Why am I so jealous?*

And I think I might have pushed it a little too far as he looks really pissed off. Sounds it, too.

"No. I loaned her the money. She's my best friend's little sister. She's my friend. I help my friends."

"Like you're helping me with my list?" I give him a look.

I'm clearly itching for a fight with him. But, why?

Liam slowly shakes his head at me, his dark eyes pinned on mine. "I think we both know that you and I are more than friends. I think my thumb up your arse while I was fucking your pussy with my cock earlier on should have confirmed that fact to you."

"God, you're so fucking crass." I flick a look at Paul, hoping he didn't hear what Liam said. It's just wishful thinking on my part because there is no way he didn't hear.

"I'm not crass. I'm just a man who knows what he wants. And when I want something, I take it. I don't pussyfoot around. Just like when I took your arse earlier. Next time, it will be my cock in there." He leans in close, so his breath is brushing over my lips. "And I will fuck you hard…so hard that my name will be imprinted on your voice box from you screaming it."

Holy fuck.

I close my eyes. I can't help the shudder that runs through my body or the whimper that leaves my mouth from the sensations that his words and nearness send rushing through me.

Liam's dirty mouth seems to be my kryptonite.

"I want you, Boston," he whispers, sliding his hand around my waist, turning my body into his. "Only you. Your pussy and arse are the only ones I'm interested in fucking. So, are we done with the jealousy?"

My eyes snap open to meet his. "I'm not jealous."

"You are so jealous. It's cute but not necessary." He taps my nose with his finger.

"Fuck off!" I bat his hand away.

He laughs. The bastard fucking laughs.

I turn away. Childish probably, but I don't care. He's pissed me off.

"Aw, babe"—he curls a hand around the back of my neck, bringing my face back to his—"you have nothing to be angry about. You are the only one I want to fuck for the foreseeable future."

"For the next two weeks," I correct him. "And I wasn't jealous. I was…well…"

"You were what?"

He's staring at me, and now, I have to given him an answer.

For once, I decide to go with the truth.

"Well, I don't share. I don't like to be with a guy if he's with other women or even if he's interested in being with other women. I know we're not in a relationship, but I just think, if we're sleeping together for the next two weeks, then we should sleep with only each other. And if you don't agree with that, then we shouldn't sleep with each other anymore."

"I agree."

"Oh." That takes the wind out of my sails. "You do?"

"Yeah. I've never been good at sharing either, and I definitely don't want to share you."

"Well then…we're agreed. For these next two weeks, we sleep with only each other."

"Agreed." His hand slides up my thigh, gripping the top, and then he presses his lips to mine, kissing me hard.

"Wow," I say breathless when he releases me. "You always close all your deals that way?"

"Only with hot list-making Bostonians." He gives a boyish grin. "Talking of lists, we're here."

"What? Where?" I turn to look out the window as the car comes to a stop.

"Cam's—my friend's bar. We're eating here, and then you're going to cross another thing off your list."

"I am?" I turn back to him, my brow raised in question.

"Yeah—*sing in public.* Cam has a resident band. Tonight is open mic night, so it's the perfect opportunity for you to cross it off your list."

"Oh…I don't know. I was thinking that I'd maybe do one thing a day. And the hair constitutes as one thing."

Liam laughs. "Stop being a chicken."

"I'm not being a chicken. I was the one who put it on my list, wasn't I?"

"So then, what's the point in waiting? Do it now."

He's right. What's the point in stalling? It's not like I have the luxury of time.

"Okay, let's do it."

He smiles wide. "This is going to be epic."

"It's going to be terrible. I'm a really awful singer."

"And that's why it's going to be epic." He flashes a grin at me.

We get out of the car with Liam telling Paul to take off and that he'll call when he needs to be picked up.

Then, holding my hand, Liam leads me into Cam's Bar.

There's music playing when we enter. Sounds to be a cover of a Kings of Leon song.

"That's the band you'll be singing with, The March. Lee over there is the lead singer and guitarist." He nods at a dark-haired guy who's currently singing into the microphone. "You can either sing with him or go solo. Your choice."

"I'll be solo when I start singing because my voice will clear this place out."

Liam snickers. "Come on, let's go see Cam and get you fed."

The bar is really nice. Modern and trendy with a warm feeling to it. And I'm relieved to see that it's not too busy either. Less people to humiliate myself in front of.

"Cam," Liam calls to a guy further down the bar.

Smiling, he walks toward us. He's Megan's brother. I can tell immediately. He's as good-looking as she is beautiful. He has the same black hair and contrasting blue eyes as she does.

"Hey, man." He reaches over the bar to Liam, and they do that handshake-and-half-hug thing that men do.

I see Cam's eyes go to me. I smile at him.

"Cam, this is Taylor Shaw from Boston."

"Hello, Taylor Shaw, from Boston." He reaches over the bar to shake my hand. "Can I get you guys a drink?"

"Beer for me," Liam says.

"I'll have the same," I tell Cam.

I take a seat on a barstool, and Liam takes the seat beside me.

Cam puts two beers in front of us.

Liam picks up a menu and hands it to me. I scan it and decide on a burger and fries, or chips as they call them here.

"I'll have the same," Liam tells me. "Cam, can you have Nancy rustle us up some burger and chips?"

"Will do." Cam disappears into the back.

"Nancy's the cook here. Makes the best homemade burgers you've ever tasted in your life," Liam tells me.

I take a sip of my beer.

"Hey! Hunter's here, and he is not alone."

I turn to the voice approaching. A guy with chestnut-brown hair, who is about the same height but not as built as Liam and more lithe than muscular, is walking toward us.

Liam gets up from his seat. "Eddie, mate."

They do the handshake-and-half-hug man thing.

"Where the fuck have you been hiding?" Liam says to him. "Feels like ages since I last saw you."

"I've been busy at the hospital. You missed me, you soppy bastard?"

"With all my heart." Liam chuckles, slapping a hand to his chest.

Eddie's eyes come to me. "And who is this beauty you've brought with you?"

Liam puts his arm around Eddie's shoulder and looks at me. "Eddie, this is Taylor Shaw from Boston. Boston, this is Eddie, one of my oldest mates. Ugly as fuck, but someone's gotta love him."

"Fuck you very much, Hunter. And Boston, eh? What is someone like you doing with this degenerate?" Eddie flicks his thumb in Liam's direction.

"He sat next to me on the plane, and I haven't been able to get rid of him since." I grin.

"Sounds like Hunter. He was like that in school. First day I met him, I just couldn't shake him off. He's like a bad smell. He's been following me around ever since."

"So, you guys met at school?" I ask.

"Yeah, first day at Eton. I met Eddie and that tosser." Liam nods at Cam, who's just appeared from behind the bar.

"Wow, you guys all went to Eton? Isn't that a really elite school?" It comes out sounding like surprise, which I totally didn't mean. I just didn't figure Liam was a private school boy.

Liam laughs loudly, and so do Eddie and Cam.

"Yes. We are from rich families, and we went to the posh boys' school," Eddie says in a preppy voice, laughing.

"But you own a bar?" I say to Cam. I slap my hand over my mouth, realizing how bad that sounded. "God, I didn't mean it like that. I just thought that people who went to Eton became, like, royalty or something."

Cam chuckles. "No offense taken." He waves me off. "I was supposed to become royalty, but it didn't quite work out that way. The call of the bar life was just too strong for me to ignore. Much to my parents' chagrin."

"I, on the other hand, did not disappoint my parents," Eddie says smugly.

Cam gives him the middle finger.

"Eddie's a doctor," Liam tells me.

"Cardiovascular surgeon, fuck you very much." He leans in, telling me, "And I'm the best heart surgeon in England. Probably the world."

"Wow. That's amazing. It must have taken you years to become a doctor."

"It took a while, but it was worth it. Still, after all those years, I don't make near a scratch of what Hunter makes in a year. What is your net worth nowadays, Hunter? You hit the billion pound mark yet?"

Liam smirks but doesn't say anything.

"Liam doesn't like to talk about how much money he has," Eddie tells me. "Because he has so much of it."

"I think he probably doesn't like to talk about his money—not because he of how much he has, but because it's not what's important to him. I think Liam's business achievements are what he cares about most," I say, staring into Liam's eyes.

His gaze softens on me.

"Oh God, she's your soul mate. Marry her, Liam. Immediately." Eddie laughs.

Liam looks at Eddie, chuckling, as he shakes his head.

"I bet your parents are really proud of what you've achieved," I say to Liam.

I instantly know I've said the wrong thing when the tenderness in his eyes disappears, and a dark shadow falls there instead.

"I wouldn't know." His voice is sharp, surprising me. "I need to go talk to Lee."

I watch him go as he walks off, his whole body rigid and tense.

I feel like crap because I know I hit a raw nerve.

"Don't worry about it." Eddie's voice comes in my ear. "Liam's touchy about his family. I won't go into his personal business because it's his shit. He'll tell you if he wants you to know. All I will say is that Liam's dad is a walking waste of good oxygen."

"Oh. He never said anything." But I never asked because I didn't want to talk about my family.

I glance back at Liam, who is now talking to Lee.

Eddie follows my stare. "Liam was raised by his grandpa, Bernie. Top bloke. You'll love him."

He was raised by his grandpa. What about his mom and dad?

I want to ask Eddie more, but I know he won't tell me. So, I'll just have to wait until Liam is ready to tell me—if that ever comes.

But would I ever tell him about my family?

I already know the answer to that one, and it's a solid no.

Cam puts a plate of burger and fries in front of me, bringing my attention to it. I didn't even realize he'd gone to get them.

"Is that one Liam's?" Eddie points to the plate with a burger and overflowing fries next to mine.

"Yeah," I answer.

"He won't miss some chips." Eddie leans over and grabs a handful of fries from Liam's plate, taking nearly half of them.

I chuckle.

Eddie then quickly eats them, and he's just finishing them off when Liam comes back and sits on his stool next to me.

"All right?" I carefully ask him.

"Yeah, I'm good." He smiles and gives my thigh a squeeze.

I immediately feel better.

He looks down at his plate and frowns. "Hey, Cam, are you skimping on the chips to save money, you tight bastard?"

I glance at Eddie, and we both start laughing.

chapter 8

We've finished eating. I'm on my third beer, and the bar has filled up with people.

"Okay, Boston, it's time. You're up." Liam nudges me.

"What? Sing now?"

"Um-hum."

I start to feel sick, and it's not from the food or beer. "I don't know, Hunter."

"Come on." He gets to his feet. Taking me by the hands, he pulls me off my stool.

"Go on, Taylor," Eddie encourages.

Liam told Eddie and Cam all about the list of things I wanted to do—except for the sex stuff. Thankfully, he didn't tell them that. And he didn't go into the details of why I have the list either, which was another thing I was thankful for.

"You've got this, Boston."

I stare up into Liam's beautiful green eyes. "No recording this, and no laughing, promise?"

I hold my little finger up to him for a pinkie swear.

He laughs and wraps his little finger around mine. "I promise. Now, go get 'em, tiger." He smacks me on the ass.

Shaking my head at him, I turn, and on wobbly legs, I walk toward the stage where the band is waiting for me.

The lead singer, Lee, holds out a hand, helping me up onto the stage.

"Hey, I'm Lee. You're Taylor, right?"

"Yeah. It's nice to meet you."

"You, too. So, you want to sing with us tonight, huh? Just one song?"

"Definitely one song." I laugh.

"Okay, so do you know the words to 'I Touch Myself' by Divinyls?"

"Um…" I roll through my mental song list. *Isn't that song about sex?* "I'm not sure if I know the lyrics."

"Don't worry. I have the sheet music. Liam chose it for you. He was very insistent that you sing it."

"Oh, he was, was he?" I meet Liam's eyes across the bar and watch as a massive grin spreads across his face.

"Here are the words." Lee hands me a sheet of paper with the lyrics on it.

I let my eyes scan the words. *Holy shit.*

This song is about a woman making herself come while she's thinking of the man she wants.

Bastard.

I glare at Liam across the room.

The smile on his handsome face gets bigger. I have the sudden urge to wipe it off.

I can't sing this.

"And here's your mic." Lee hands me a microphone.

"Thank you."

"You ready to do this?"

Nope. "I guess…"

Liam is so going to pay for this later. He can forget hair-pulling and fucking later. At this rate, dude is going to be sleeping alone with only his hand for company.

I blow out a breath and put the microphone to my lips.

"I'll count us in, and then we'll start playing. You count to sixteen in your head and then start singing. Okay?"

"Sixteen. Okay."

My heart starts pounding, and nerves are swimming in my belly. My palms start to sweat around the microphone.

You can do this, Taylor. No fear.

The band starts to play. I shut my eyes and begin counting. When I reach sixteen, I flick my eyes open, stare down at the first words, and then I start to sing.

Oh my God, I'm singing. In a bar filled with people.

I'm singing in a bar full of people, and…I'm actually not that bad.

Hell yeah. I've got this.

By the time we reach the chorus, I'm totally into it, shaking my hips and ass on stage and belting out the words. Liam, Eddie, and Cam are all cheering me on. People in the audience are singing along. Some are even getting up from their seats and dancing.

My confidence is soaring.

Maybe Liam was actually onto something with this song.

I feel awesome!

He's totally getting a blow job later.

And then we're on the last chorus, and the song is over way too quickly for my liking.

People are clapping and cheering. I see Liam standing up on his stool, whistling.

I give a little bow.

I have never felt so amazing in all my life as I do now—well, apart from when I'm in Liam's bed.

"You were great." Lee smiles at me.

I hand him back the microphone and sheet music. "Thanks." I beam. "And thank you for letting me sing with you guys."

"Anytime. You can sing with us anytime."

My smile gets even bigger.

Heart pumping with adrenaline, I turn to leave the stage, and Liam is there. He puts his hands on my waist, lifting me down. My body slides against his, and he pauses me when our faces are close. His lips meet mine in a soft kiss.

"That was fucking amazing, Boston. I'm so proud of you."

"I'm proud of me, too." I smile.

"One more thing crossed off your list."

"It is."

Liam puts me on my feet, and holding my hand, he leads us back to our seats at the bar.

"That was really great, Taylor." Cam smiles at me.

"She was better than great, fuckwit. She was hot as fuck up there," Eddie says to him.

Liam reaches over and slaps Eddie on the back of the head.

"Oi!" Eddie complains, rubbing his head where Liam just smacked him.

"Don't call her hot."

"I was giving her a compliment."

"You can give her compliments without calling her hot, dickface." Liam gives him a stern look.

"You did really great," Cam tells me again. "Let me get you a drink on the house."

"I still have my beer left, but thanks."

"I'll take Taylor's free beer," Eddie says.

"You can pay for yours, you cheap bastard," Cam tells him. He grabs a bottle and pops the cap, putting it on the bar in front of Eddie.

"What about me?" Liam says. "Don't I get offered a drink around here?" He waves his empty beer bottle around.

"I'll have a beer waiting for you when you're done."

"When I'm done?" Liam's brows draw together, puzzled.

"You're up to sing. I thought you'd want to show off your killer serenading skills to Taylor. Because we all know how you *want it that way*." Cam chuckles, a shit-eating grin on his face.

Liam looks confused for a moment. He glances at Eddie, who is also wearing a huge grin.

Then, something dawns on Liam, and his expression drops. "You didn't?"

"*Ye-ah,*" Eddie sings from behind us.

"*You are…*" Cam sing-laughs.

"You set of cunts," Liam growls.

"Aw, don't be like that. *You're my fire!*" Eddie bursts out laughing.

"I fucking hate you both. Why the hell am I still mates with you?"

"*Tell me why!*" Cam barely gets the words out because he's laughing so hard.

I can't help but laugh. I have no clue what I'm laughing about, but I have a feeling I'm about to find out.

"Hardy-fucking-har. I hope you both fuck hookers, and your dicks fall off."

"You do realize that's medically impossible, right?" Eddie smirks at him.

Liam looks murderous, which only makes Eddie and Cam laugh harder.

He sighs and gets up from his stool. He turns to me, cupping my chin in his hand, staring deep into my eyes. "Whatever they tell you, it's a lie." He lifts his eyes over my head, leveling them both with a harsh glare. "And if I were you two, I'd sleep with your eyes open from now on." His eyes come back to me. "Remember, Boston, all lies."

"All lies. I got it."

He kisses me firmly on the lips and then leaves me. Walking in the direction of the stage, he looks defeated, like a man heading for execution.

Liam climbs up onto the stage and takes the microphone that Lee was holding out for him.

The next thing I hear is the intro for "I Want It That Way" by the Backstreet Boys, and Liam starts to sing. Rather badly.

Okay...

I turn back to Cam and Eddie, barely able to control my laughter. "So, which one of you is going to tell me the story behind this song and why Liam looks like he wants to kill you both?"

Cam grins and rests his arms on top of the bar while Eddie moves his stool closer.

Leaning forward, Cam says, "Okay, so we were sixteen years old. We were in an all-boys boarding school, and girls were like gold dust to us. So, when you got a girl...well, it was like Christmas. Anyway, Liam was seeing this girl, Sophie Forester, from a neighboring school. And she dumped him because she'd heard that he'd shagged another girl."

"Had he?" I ask.

"Oh, yeah, totally," Eddie says.

"But Liam was all cut up because he realized that he'd made this huge mistake by sleeping with this other girl." Cam slaps a hand to his chest, feigning drama. "He was down and driving us fucking nuts, so we snuck out of school and took him to the off-license to buy some booze. We thought if we got him drunk, he'd shut the fuck up about Sophie. Only it didn't quite work out that way."

Eddie tells me, "We were sitting at the park, getting hammered on cheap cider, when Liam gets to his feet and suddenly announces that he has this *amazing*"—he emphasizes with his hands, laughing—"idea and that Sophie will forgive him and get back together with him."

Cam laughs. "Of course, we encouraged this line of thinking because...well, we thought it would be funny to watch Liam do whatever he was going to do to win this chick back."

"So, we walked to Sophie's house," Eddie continues, "which wasn't that far from the park. When we got there, all the lights were on. I thought that Liam was just going to go up and knock on her front door, so he could talk to her. But, oh, no, that wasn't what Liam had in mind at all. He was planning something…bigger. So, he staggered across her front garden, trampling all over her mother's flowers in the process, and he stood beneath Sophie's bedroom window, which faced out onto the main street. Then, he just started…singing—loudly."

"Oh my God!" I cover my mouth with my hands. "'I Want It That Way.'"

"The very song." Eddie fist-bumps me. "Sophie was a massive Backstreet Boys fan. So, dickhead over there thought he could win her back by serenading her with her favorite song."

"And the best part was, not only was he a fucking terrible singer—as you can currently hear—but Sophie wasn't even home," Cam tells me. "She was out at a party with her family. So, the silly cunt was singing to an empty house."

I'm laughing harder now, clutching my stomach.

"It was fucking brilliant!" Eddie laughs.

"So, what happened when he realized that Sophie wasn't home?" I ask.

"He didn't. He thought she was holding out on him, so he just kept on singing—until the cops arrived, that is."

"The police came?" I gasp.

"Oh, yeah," Eddie tells me. "Sophie's next-door neighbor had rung the police. Next thing we knew, Liam was arrested for underage drinking and disturbing the peace. They rang his granddad, and he had to go down and bail Liam out."

"It was the single greatest moment of my life." Cam grins. "And one we've never let him live down."

"Oh my God!" I'm laughing so hard, imagining a sixteen-year-old Liam serenading his girl to win her back. "So, did he get back together with Sophie?" I ask, wiping tears of laughter from my eyes.

"Nope." Eddie chuckles, shaking his head. "The neighbor who had called the cops told her and her folks what had happened when they got home. Sophie wouldn't even look in his direction after that."

"Aw, poor Liam."

"Don't feel too bad for him. He had a line of chicks waiting to shag him after they'd heard what he had done. For some reason, they all thought it was really romantic, putting his heart out there and singing to Sophie. Hunter got laid *a lot* that year," Cam tells me.

"He always was a lucky bastard when it came to women. Present company included," Eddie says, making me blush.

I hear Liam's song coming to a close, so I turn to the stage, watching and listening as he murders the end of the song.

And when he's finished, Cam, Eddie, and I all start cheering and clapping. I stand up on the edge of my stool and whistle loudly.

Liam gives his microphone to Lee, jumps down off the stage, and walks over to me.

"You were great!" I beam at him.

He slides his arm around my waist and presses a kiss to my temple. Then, he takes his seat beside me. "So, you told her then, you pair of bastards."

"Of course we did." Eddie smirks.

"I think what you did was really sweet." I turn in my seat to face him. "Singing like that to try to win your girl back? No one has ever done anything like that for me."

He slides his hands up my thighs, parting my legs, ensuring my skirt is still covering me, he tugs me closer, so I'm all but straddling him. "I'd sing for you, Boston."

That puts a smile onto my face and sends a flutter in my chest. Then, Liam leans in and presses his lips to mine, and that flutter turns into a swarm of butterflies. His hands move around the outside of my thighs until they are on my ass, and he pulls me onto his lap, so I'm actually straddling him. Thank god my skirt is knee-length or everyone would be getting a good show right now.

His kiss deepens, setting my insides on fire. And for a moment, I forget where I am with all the people around us, and I just revel in the feel of his tongue in my mouth and his hands on my ass.

"Okay, enough of the PDA. I don't have a lap-dancing license. And you're making Eddie jealous."

I break away from Liam's mouth, panting, my cheeks instantly flushing.

Liam grins at me, touching the pink with his fingertips. "Everything I've already done to you, and making out in a bar embarrasses you."

Smiling, I shake my head at him. Then, I disentangle myself from him, sitting back on my own stool. But he doesn't let me go completely. He takes ahold of my hand, holding it against his thigh.

"So, do I get that beer or not?" Liam lifts his chin at Cam.

"One beer coming up," Cam says.

"I'll have another beer," Eddie tells Cam. "I'm just gonna go take a piss first."

"Taylor, you want anything?" Cam asks me.

My beer is nearly finished. If I keep going this way, I'll be marking off another thing on my list—getting wasted and puking.

I pick up my beer and finish the last of it off. "Yeah, I'll take another beer," I tell Cam.

Cam gets three bottles out of the fridge. He pops the caps off and puts them down on the bar. Then, he seems to freeze. His eyes are fixed on something over the top of my head.

He darts a look at Liam and then says, "I didn't know he was coming in tonight."

Who came in?

Liam frowns and then turns to where Cam's staring.

The look on Liam's face…is one of pure anger. His whole expression darkens. His jaw clenches tightly. I can feel the tension pouring off him.

I follow his stare. There's a blond guy, about six feet, standing there. I'd say he's in his thirties, but it's hard to see him properly from here.

The guy seems to hesitate. Then, he makes a decision and walks toward us.

"Jeremy." Cam lifts his chin in greeting.

"I just came to pick up Nancy after her shift," Jeremy says.

"I'll let her know you're here." Cam casts a nervous glance at Liam, who is just staring at Jeremy like he wants to kill him.

Jeremy is looking at anything but Liam.

And I have never felt so uncomfortable in my life.

Cam reluctantly leaves to get Nancy.

There's a horrible, tense silence. Then, Jeremy seems to pluck up some courage and turns his face our way. "How are you doing, Liam?"

"I was doing just fucking great until about thirty seconds ago," Liam says, through clenched teeth.

"I won't be here long. I'm just picking up Nancy."

"I didn't realize Nancy was your type, her being single and all. And I thought she had better taste but clearly not."

I expect Jeremy to be angry, but he doesn't look angry, just sad.

"Look, Liam…it's been seven years. Don't you think it's time we bury the hatchet?"

"No. The only place I want to bury the hatchet is in your face."

Oh Christ.

"Jesus, man, I've said I'm sorry a million fucking times. What do I have to do?"

"Nothing." Liam slips off his stool and takes a menacing step toward him. "I don't care if you're sorry. Nothing you say will ever change what you did!" Liam roars.

A hush falls over the bar.

Jeremy's nervous eyes flicker to me.

"Don't look at her." Liam steps in front of me. "Don't ever fucking look at her. Don't even breathe the same air as her. If you do—you remember the last time I hit you? Well, that will look like a fucking tickle compared to what I'll do to you if you go anywhere near Taylor."

Holy fuck. Angry Liam is Hot Liam. But he's also scary as hell.

I need to defuse this situation. I'm just not sure how.

"Liam?" I touch his arm, but he doesn't seem to feel me.

He's just glaring at Jeremy, his chest pumping up and down. Then, I see Eddie coming back, and I nearly fall off my stool in relief.

I watch Eddie as he sees Jeremy. His eyes go to Liam, and his steps seem to falter.

Then, I see him mouth, *Oh, fuck.* And he's speeding over to us.

He comes to a stop between Jeremy and Liam. "All okay here?" Eddie asks Liam.

"Everything's just fucking great. Jeremy was just leaving, weren't you, *Jeremy*?" The way Liam says his name is with total distaste.

Jeremy sighs and takes a step back.

Cam appears back behind the bar, a harried look on his face. "Nancy will be out in a few," Cam tells Jeremy.

"Tell her I'm waiting outside." Jeremy tips his head in the direction of the door as he takes another step back. His eyes go to Liam. "For what it's worth, man, I am sorry. More than you'll ever know."

"Tell it to someone who gives a shit," Liam says in a tone that makes the hairs on the back of my neck stand on end.

Jeremy lifts his hands in defeat. Then, he turns and walks out the bar.

Jesus Christ, that was tense.

I hear Eddie blow out a breath that sounds an awful lot like relief, and I know exactly how he feels.

Angry Liam might be Hot Liam. But he's also Scary Liam.

Liam turns to face Cam, his hands curling around the edge of the bar. "He's seeing Nancy?" Liam says low.

"For a couple of months now," Cam answers him carefully.

"Why didn't you tell me?" Liam's tone is accusing.

Cam frowns. "Because I didn't think it was newsworthy. And it's not like I can ever mention Jeremy's name in front of you without you turning into the Hulk." He exhales a tired sound. "You used to be friends once."

"And, now, we're not."

"Yeah, and none of us know why, except for you and Jeremy. And Jeremy won't tell us a fucking thing because he's protecting you."

"Protecting me?" Liam gives a bitter-sounding laugh. "That's fucking rich. He actually said that?"

"No, he didn't say that. He never says anything, just like you. So, we have to jump to conclusions, and considering you were the one who punched him in the face at Kate's funeral, I'd say he's covering for you."

"Because, of course, it would be something I did. Sounds about right." Liam's laugh is dry, but I can hear the hurt beneath it, and it cuts me. "Not perfect fucking Jeremy Bentley. He would never do anything wrong. But me, the bastard son of a stripper? Yeah, I'd definitely do something wrong." He steps away from the bar.

He's the bastard son of a stripper? And who is Kate?

"I never said that. Jeremy isn't perfect—far from it. None of us are. We're all a bunch of fuckups, except for you. You're the one who made something of himself. And I'm so fucking proud of everything you've achieved, man." Cam tries to reason, but I can see Liam is already gone, not listening to anything he's saying. "But if we just knew what went down between you and Jeremy, then maybe we could help."

"You can't help. No one ever could." He stares hard at Cam before looking at me. "We're leaving." Liam grabs my arm and all but pulls me off the stool.

I have just enough time to grab my bag off the bar before I'm being dragged along.

I hear Cam and Eddie calling his name, asking him to come back, but he doesn't stop. He just strides out of the bar, and I have to jog to keep up with him.

Thankfully, there's no sign of Jeremy when we get outside.

Liam doesn't stop walking. He continues on along the roadside, pulling me with him, and he lifts his hand for an approaching taxi.

"Will you just slow the hell down?" I yank my arm from his grip.

"No." He grabs my arm again as the taxi pulls up beside us. He opens the door and manhandles me in. He barks his address at the driver. Then, he finally sits back in his seat.

I fold my arms over my chest. "I don't appreciate being manhandled like that. And I didn't even get to say good-bye to your friends. You were really rude to them, you know."

"I'll buy them a fucking card to apologize."

"You're acting like a total dick. You don't like that Jeremy guy, fine. Doesn't mean you get to act like a prick toward me."

His eyes swing to mine. The look in them makes me want to shrink back in my seat. Possibly get out of the cab—while it's still moving.

"I thought you liked it when I acted like a prick?" His voice is low and dark.

I don't get a chance to respond because he grabs the back of my head and slams his mouth down on mine.

His kiss is hot and hard, angry and so fucking hot.

He's devouring my mouth, his tongue sliding along mine. His hand grazes up my leg and pushes under my skirt, slipping between my thighs.

And I don't even stop him.

He strokes his fingers over my panties. "The second I get you out of this taxi, I'm going to fuck you. Hard."

Then, he's kissing me again. The whole time, his fingers are rubbing my clit through my panties, driving me wild. And all I want is for my panties to disappear and for him to be touching me, skin to skin.

I don't care that we're in the back of a taxi and that the driver can probably see what Liam is doing to me.

I don't care about anything but him.

I'm mindless, lost in Liam's touch, his body…his kiss.

Almost as if reading my mind, he brushes his lips over my cheek and says into my ear, his words hot against my skin, "Does it turn you on that he might be watching what I'm doing to you?"

I turn my head, staring into his dark eyes. "Yes, it turns me on."

"You make my dick so fucking hard."

He pushes my panties to the side and slides a thick finger inside me.

I can't help the moan that escapes. Liam swallows it with his kiss.

"I'll never tire of fucking your hot, tight pussy," he rumbles over my lips, curling his finger inward in a come-hither motion, pressing against my inner walls.

I'm squirming and bearing down on his hand, riding his finger.

"That's it, babe. Fuck my finger. Just like I'm going to fuck you with my cock. God, I want to fuck you now—so bad. I want to bend you over this seat, lift your skirt, pull your knickers down, and slam my cock deep inside you. I want to fuck you right here, in the back of this taxi, while the driver watches, jealous because I'm the one inside you, fucking you."

"Oh God," I whisper.

If he tries to fuck me in this taxi, I don't even know if I'll stop him because I'm so turned on that I can't even think straight.

He's just that sexy and so fucking dominant.

He's like a sexual force of nature that I wouldn't know how to stop…and I don't want him to stop—ever.

Liam's fucking me with his finger, and I'm so ready for more. Then, he abruptly pulls his finger out of me, and I whimper at the loss.

I quickly realize that the taxi has stopped, and we're outside Liam's building.

Without a word, Liam pulls some bills from his wallet and throws them at the driver.

He opens the door and grabs ahold of my hand, pulling me out of the taxi. He starts speed-walking to his building, and I have to rush to keep up.

He doesn't even stop to return the hello to the night watchman. He just marches straight for the elevator and jabs at the button. The door slides open, and he yanks me inside the elevator. He presses the button for his floor, inputting his number on the keypad.

Next thing I know, I'm being slammed up against the wall, and his mouth is on mine before the door even closes.

His kiss is deep and passionate, even more so than in the taxi. It's like nothing I've ever felt before.

He's like nothing I've ever known before. And I don't ever want him to stop.

I slide my fingers into his thick hair and start sucking on his tongue.

He groans, his hands going to my skirt. He yanks it up over my hips, leaving me naked from the waist down—all but for my panties, which he proceeds to rip off with one snap of the elastic.

I don't even care enough to be pissed that he just tore up my good panties because the moment is so intense and so incredibly hot.

I just want him. Now. No matter what, I just want him inside me.

Both of our hands go to his jeans. I undo the button. He pulls down the zipper and pushes them down his hips with his boxers, too, just so his cock is free.

Our mouths are still connected, desperate and hungry.

His hands go under my thighs, pushing me up the wall of the elevator.

His eyes are dark on mine.

He shoves a hand between us and starts rubbing his fingers over my clit. "Always so wet for me." He gives my pussy a teasing slap, making me gasp. Leaving me, his hand goes to my ass along with his other one, too. "Gonna fuck this ass soon," he says roughly, digging his fingers into my ass cheeks.

Then, he spreads me open for him and slams his cock up deep inside me.

My head falls back against the wall with a thud, my eyes closing at the feel of him filling me so fully. "Liam," I moan.

He hasn't moved, so I open my eyes.

He's staring at me. His eyes are dark and filled with a need that I don't understand.

"I have never wanted anything as badly as I want you right now," he says, his voice low with meaning.

I curl my fingers into his hair. Leaning in, I brush my lips over his. "You have me. So, stop wasting time, and fuck me."

My words seem to have an effect because his mouth slams down on mine, and he starts to fuck me hard against the wall.

When the elevator door opens, he carries me out of there, his cock still inside me.

He doesn't bother going inside. He just presses me up against his front door and continues to screw me senseless there.

"Lift your top. I want to see your tits," he rasps out.

Freeing a hand from his hair, I do as he asked, and I lift my top, taking my bra up, too, revealing my breasts to him.

"Fucking perfect," he growls. Then, his mouth is on one. Licking and sucking on my nipple, he continues to fuck me against his door.

I catch sight of us in the reflection of the glass on the emergency exit door. Liam has his pants hanging around his thighs, and I have my skirt around my waist, my top pulled up and my breasts hanging out, while he fucks me with a desperation I've never known. It's the hottest thing I've ever seen, and it has me coming seconds later.

I'm screaming his name—my hands pulling his hair, my thighs locked around him—while he continues to pump in and out of me with desperate movements.

He slaps my ass. "You're so fucking hot. So fucking hot…" he grunts. Then, he buries his face in my neck. "You make me come so hard."

He starts fucking me with short, hard thrusts, his hand squeezing my ass. Then, I feel him start coming inside me, coating my insides with his cum.

We didn't use a condom.

I'm not worried about getting pregnant. That's not a possibility for me. The radiation treatment from my first tumor saw to that. Though I did have my eggs frozen. For all the good it will do me.

But sexually transmitted diseases…I could catch something.

Really, what does it matter?

I'm not going to be around long enough for it to matter if I get one. And it was worth it just to feel him bare and hot inside me.

Liam lifts his head from my neck, and his mouth seeks mine out. He trails those kisses across my cheek to my neck in a gentle way, so different and in stark contrast to the way he just fucked me.

Then, he frees a hand from underneath my thigh. I tighten my grip, so as not to drop to the floor.

He keys in the number on the keypad by his door. The lock clicks open. Liam pushes the handle down, opening the door. Then, his hand goes back under my thigh, and he carries me through, kicking the door shut with his foot.

He walks us through his darkened apartment, going straight to his bedroom, his cock still inside me. He lays me down on his bed, pulling out of me. I feel his cum slip out of me and onto my thighs.

I watch as he pulls his shirt off, kicks his shoes off, and removes his jeans.

Then, he reaches for my skirt. I lift my hips, letting him pull it down my legs. Then, he removes my top and bra.

He walks from the bedroom into his bathroom. I hear running water. He comes back with a cloth and cleans between my legs.

His tenderness makes my heart clutch.

"I didn't use a condom," he says softly as he cleans my thighs. "I'm sorry."

"It's okay." I touch a hand to his face. "I can't get pregnant."

"I'm clean," he tells me. "My last checkup was four weeks ago. And you're the only person I've slept with since then."

"I'm clean, too," I feel the need to tell him.

He finishes cleaning me up and then takes the cloth back to the bathroom. He comes back, and he just stands at the end of the bed, staring down at me.

"Do you want to talk about what just happened at the bar with Jeremy?"

I see his eyes close off to me. "No."

"Are you sure? Because you were really upset, and—"

"Do you want to talk about your family?" he cuts me off. His voice is like a blade.

Tears instantly sting the backs of my eyes.

"No," I say in a small voice, shaking my head.

His hands curl around my ankles, and he yanks me down the bed. "Neither of us wants to talk, and I know I sure as hell want to forget. Do you want to forget, Taylor?"

"Yes," my voice whispers into the darkness.

"Then, let's forget together." He climbs up onto the bed over me, kneeing my legs apart. He grabs my hands and pins them to the bed above my head.

Without another word, he thrusts his cock deep inside me, and then he starts fucking me like it's all he knows…like I'm all he needs.

And he spends the rest of the night buried deep inside me, making sure the only thing I remember…the only thing I know…is him.

chapter 9

I blink my heavy eyes open to the bright sunshine and the sound of Liam banging around in the kitchen.

I grab the alarm clock from his nightstand, checking the time. Ten thirty.

We didn't get to sleep until late. Or early.

Liam had a lot of anger to fuck out, and I was more than willing to be his companion in his endeavor.

He was angry last night though.

But hot. God, was he hot.

I giggle at the thought of what we did in the taxi. And the elevator. And in his bed.

The stamina he has…it's inspiring.

I stretch out my aching limbs. My muscles are deliciously sore from all the sex with Liam.

Then, my bladder tells me that it's time to get up. I kick the covers back and head to the bathroom.

When I'm done in the bathroom, I pick up Liam's shirt from last night off the floor and put it on. I'm sans panties, considering he wrecked them last night. I don't actually know what happened to my panties. I have visions of them still on the floor of the elevator, riding up and down all night.

I walk into the kitchen. Liam is at the stove, wearing only boxer shorts, and I get the distinct whiff of bacon frying. It makes my tummy rumble.

"Hey," I say, padding into the kitchen toward him.

"Morning." He smiles at me from over his shoulder.

I reach him, putting my hand on his warm back, sliding my other one around his waist. He leans his mouth down to mine, softly kissing me.

"You should have a shirt on." I pat his stomach, nodding at the frying bacon.

"I'm hard-core, Boston." He grins. "You hungry? I made eggs and bacon."

"I'm starving," I tell him.

"Take a seat." He nods at the breakfast bar, which is set up with plates and cups and a pot of coffee.

I sit down and pour us each coffee while Liam serves up the eggs and bacon. He sits down opposite me and picks his coffee up.

In the light of day, I notice a roof terrace through the full-glass panel in the kitchen. "You have a roof terrace?"

"Yeah. We can sit out there to eat if you want? It's a warm day."

"Heights are not my friend. I'm happy to just sit here, from the safety of being inside, and admire the view."

Liam chuckles and puts some bacon in his mouth. "What are your plans for today?" he asks me as he chews his bacon.

"I'm not sure. I'm not really a planner. I'm more a fly-by-my-pants kind of girl."

I put some scrambled eggs in my mouth. They're really good. Guy can really cook.

"Good because I've got something arranged for you for this afternoon. If that's okay?"

"Depends on what it is. You're not going to make me strip naked and walk around London, are you?"

"No." He laughs.

Smiling, I eat some bacon. "So, what are you taking me to do?"

"It's a surprise."

"Okay," I say, dubious. "But I've gotta say, I'm not a fan of surprises—you know, in case I don't like it."

He smiles. "You'll like it. I promise."

We eat the rest of our breakfast in amiable silence. When I've finished, I get up and take away my plate, and then I come back for Liam's.

I pick up his empty plate and tell him, "I'll need to go to the hotel to get changed—"

It hits me out of nowhere. The pain in my head is so severe that I can't see. My vision blurs. The plate slips from my hand. It hits the floor and smashes. I can't do anything but clutch my head and cry out in agony.

This is bad. The headaches are getting worse.

"Jesus, Taylor. Are you okay?" Liam's voice sounds like he's underwater.

Everything starts to fade to black.

I register my legs giving out right at the time he lifts me into his arms. He carries me over to the sofa in his living room.

"What's wrong, babe?"

I can hear the worry clear in his voice.

"Head…ache," I manage to get out.

"What can I do?"

"Tablets. My bag."

I hear Liam leave me. I turn onto my side, curling into a ball. My hands clutch my head, my eyes squeezing tightly shut, as I will the pain to stop.

Not now. Not in front of Liam. Please.

"I got them." He's back. He sounds out of breath. "This was the only pill bottle I could find in your bag. I got water, too. How many do you take?"

"Two," I whisper, everything sounding loud.

I hear him shake out two pills.

"Open up, sweetheart."

I feel the pills pressing against my lips. I part my lips, and Liam drops the tablets into my mouth. Then, I feel a water bottle at my lips.

"Drink," Liam tells me.

I let the water in my mouth and swallow down the tablets.

"Better?" he asks.

I murmur a sound, waiting for the pills to do their job.

Liam sits on the floor beside me, his hand gently stroking my hair.

The headache begins to subside after what feels like forever, but in reality, it's probably only been five minutes.

"Hey," Liam murmurs when I blink open my eyes. "You doing okay?"

"I'm better. Thanks." I touch his hand still stroking my hair.

"Do you always get headaches that bad?"

I press my lips together. "Sometimes."

"Is it because of the tumor you had when you were younger?"

I press my lips together and slowly nod my head.

I'm lying to him. It doesn't make me feel good. But the alternative is telling him the truth, and I won't do that.

"The tablets make it better?"

"Yes."

"Good."

"I broke your plate," I say regretfully.

"Forget the plate, so long as you're okay. That's all that matters."

I swallow past my lies and touch a hand to his face. "I'm okay."

He turns his face into my hand, kissing my palm. "Did I…" He meets my eyes. "Did I overdo things with you last night?"

I give him a questioning look.

"The sex. You didn't get much sleep last night."

"It wasn't that. I just…I get headaches sometimes. Nothing to worry about."

He's staring at me.

"The sex is amazing. I love the way you fuck me, Liam."

His eyes darken with lust, and I know I've gotten him back to where he should be.

"I can't believe I let you finger me in the back of a taxi." I grin.

A smile teases the corner of his lips.

"Do you think we scarred the driver?" I ask.

"I think the guy probably went straight home and had a wank. I know I would have." He leans in and brushes his lips over mine. "You, in the back of that taxi last night…riding my fingers—hottest fucking moment of my life."

I let out a nervous giggle. "Surely not. I bet you've done way hotter things than that."

Holding my gaze, he slowly shakes his head. "Nope. What we did last night was the hottest thing I've ever done." He kisses me again, sucking on my lower lip. "You, Boston, are the most sexually adventurous woman I've ever known."

I can't tell him that I'm only that way because I have nothing left to lose, so I have nothing to fear. And I want to experience as much of everything that I can, even the things that scare me, before I go to my family.

So, I just smile and slide a hand down his bare chest, heading south, as a distraction for myself, but Liam catches my hand.

"But no fucking today, my Boston temptress, and I'm going to cancel our plans for this afternoon. You need to rest."

"No." I push myself up to sit. I hide the wince I feel at the ache that remains in my head. The ache no pills will ever take away.

"Yes," he says in a firm voice.

"But I'm better, I promise."

"You just flinched in pain from sitting up."

Shit, I thought I hid that. Apparently not.

"You're not better."

"I am. That was just a little vertigo after lying down for so long."

"Bullshit." He gives me a disbelieving look.

"Hey…I'm not bullshitting. I want to go out. I want my surprise."

He continues to stare at me.

"I'm fine now, Hunter. I promise. It was just a headache, and it's gone. I'm all better." I give him my best smile.

"I don't know, Boston. That headache knocked you off your feet…"

"I'm fine."

"What if it happens again when we're out?"

"It won't. And if I feel even the slightest twinge of a headache, I'll tell you, and we can come home straightaway."

He's still staring at me.

"I flew all this way to come to England. I don't want to spend it stuck inside." I get to my knees and press my hands together in front of me. "Please," I say in a soft begging voice. "I'm only here for a few weeks. I don't want to waste my time. I want to be out with you, having fun." I pout to finish it off.

He lets out a sigh. "Okay. But if you feel ill at any point—"

"Then, I'll tell you. We can come home, and you can be my nurse." I smile winningly.

"Fine. But I'm not wearing a nurse outfit, just so you know."

"I wouldn't dream of asking."

Liam gets to his feet. Then, he leans down and picks me up, holding me in his arms.

"What are you doing?"

"Playing nurse before we go out." He starts walking through the living room. "I'm gonna put you in the bath. Maybe wash your hair. Then, I'll get you off with my hand while you suck my cock."

A laugh escapes me. "I thought, a minute ago, I was too ill to go out. But, now, I'm okay to suck your cock?"

"Boston, you are always okay to suck my cock. All you have to do is ask, and I'll whip him out for you. Anytime of the day, no matter where we are, just ask, and my cock is yours to do with as you please."

"Gee, you're so kind." I giggle.

"I'm a philanthropist. Didn't I tell you?" He grins as he pushes open the bathroom door with his foot and carries me inside.

chapter 10

Liam dropped me off at the hotel earlier and told me he'd be back to pick me up in an hour.

That hour gave me ample time to get ready for my surprise afternoon outing with him.

I don't usually like surprises. I normally like to know what to expect. But something about Liam surprising me has me all excited. Butterflies-in-the-tummy excited.

The hour is almost up, and I'm ready and waiting for the main man to make an appearance.

I've got makeup on—light beige eye shadow and pale pink gloss on my lips. My pink hair speaks volumes nowadays, so the makeup definitely needs to be neutral so that I don't look like a doll. Because it's warm outside, I've opted to wear my denim shirtdress with a brown belt on the waist, and I've got my brown ankle boots on, which only have a small heel, as I don't know if we're going to be walking or not.

I'm looking good—well, for someone with a brain tumor, that is.

And that's enough of the depressing shit.

But I did take some pain pills just in case another headache decides to attack, and my pills are also in my bag.

I don't want the headaches to become a regular occurrence in front of Liam; otherwise, he'll start to notice. He's far from stupid.

But it's going to be hard to hide them when I'm hardly away from him. I've seen him every day since he sat beside me on that plane.

And, now, I'm starting to wonder if seeing so much of Liam is a good idea.

I don't need to be getting too close to anyone. Or to let anyone get close to me. Close equals attachment, which means complications.

I don't need complications.

But then Liam isn't exactly a complicated guy, and I can't imagine him getting attached to anyone.

We both know where we stand. Two weeks, and then we're done.

Liam will go back to his life, and I'll go back to…well, I'll just go, and Liam will be none the wiser.

He'll never know what became of me. I'll just be a fond memory—that American girl he once spent two weeks with.

And for me…he'll be the last good thing I had.

My cell phone starts to ring on the nightstand.

Liam and I exchanged numbers earlier. As many times as we'd slept together, it was weird that we didn't have each other's cell numbers.

"Yes, Mr. Hunter?" I say on a smile.

"Are you ready?"

"I am." I brush my hand down my dress.

"Good. Come down. I'm waiting outside the hotel for you."

"I'll be down in a few."

I pick up my cardigan in case it gets cold later and put it along with my cell in my bag. I check to make sure I have my wallet. Then, I hang my bag on my shoulder. I grab my room key on the way out and let the door lock behind me.

I don't have to wait long for an elevator. I ride the four floors down, excited to see Liam, which is crazy because I saw him only an hour ago.

But still, I have flutters in my tummy at the thought of seeing him again.

It's going to suck when it comes time for me to leave him.

I push through the door of the hotel, stepping out into the lovely sunshine. And I see Liam standing by a…bus.

Smiling, he walks over to me. He looks gorgeous. He's wearing dark blue jeans and a black polo shirt. His wavy hair is parted down the side and slicked back. He looks hot. So very hot.

"Hey." He hooks an arm around my waist and kisses me.

He tastes delicious, like mint and coffee.

"Hey." I smile at him.

"You look beautiful."

"You're looking pretty good yourself." I smile at him.

"I know." He smirks. "Your chariot awaits you, madam." He steps to the side, waving his arm out in the direction of the bus.

"We're going on a bus?" I stare up at him.

"We're going on a tour bus. I've hired it to take us around to the sights of London. I thought it was time you got to see some of my great city."

"Really?" I beam at him.

I'm going to see the city where my mother grew up in the comfort of my very own bus. It doesn't get better than this.

"Really." He smiles down at me, a soft look in his eyes.

"You're the best!" I throw my arms around his neck and slap a kiss to his cheek.

Then, I let go of him and skip my way over to the bus.

The doors are already open. The driver is sitting in his seat, waiting for us to board.

"Hi." I smile at him.

"Good afternoon. I'm Derek, your driver for the next few hours." He smiles at me.

"Nice to meet you, Derek. I'm Taylor."

I don't think he actually cares about my name, but I always feel the need to introduce myself when people tell me their names.

I feel Liam's hand on my lower back. I turn to him.

"So, where do we sit?" I ask.

"Upstairs. It's an open top, so you can see everything London has to offer."

A frisson of excitement passes through me. "We really have the whole bus to ourselves?" I ask as I walk toward the stairs.

"We really do."

I stop, my foot on the first step. "You're awesome." I grin at him.

"I know." He gives my ass a slap. "Now, hurry up and get your hot arse up the stairs, so we can get this show on the road."

I quickly make my way up the stairs.

When I reach the top, I look around. "Where should we sit?" I ask him.

He stands behind me, his hands resting on my hips. "Front seat. Best in the house."

I tilt my head back against his chest, looking up at his smiling handsome face.

"Thank you for this," I say softly. "It's really great."

His fingers stroke down my cheek, his touch featherlight. "You're only here for two weeks. I want every day to be great for you." He leans his face down to mine, gently pressing his lips to mine.

"Mr. Hunter, Miss Taylor, I'll be setting off in a few minutes. Make sure to take your seats." Derek's voice comes over the intercom.

"Guess we'd better take our seats," I whisper to Liam.

He gives me another quick kiss, and then I release myself from his touch, walking to the front of the bus.

A big smile spreads across my face when I see what's sitting on the front seat. "They've provided a picnic as well."

There's a picnic basket and a tartan blanket folded up beside it, sitting on the seat.

His hands touch my shoulders. "I brought the picnic," he says.

My smile grows wider, my heart swelling.

I turn to face him. "You made me a picnic?"

"I did."

I touch a hand to his face. "You're kinda perfect right now, you know that?"

He gives me a mock-offended look. "I think you meant to say that I'm *always* perfect."

I smile at him. Then, I reach up on my tiptoes and press a kiss to his cheek. "You're always perfect in bed," I whisper in his ear, my lips brushing over his skin.

I love the shiver it elicits from him.

"Damn fucking right I am." His voice is a low rasp. "Now, sit down before I show the whole of London just how good at fucking I am when I bend you over this seat and screw you right here."

"You wouldn't dare." I meet his eyes.

"I guess I haven't shown you just how far I am willing to go when it comes to you. Looks like I'm going to have to rectify that."

Then, he takes my mouth with his, kissing me like he means it. His strong hands gripping the back of my dress, he brings me into his hard body. His hips press into my stomach, and I feel his erection against me.

He wasn't kidding. *But is he really going to screw me on an open-top bus in the middle of London in broad daylight?*

The bus suddenly lurches forward, breaking our hot little moment.

Liam's eyes are blazing down on mine. His hand caresses my cheek. "We'll save the sex for later. Right now, you're going to see the sights that London has to offer."

I take my seat, squirming in it. My panties are soaked to hell, and I'm wondering just how long this tour is going to take, so we can get back to my hotel and get on with the sex.

Yes, I've turned into a total sex maniac, and I blame Liam Hunter entirely for being so damn good at it.

chapter 11

"A carnival. You've brought me to a carnival." I smile warmly up at Liam.

It's early evening. The bus dropped us off at Hyde Park, and a carnival is happening here.

"Well, we don't call it a carnival. It's a funfair to us English folk. But is it okay, bringing you here?" Liam stares down at me. "I know it's not something on your list, but—"

"It's great." I beam. "I love carnivals or funfairs or whatever they're called!"

Well, I don't like the rides—at all. I don't mind the small rides—okay, the kiddie rides, which I can't get away with riding because I don't have a kid. But I just love playing the games in the booths along with the popcorn and cotton candy and candy apples. I have a sweet tooth, if you didn't guess.

I love it all, the atmosphere and fun to be had, and I am so ready to have this kind of fun.

Not that the tour of London wasn't fun. It was amazing, seeing all the sights and sharing the picnic that Liam had made for us. I swear, if he ever decides to give up being a businessman, he'll make someone a great house husband one day. But the day was tainted with a little sadness for me. I couldn't help but think about my mother growing up here, especially when we drove around Knightsbridge.

And thinking about my mother leads to thinking about the rest of my family…and it hurts.

But I'm not here to hurt or dwell. I'll be seeing my family really soon.

Now is the time for me to live in the little life that I have left.

And I want to do that living with Liam.

Grabbing ahold of his hand, I start speed-walking us into the carnival.

"I take it, this was a good call to come here then." Liam chuckles.

"It was a great call." I slow down, so we're walking side by side.

Liam drops my hand and puts his arm over my shoulder, pulling me close to his side.

"What do you want to do first?" Liam asks as we start walking down the path lined with booths selling trinkets and food.

"You choose," I tell him.

A smile crosses his face. "Do you like rides?"

I grimace. "No," I respond immediately because I really dislike rides.

Being strapped in while you go at crazy speeds and up to stupid heights or get thrown around? No, thanks.

Then, I stop myself. Like, literally, I stop walking.

Liam stops, too, and moves to stand in front of me. "You okay?" he asks, a touch of concern furrowing his brow.

"Yeah." I nod. "Just…I hate rides. Well, maybe not hate, but I definitely dislike them a significant amount."

"That was very specific."

"I'm a specific kinda girl." I flash my eyes at him.

"Okay, Miss Specific, how about we just hit up the stalls and eat food, and then I can kick your arse at games?"

I pause again, caught in my thoughts.

"You there?" Liam waves a hand in front of my face.

"I'm thinking," I tell him.

"Do I need to sit down for this? Is it going to take a while?"

"No. But then again, five minutes is a long time for an old man like you, so maybe you should sit." I smirk.

He shakes his head at me. "I might just sit down, so I can put you over my knee and spank your arse for being smart."

"So, I get spanked for being smart? Sounds like a win-win to me." I widen my grin.

He chuckles. "See? That's why I like you, Boston."

"'Cause I let you spank me?"

Stepping closer, he pushes his fingers into my hair. "That, and"—he brushes his lips over mine—"because that smart mouth of yours gets my dick hard at the most inappropriate moments."

His lips touch mine again, and I feel his erection press into my hip.

"Do you need to stand here for a moment while he goes down?" I flick a look south, my lips pushing up.

"Yeah." He chuckles. "Tell me where we were before spankings and my erection?"

"I was thinking."

"Oh, yeah. How's that working out for you?"

"Quite well." I meet his smiling eyes. "I think I should go on the rides because I dislike them."

"Did you drink alcohol before you came out today?"

"Funny." I stick my tongue out at him. "No, it's on my list. I have to do something that scares me."

"If I remember rightly, it said, do something that terrifies you to the point of pissing your pants."

127

"Do you remember everything? Like literally everything?"

"Only the things that matter."

"My list matters to you?"

"It matters to you."

Oh. Wow. Breath is knocked from my lungs.

"So, which ride scares the shit out of you?" Liam is talking again, back to normal, while I'm still gasping for air.

"Roller coaster," I say without hesitation. "They always look rickety and unsafe, and they take you up to stupid heights and then drop you back down at stupid speeds."

"Roller coaster, it is then." Liam grabs my hand and starts walking, dragging me behind him.

"Now?" I squeak.

He looks back at me but keeps walking. "Yep. If you don't ride the roller coaster now, you won't ever do it."

True.

"But…what about your erection?" Okay, I said that quite loud, and it earns me a few looks.

Liam bellows out a laugh. "Down for now. Although keeping talking like that, and he'll make another appearance."

"Okay, well, what about food? Shouldn't we eat first?" I'm totally stalling.

Stop stalling, Taylor.

Liam stops abruptly, and I almost crash into the back of him.

That's when I see that we're standing in front of a roller coaster ride.

"No one eats before a roller coaster unless they intend on puking. So, it's decision time, Boston. We either ditch the roller coaster and go get food—even though I know you're not hungry because we only ate an hour ago and that you're just stalling before making another excuse, and then we'll never end up riding this roller coaster because you'll let your fear talk you out of it—*or* you can pull your big-girl knickers on and ride the fuck out of this roller coaster."

"Big-girl knickers? Seriously, Hunter? That might be the unsexiest thing I've ever heard."

He tilts his head to the side. "Seriously? Because I think you'd look hot in big knickers."

"Really?" I blink, trying to picture that.

Nope, not working for me at all.

"Really." He gives me a sexy smile. The look in his eyes is like he's actually imagining me in them right now.

And, now, I'm thinking about where I can find a store in London that sells big knickers.

"But we're saving big knickers for later," he says.

"We are?"

"Quit stalling, Boston." He gives me a look.

He's right. I'm totally stalling. Again.

"Now, are we riding the fuck out of this roller coaster or not?"

I take a breath and blow it out. "We're riding the fuck out of it."

A smile lifts his gorgeous lips. "Good girl. And, just so you know, I intend to ride the fuck out of you later tonight."

Sweet baby Jesus. He's so fucking hot.

Liam gives me a quick firm kiss on the lips and grabs my hand, and then I'm moving again.

He brings us to a stop at the ticket booth. "Two tickets, please," he tells the woman sitting in the booth.

"Twenty pounds," she tells him.

Liam hands her a bill, and she passes him two tickets. He grabs my hand again, and we move up the walkway to the ride together.

We've come at the right time, as the roller coaster has just finished unloading the last lot of passengers and is starting to fill up with new ones.

So, at least I won't be waiting around.

Even still, my heart is beating like a bitch in my chest, and I'm shitting my pants.

I know. I have a tumor literally growing in my brain, killing me—and I'm letting it…I'm doing nothing to try to stop it—but I'm afraid of a stupid roller coaster.

Doesn't make sense, does it? But then fear isn't exactly rational. It doesn't let us pick and choose. It just is.

And dying to me isn't the thing I'm afraid of. Not since I lost my family anyway.

It's living that scares me.

Living without them—that's what terrifies me.

Dying and being with them—that will be a welcome relief.

I stare up at the roller coaster, which looks a hell of a lot bigger and higher than it did the first time I looked up at it. It must be at least a couple of hundred feet at its highest point.

"Do you think it looks safe to you?" I whisper to Liam as we're in line to get on.

"It's safe." He squeezes my hand.

If I don't care about dying, then why do I care if this ride looks safe enough?

Because I don't want anything to happen to Liam.

And fear, like I said, is not rational.

But it is a state of mind.

I squeeze my eyes shut and force the stupid fear out of my thoughts.

Liam tugs on my hand, and I see the ride attendant waiting to let us on the ride.

"You sure you want to do this?" Liam leans his head close to mine, his voice just above a whisper.

I stare back at him and force a loose smile onto my lips. "I'm sure. Just…don't let go of my hand, okay?"

His eyes move down to my hand that he's holding, as if he's just realizing he's still holding it. Then, he looks back to my face. "I won't let go, Boston. I promise." Then, he leads me onto the ride.

What is it about someone holding your hand that makes you feel safe?

It's not that they can save you or change things or make a difference by holding your hand.

But, somehow, someone just holding on to you in that small way can make the scariest things seem a little easier.

Because you know that, no matter what, they have you, and they're not letting go.

And, right now, Liam has me, and he's not letting go.

The ride attendant secures us in our seats with the harness, and then the metal barrier comes down over us.

Liam squeezes my hand that he's still holding. "You doing okay there, Boston?"

I move my eyes to his and off the roller coaster that I've been examining to make sure it's fixed together properly—like I would actually know.

"Mmhmm."

"There's nothing to be worried about."

"Mmhmm."

He chuckles. "Do something for me. Think about when we get to the top of the ride."

"I really don't want to think about that. That's actually the last thing I want to think about."

Thinking about being up there, in this rickety car on a set of tracks a couple of hundred feet off the ground, while it pauses to scare the crap out of me more before it drops back down those couple of hundred feet…um…no, thanks.

My heart starts pumping in my chest, and my hand tightens around Liam's, a pulse starting in my head.

God, please don't let me have a headache now. Not now.

And I swear, if I die on this roller coaster, if the tumor decides to take me out on here, I'll be really pissed.

"Boston," he softly says my nickname, "when we reach the top, we'll be at one of the highest points in London,

131

aside from the London Eye. From up there, you'll be able to see all of London at sunset. And, trust me, the sight is so fucking beautiful that you won't care about how high you are or how afraid you feel. You'll just care about the view and the way it makes you feel."

I close my eyes and release a breath. "How did you get to be so brave?"

He chuckles low. I open my eyes.

"I'm not brave, babe. A lot of things scare me." He's staring into my eyes, and the look in them is making my heart beat faster. "I just refuse to let those fears control me."

Our car jerks forward and starts moving. My hand tightens around Liam's, my mouth drying.

"Just keep looking at me," he says gently.

So, I do. I stare into his eyes that remind me of autumn, and I don't look away.

"My grandpa used to be in the Royal Air Force when he was younger," Liam tells me. "He loved to fly. He had his own airplane. Still does. When I was twelve, he told me that he thought it was time that I learned how to fly a plane."

"You flew a plane when you were twelve?" I give him a shocked look.

"My grandpa's not exactly on the conventional side." The fondness on his face tells me that his grandpa means a great deal to him. "And when I say 'fly'"—he air quotes— "it was him flying and me being copilot. But twelve-year-old me thought that he meant literally fly the plane. So, I was shitting myself."

"I can imagine. I'd shit if someone said that to me now, and I'm twenty-two."

Liam laughs. "I think you'd probably surprise yourself."

"No, I'm pretty sure I'd surprise the person sitting with me—you know, after I shit myself."

The laughter that comes from him this time is deeper and louder, and it brings a glow to my chest.

"So, did you fly this plane when you were twelve?" I ask him. I could totally see him doing something crazy like that.

"Well, I'd been flying with my grandpa since I started walking," he says, not answering my question directly.

I get that there's a point to what he's telling me.

"He used to take me up in his plane, and we'd fly for what felt like hours. We'd just be up there, and I loved it. But the thought of being the one in control of the plane...totally different ball game."

"No kidding," I say.

"Grandpa told me that we'd go out on the weekend. So, for the whole week leading up to it, I was worried, and the more I thought about it, the worse I felt. It wasn't about being up in the sky. I loved that. It was the thought that he wanted me to do something...so big. The closer we got to the weekend, the more afraid I got. I even thought about faking an illness, so I wouldn't have to go. But then I knew he'd just reschedule for another time. And..."

He briefly looks away from me, and I wonder if it's because he doesn't want me to see what's in his eyes. But then he's back looking at me, and I feel better for it. His eyes on me...just makes me feel better.

"He'd taken me into his home and cared for me, and I guess...I didn't want to let him down. So, I told myself that I had to man up and do it."

I keep getting these snippets of Liam but nothing tangible to tie any of them together.

"Saturday morning rolled up, and Grandpa got me up early. He drove us to the airfield, and I felt like vomiting the whole way there."

"I would have vomited without a doubt."

He chuckles. "So, we got there. Got out of the car. Walked over to his airplane. The whole time, I'm telling myself I can do this. Then, I got up to the plane, and I just froze. I literally couldn't move. Total freak-out moment."

"Understandable. You were twelve, and your grandpa was asking you to fly a plane."

His laugh is rich and deep. "Grandpa realized I wasn't moving, and he asked me what was wrong. I was embarrassed to tell him the truth—that I was afraid—but I also didn't have another excuse to get out of it. I felt cornered, so I told him that I didn't want to fly his plane because I hated flying with him, which wasn't true. I loved being up in the sky with him. But my fear had gotten the better of me, so I lied. And, in turn, I hurt him. I saw it in his eyes, and that made me feel sick for real. So, I fessed up the truth. I told him that I didn't want to learn to fly because I was afraid."

"What did he say?"

"He hugged me. My grandpa's kind of a hugger. You'll learn that when you meet him."

I'm going to meet his grandpa?

"And then he said to me, 'Liam, there's nothing wrong with being afraid. Everyone feels fear. But the day you let your fear control you is the day you stop living. *Really* living.' Then, he asked me if I wanted to live."

My eyes are on Liam's face. I'm riveted. I've forgotten that I'm on a roller coaster and that it's currently climbing hundreds of feet in the air. Well, I haven't forgotten, but it's not at the forefront of my mind. What Liam is telling me is. Because it matters to me, more than he could ever realize.

My mouth is dry as I ask, "What did you say?"

He grins, his eyes lighting up. "Well, I was twelve years old, and I didn't really have a fucking clue what he was trying to tell me. He'd just hugged me, and I always felt better when my grandpa hugged me. But I knew he was talking about living, and I definitely wanted to do that. And I wanted to make him happy. So, I got on the plane. And it was the best decision I've ever made. I copiloted the fuck out of that plane, and I loved it.

"If I hadn't done that, then I wouldn't be the man I am today. I wouldn't have the businesses I have. My airplanes wouldn't be flying millions of people all over the world to exotic locations. And I wouldn't have met you, and I wouldn't be sitting here next to you on this ride, helping you conquer this fear. My choice to conquer my fear brought me to this moment. It brought me to you."

Sweet Jesus.

There's a lump the size of this roller coaster stuck in my throat. Out of nowhere, I feel tears start to creep in. I blink away from him and turn my face forward as I close my eyes.

I feel Liam's body move closer, his shoulder pressing to mine.

"Open your eyes, Boston." His breath brushes over the shell of my ear, making me shiver.

I take a deep breath, making sure I'm not going to bawl like a little girl, and I open my eyes to see that we've stopped.

And we're at the top of the roller coaster track.

I can see the whole of London from up here. The sun is setting in the distance, and the sight is incredibly beautiful—just like Liam.

My eyes sweep the view, looking at the dusky pink and orange glow from the sun, as the last remnants of it brush over the tops of the buildings, like an artist's paintbrush. And below, the streetlamps are coming on, and lights inside the buildings are turned on.

It looks like a painting. A beautiful painting.

"You were right," I whisper. "It's beautiful."

"Most beautiful thing I've ever seen." Liam's free hand touches my cheek, turning my face to his. He presses his lips to mine. Then, he slides his lips over my cheek and says into my ear, "*He who has overcome his fears will truly be free.*"

135

I tilt my head back a touch to look in his eyes. "You're quoting Aristotle to me?" I grin.

An impressed look flashes through his eyes. "Boston, I'm as smart as I am good-looking, which is *extremely*, in case you had any doubt."

"Nope. Never doubted that for a second." I shake my head, a smile still fixed on my lips.

"So"—his eyes leave mine to look over the view—"do you feel free right now?"

"Yeah," I exhale. "I guess I do."

"Good. You're about to feel a whole lot freer—"

His words are cut off by the loud screams around us as the roller coaster plunges forward at breakneck speed.

Actually, I think I might have broken my neck. Not that I can feel anything or move.

My head is stuck to the headrest. My hair is plastered back to my head. The wind is rushing in my ears along with screams of delight from other riders, and I'm pretty sure my stomach is still at the top of the ride.

And even though I'm terrified out of my mind and I just realized that those screams I hear are actually coming from me…even with all of that, my heart feels light.

And that's because of the man sitting beside me. The man who is still holding my hand, just like he promised he would.

With some effort, against the g-force, I manage to turn my head to look at him.

Liam's stare is on me, and he's smiling and laughing. Probably because I've been screaming like a little girl.

Even still, my heart squeezes in my chest at the sight of him laughing.

I smile back at him—at least, the best I can with my lips that have been g-forced to my face.

I feel happy and free. I feel alive.

The shock of those words reverberates around inside me. Like a ball spinning around a moving roulette wheel.

I feel alive.

For the first time in a really long time, I feel alive.

And it's because of him.

I'm smiling and laughing and doing something that scares the crap out of me.

I'm *living* because of Liam.

And that thought alone brings with it a whole new brand of fear in me. A fear that terrifies me in a way that I have never known before.

"You really suck at this." I laugh, putting cotton candy in my mouth—or *candy floss*, as they call it here.

Liam bought it for me when we passed the last food booth. I needed sugar. The choice of cotton candy was blue or pink or both. I chose both. I've already eaten all the blue. I'm onto the pink now, which is pretty close to my hair color.

I lick the cotton candy off my sticky fingers.

Liam gives me a dirty look. "If you think you can do any better, then, by all means, try." He holds out a ball to me.

He's playing a game called Knock 'Em Down, which is basically nine cans stacked up into a pyramid—four at the bottom, three in the middle, and two on the top. You have to knock the cans down by hitting them with a ball, and if you knock off the two top rows, you win a medium prize. Knock all the cans down, and you get a big prize.

Sounds simple, huh? Apparently, it's not.

I've sat this game out, so I can eat my cotton candy.

But we played darts and Bull's Eye, which is basically archery and you had to hit the bull's-eye to win. And we played a shooting game where you have a pellet rifle and you have to hit a playing card with a pellet. I was especially bad at that.

But, so far, we haven't won a thing, and I really want a stuffed animal. Something to keep. A keepsake of this day with him.

But then what's the point? It's not like I'll get to keep it for long.

Even still, I want one.

Tucking my sad thoughts away, I put my bag of cotton candy under my arm and hold my hands up. "My hands are sticky from the cotton candy."

"Excuses, excuses."

I stick my tongue out at him.

"Your tongue is blue from the candy floss." Liam chuckles.

I lean in close to him and whisper into his ear, "Well, if you're a good boy and win me a prize, I'll lick your cock with my blue tongue."

I lean back a little, staring into his eyes, which are currently dark and lusty.

"Deal," he growls, sending shivers hurtling through me.

I move back to my standing spot and watch him get back to the game.

He picks up a ball and throws it. Hits the edge of a can, but it doesn't go down.

Guess he doesn't want a blow job.

"I'm sure these cans are fucking glued down," he says in a low growly voice, making me laugh.

"I don't think they are. I'm pretty sure that's illegal. You just have a weak arm, Hunter, and your aim sucks."

That earns me a dirty look.

I love winding him up. Seeing him flustered and off his game like this...it's fun.

"You seriously used to play rugby in college?" I tease.

Liam told me that he used to play rugby. It was how he broke his nose—twice apparently. Men and sports—I'll never understand it.

"How did you ever manage to throw a touchdown?"

"You don't have touchdowns in rugby." He grits his teeth, so his words come out in single syllables. "It's called a try, and the position I played, was Winger, and it mostly required me to run fast and score a try."

"Good job. Otherwise, you'd have lost a lot. Did you lose a lot?" I grin.

He flips me the bird. I laugh.

He exhales through his nose, which makes him sound like an angry bull. That makes me laugh harder.

Ignoring me, he pivots and sets up to throw his last ball.

He's managed to knock the top two off, so he only has seven more cans to go.

Seven cans and one ball. I don't see it happening, but if he manages to knock the next three off, he'll win a prize— meaning, I win a prize.

Thing is, he only has one ball left, and his aim is appalling.

Sheer concentration is on his face.

Leaning over, I tilt my head to the side in front of him.

"What?" he grumbles without looking at me.

"You're totally pulling your sex face right now."

He frowns. "I don't have a sex face."

"You so do. Just as you're coming, your face looks…well, just like it does right now." I gesture a hand to his face.

"Stop trying to put me off with sex talk. Back the fuck off, Boston, and let me throw my ball."

I splutter out a laugh. He almost cracks a smile.

"Sorry. Please continue." I flutter a hand at him and move away.

His sex face is back. I stifle a giggle.

141

SAMANTHA TOWLE

Liam draws his arm back and throws.

And misses.

I clamp my hand over my face to stop from laughing.

He's scowling at me. "That was your fault."

I move my hand from my mouth. "How was that my fault?"

"You talk about sex, and I get distracted."

"Okay." I give a contrite look. "Have another turn. My treat."

"So, you can take the piss out of me. No thanks."

"Aw, come on. I want a stuffed animal."

"I'll buy you one."

I give him a look of disgust. "You can't bring a girl to a carnival and then buy her a stuffed animal. You have to win it."

"For fuck's sake," he growls. He sticks his hand in his pocket and slaps a bill on the counter. "Another go," he tells the guy behind the stall, who is only happy to take Liam's money.

The guy picks up the bill and places three balls on the counter in front of Liam.

"I said I'd pay." I frown.

He won't let me pay for anything. It's seriously annoying.

"You pay for the game, and it's like you're winning the prize yourself."

Fair point.

"So, you are actually going to win me a stuffed animal?"

He ignores me, which oddly makes me smile.

I put the last of my cotton candy in my mouth and deposit the wrapper in a nearby bin. Then, I go sit up on the counter beside where Liam is standing, angling my body, so that I can watch him throw the balls.

Liam picks up his first ball and gets read to throw. His sex face is back on—sorry, his face of concentration. I hold in a laugh and watch him throw it.

142

He knocks off the top two.

"Yay!" I clap my hands although I don't know why I'm excited because he managed that last time.

He picks up his second ball, and wasting no time, he throws. He knocks off two of the three cans on the second row.

My cheer is louder this time.

He looks at me, a prideful glint in his eyes.

Picking up his last ball, he takes aim and throws.

He manages to knock off the last can on the second row.

"Any prize off this bottom row," the guy tells us, walking away to a waiting customer.

"You did it!" I jump down off the counter and wrap my arms around his neck. "You won me a prize!"

"Thank fuck." His arms wrap around me. "I was starting to worry for a moment there. Felt like I was losing my man card."

I reach up on my tiptoes and kiss his lips. "Never. And thank you." I tip my head back to look into his face.

His hands slide down my back to my ass, and he gives it a squeeze. "Go pick your prize, Boston."

Leaving Liam, I head back to the counter and lean over, looking at the bottom row of prizes. I see all kinds of crap here, including really cheap-looking stuffed animals and dolls.

I definitely do not want a doll. They freak me out.

Then, I spy this sad-looking odd toy. Reaching over, I grab it.

Liam comes up behind me as I right myself. His chest is pressed to my back. "Is that a…fucking knitted jellyfish?"

I turn my head to look up at him. He's squinting at the toy I've picked up.

I look back down at it in my hands, and I think he's right. It is a knitted jellyfish toy. "I think so."

It's white and pink and looks like a little princess jellyfish. And the more I look at it, the cuter it becomes…in a weird knitted jellyfish way.

"She looks like a jellyfish princess," I say.

"It looks like a piece of shit."

"Hey! You'll hurt her feelings." I jab him in the arm. Then, I hug her. "I shall call her Squishy, and she shall be mine." I laugh, meeting Liam's blank expression. "*Finding Nemo*? No?" I say.

Liam slowly shakes his head, looking at me like I've lost my mind.

"Okay, makes sense. You were probably too old to watch it when it first came out—you know, when I was still in diapers and you were out serenading teenage girls with the Backstreet Boys—hey!" I squeal when he digs me in the ribs with his fingers. "We'll watch *Nemo* later, and then you'll get the reference."

I turn to the guy. "I'll take Squishy," I tell him, holding the stuffed animal up.

"Okay, what's next?" I hook my arm through Liam's, holding Squishy to my chest.

"Hook a Duck."

"Hook a what?" I give him a confused look.

"Duck."

"And what's Hook a Duck?"

"You don't know what Hook a Duck is?" Liam looks appalled.

"No…but I feel like I should."

"You should."

"What's so special about it?"

"Well, nothing special per se, but it's like a rite of passage. Every kid plays Hook a Duck when they come to the fair."

"Hate to break it to you, Hunter, but we're not kids."

"Maybe not. But it's your first time at a fair in England, and you have to play." Liam grabs my hand and sets off, I assume, in search of this Hook a Duck game.

We find one a few minutes later, and it's closed. All shut up with the tarpaulin covering the booth.

"It's closed. Never mind," I say to him.

I start to walk away, but Liam tugs me back by the hand he's holding.

"Like a little thing like it being closed is going to stop us from playing."

He gives me a grin and drops my hand. I watch as he unhooks the tarpaulin at the bottom and lifts it just enough so that he can sneak in underneath it.

"Hunter, what are you doing?" I hiss.

He ducks his head back out. "Come on," he whispers, holding the material up for me to go under.

"I'm not going in there."

"Yes you are. Now hurry the fuck up, or you'll get me arrested for breaking into a Hook a Duck tent," he whispers.

"Ugh," I complain.

I do a quick look around to make sure no one is watching, and then I duck under. Liam drops the tarpaulin, and we're inside the Hook a Duck tent. Thankfully, there's a dim light on in here otherwise it'd be pitch black.

"Okay, so we're in here. Now what?"

"Now, you hook a duck." He grins and picks up a stick that has a wire hook on the end. He points to what can only be described as a fake pond in the middle of the stall with rubber duckies floating around it.

"So, that's it? I just use this stick and hook a duck on it."

"Well, yeah." He gives me a stupid look. "It's not as easy as it looks."

"Sure it's not." I snatch the stick from him.

Liam leans against the edge of the fake pond and folds his arms, watching me. "Go on then. Hook a duck, Boston."

I chuckle, shaking my head. I put my bag on the floor and set Squishy on top of it. Then, I hover my stick over the water.

I try to catch one of the little fuckers—I really do—but they're moving a lot quicker than I realized, and they're all bumping into each other, knocking the others away.

I nearly catch one, but another bumps into it and knocks the fucker away from my hook.

"Little bastard," I hiss.

Liam laughs. "You can't call a duck a bastard."

"It's not a real duck." I give him a look. "Aha! Got one!" I proudly lift my stick with the duck hanging on the end of it. "So, now what?"

"What do you mean, now what?"

"I mean, now what happens?"

"Nothing. That's it. Well, you win a prize, but considering that we broke in here, taking a prize would be stealing."

"Oh." I take the duck off the stick, stand the stick against the pond, and set the duck on the small ledge below. "Well, it just feels kind of…anticlimactic now." I lean against the pond next to him.

"Anticlimactic, huh? How about I make you feel climactic?"

I turn my face, meeting his gaze, and see the desire right there in his eyes. "Here?" I whisper.

"You wanted to have sex outside. It's on your list."

"Yeah, but this is hardly outside. We're in a tent filled with a fake pond, rubber ducks, and cheap toys."

"Well, I've always wanted to fuck before an audience." He gives me a sexy smile. Putting his hand on my thigh, he slides it upward, taking my dress with it.

"You're not a stranger. I said I wanted to fuck a stranger."

He leans his face down to mine. His breath is burning over my lips, and I'm suddenly in dire need of his kiss.

"So, pretend I'm a stranger."

I lift my eyes to his. "So…just pretend like I don't know you?"

"Mmhmm." He brushes his lips over mine, softly, teasingly. "You don't know me, and I don't know you. We're two strangers with insane chemistry that we need to fuck out."

I graze my lip with my teeth.

Next thing I know, he's in front of me, pulling me against his body and kissing me, hard.

I wind my fingers into his hair, gripping, as his tongue explores my mouth.

He steps forward, moving me back against the pond. His hand comes up my side to cup my breast.

"The rubber duck is jabbing me in the ass," I whisper against his mouth.

Liam rumbles out a laugh. "Lucky fucking duck." He reaches behind me and moves the duck out of the way. "Better?" he asks.

"Much," I say, cupping his face and bringing his lips back down to mine.

The kiss quickly turns heated. I reach for Liam's zipper and pull it down. I put my hand inside, and moving his boxer shorts out of the way, I wrap my hand around his hard cock.

He moans over my lips. He grabs the hem of my dress and pulls it up over my hips, running a hand over my ass.

He pauses and stares down at me. "Thong?" he asks, fingering the thin scrap of material between my ass cheeks.

"Easier access." I shrug.

A grin covers his face. "God, you're so fucking hot. Turn around, and bend over," he orders.

I do as he said. In practice, it is not easy on a fake pond. So, I have to hold onto the pond edge with my hands.

Liam's hand smooths over my ass cheek. Then, he spanks it.

"Shit," I hiss, more surprised than hurt. Actually, it didn't hurt at all. It actually felt good.

"Did that hurt?"

"No." I can hear the blatant sex in my voice, so I'm sure he can, too.

His hand is stroking my ass cheek. "All that talk of spanking earlier...I thought you deserved one before I fucked you."

"Just the one spank?" I grin back at him.

He slaps my ass again, and I moan.

"You like being spanked?" he asks. His voice is low and gravelly. So incredibly sexy.

But then everything about him is sexy. Like the way he's taking his time to fuck me in here, a place where we could be caught at any moment.

I think part of that is what turns him on. And it turns me on, too.

I never realized I was an exhibitionist. I'm learning a lot about myself from being with Liam.

I glance back at him. "You know I do."

"Do I?" He tilts his head to the side. "I thought we were strangers, you and I."

"Screw being strangers. Just be you. Because I like you, Liam Hunter. And I love what you do to me. How you make me feel when you're inside me, fucking me."

"Jesus Christ," he moans. "You're gonna be the death of me, Boston."

His words are a stark realization for me. But I don't allow them to bother me or ruin the moment.

So, I push aside what they mean to me, and I smile at him. "Yeah, but what a way to go."

His darkened eyes on mine, he yanks open the button on his jeans and shoves them down, leaving them low on his hips. He takes his cock in his hand, stroking it.

He hooks a finger around the string of my panties, moving them out of the way. He groans, and then he pushes a finger inside my pussy. "Fucking soaked."

"For you," I breathe.

"Damn right for me."

I push back on his finger, fucking it. "So good. Make me come, Liam."

He pulls his finger out of me. "Don't get greedy, Boston." He slaps my ass, making me wetter. "You'll get to come at the same time I do. Now, spread your legs."

I spread my legs.

He slaps my ass again, harder this time, leaving a sting. "Wider."

I give him a look even though that slap was hot as fuck as I part my legs as wide as they'll go.

"Good girl," he rumbles.

He comes up behind me and rubs his cock down my ass, passing my puckered hole and going straight to my pussy. Then, he slams inside me.

"Liam," I cry out.

His hand comes over my mouth. "Shh," he tells me. "People will hear."

I bite down on his hand, so he frees my mouth.

I glance back, meeting his eyes. "I thought you liked the thought of people watching you fuck me."

He grins, as his eyes flare. "Such a dirty girl. Now, get your tits out for me. I want them in my hands while I fuck you," he commands in a low voice.

He starts to fuck me, his hands gripping my ass.

One hand holding onto the pond to steady myself as he pounds into me, I use the other to undo the top few buttons on my dress. I push the cups of my bra down, freeing my breasts. Liam's hand immediately is on one cupping it.

The carnival is going on around us. Calvin Harris & Disciples "How Deep Is Your Love" is playing from one of the nearby rides, and people are walking all around, only serving to intensify the moment.

Anyone could come in and catch us, and I don't care. If anything, the thought of being caught turns me on.

He pinches my nipples, and I moan loudly.

"You really want someone to hear and come in here, don't you?" he rumbles, giving a nipple an extra-hard tweak. "You're a little exhibitionist, and I fucking love it. Just as much as I love your tight little pussy."

His hand leaves my breast and slides down my side. He grabs ahold of my ass cheek, his fingers biting my skin.

"One of these days, I'm going to fuck you where everyone can see. Where they can watch me fuck your hot, tight pussy." The words drip from his mouth.

"God, yes," I whimper, the visual turning me on even more.

I didn't realize until now just how much it does actually turn me on—the thought of being caught having sex or having someone watch him fuck me.

Or maybe it's just him. Being with him. Every thing Liam does and says turns me on.

I'd let him fuck me anywhere, so long as I get to have him inside me, making me feel this way.

"Jesus," he growls. "You're so fucking hot. I want to spend all my time fucking you." He reaches around and pinches my clit with his fingers.

I don't have a chance to tell him that the feeling is mutual because my orgasm hits hard, taking everything with it but the ability to cry out his name as my inner walls convulse around his cock, squeezing him hard.

"Fuck yeah, that's it…I'm coming, babe…" His grip on me increases, and his cock pulses inside me as he comes, coating my insides.

He presses a kiss to my shoulder, grazing his teeth over my skin, making me shiver. "So hot," he whispers.

"I guess that's *sex outside* checked off the list." I laugh softly.

Liam chuckles and kisses my shoulder again. "We should make a move, get out of here." He sounds disappointed.

I'm disappointed, too. I could live with him inside me permanently—well, not permanently, but you know what I mean.

He gently pulls out of me, leaving me with that empty feeling I dislike so much. Then, he helps me up. The moment I'm upright, I feel his cum trickle out of me.

"I need something to clean myself with." I point to the offending drip, and then I pull my bra back up, covering my breasts.

Liam looks around and then picks up Squishy.

"No way! I'm not cleaning myself on Squishy."

Laughing, he drops Squishy back onto my bag.

Then, I spy a roll of blue paper towels down the side of the pond. "Grab me some paper towels. I'll use that."

Liam tucks himself back into his pants, fastening them up, and then he gets me some paper towels.

I clean myself up and then look for somewhere to dispose of the towels. I find a bin under the pond.

"Here, you forgot your buttons." Liam stands in front of me. He starts to button up my dress. Then, he cups my face and presses a soft kiss to my lips. "Perfect," he murmurs.

Yes, you are. So perfect that you make me wish things were different.

But they're not.

151

Liam picks up my bag and Squishy. He hangs my bag on my shoulder and hands me Squishy.

"We should go," he says.

I follow behind Liam. He lifts the tarpaulin and ducks his head out.

"Clear," he whispers, stepping out.

He holds the tarpaulin, letting me out.

Then, we're back out in the carnival, and it's almost like it never happened.

But it did.

"I can't believe we just did that." I grin up at Liam.

"Believe it, babe. And I got you this as a memento"—from his back pocket, he pulls out the rubber ducky that was sticking me in the ass and hands it to me—"so every time you look at it, you'll remember the time when you had sex with that hot English dude in a Hook a Duck tent."

I don't tell him that I don't need the duck to remember him because I will always remember him. Even when I close my eyes for the very last time and go join my family, Liam will be the last thing I see.

Instead, I smile and swallow. I take the duck from him and hold it with Squishy to my chest.

"Ducky can be a friend for Squishy," I tell Liam.

He laughs. "Ducky and Squishy. Has quite a ring to it. But not as good as Hunter and Boston sound together." He puts his arm around my shoulder, as we start to walk back into the crowd at the carnival.

Hunter and Boston. Together.

If only.

Some things in life just aren't meant to be forever.

Liam and I are one of those things.

chapter 13

I stayed at Liam's place after the carnival. He woke me up in the morning, bright and early, to tell me that something had come up at work and he had to go into the office.

I was a little disappointed about not spending the day with him. I was kind of used to being around him.

But then he told me that he had booked me a spa day at my hotel—well, his hotel—and that it was his treat. I thanked him but told him that I'd pay for it myself.

He just smiled and said he'd have them add it to my bill to pay when I left the hotel.

He was so lying. He wouldn't have them add it to my bill.

But I didn't argue. I just got up, and he made eggs and toast for me before he left to go to the office.

Honestly, the guy is perfect. If I had a lifetime left, I'd be hanging on to him.

After breakfast, I headed back to my hotel. Liam had sent Paul back to drive me, which was sweet.

Then, I spent the day getting pampered. I had a massage, facial, and manicure and pedicure.

It was awesome.

I'd never had a spa day before, so I mentally added it to my list and ticked it off.

When I got back to my room, all relaxed and feeling pretty, a garment bag was lying on my bed, waiting for me, with a note on it from Liam.

It said I had to wear the dress—no arguments—to pack an overnight bag, as I'd be staying at his apartment, and that he'd be at the hotel to pick me up at seven thirty.

So bossy. But it's one of the things I like about him. Liam knows what he wants, and he just goes for it.

I pulled open the zipper on the garment bag, and inside was a gorgeous long black dress that had diamantes covering the shoulder straps and a fitted diamante belt sitting just under my breasts. A pair of strappy high-heeled sandals were also included in the garment bag, too.

It was all very *Pretty Woman*. I did wonder if I could put it down as my romantic movie moment—except that I wasn't a hooker.

So, I did as I had been told.

I applied my makeup and did my hair, styling it up into a pretty chignon with the help of a How to Do a Chignon YouTube video. Got to say, when I was finished, my hair was looking good, and I was feeling mighty proud of myself.

I put on my nicest and sexiest black underwear, and lastly, I slipped into the dress and shoes.

I looked in the mirror, and I barely recognized myself. I looked grown-up. And I felt like a movie star.

For that moment, I wasn't Taylor Shaw, brain tumor girl.

I was Taylor Shaw…pretty woman.

Minus me being a hooker or snagging Richard Gere.

But I did have my own businessman, Liam Hunter, and that was way, way better.

Liam picked me up, as promised, at seven thirty. I loved the look on his face when he saw me wearing the dress. Like a kid in a candy store with a hundred dollar bill in his hand.

He had Paul drive us to an exclusive French restaurant in London. We ate crazy food, like escargot, and drank champagne all night. We had the best time just laughing and talking.

He didn't push me to talk about my past. He just asked what I wanted for my future.

I didn't have anything to tell him because I wouldn't have a future.

So, I told him the things I used to want before losing my family.

I said that I was thinking about getting a master's in English literature when I got back to Boston.

That took us onto talking about his college days.

Liam told me that he went to Cambridge, and he had a degree in business.

Then, he told me more about his companies and his business goals for the future.

But, honestly, it didn't matter what he was talking about. I was just happy to listen to him. I could seriously listen to the man talk all night.

Partly because of his hot accent. But, mostly, I just liked listening to what he had to say.

I saw just how smart and driven and incredibly ambitious he is.

Listening to Liam talk about his company and his business plans for the future made me happy.

I knew I wouldn't be here to see it all happen, but at least I knew that he'd be happy, doing what he loved.

I truly had the best night with him. But then again, every night…every moment spent with Liam was amazing.

I'm so thankful that I met him. I couldn't imagine being here without him and completing my list without him. *The thought of taking Liam out of the equation…makes the list seem dull.*

He's added color to my life. He's brightened up the time I have left, and for that—though he'll never know—I will be eternally grateful to him.

After we finished dinner and I was obscenely full and a little drunk, Paul drove us back to Liam's apartment.

Liam and I just made it inside his apartment before we started having sex. It wasn't like when we'd ended up doing it against his front door, but it was just as hot.

He carried me to the sofa, and I rode him to climax while still wearing my dress and heels.

After sex, he carried me to the bathroom. He set me down on my feet, took my dress off, and turned on the shower. We spent time washing each other. When the soap was all rinsed off of him, I got down on my knees, took his cock in my mouth, and let him fuck my mouth.

After the blow job and shower was over, we got out and dried off.

We got in bed, and as it turned out, we weren't done because we ended up having sex again.

Clearly, I can't get enough of the man.

But the sex was different that time. It was slower. Not the crazy sex or frantic fucking we normally did.

It was passionate and intense.

After we both came, Liam stayed inside me for a really long time, just holding me and kissing me, before he eventually had to move to clean up.

When he was finished, he came back to bed and wrapped me up in his strong arms, and that was where I slept all night.

But not now, as I'm alone in bed, and the space where Liam was is empty and cold.

I open my eyes and look at the clock on the nightstand. Squishy and Ducky are sitting beside it. I smile at the memory of the carnival and the fun we had in the Hook a Duck tent.

The clock reads seven fifteen. Too early for me.

Part of me wants to put my head under the pillow and go back to sleep, but the bed feels weirdly empty without Liam here, and my head has started buzzing a little. I really hope it's the aftereffects of the champagne last night, as I really don't want to deal with a headache right now.

I didn't have one at all yesterday, not even a twinge. So, I worry that I might pay for that today.

I should get something to drink, rehydrate, and try my best to ward off a coming headache.

But I know all the water in the world won't fix what causes my head to scream in pain.

Getting up, I reach for Liam's shirt, which he tossed on the floor last night, and pull it on, fastening up some of the buttons.

It's all wrinkled, but it smells of him, and that's what I like—having Liam's scent all around me.

I use the bathroom and head into the kitchen, as that's where I usually find him. But the kitchen's empty.

I check the living room, but he's not there either.

Considering the amount of time that I've spent in Liam's apartment, I haven't checked it all out. I've seen the living room, kitchen, guest bathroom, and Liam's bedroom—multiple times—but that's it.

I pad down the hall, my feet cold against the hardwood floor after leaving the warmth of his plush bedroom carpet. I walk past the guest bedroom and pause at the doorway of the guest bathroom that I used the first night I came here.

God, that seems so long ago. In reality though, it was only a handful of days ago.

It's like time has slowed down since I met Liam. I'm thankful for that. If these two weeks with him end up feeling like a lifetime, then I will forever be grateful for that.

I just pray the tumor lets me last that long.

Truth is, I don't know how long I have left. Could be months. Weeks. Days…

And that's why I have to make this time, here right now, count.

With Liam and completing my list before I go to join my family.

I keep walking, and my ears suddenly become alert to the sounds of heavy breathing.

What the…

I pick up my pace and realize that the heavy breathing is coming from behind a door toward the end of the hallway. I walk toward it, my heart rate picking up a little, until I get close enough to register the telltale sounds of someone exercising.

Liam must be working out in there.

I open the door to a fully equipped out gym. *Fancy.* And it's clearly how he manages to keep that awesome body of his…well, awesome.

The opposite wall to me is solid glass. I can see the whole of London from it.

Liam is on a treadmill facing the view. Earbuds are in his ears. There's also a flat screen up on the wall to the right of him, and the business channel is on.

But, as he runs, his focus is on the view.

I'm stuck on his powerful body as he moves. Sweat is running in rivulets down the nape of his neck and over the muscles on his back. His skin is glistening.

I'm starting to sweat from just watching him.

Not to be a total pervert and ogle him, I walk over to him, moving around to the side, so as not to come up behind him and startle him.

He catches sight of me and smiles. He yanks his earbuds out. "Morning, gorgeous." He slows the treadmill down a touch, bringing him to a jog.

"Morning yourself." I take a seat on what looks like a weight bench.

"I thought you'd sleep longer since I kept you up so late last night."

The glint in his eyes tells me that he's thinking about everything we did. It sets off a warm shiver down my spine and sends my stomach butterflying.

I bite my lower lip. "The bed was cold without you."

"Sorry, babe. I'm an early riser. I sleep six hours, if I'm lucky. And if I stay awake, lying next to you, then I'll only end up waking you up for more sex."

"And I totally wouldn't mind if you did that."

The look I get this time is seductive. It sends the butterflies into overdrive.

"I'll remember that for next time." Liam picks up a bottle of water from the cup holder on the treadmill, and he takes a drink.

The buzz in my head intensifies. The room spins, and a pain shoots across my forehead.

Not now. Not in front of Liam again.

"Hey, you okay?"

I hear a hint of concern in his voice.

I realize my eyes are shut, and my hand is pressed to my forehead. My other hand is curled around the edge of the bench. I blink open my eyes and rub the heel of my hand against my forehead, trying to force the pain away, wanting to downplay it so that he won't worry.

"Yeah, I'm fine," I lie with a forced smile. "Just all that champagne last night. My head is a little fuzzy."

I hate lying to him, but the alternative isn't an option. If I tell Liam the truth, I know what will happen. He'll try to talk me out of my decision.

I don't want to be talked out of it.

"Have you had anything to drink?" he asks.

"It was the drink that got me in this state." I convey humor in my voice as I lift my eyes to him.

"I mean, water, smart-arse."

"No." I shake my head. Then, I immediately regret doing it as the pain increases.

"Here, drink this." He lifts his half-full water bottle and then throws it to me, and I catch it. "You need something to eat, too. I'll feed you after I've finished up here."

"You'll make someone a good husband one day, Hunter." I manage a teasing smile.

His return look is less than humorous.

I unscrew the cap on the bottle and put it to my lips. I can taste Liam on it. I like that a lot. Might make me weird or a little gross, but I don't care. I drink the water he gave me. Once the bottle's empty, I screw the cap back on and put it down.

My headache is now a low throb. I need to grab some pain pills from my purse before it comes back with a vengeance.

"What are your plans for today?" Liam asks.

"Dunno." I lift my shoulders.

He gives me a contrite look before saying, "I've got to go into the office again today." He checks the time on his Apple Watch. "Pretty soon, in fact."

"Everything okay at work?" I ask.

"Yeah, just a few issues with a company I'm buying out. I need to call some people. Shout at them." He gives a slow smile.

"Such a big boss man."

"And don't you forget it." His smile curves into a sexy one, and then it suddenly downturns. "I feel like shit for leaving you alone though."

"Don't feel bad. I'm a big girl, Hunter. It's not your job to entertain me twenty-four/seven. Your job is to run your businesses."

With all the time he's been spending with me since I arrived in England, it's easy for me to forget that Liam has a day job—an I-own-multiple-multimillion-dollar-companies day job.

"I'll find a way to entertain myself."

His brows pull together. "But I like to entertain you, Boston. It's become my new favorite pastime."

"I'm your *new* favorite pastime? I'm afraid to ask what you did before me." *Screw other women probably.*

I suddenly feel a little sick. Probably because of the headache.

"When I say that, what I mean is, fucking you is my new favorite pastime. Getting to spend time with you is, of course, the bonus."

"Nice save."

"I thought so." He grins. "So, today…what about shopping?"

"What about shopping?"

"Why don't you go shopping? You haven't hit up any of the stores since you've been here."

"Um…" I curl my toes in against the hard floor. "Shopping's not really my thing."

Well, it is. I love to shop as much as the next girl, but there's no point in buying new clothes if I'm not going to be here to wear them.

But then I could always buy my funeral outfit.

Wow, that was morbid, even for me.

Definitely no to the shopping then.

"Isn't shopping an all women's thing?" Liam says.

I raise a brow. "That's a stereotypical thing to say, Mr. Hunter."

"You got me. Sorry, Miss Shaw." He lifts his hands in surrender, but the smile on his lips says otherwise. "So, no to the shopping. Why don't you hang out here until I get back? Watch a movie in the cinema room."

That gets my attention. "You have a cinema room? How am I just finding this out now?"

Liam chuckles. "The door at the end of this hall—that's the cinema room. It's well stocked with movies."

"And that's my whole day planned." I smile. Leaning back on my hands, I stretch my legs out.

"Popcorn and sweets are in the kitchen, so just help yourself." He stops the treadmill and steps off.

"What are sweets?"

He walks toward a cupboard, opens the door, gets a towel out, and turns back to me. He presses the towel to his face, drying the sweat from it. "Candy to you."

"Ah. I think I'm going to need an English phrase book to learn these new things."

"Don't worry. I'll teach them to you. You'll be an expert in English lingo in no time." He hangs the towel around his neck and tilts his head in the direction of the door. "I'm gonna go take a shower. Wanna join me?"

I get to my feet and tread softly toward him. He watches me the whole time.

Stopping just before him, I press a hand to his sweat-slicked chest. I have the sudden urge to lick the place where my hand is.

Looking up at him, I seductively bat my lashes. "Are we going to have sex while we're in the shower?"

A smile teases his lips. He leans down and presses his lips against mine, kissing me. I can taste the salty sweat on his lips. It's a surprising turn-on.

"Of course."

"And are you going to spank me again?"

Fire sparks in his eyes, and his smile returns, wider this time. "Only if you're really dirty."

"Oh, I'm really, *really* dirty." I lift my lips.

"Then, get your arse in the shower. Now."

"Wake up, sleepyhead."

Warm fingers are stroking my cheek, and I can hear a television on in the background.

Where am I?

Liam's apartment. Cinema room. I was watching a movie. I must've fallen asleep.

I blink open my heavy eyes to see Liam's autumn eyes staring back at me.

God, he's beautiful.

"Hey." I stretch my arms out, smiling at him. "I fell asleep, watching a movie."

"So I see. Which movie was it? Just so I know not to watch it. Couldn't have been that good if you passed out."

I don't tell him half the reason I fell asleep was because I'd been fighting a headache that hit not long after he'd left for work, and I'd spent most of the morning either in the bathroom, vomiting up the breakfast he'd made me, or lying in his bed with the shades drawn.

It wasn't until lunchtime that I'd felt half-human, so I'd showered the smell of vomit off me while remembering what Liam had done to me in the shower that morning.

Even though it'd made me smile, it'd actually made me feel lonely, too.

Lonely for him.

After my shower, I had taken some more pain pills, and then I'd come into the cinema room and put a movie on.

"Latest Bond film," I tell him.

"I'll give it a miss then." Lifting my legs, he sits on the sofa beside me and puts my legs back in his lap.

Liam's cinema room is amazing. Instead of separate cinema chairs, he has one huge black U-shaped sofa that is loaded with these über soft gray-and-black cushions. It's the comfiest sofa I have ever sat my ass on.

In the center of the room is a glass coffee table, and the walls are padded. On the far wall is the screen, which is quite possibly the size of the ones you see in a theater. It's freaking awesome.

"How was work?" I ask him, turning to lie on my back.

"Dull. I would have much rather been here with you." His hand is running absentmindedly up and down my bare leg.

I'm wearing shorts and a T-shirt, which I packed in my overnight bag to sleep in. As I ended up sleeping naked last night, I thought I'd wear them as my lounge-around clothes.

"Here with me, watching a boring film?" I chuckle.

"Yeah, but boring with you is much better than being stuck in a meeting with a bunch of men. With you, if we're both bored, then at least we can make up our own fun together." His eyebrows rise, his lips lifting, and pure sex is written all over his face.

"True." I grin, biting my lower lip.

I touch my feet together and realize they're cold. Lifting my legs, I tuck one foot inside his suit jacket and the other between his firm thighs.

He's wearing a navy blue three-piece suit. He looks incredibly sexy in a suit. But then again, he looks just as sexy without one…more so actually.

Naked Liam is a beautiful sight to see.

"Comfy?" he asks, grabbing the foot that's burrowed inside his jacket through the fabric.

"Very. Thanks."

He starts massaging my foot.

"Mmm, that feels good." I shut my eyes.

"Don't fall asleep again. We're going out soon."

"We are? Do I have a say in this?"

I have a feeling I already know the answer. And I know I shouldn't be lazy because it's not like time is my luxury, so I shouldn't waste it. I've already lost enough time today being sick and sleeping.

But I'm just super comfy right now.

"No. But trust me when I say, you're going to want to do this. Tonight, we're going to be checking something else off your list."

My mind starts to work quickly, running through my list and what I have left to do. "Ooh, what?"

He smiles. "I'm taking you to a rock concert."

That gets my attention. I pull my foot from between his legs and the other from his hand. I sit up. "A rock concert. Really?"

"Really." He smiles again.

"Who are we going to see?"

"The Mighty Storm."

"Holy shit!" I get up onto my knees. "Are you serious?"

His lips creep up into a smile. "As serious as a heart attack."

I tilt my head, confusion furrowing my brow. "I have no clue what you just said."

"You've never heard of that saying?" Liam looks surprised.

"Nope. But then I'm not an old man like you," I tease, shrugging.

He grabs ahold of my waist, his fingers digging in, and he tugs me onto his lap, so I'm straddling him. I rest my hands on his shoulders.

"Any more of your lip, and I'll spank your arse."

"Ooh, is that a promise?" I grin.

Liam chuckles, shaking his head. "Dirty girl. And when I say that I'm as serious as a heart attack, I mean, yes, I'm serious."

"So, why not just say you're serious?"

"Because I'm old, and us old people like our sayings."

That makes me laugh.

"So, Boston, you and I are going to watch The Mighty Storm in concert tonight, and we're also going to meet the band backstage."

"Holy fuck!" I scream. I actually scream, making Liam wince. "Sorry," I say. "But this is exciting! I fucking love The Mighty Storm! They're my favorite band ever!" *Did Liam know this? Did I tell him? Or is it just a coincidence?*

Either way, who cares? I'm going to see The Mighty Storm!

"I can't freaking believe we're going to see them! And actually meet them in person! Oh my God! I'm going to meet them for real!" I scream again. "How did you manage to score backstage passes for The Mighty Storm? Not that I'm complaining because I'm totally not. I'm the absolute opposite of complaining right now. I'm like the most grateful person ever."

Liam chuckles.

"But, seriously, how did you get backstage passes? I imagine getting backstage passes to meet The Mighty Storm would be like trying to win a golden ticket to get inside Willy Wonka's Chocolate Factory."

Or like getting gold dust.

He got me gold dust.

I don't know whether to hug him or kiss him or give him a blow job right now.

He smiles again and gives a lazy shrug. "I got them because I'm me."

And that's all he says. Because it's all he needs to say.

Sometimes, I forget just *who* Liam is and how rich he is. I guess it's because he doesn't live an excessively wealthy lifestyle. Sure, he has a nice apartment, but he's not flashy. He goes to the pub with his friends and takes me to the carnival.

To me, he's just Hunter. Amazingly sweet, hot, funny, fantastic-in-bed Liam Hunter.

Leaning my face to his, I plant a firm kiss on his lips. "You are awesome," I tell him.

"Only awesome?"

I tip my head back and look in his eyes. "Nope. You're phenomenal." I kiss him again on the lips. "And wonderful." Another kiss. "And incredible." I place my hands on his cheeks. "You are perfect, Liam Hunter." I brush the tip of my nose over his, staring down into his autumn eyes.

"I'll take all of those." He tugs me down to his mouth, leaving a whisper of air between our lips. "But I want a proper thank-you kiss."

So, I give him one.

And when I let him up for air, he's breathing hard, and he's also hard beneath my ass.

"You need help with that?" I wiggle my ass against his erection.

His eyes move from me to the clock on the wall and then back to me. He sighs. "It'll have to wait until later, babe. We need to get ready and head to the stadium soon." He gives my ass a slap.

So, I climb up off him and excitedly head to get dressed for my date with The Mighty Storm.

I'm going to meet The Mighty Storm! I'm going to meet Jake Wethers!

Oh God. What in the hell am I going to wear?

" A re you sure you're okay in the standing area?"
I tip my head back against Liam's chest and smile up at him. "I'm sure."

"We can use my company's private box if you change your mind. Just say the word."

I can see his company's private box. It's way up high above the seating. I know company boxes are supposed to be exclusive, but it just seems too far away from the stage and the action.

I want to be right where we are, in the thick of it.

Sure, it's pretty cramped, bodies all squished together, and I'm also sure the squishing will increase when The Mighty Storm comes onstage. But I honestly don't mind.

I want to experience a rock concert.

This right here is the experience.

It also helps that I have Liam pressed up against my back, his hands resting on my hips with his fingers hooked through the belt loops on my jeans, while he acts like my very own personal body shield.

Seriously, no one can get too close with his six-three huge body covering mine.

He's already warned one guy for getting too close. Poor guy. I told Liam to chill, which earned me a rumble of displeasure in response.

On the drive to the stadium, Liam said he'd gotten tickets for standing near the stage, or we could use his company box. The choice was mine. Of course, I said standing.

Being down here with him feels right.

Liam might be wealthy, but he just fits in just fine with me and everyone else.

Dressed in blue jeans, brown working boots, a fitted black T-shirt, and a biker-style jacket, he looks droolworthy. And more like he should be a member of The Mighty Storm than the businessman he is.

We unknowingly coordinated our outfits, which caused us to laugh.

I'm dressed in a black tank top and blue jeans with brown flat ankle boots and a leather jacket that I brought in my overnight bag with me to his place. I thought I'd wear these clothes to save me from going back to the hotel to change.

"I'm fine here," I tell him, looking back to the stage. "And you can bet I won't be changing my mind. I'm near the front of the stage—meaning, I'm literally within grabbing distance of Jake Wethers." I grin, rubbing my hands together.

We're on the second row back. I had a clear view of the opening band, who just finished five minutes ago. We're so close to the stage that I could make out the words the guy had tattooed on his neck. That means I'll be able to see Jake Wethers's tattoos and his face and super hot body up close as well.

I know I'm meeting Jake and the rest of the band after the show. But, seriously, I want to pee just at the thought of them coming out onstage. *What will I be like when I'm actually face-to-face with them?*

God, please don't let me act like a total basket case when I meet them.

My only saving grace is that Liam will be there to keep me under control.

Speaking of, he's been quiet for a while.

I tilt my head back again to look up at him.

His face looks tight. I can see the muscles in his jaw working, like he's grinding his teeth, and his lips are pressed together in a firm line.

His eyes move down to look at me. When I say *look*, it's more of a glare. He doesn't look happy.

"What's the matter with you?" I say in an overly high-pitched voice to try to make him smile.

He doesn't smile. But he does speak, "No grabbing Jake Wethers when he comes onstage or later when you meet him, Boston. I mean it." His tone is really off. He sounds like he's angry with me.

I feel a little uncomfortable because I'm not exactly sure why he's being so off with me. But I cover my discomfort with a laugh and say, "Not even a little grab?"

"No, not even a fucking little grab, Taylor."

Wow, he first-named me. Must be serious.

But I don't let his pissy attitude deter me. So, I keep on with winding him up to help me get to the source of his stinky attitude.

"You worried I'm gonna get arrested, Hunter? Because I'm thinking that might be a lot of fun. Handcuffed and thrown in a cell...mmm, yeah, that sounds really hot. I could add, *Go to jail*, to my list. I think I'd look good in one of those orange jumpsuits." I give him a part-teasing, part-sexy grin with the hope that he lightens the fuck up.

He frowns, his eyes crinkling up at the corners.

Okay, so that didn't work.

I definitely thought the handcuffs and jumpsuit would at least get me a smile.

I really don't like Moody Liam.

"I'm not worried about you getting arrested," he says in that low and pissy voice he seems to have adopted.

Okay, Mr. Grumpy Pants. Fuck you very much.

I turn my face back to the front.

Anger is gathering in my chest because he's being a dick. Well, whatever has crawled up his ass can just stay there because he's not spoiling my night or my ogling of Jake Wethers.

Then, it hits me.

And I can't help the grin that spreads across my face.

I turn in his arms, so I'm facing him. His hands slide away from my hips.

I press my hands to his chest and stare up at his face. "Liam Hunter, are you jealous right now?"

His brows draw together so hard that I'm surprised he isn't straining the muscles in his forehead.

"I'm not jealous. I just don't share," he grumbles that last sentence.

"Ha!" I laugh. "You are so jealous!"

He stares me in the eyes. "Fuck off."

That makes me laugh harder.

"Aw, Hunter." I reach up and pat his cheek with my hand. "You've got nothing to be jealous of." I remember him saying something similar to me when I got all bent out of shape over Megan.

Got to say though, it feels good to be on the other side of the jealousy. Though I never pegged Liam Hunter for the jealous type. But then again, I never had myself down for the jealous kind either—until I met him.

I'm not sure what that says about my feelings for him. Honestly, I'm not going to think too hard about it because it could be a rabbit hole I don't want to venture down.

"I'm pretty sure Jake Wethers wouldn't ever be interested in sharing me, so you needn't worry."

His frown reaches epic depths, and his eyes darken infinitely.

There's a definite pause, and I shift a little with unease 'cause I'm fairly sure I just said something wrong. I'm just not sure what it was.

Then, he says in a low and deadly tone, "And if he *were* interested?"

I give him a look. "Come on, Hunter, this is Jake Wethers we're talking about. Who would turn him down? I bet even you wouldn't say no."

"I might like *ass*"—he mimics my American accent on the *ass* part—"but I like my *ass* to be a few inches from the pussy."

That makes me laugh.

And the woman next to me turns her head in our direction, clearly hearing what he said.

I pretend not to notice, and I just focus on Liam. "Hunter, you're being ridiculous about this. For starters, I wouldn't even be on Jake Wethers's radar."

"But just to be on Jake's radar or on anything or any part of his body would be amazing," the woman next to me says with a sigh in her voice.

Yep, she's clearly been listening in on our conversation. After the ass and pussy comment from Liam, who can blame her?

I glance at her over my shoulder. "Amen to that, sister."

I lift my hand to her, and she high-fives me.

I'm laughing when I look back to Liam. My laughter quickly disappears because of the expression on his face. He's über pissed. His eyes are like lasers, burning me to a crisp.

He flicks an angry glare in the direction of my high-five sister, and she promptly faces back front.

I kind of want to turn around and face the front now, so I don't have to deal with Moody Bastard Hunter.

I swear, I'm going to kick him in the nuts if he doesn't chill out. He's kind of dousing my rock concert high.

He leans his face close to mine, leaving a whisper of space between us. "Boston, you would definitely be on Jake Wethers's radar," he says, his breath gusting over my lips.

Even though he's annoying me, he's being all alpha, and it's kind of a turn-on. Okay, it's a massive turn-on.

"You'd be on all men's radars," he continues. "The only ones whose radars you wouldn't be on are the ones who like cock with their ass. I'm almost positive that Jake Wethers likes pussy. And he's a rock star. Rock stars like to fuck hot groupies."

I reach up and slide my fingers into his thick hair, winding it around my fingers, holding his face in place. "I'm not a groupie, you idiot. And do you know nothing? Jake Wethers is happily married to his childhood sweetheart, and they have, like, a hundred kids together."

I might know a thing or two...or, like, pretty much everything about The Mighty Storm. I'm a fan of theirs, if you hadn't guessed.

I lift my mouth to his and softly kiss him. "You're acting out for no reason," I say against his mouth.

Liam's response is not with words.

His hands come up into my hair, gripping it tightly, and he answers me with his lips and his very skilled tongue. He kisses me hard, demanding, leaving me boneless and breathless.

Suddenly, he releases me. The look in his eyes instantly makes me want to get out of here and find a dark corner where I can do all kinds of dirty things to him.

His eyes are filled with desire and fixed on me. My skin feels feverish, and my nipples are hard. And I'm almost certain that my panties are soaking wet, too.

His hand slips from my hair and goes down my back. He possessively grabs my ass, pulling me closer to him.

Suddenly, the lights in the stadium go out and plunge us in total darkness, taking Liam from my sight.

Screams and cheers erupt around us. It's sheer excitement. I can practically taste it in the air, feel it brushing over my skin.

I know this means the band is coming on.

My own level of excitement is at an all-time high right now.

But it's not because of the reason I thought it would be. It's not because The Mighty Storm is about to appear any minute now.

It's because of this man pressed up against me, holding me like I belong to him. Being here in the pitch-dark with Liam, surrounded by all these people, where we could do anything we wanted and no one would be able to see—it's a major turn-on. It's intoxicating.

He's intoxicating.

All I can feel…smell…taste is him.

I want him.

I slide my hand down between us and cup him through his jeans. He's hard as a rock.

I feel his chest jump on a breath. Then, he grabs my hand on his cock and pushes himself against it.

He brings his mouth down to my ear. His lips brush over my skin as he speaks, making my toes curl, "When I get you home later tonight, I'm going to fuck you for days. Fuck you so hard and thorough that you'll feel me weeks later. That'll be your punishment for making me feel jealous. Because I don't like to feel jealous, Taylor."

A shiver runs down my spine and quickly spreads throughout my body.

Jesus…he calls fucking me for days punishment?

I call it a reward. Or a gift. Like probably the best gift ever.

Maybe I should make him jealous more often if it elicits this kind of a response.

Strobe lights in the stadium suddenly come on.

Liam's eyes are on mine, staring intently with meaning.

It's like nothing else around us matters.

It's just him and me.

I'm transfixed on his gaze.

My eyes flicker down to his mouth, and I'm suddenly feeling parched.

My heart starts to race, and I have this intense feeling that I'm very much out of my depth with Liam.

His eyes move past me and then immediately return. He leans in close again and says, "I meant what I said, Boston. Fucking for days," he enunciates the last three words.

And, I swear, I almost come.

"Now, turn the fuck around and watch the show. Sooner it's over with, sooner I can get you home and make good on my promise."

I seriously don't think I can move my legs. They feel like Jell-O, but I force myself to turn and face the front.

Honestly, I'm just confused and jittery and all over the place, but I'm massively turned on. I've never needed to orgasm as much as I do now.

I don't know what to do with myself.

Liam's hands go back to my hips. His fingers hook through my belt loops, and he yanks me back against his body.

His hold is possessive. And I like it.

His hips are nestled nicely against the top of my ass. He's still as hard as stone, and having his erection pressed up against me is doing nothing to help the itch I need to scratch.

For a moment, I just wish the lights would go out again, so I could put Liam's hand to good use.

The strobe lights stop, and the huge screens onstage illuminate The Mighty Storm logo.

Elation unfurls in my stomach, and I'm instantly right back to being excited to hear the band play.

I feel like a fucking yo-yo, going up and down, not exactly sure where I'm at emotionally or physically.

The crowd around us erupts in screams, and then I see that The Mighty Storm is starting to walk onstage.

Jake is coming!

God, I wish I were.

Denny is first out onstage. He climbs up behind his drum kit, which is set up at the back of the stage on a little stage of its own, putting him higher than the rest of the band.

Next, Tom appears, his bass guitar already strapped to his chest. The screams get louder. He looks even bigger and seriously hotter in real life than he looks on TV or in photos.

Smith, the guitarist who replaced the late, great Jonny Creed, comes out onstage.

When Jonny Creed died, I cried for a week straight, like the rest of the world did. I only wish I'd had a chance to see them live when Jonny was still alive.

But Smith looks cool as hell, and he's easy on the eyes.

It seems like forever, but then Jake Wethers walks out onstage, and the stadium goes mental.

My heart stops beating for a few seconds.

I watch, transfixed, as Jake walks straight up to the microphone.

Holy crap, he's like fifteen feet away from me.

Please don't let me faint. Please don't let me faint.

His eyes sweep over the crowd. He doesn't say anything. But then he doesn't have to because he's Jake fucking Wethers.

The guy could stand there all night and not say a word, and people would still walk out of this place, saying how awesome he is. He just has presence and charisma and charm and that likeability factor about him. Also, he breathes sexuality, which definitely helps.

Exactly like Liam does.

Guess I have a thing for the alpha men.

I press my back into Liam, feeling he's still hard against my butt. A secret smile sneaks onto my lips.

I reach back and wrap my arms around him. I glance up. His eyes are smiling down at me.

Yay, Happy Liam is back.

I smile at him. He sweetly kisses my forehead.

My heart squeezes with affection and happiness.

I move my face and eyes back to the stage at the exact moment Jake curls his hand around the microphone and leans in close to it.

Then, he starts singing the intro to their latest hit song in a cappella.

A few beats later, the rest of the band joins in.

And here, in Liam's safe hold, I float off to TMS heaven.

My hand is firmly in Liam's as he leads me backstage to meet The Mighty Storm.

Still on a high from the phenomenal concert, I'm close to peeing at the thought of actually meeting the band.

I really hope I don't act like a total freak.

The concert was amazing and everything I'd hoped a rock concert would be. I get to tick that off my list now. And I can add meet The Mighty Storm and tick that off, too.

And all because of Liam. He truly is the best.

Liam shows our backstage passes to a burly security guy who is guarding the entrance. He lets us through, and then we're backstage.

It's total mayhem back here. I'm guessing the people bustling about are the roadies working to pack up all the stuff.

"The band should be in the green room, so we'll head there," Liam tells me.

Leaving the backstage area, we walk down a long hallway until we find the green room.

I can hear music and the chatter of voices behind the door.

"Ready?" Liam stares down at me.

"No. Yes."

"Which is it?" He chuckles.

"Just don't let me act like an idiot. I have a tendency to ramble and go a little crazy when I'm nervous."

A grin slides onto his lips. "Like kissing strangers who sit next to you on airplanes?"

"Exactly like that."

His eyes darken a little, but the smile remains. "Yeah, well, no kissing anybody in there but me. Got it?"

"Got it." I smile, giving him a thumbs-up, appeasing him.

I don't want Moody, Jealous Liam to make a comeback. Not that I'm going to be kissing anyone in there.

But…if Jake Wethers did ask for a kiss, who would I be to say no?

Just kidding.

Sort of.

Liam pushes open the door, leading me into the green room, and—

Holy fuck.

They're here. The Mighty Storm is here. In this room. With me.

Oh my God!

There are other people here, but I can't see anyone else because all I can see is Jake and Tom and Denny and Smith.

I think I actually just peed a little.

Jake looks over at us and smiles.

Holy shit. Jake is smiling at me!

Okay, so it's not exactly me he's smiling at. It's Liam. But whatever. He is smiling in my vicinity, and that's good enough for me.

Jake starts to walk toward us.

Shit. He's coming over here. Holy fuck!

Okay, calm. Be calm. And cool.

Don't act like a tool, Taylor. Act…normal.

"Hey," Jake says to Liam. "Liam Hunter, right?"

"And you're Jake Wethers."

"The one and only." Jake chuckles, putting his hand out to shake Liam's. "It's good to finally meet you, man."

Liam takes his hand and shakes it.

Hang on…Jake is saying it's good to finally meet Liam? Um, not that Liam's not awesome because he is, but—and this is a big but—this is Jake Wethers we're talking about here.

"Jake, this is Taylor Shaw. Big fan of yours."

I hear the tone in his voice on that last part, but I refrain from looking at him.

Jake smiles at me. "Hey," he says.

Oh my God. He's talking to me. What am I supposed to do?

Speak, you freaking dummy.

Liam gives my arm a nudge, and I come to, realizing that I'm just staring at Jake with my mouth open, like a total basket case. I wouldn't be surprised if drool was on the corner of my mouth at well.

"Hi." I smile at Jake. Then, I lift my hand and wave at him.

I waved at Jake Wethers.

Why, God? Why?

Jake chuckles. "Big fan, huh?"

"Uh-huh."

"What did you think about the show?" Jakes asks me.

"It was really great." I start enthusiastically nodding my head. "Like, amazing. Best concert I've ever been to. Actually, it is the first concert I have ever been to. But I have no doubt that, if I had been to other concerts, this one would have been the best—ever. Like, really. I'm positive. It was just amazing. Really."

Oh God. Stop talking. Please stop talking.

I bite my lip to stop the verbal diarrhea. And I know my face is bright red because it feels like I just stuck it in a furnace.

Jake chuckles again. "I'm glad you enjoyed it."

"Jake," Liam says, "I just wanted to thank you again for meeting with the kids. They were seriously excited about it."

Kids?

I glance around and see that some of the people are actually little people—well, not little people, but kids. Maybe twelve or thirteen years old. They're all sitting with the rest of the band, talking with them.

"No problem. Like I said on the phone, anything to do with charity, I'm in. And the kids are great. I did want to talk to you about donating some money," Jake says.

Charity?

"That would be great," Liam tells him, happiness clear in his voice.

"Charity?" I say to Liam, looking up at him.

For the first time ever, I see a blush in his cheeks.

He lifts a shoulder in a half-shrug and says, "A while back, I set up a charity for children from underprivileged families and children in foster care. Basically, any kid who needs help, we get them what they're lacking—clothes, shoes, food, school supplies, anything to try to give them a better chance in life. We also fund education and sports programs, and we organize outings for the kids every once in a while. This is one of the outings. The kids got to come watch The Mighty Storm from the comfort of my company's box, and then Jake and the guys were kind enough to agree to meet them—after I'd called up Jake and begged him."

Jake laughs. "He hardly begged."

"He made me beg." Liam chuckles, winking at me.

"So, the donation," Jake says. "I'll have my assistant, Stuart, contact your people to sort out the details, and we'll send some money over."

"And just so you know, the charity runs on a hundred percent donations, so anything you send will go straight to the kids," Liam tells him.

"You fund the charity yourself?" Jake asks, seeming impressed.

Liam nods. He seems a little uncomfortable, and that blush in his cheeks is back. "It's not a big deal, but my accountant seems to think so. He doesn't like it very much."

"I can imagine." Jake chuckles.

"That is incredibly generous of you," I say to Liam, turning to him.

It's just…such an amazing thing to do. He runs the charity out of his own pocket, so the children see all the donated money. Not many people would do that.

His eyes come to mine. "It's nothing someone in my position wouldn't do."

"That's not true," I say emphatically. "There are a lot of rich people out there who don't even do half of what you're doing." Then, I say to Jake, "And I'm not including you in that statement because, clearly, you're a generous man with your time and money." And I'm babbling again.

I turn back to Liam. "It's just…wonderful."

"It's not like I can't afford it." He shrugs, like it's no big deal. "I mean, what else am I going to do with my money?"

I…I don't know what to say. There are so many things he could do with his money.

But he doesn't. He doesn't exactly live a lavish lifestyle. Sure he has a nice apartment and nice clothes. But I don't see him splurging like others would. He flies economy on his own airplanes, for God's sake.

"Well, I think Taylor is right, man. It's commendable, what you do. Makes me want to do more." Jake rubs a hand over his chin. "I'll have Stuart speak to your people about us getting more involved, fundraising or something. My wife, Tru, owns a magazine. She runs the LA office, but the office here in London is run by her business partner, Vicky. I'm sure Tru and Vicky will also want to get involved."

"That would be…great," Liam says. He sounds a little choked up. "We'd really appreciate that."

I wish I could do something, too. Help his charity in someway. But I'm not exactly in a position to do so.

I do have some money—the money my parents left me and the money from the insurance settlement from the fire and the deed to my family's home. I could sell the house, and give all the money I have to his charity. Help those kids that Liam cares about. It's not like I need the money. I could donate anonymously.

But, first, I need to know the name.

"What's your charity called?" I ask Liam.

"We're All the Same."

We're All the Same.

I love that.

It's perfect.

It's him.

"Do you want to meet the guys?" Jake asks. He nods in the direction of where the band is still sitting, talking with the kids. "I'm sure they'll want to donate to your charity as well."

"Love to," I say quickly.

I might be in awe of Liam right now, but I'm still totally aware that I'm in the presence of rock royalty. I've met Jake. Now, I want to meet the rest of the band.

Liam chuckles from beside me, and I grin up at him.

As we walk over to meet the rest of The Mighty Storm, I can't take my eyes off Liam.

I feel like I'm seeing him through new eyes tonight.

Of course I knew he was great. He's wonderful and charming and funny and smart and fucking amazing in bed.

But this—his charity and what he does to help these kids who don't have much in life—I guess it's making me see just how special Liam really is.

And I'm starting to see just how special he is to me.

What he's starting to mean to me.

This is the exact moment, as I walk over to meet the band whose music I've been listening to since I was a teenager, that I realize I have feelings for Liam.

Real, actual feelings that move beyond the realm of just sex.

I can't tell if these feelings are that of friendship.

Or something more.

Either way, I have feelings for him.

And that knowledge scares the hell out of me.

chapter 17

"Oh my God," I breathe, waking to find Liam's head between my legs and his tongue licking me with gusto.

At the sound of my voice, Liam's eyes lift to mine. "Good morning," he rumbles. His chin rubs on my clit, the scratch of his morning stubble feeling strangely erotic.

"It certainly is." I smile, biting my bottom lip.

"Well, I did tell you if I stayed awake in bed next to you, I'd end up waking you up for sex."

"I'm glad you did—wake me up, that is."

He tips his head back down and runs his nose over my clit, making me shiver.

Then, he puts his mouth back on me and sucks on my clit, sliding two fingers inside me, making my hips jerk upward.

He presses his free hand on my hip, holding me in place, as he drives me crazy with his skilled tongue.

My heart is pounding in my chest, my fingers pulling at his hair, and I'm coming against his mouth seconds later.

I'm lax in the bed, my heart still beating hard and my breaths are coming fast.

Liam climbs up my body. "Hi."

He brushes his mouth against mine. I can taste myself on his lips.

"Hi yourself." I grin.

I part my legs wider, letting him know what I want—him inside me.

Liam smiles against my mouth, kissing me again, as he pushes himself inside me.

"Liam," I moan between kisses.

"Jesus, Taylor." He presses his forehead to mine and starts moving in and out of me in long, measured strokes.

Liam rarely says my name, but when he does, it's when he's inside me or angry with me, as I learned last night. But I like hearing him say my name, especially when he's moaning it in sexual pleasure.

The slow sex doesn't last long, and very quickly, he's fucking me fast and hard. His hand goes under my ass, tilting it up, so he reaches deeper. His mouth kisses down my neck to my breast, taking it in his mouth. Then, his tongue is licking around my nipple.

My hands are on his back, my nails scoring into his skin.

"I'm not gonna last much longer, babe. Are you close?"

"Come," I tell him. "I want to feel you come."

Liam always thinks of me first in sex. But, right now, I want this moment to be about him.

His mouth finds mine again, and he kisses me deeply. Not much later, he's coming long and hard. He collapses on top of me, making sure not to crush me, with his face buried in my neck as he catches his breath. Then, he kisses a path up my neck to my mouth and gives me a soft, sweet face.

"I'll get something to clean you up. Give me a minute." One last kiss, he pulls out of me and leaves the bed, walking into the bathroom.

I hear the telltale sound of running water, and then Liam reappears with a damp cloth.

"I can do it." I hold out my hand.

"I know, but I like to do it." He sits on the bed beside me and presses the damp cloth to me, cleaning me up. "It's my last chance to feel you up—well, until the next time I get to do it." He lifts his smiling eyes to mine.

I giggle, shaking my head at him.

He takes the cloth back to the bathroom, and then he's climbing into bed beside me. I curl up against his body, resting my head on his chest. I listen to his heart beating, my fingers running through his soft chest hair.

"I wanted to ask you something," Liam says.

I tip my head back, so I'm looking at him. "Sounds ominous."

He smiles. "It's nothing bad. It's just Grand Prix weekend, and I always go down to my grandpa's place. I usually drive down on Friday night. We hang out and go flying on Saturday, and then we head to the Prix on Sunday."

"You go to your grandpa's often?"

"As often as work allows."

"Then, you should definitely go. Don't worry about me here. It's London. There's plenty to entertain me."

I could actually go down to Oxford. I was planning on doing it at the end of my trip. But I could go this weekend while Liam's away. I could catch the train and spend the day down there.

The thought of going alone, without Liam, makes me feel…lonely. But it's important that I go.

He shifts, forcing me to move. He lies on his side, his head on the pillow, facing me. He brings his hand to my face and tucks my hair behind my ear. Then, he brushes his fingers down my neck, over my shoulder, and down my arm. He takes my hand in his. "Well, I was wondering if you wanted to come with me. I know going to my grandpa's house isn't on your list. But we could probably do some of the things left on your list while we're there. And we still have next week to complete it."

Next week—that's all I have left with him.

The level of sadness I feel from that knowledge is…concerning.

It should stop me from wanting to be with him this weekend. It should make me want to say no.

But it doesn't. It has me wanting to say yes.

I bite my lip. "I don't want to intrude on your time with your grandpa."

"You wouldn't be intruding, and I know that my grandpa would love to have you there. He's a people person." Liam smiles wide. "And I bet you've never been to the Grand Prix, right?"

"Right."

"So, we can add it to your list. You'll love it, Boston. It's an amazing experience."

Say no, Taylor. You're getting too attached. Let him go to the Grand Prix with his grandpa, and you go to Oxford alone.

"Where does your grandpa live?"

Don't ask that. Say no. Thank you for the offer but no.

"Oxford," he says.

My breath catches.

"My parents met at Oxford University." The words are out before I can stop them.

I'm surprised at how easily they came out. I feel my heart start to beat faster.

Liam's hand tightens around mine, his eyes softening on me. "Do you want to go…to Oxford? See the university?"

I can feel my throat thickening, so I don't attempt speech. I nod my head.

Liam brings his mouth to my forehead and kisses me there. I close my eyes, my chest feeling too full…with everything.

"So, it's settled. You'll come with me to Oxford." He tips my chin up with his hand and kisses me once more on the lips.

Then, he gets up from the bed. "I'll make us breakfast," he says, pulling some black pajama pants from the drawer and putting them on. "After breakfast, we can swing by the hotel, you can pack a bag for the weekend, and then we'll head to Grandpa's place. Scrambled eggs and bacon good for you?"

I feel mute. Because I'm feeling too much.

"Eggs and bacon are fine," I force out the words.

Liam heads for the door. "I'll get breakfast started, and you can get your hot arse out of bed and make the coffee." He tosses a smile back at me before leaving the room.

I push myself up in bed and just sit there for a moment.

His grandpa lives in Oxford. The place my parents met and fell in love.

I don't know if it's just a coincidence or meant to be.

Coincidence. It has to be.

Why did I tell him about where my parents met?

Because you want him to know you.

No, I don't want Liam to know me.

And, in many ways, I don't want to know him. I don't want to get close to him.

This here, with him, was just supposed to be sex and fun.

But, now, it's starting to feel like more than that.

On my part at least.

Last night, I wasn't sure if the feelings I had for Liam were friendship…or something more.

Now, I'm sure. They're something more.

The only saving grace I have is that Liam doesn't reciprocate my feelings. At least, I don't think he does. If he did, then that would make things messy.

No, Liam's not a relationship person. His job is everything to him, the only thing he cares about. It's his life.

He has no room in it for anyone else—aside from his grandpa and his friends.

He might be spending this time off work with me, but this, for him, is just a vacation.

I'm his at-home holiday romance.

When I leave London, Liam will be someone I have to let go of, and it will hurt.

For Liam, I'll just be that American girl he had two crazy weeks with. In time, I'll just be a memory. A fond memory, I hope.

But one thing is for certain. This thing between Liam and me will end the way it was always supposed to end, irrespective of the feelings I have for him.

One more week, and I will leave London and go back to Boston.

And soon after…I will die.

"This is your car?"

Liam stops by the trunk of the car and looks over at me. We're in his building's parking garage, and I'm staring at the hottest car I have ever seen.

"It is." He smiles.

He pops the trunk and puts his bag in along with the empty one I've borrowed from him. We're stopping by the hotel, so I can get my stuff before we head to Oxford. All I have with me is my handbag that I've been using for overnights at his place, and sure, it's big, but a weekend away requires more stuff. The only other thing I have with me is my big-ass suitcase, and I'd prefer not to drag that to Oxford with me, so Liam lent me one of his weekend bags.

And remember when I said that Liam doesn't spend money to the excess? I take that back.

I might not be a car expert, but I know a Bugatti Veyron when I see one. And that's what I'm looking at right now.

A sexy-as-hell Bugatti.

"This car is a total babe magnet." I run my fingertips over the smooth, shiny black paintwork.

"Like its owner," he says, shutting the trunk with a soft clunk.

"Ha!" I laugh. "Seriously though, you could look like the Hunchback of Notre Dame and still score a supermodel if you had this car."

Liam gives a mock-offended look. "I hope to fuck you're not implying that chicks only dig me because of my car."

I laugh again. "As if. This is the first time I've seen your car, and I totally dug you long before this."

He comes around the car, toward me. Standing before me, he takes my face in his hands, tipping it back so that I'm looking up into his eyes.

Leaning in, he softly kisses me on the lips. "I kinda dig you, too, Boston."

I don't know why, but the sentiment really touches me. More than it should. More than I should allow it to.

I blink my eyes open. His are on mine.

My heart bumps around my chest.

He kisses me again and then whispers over my lips, "Now, get your hot arse in my hot car, so I can get her out on the open road."

He releases me with a chuckle. Then, he walks over and opens the passenger door for me.

"Boys and their toys." I smile as I climb inside, setting my heart back in place.

Wow. The car is just as nice on the inside as the outside. It's rich leather and glossy everything. I'm afraid to touch anything in case I leave a mark.

For a two-seater, it's surprisingly roomy. It even fits Liam's big body as he climbs in.

I put my seat belt on. "I'm so going to enjoy this ride," I tell him.

He stops with his seat belt in his hand and looks at me. "I promise that this ride will be as good as the ones I give you every night in my bed." A grin spreads over his gorgeous face, making me laugh again.

I really like how much I laugh around Liam.

Another thing I like too much.

"Is the car new?" I ask. It looks brand-new.

"I bought her a few years ago. A present to myself when I turned thirty. I don't get to drive her as much as I'd like though."

"Ah, she's your midlife-crisis car," I deadpan.

His lips press together, battling a smile. "Laugh it up. You'll be thirty one day, and when that day comes, I'll remind you of this conversation."

Everything inside me pauses.

No, Liam, I won't.

But, of course, that isn't what I say.

I really shouldn't say anything. I should just laugh it off and change the direction of the conversation. But the concern that he's talking like he'll know me beyond these two weeks has me saying, "You think you'll know me when I'm thirty?"

He lets out that smile on his lips. It reaches all the way to his eyes. "If you're lucky."

If I'm lucky.

I really wish I were.

Recently, I've found myself wishing for a lot of things. Things I have no right to wish for.

But the heart can be a selfish and foolish thing.

And mine is certainly both.

I can feel the conflict inside me between this man in front of me and what I know is right, what I deserve…and it isn't him. I know that.

So, I paste on a smile, and I force a laugh, giving a shake of my head, to show that everything is just right when it couldn't be further from it.

Liam puts the key in the ignition and then presses a button on the console beside him. The car purrs to life.

He looks at me. "Hotel first and then my grandpa's place," he confirms.

"Perfect," I say even though things aren't.

Except for him. He's perfect.

Liam stops by the hotel, and I run inside with the weekend bag.

As I'm wearing last night's clothes since they were all I had with me at Liam's, I do a quick change and opt to wear a pale pink knee-length summer dress, the color matching my hair. I want to make an effort to look nice since I'll be meeting his grandpa. My makeup and hair are already done because I showered at Liam's before we left.

I slip on my silver ballet pumps and put the ankle boots I wore last night in the overnight bag to take with me. Then, I fill the bag up with essentials—clothes, underwear, and toiletries. Before leaving, I grab the photo of my family off the nightstand and put it in the bag.

Then, I head back out to Liam.

"Sorted?" he asks as I climb into the car, the bag safely in the trunk.

"Yep."

He pulls out into traffic, and soon, we're on the highway, heading toward Oxford, with music playing on the radio and a companionable silence between us.

"Boston…can I ask you something?"

The tone in his voice has me feeling like it might not be a question that I'll want to answer.

My head against the headrest, I turn my face to look at him.

He looks so strong, so beautiful, driving his car.

Those feelings I have for him twist inside me.

I swallow against them. "Sure." My voice comes out scratchy, so I clear my throat.

He flickers a glance at me before looking back to the road ahead.

There's a pause before he says, "I know you said you don't talk about your family—"

"I don't. And I meant that." My words are hard. I hate the way my voice sounds.

He doesn't deserve my harshness. He's been nothing but good to me.

I turn my face away, feeling ashamed. "I'm sorry," I whisper. "I didn't mean to snap."

His hand touches my hand, surprising me, bringing my eyes back to him.

"Don't be. I didn't mean to pry. I was just wondering about how they met. You said they met in Oxford…and curiosity just got the better of me. I'm the one who's sorry, babe."

His apology makes me feel worse.

And it makes me want to tell him. Talk to him.

I've never felt the urge to talk about my family out loud since they died. In my head, I think about them all the time. I talk to them all the time.

But it always felt like if I talked about them…then it would make everything so much more real. Would make me feel their loss even more than I already did.

Maybe now is the time to talk about them, right before I go to join them.

If they can hear me, then they'll know that I think of them all the time.

Maybe I should have been talking about them all along.

But then again, I've never let myself get close enough to anyone to talk about my family.

Except for Liam. He's become my exception to my rule.

I've let myself get close to him. I know how stupid that was.

But I've already crossed that line of stupidity. There's no going back.

What more harm can I possibly do?

197

"My parents met at Oxford University." I stare down at our entwined hands. "My mom was a student there. She was in the first year of earning her master's degree. My dad…he was a professor."

"He was her professor?" Liam asks softly.

I lift my eyes to him. "No. My dad taught English literature. My mom was studying politics."

I know what he's thinking—teacher-student relationship and the age difference between them. Like there's an age difference between him and me.

"My dad was seven years older than my mom," I tell him.

"And I'm ten years older than you. Should I take it that you Shaw women have a thing for older men?"

"Actually, you're the first older guy I've dated."

Dated?

Is that what Liam and I are doing—dating? Because all we were supposed to be doing was having sex.

But when we're not having sex…we spend all of our time together. And we don't act like friends during that time. We act like a couple. Isn't that considered dating?

This is bad. And wrong.

While I'm internally agonizing over this, Liam doesn't seem fazed by what I said because he responds with, "Glad to hear it." His tone is gruff and very alpha-sounding. The alpha that usually sends a shiver down my spine.

But not this time because my mind is in overdrive.

"So, your dad was a professor dating a student…" Liam prompts when I haven't said anything.

"Yes." I come back around, back to my parents' love story and away from my own.

Not that Liam and I are in a love story…

Oh God.

"They met on campus one day. My mom used to ride her bike to class. She was late, rushing and not paying attention, and she ran my dad over. Literally ran him over."

Liam laughs, and I smile at the memories of my mom telling me this story. I used to love to hear it.

"He was fine, but my mom was mortified. He'd grazed his hand as he fell. So, she insisted on fixing up his hand. Her dorm was far away, but my dad had a first aid kit in his office. She went with him, cleaned up his hand, and put a Band-Aid over the cut, and then she left for her class, late." I laugh softly.

"Then, she started seeing him on campus all the time. My mom told me that she'd never seen my dad before that day. Suddenly, he was everywhere. My dad later told her that he started taking different routes to class just so he could bump into her.

"And I guess…they fell in love. My mother always said she fell in love with him at the exact moment when she looked into his eyes, right after sticking that Band-Aid on his hand. But they had to keep their relationship a secret because, technically, it was wrong. Even though my mom was twenty-two, an adult, she was a student, and my dad was a professor. So, they hid their relationship."

It's in this moment I realize that my mom was twenty-two when she met my dad.

I'm twenty-two now.

And I met Liam at twenty-two.

And I'll be twenty-two when I die.

"My grandfather, my mother's father, was a well-known politician here in the UK. You might have heard of him. Marcus Grant?"

"The name sounds vaguely familiar," he says. "But I have never been big on politics. My grandpa would probably know."

"Ah, well, he died years ago. But my grandfather had found out about my mom and dad because of her sister—my aunt whom I've never met. My mom had confided in her about my dad, just wanting someone to talk to, and my aunt had gone home and told my grandfather."

"Wow, what a bitch," Liam says. Then, he immediately says, contrite, "Sorry. I shouldn't have said that about your family."

"No, you're right. She was a bitch. My mom had trusted her, and she'd stabbed her own sister in the back. They never spoke again after that. After my grandfather had learned of their relationship, he hit the roof. His main concern was his political career. If it got out that his daughter was having a relationship with a professor at her university…apparently, it would have looked bad on him."

"The British press have a great way of angling a story to make it sound juicy." He sounds like he's speaking from experience.

"My grandfather told my mom to end the relationship. He told her that he'd have my dad's job taken from him and that he'd have my dad deported back to the States. My dad was from Boston and here on a work visa," I tell him. "My mom didn't want to be the reason that my dad lost his job, and she didn't want him to be deported. So, she did as my grandfather had told her, and she ended things with my dad."

"But that didn't stick," Liam says, gesturing to me.

"No." I laugh. "My dad is…was…" I take a deep breath. Talking about them like this…for a moment, it almost feels like they are still here. "My dad was stubborn. He wasn't going to let my mom go. He finally got the truth out of her, and the next day, he handed in his resignation. But giving up his job meant his visa went, too. He tried to get another teaching job in the UK, but he couldn't get one. I don't know if that was because of my grandfather, but my mom believed it was.

"Then, he got offered a professorship at Harvard. He couldn't turn it down. So, my mom went with him. She finished her degree in Boston. Then, she got a job working for *The Boston Globe* as a political journalist. She scaled it back when she had me and Parker, and then when Tess was born, she left her job and stayed home."

"Parker and Tess…" His words are soft, hesitant.

"My brother and sister."

Liam glances at me. The sadness in his eyes nearly unravels me.

I feel myself shutting down. This is getting too close to talking about what happened, and I can't talk about that.

Liam seems to sense that because he doesn't ask me anything more.

I lay my head back on the headrest, turning my face to stare out the side window, while the sound of the radio softly plays Zara Larsson and MNEK's "Never Forget You."

And I just let myself think of my family.

I let myself feel the agony of their loss. I let it curl around my insides and crush my heart.

Because I need the reminder.

I need to remember the reason I'm doing all of this. Why I've chosen the path I have.

For them. To be with them.

And Liam is making me forget that.

He's making me feel things I shouldn't feel.

It shouldn't be easy to talk about them. It shouldn't make me smile.

It should hurt. It should cut me to the core.

But, in that moment, talking about my parents with him…it felt…good. Manageable.

I want to blame him for that. I want to feel anger toward him.

But it's not Liam's fault. It's mine.

I have no one to blame for everything that's happened in my life and everything that I have coming to me but myself.

And I need to stop feeling…for him.

We don't talk on the journey after that. It's not an uncomfortable silence. More that Liam knows I need time with my thoughts, and he gives me it.

When I see the first sign for Oxford University, I wonder if Liam's grandpa lives near here.

But when he pulls onto campus, I know that's not the case.

He's come here first for me.

Tears push at my eyes. I have to take a few calming breaths before I speak, "You came here." My words come out quieter than I intended. I bring my eyes to him.

He presses his lips together before casting a glance at me. "Was that the wrong thing to do?"

No, it was the right thing to do.

Everything you do is right.

I need now more than ever to remember my parents...my brother, and my sister. I need to remember why I'm letting myself die.

Because, sometimes, with Liam...it doesn't seem so clear anymore.

"It…" My throat thickens on the word. I pause and take a breath. "It was the right thing. Thank you."

The smile that touches his lips is beautiful. And it hurts me.

It hurts even more when he says, "Don't thank me. I know, coming here…it's important to you. That makes it important to me."

I'm important to him?

My brain is screaming to me that I have to stop this—whatever this is that's happening with Liam—before it goes any further.

But the selfish part of me…my heart…doesn't care.

My heart wants to be with him for every single moment I have before it's time for me to go.

My heart wins out.

I'm not usually selfish…well, not since my selfish acts caused the loss of my family.

Maybe my heart is just stronger now because my brain is sick. It's making me weak.

I can only hope that my selfishness doesn't hurt Liam.

"We're good for as much time as you need here," he says to me.

"Your grandpa isn't expecting you?"

"I'll text him and let him know that we're running a little behind schedule."

"You told your grandpa I was coming?"

"I called him while you were in the shower." He glances at me and smiles. "He's looking forward to meeting you."

"I'm looking forward to meeting him, too." I smile.

Liam navigates the car, following the signs for the English Faculty Library. When we reach the building, he slows the car to a stop and parks up on the street outside of it.

"The university is probably pretty much closed up for the summer," he says, turning off the engine.

Then, he pulls his cell out of his pocket and starts tapping. I'm assuming he's texting his grandpa.

He continues, still texting, "But I'm sure there are some summer classes, so if we're lucky, the doors might be open, and we can have a look around. Then, we can check out the politics department where your mom would have studied. Maybe have a walk around the grounds. How does that sound?" He puts his cell back in his pocket and looks at me.

I press my lips together. Emotions are choking me. I clear my throat. "Sounds perfect." *Like you.*

Liam opens his door and climbs out of the car. I follow suit. Leaving my handbag behind, I meet Liam at the front of the car. He locks it using the key fob.

Then, he puts his hand out for mine. I place my palm against his. Liam threads his fingers through mine, and the riot of emotions I was feeling calm at his touch.

It surprises me. Nothing has been able to calm the way I feel inside when it comes to my family. But with the simple touch of Liam's hand, the pain that always comes when I think of them seems manageable in that moment.

The sign says the building is called the St. Cross Building. Liam and I walk up the steps. I think of my dad walking up these steps every day, going to work.

Liam tries the door. It opens. He gives me a smile of success.

I follow him into the building. The smell reminds me very much of a library filled with old books.

It reminds me of my dad.

"Where to first?" Liam asks.

"Let's just…walk," I tell him.

So, we do. We just wander the halls, and I think of my dad being here.

Liam opens the door to a lecture theater just a crack. "Empty," he tells me in a whisper.

"Why are you whispering?" I whisper back.

"I have no clue." He laughs.

He opens the door, letting me in first.

It's a large lecture theater, and we're on the ground level.

I look at the floor before me and the row of seats going up, wondering if my father ever lectured in here. I close my eyes and let myself hear his voice.

"Taylor, words and the ability to write…they are the guide in life that God gifted us with."

Liam's hands touch my shoulders from behind. I open my eyes and look back at him.

"Okay?" he checks.

"Yeah." I lift my lips into a half-smile. "Just remembering."

We leave the lecture theater and come across the library.

Liam tries the door, and it opens. "Must be our lucky day." He grins. "Ladies first." He stands aside, gesturing me through.

Even though being here is hard, it is impossible not to smile at him.

We venture into the library, which is empty, except for us.

I head straight for the book stacks with Liam following behind me.

"Do you read much?" I ask him as we walk beside the shelves, my fingers trailing over the books stacked on them.

"Not as much as I should." He chuckles. "You?"

"I try to."

"I haven't seen you with a book in your hand since you've been here."

I give him a glance over my shoulder. "You've been keeping me busy."

"True." He gives a wicked grin.

"I studied English lit during my undergrad," I tell him.

What I don't tell him is how I ghosted through those years, living in the stories of others, just to get through each day. I only went to college because I had applied and been accepted before my family died.

"Following in your dad's footsteps?"

"Mmhmm." That was true a long time ago. I wanted to be an English professor like my dad.

That option isn't available to me anymore.

"So, when you go back to Boston, that's what you'll do—get your master's and become a professor like he was."

"I haven't decided yet," I lie. I stop and turn to him. "Shall we go find the Department of Politics now?"

He steps close, cupping my face with his hands. He brushes his mouth over mine. "If that's what you want to do." His voice and breath are gentle against my lips.

"It is."

Turns out that the politics department is on the same street as the English building.

We walk around the empty building, and I imagine my mom rushing through the halls with books under her arm. She was always rushing, always busy. But never too busy for us. She always made time for me, Parker, and Tess.

There's not much to see inside the building, and I don't see anything related to my mom here, not that I thought there would be. I just hoped, I guess.

Liam and I walk back outside, following the path.

There's a bench that overlooks the grounds with a bush surrounding back edge of it, pretty pink flowers filling it.

"Sit?" I suggest to Liam.

He nods.

I take a seat on the bench. Liam sits beside me.

"Those flowers are pretty," I say to him.

Liam glances back at them. "Peonies," he tells me.

"You a secret gardener?"

He smiles. "My grandpa likes to garden."

He reaches back and plucks a flower from the bush. Then, he brushes my hair behind my ear and places the flower there.

"Almost the same color as your hair," he says softly, his fingers lingering on my face.

I take his hand and kiss the tips of his fingers. "Thank you…for bringing me here."

His eyes stare into mine. "Boston…I told you…it's important to you; it's important to me."

And there it is again.

My heart sings, and my head weeps.

Letting his hand go, I pull my eyes from his and stare ahead.

This is the place where my parents met and fell in love. It feels magical to me. But even more so because Liam is here, sitting beside me.

I force my thoughts onto my parents, and closing my eyes, I let their meeting play out in my head—my mom rushing around on her bike, crashing into my dad.

If they'd never met…then I wouldn't be here.

I would never have had the privilege of knowing and loving them.

But if they had never met, they would never have had me. I would never have been the cause of their deaths.

I don't know which I would want more.

To have had my parents as I did, for the time I did…or for them to have never met.

But then Parker and Tess would never have been born.

And that is inconceivable to me.

I can't allow myself to think those kinds of things. I can't change what was.

But I can change what is to be.

So, I let my mother's voice into my head, and I listen to her as she once again tells me their love story.

"You okay?" Liam's voice is quiet beside me.

"Yeah." I open my eyes and turn my face to him. "Just thinking."

"About your family?"

I look away and nod. It's too hard to stare into his eyes and talk about them.

"I'm sorry you lost them…your parents…and your brother and sister."

I press my lips together and move my head forward slightly, acknowledging him.

Silence falls between us.

Liam breaks it. "My mother died when I was ten."

His words surprise me. Because I had no clue. No clue at all.

I turn in my seat to face him. My knees press up against his thigh. I stare into his face.

Liam brings his eyes to mine. "I know what it's like to lose someone you love, Boston. Maybe not to the extent you have…but I do know."

"I'm sorry." I reach for his hand, and he lets me take it. "I'm so sorry that you lost your mom. How did she…die?" I immediately regret asking because I'm prying.

When Liam asked me about my family's passing, I tore into him.

"My mother was…" He looks away from me, his eyes focused on the grass beneath our feet, and he takes a deep breath. "She was murdered by her boyfriend."

"Oh God, Liam. I'm so sorry."

He shakes his head but doesn't look at me. "The way she died…it was horrific and brutal…but the life she lived…" He brings his eyes to mine. I see the pain buried deep in them. "It was difficult."

"Difficult how?"

He lets out a breath. "She was an addict—heroin—for as many years as I can remember. I don't think she was in the beginning though when she met my father and got pregnant with me. I figure she probably used recreational drugs. But, after I was born, I guess things got worse. I know she had a hard time, growing up. She didn't talk much about it, but she didn't have anything to do with her family.

However, her childhood was…I do know it wasn't easy. When she met my father, she was twenty-one and working as a stripper."

There's clear bitterness in his voice. I don't know if it's because of the mention of his father or the fact that his mother worked as a stripper.

"My father liked—probably still does—to frequent strip clubs. Well, any club really. He likes the party lifestyle. My father was…what you might call rebellious. Charles Hunter, the son and only heir of Lord Hunter…had everything a man could want, and my father chose to piss his life away on women and alcohol and partying."

"Lord Hunter? Your grandfather is a lord? The grandfather I'm going to meet really soon?"

"Mmhmm." He doesn't meet my stare.

Wow. A lord. I'm glad I put on a nice dress.

"I'm guessing my mother fell in love with my father," Liam continues, a hard tone to his voice. "Or she fell in love with his wealth, maybe the life she thought he could give her. My father, on the other hand, fell in lust with my mother. She had a hard life, but she was a beautiful woman. The minute she told him she was pregnant with me, he was out of there."

"What an ass." The words are out before I can stop them. "I'm sorry." I look at him, contrite.

"Don't be." He laughs. "You're right. My father is an ass."

"So…when your mom died, you went to live with your grandpa?"

"Yeah." His expression warms at the mention of his grandfather. "My dad wasn't really around, too busy traveling the world with whomever he was fucking at that time, moving from party to party.

"My grandpa has been involved in my life from the very beginning. He tried to get my mother out of that lifestyle. He wanted her to move to Oxford to be close to him, but she wouldn't do it. She wanted to stay in London. So, he bought her a house in a nice part of London. Gave her an allowance to use to care for me. My father never gave us a penny. But I guess…no matter how much money Grandpa gave her or how much I…loved her."

I hear the break in his voice, and it hurts. A lot.

He clears his throat. "Sometimes…whatever broke someone in the first place is embedded so deeply inside them that nothing can fix it or root it out, and all the love or money in the world isn't going to change that. Maybe my father tossing her aside was the tipping point for her. And that's where the drugs helped her…made her feel better when nothing or no one else could." He looks at me with something so painful in his eyes that I feel his hurt like it's my own. "She wasn't a bad mother…not in the beginning…but she lost her way…with the drugs…and the dealer boyfriend who fed her addiction. Along the way, she forgot she had a kid to care for."

My heart is breaking for him. For the boy who just wanted his mother.

My life might be as it is now, but my mother loved me and cared for me, as a mother should.

Liam should have had that, too.

"The money Grandpa gave her for me, she was spending it on drugs. When Grandpa would question my lack of clothes or the wear on my shoes, I would make up lies to cover for her. I lied because she was my mother. I loved her. And I guess…I was worried about what would happen if my grandpa found out where his money was being spent. I didn't want him to walk out of my life. The weekends I spent with him at his house were…important to me."

"I don't think he would have left you. It sounds like he loves you a lot."

"Yeah." He gives a sad smile. "I know that now. But, back then, I was a kid who didn't know better. Just before she died, my grandpa grew suspicious. He turned up early one Saturday morning to pick me up, and he caught her drug dealer boyfriend leaving the house. My mother always made sure not to have him around when my grandpa came for me. She didn't want him figuring out where his money was going and cutting her off. But Grandpa saw him. He's not a stupid man. That's when the problems began. I remember my grandpa asking me questions about Russ, my mother's boyfriend. I tried not to give anything away, but the seed of doubt was there…and I guess he figured out the rest.

"The following weekend, my grandpa came to collect me, but he came early again, said he wanted to talk with my mum in private before we left to go to his house. I was told to go to my room. But I sat on the landing and listened in. They were arguing. Grandpa told her that he knew she was a junkie. He said she either stopped using, cleaned herself up, and dumped her dealer boyfriend, or he'd have Russ arrested, and he'd take me from her. He told her that he wouldn't have her putting me at risk like she was. My mother told him that he couldn't have me. Grandpa said to her that no court would stop him because of her drug use and the danger she was knowingly placing me in. My mum called his bluff. Told him to get out, that he would never see me again.

"I remember the panic I felt when I heard him leaving the house. I ran down the stairs and out of the house after him. I caught up with him at the garden gate. I pleaded with him not to leave. I could see how much it was hurting him in that moment. I didn't want him to leave. I was hanging on to his jacket, but my mother pried me off of him. Before she dragged me inside the house, my grandpa knelt in front of me, took my face in his hands, and told me that it would just be this one weekend that I wouldn't see him. He promised me that he'd be back the following Saturday to pick me up. Told me that he loved me, and he'd always take care of me. Then, he hugged me, and he got in his car and left."

I discreetly wipe away the tear on my cheek. "He came back," I whisper. "He kept his promise."

"Yeah, he did." Liam's expression softens. But then his eyes harden. "But I didn't see him for three months. My mother kept her word and wouldn't let him see me. I knew he was fighting her for access. I saw the letters from the lawyers. I might have been ten, but I knew he was fighting for custody. And…I hated my mother for keeping me from him." His voice catches.

I look at him, and I can see the agony clear in his eyes.

"I told her I hated her." His pained gaze comes to mine. "I argued with her a week before she died. I told her that I hated her for keeping my grandpa from me. I didn't speak to her for a whole week. I ignored her, pretended that she didn't exist. And then…she didn't anymore."

I catch another falling tear, rubbing it away with the back of my hand. "It wasn't your fault."

"My last words to her were my fault. They were in anger, yes, but a part of me meant them at that time."

"You were ten, Liam."

He lifts a shoulder, like that doesn't matter. "My mother died, thinking I hated her. I never got the chance to tell her that I didn't."

"She knew you didn't hate her," I say the words softly.

In my opinion, his mother didn't deserve his love. She didn't deserve him, period. But he did love her…still does, I think, and it's important to him that she knows that even though he thinks she doesn't.

And I understand needing those you loved who are gone to know just how much you loved them. How much they meant…still mean to you, and just how sorry you truly are for everything.

I'm willingly, without regret, giving up my life to show the ones I love how sorry I am for the way I hurt them.

"She was a lot of things…but she was my mother, and I did love her."

"*She knew*, Liam," I emphasize the words to push them home. I want him to know this.

He shakes his head, like he's clearing it of those thoughts. "Things were crap in those last three months without my grandpa around," Liam says quietly, the ache painfully evident in his voice. "I mean, they were never particularly great before, but they got bad. Grandpa cut my mother off financially after she'd stopped him from seeing me. I know now that he was trying to make her see sense. But cutting her off meant he cut me off. I didn't eat well in those three months." His eyes slide to the ground. "The money she did get from the government would go straight into the needle that went into her arm.

"I didn't see my grandpa again until the day my mother was murdered. That morning, I'd gotten up, gotten myself ready for school, and left the house. She hadn't gotten out of bed, but that wasn't unusual. And, from what I know, from what the police told us, Russ turned up at our house at lunchtime. They got high on heroin. Then, they got into an argument. Russ had been accusing my mother of cheating on him for a while now. I'd heard and been witness to the fights—some physical." He meets my eyes. "They argued that day about the same thing…him accusing her of cheating. Guess the drugs were fueling his paranoia. When Russ was arrested, he said they were arguing, he hit her, she fought back…and the argument…got out of hand. Then…" He trails off, lifting a shoulder.

"Was she cheating on him? Not that she deserved to die because of it," I quickly add, worrying how that could sound to him.

Liam shakes his head. "No, I don't think she was cheating. But, that day, Russ believed she was. And he stabbed her to death in our kitchen. Our neighbor heard the commotion, saw Russ running from our house, covered in her…blood." He exhales harshly. "My grandpa got the call. He was actually listed as my mother's emergency contact. I guess he was the only family she had. Me, too. I was still at school. The teachers made me stay after everyone had left for the day. I was sitting in the headmaster's office. I remember the way he kept looking at me. I knew something was wrong. Then, my grandpa turned up and took me straight to his house. He sat me down and told me what had happened to my mother. He hugged me for what felt like forever. I stayed at his house, and I never left."

"Your father…"

He shakes his head. "He didn't even come home for her funeral. He and Grandpa haven't spoken since."

"What about you and your dad?"

He lets out a laugh, a sardonic-sounding one. "I fund his lifestyle. Grandpa cut him off, and his trust ran out. I was a man by that point, and my business was doing well. He came begging." He shrugs. "My father has never worked a day in his life. He wouldn't even know how to earn money. I might have my issues with him…but he's my father, so I couldn't see him on the streets."

This is the exact moment I realize just how deep my feelings run for Liam. And it frightens the hell out of me.

He looks at me, his lips lifting a touch. "The day I met you on the plane, I was supposed to be meeting him for dinner. He needed more money. He's living in Boston at the moment. His latest squeeze is there. She's about your age." He rolls his eyes.

"I was there on business. He must've heard because he called me up the day before, asking me to meet him. Being the sucker I am, I went. I pushed back my flight a day. I waited at the restaurant for him. He didn't show— unsurprisingly. Then, I got a text as I was leaving the restaurant, saying he couldn't make it, something had come up, and asking if I could just transfer some money into his account for him. So, I decided to fly home early. Caught the next flight out. And there you were." His eyes focus on mine, warmth in them.

"There I was." I smile. "And I'm glad I was."

I mean that. More than I can say.

Even if having Liam in my life is causing me inner turmoil, I don't regret a second of the time I've spent with him because the thought of never having met him seems inconceivable to me now.

I don't have forever, but I have this point in time. And that's what matters. Spending my remaining time with him.

Because he matters to me.

"I'm glad, too," Liam says, giving me the look that always makes my skin tingle and heat.

Sitting forward, I curl my hands around the edge of the seat. "What happened to your mother's boyfriend?" I ask softly. I hope he went to prison for a very long time.

Leaning back, Liam looks away and pushes his hands into his pockets. "He hung himself in his prison cell before his trial."

"Good," I say, and I mean it.

Without warning, Liam gets up from the bench. "We should go." Staring down at me, he pulls a hand from his pocket and holds it out to me.

I slip my hand into his and let him pull me to my feet.

He holds my hand all the way back to the car, breaking from me only to get inside. Then, he's back to holding it again. Holding it like he has to, and I know the feeling because, right now, I need him just as much.

Liam starts the engine. The song playing on the radio is James Blunt's "Goodbye My Lover."

Liam pulls away from the university, my hand safely in his.

I touch my free hand to the flower still in my hair. I pull it free and press the peony to my nose, inhaling. It's sweet but not overpowering.

I put the flower back in my hair and watch the buildings pass by as we leave, and I have this feeling of letting go.

The only problem is…I'm not sure what I'm letting go of.

chapter 20

"You grew up here?" My eyes widen to saucers as I take in the place. "It's a castle. An actual castle. Is that a moat?"

I squint, trying to see the water around the huge-ass castle in front of me, as Liam drives us down the tree-lined driveway, which is longer than the street I grew up on.

Liam chuckles. "Technically, it's not a castle. It's called Hunter Hall. No, that's not a moat. It's a lake that encircles the back of the house. It doesn't come around the front. To be a moat, it has to totally surround the house. And, yes, I lived here for the better part of my life."

The better part of his life.

That sentence alone makes me want to wrap my arms around him and hold him tight. After learning how his early years were, the feelings I have for him have grown. Knowing how hard he had it in the start of his life to where he is now—where he's brought his life to be—makes me admire and respect him even more.

And like him more.

It's not good, I know that, but it is what it is. And, as long as I keep my feelings to myself, which I intend to do, then everything will be fine.

I can't stop thinking about his life, how he was raised in two completely different ways.

Thank God for his grandpa.

I was already looking forward to meeting him. Admittedly, I feel a little intimidated after discovering that he's a lord. An actual freaking lord. And he lives in a castle. I don't care what Liam says. It's a castle. But after learning everything his grandpa has done for him, I'm more than looking forward to meeting him.

"So, what do I call your grandpa? Lord Hunter or just Lord? Or, like, Your Royal Highness."

Liam laughs loudly. It's a really good sound to hear after the intensity of today.

"Boston, Royal Highness is reserved for the monarchy. Kings, princes, that kind of thing."

"So, he's not actually royalty? I thought lords were royalty." Not that I know much about lords or anything to do with the British monarchy—except the Queen is cool, and Prince William and Kate produce the cutest kids ever.

"My grandpa's title was given to him by the Queen. And he is distantly related to the royal family but way, way down the line. Tenth cousin once removed or something."

"But he's actually related to the Queen?"

"Technically, yes."

"That means *you're* related to the Queen."

He chuckles. "Well, no…"

"Um…your grandpa is your blood relative, and he's related to the Queen—I don't care how many times removed." I stop him when his mouth opens to speak. "So, that means you're related to the Queen."

"I guess, if you look at it that way, then, yeah, technically…but not really."

"Oh my God!" I cover my face with my hands. "I've been having sex with royalty!"

"Boston, I'm not royalty."

I wave him off with my hand. "Oh, you are so royalty! I can't believe you didn't tell me this before! I'm *so* adding that to my list. This…*you* being royalty…and you and me doing the dirty—like, *numerous* times—I think this might actually top meeting Jake Wethers."

His brow creases. "So, you have to discover there's a drop of seriously diluted royal blood in me in order for me to top Jake Wethers? God, I feel so fucking special."

I can tell from his tone that he's playing with me.

"What can I say? Monarchy just marginally tops rock royalty."

He laughs again. The sound is so rich and pure that it reaches a hand inside my body and wraps around my heart.

"Anyway, don't worry, Hunter. You already made my list way before Jake Wethers did."

"I did?" He glances at me, the look in his eyes suddenly tender.

"The first thing I checked off my list—*kiss a stranger*. You were my stranger."

He reaches his hand over and takes mine. He lifts my hand to his mouth and kisses it.

That theoretical hand he has around my heart squeezes.

We're coming up close to the castle, and he still hasn't answered my question.

"So, what do I call your grandpa then?" I ask again.

"Most people just call him Bernie."

"Bernie?" I frown. *Doesn't sound very lordlike.*

"It's his name—well, Bernard is, but I haven't heard anyone ever call him by his given name."

"You're sure I should just call him Bernie?" Feels weird to address someone of nobility by their first name like that.

"Well, you can call him Lord if you want, but I don't think it'll stick. It's just not him. You'll know what I mean

221

when you meet him. Now, me, on the other hand? If you at any point want to call me Lord or Sir or…God, then feel free, babe."

That earns him a jab in the arm.

"Hey!" He rubs the spot I just hit. "Easy there, Boston. I bruise like a fucking peach."

"Sure you do." Fighting a smile, I shake my head at his smirking face.

"Still, you pack a hell of a punch there for such a tiny person."

"Yeah, well, make sure to remember that the next time you have a smart comment ready to roll off your tongue."

"I'd much rather roll *you* off my tongue."

Oh my God.

A shudder runs up my spine, desire suddenly coiling in my stomach.

I love it when he says things like that to me.

Liam brings the car to a stop outside the castle just as a man comes out the front door and heads straight for the car.

Liam's grandpa.

Lord Hunter.

Or Bernie.

I can't call him Bernie. It doesn't seem respectful enough.

I don't know what I was expecting…but the guy walking over to the car isn't it.

He's an older version of Liam. Tall and distinguished, his short hair silver, face clean-shaven—he's handsome for an old guy. I bet he was seriously good-looking when he was younger. I can see where Liam gets his awesome looks.

Looking at Lord Hunter, it's hard to pin an age on him.

Liam gives me a smile and then gets out of the car. I climb out my side and shut the door.

"Been way too long since I last saw you, boy." He hugs Liam.

Out of nowhere, a lump appears in my throat, and tears prick my eyes. Apparently, I'm an emotional wreck today. I blink furiously to rid myself of the tears.

"I was here only a few weeks ago," Liam says as his grandpa releases him.

"Like I said, too long." He claps his hands on Liam's shoulders. "Have you grown since I last saw you?" His head tilts to the side, his eyes squinting at Liam.

Liam laughs. "I stopped growing a long time ago, Grandpa."

"You look taller. Maybe I'm just shrinking." He shrugs.

Then, his grandpa's eyes come over to me. I'm standing by the hood of Liam's car.

"You must be Taylor." He leaves Liam and walks over to me, stopping just in front of me. "So, you're the one who finally got my grandson to take some time off from that business of his."

"That would be me." I smile. "It's really nice to meet you, Lord Hunter."

He laughs a rich and deep sound. "We don't stand on formalities here, Taylor. Call me Bernie."

"Okay"—I smile—"Bernie."

"You have the most interesting hair color."

"Oh, thank you." I touch a hand to my hair. "I just recently had it done."

"It really suits you." He smiles. Then, he hugs me.

He actually hugs me.

He wraps his arms around me and squeezes.

I freeze.

I'm not sure what to do. In this moment, I realize that, aside from Liam—who mostly hugs me after he's screwed my brains out—Bernie is the only other person I've hugged since my family died.

I shake off the shock and hug him back so as not to be rude.

Bernie releases me and stares down at me. "Thank you," he says softly.

I'm not sure if he's thanking me for the hug or for Liam taking time off work. So, I just shrug and say, "No probs."

He smiles wide. "I just adore the American accent. My wife was from America—New York. Amazing woman. Far too good for me. So, Liam tells me that you're from Boston." Bernie has his arm around me and is now steering me toward the house.

"Um, yes, I'm from Boston," I answer.

"Leave the bags, Liam," Bernie says over his shoulder.

I glance back to see Liam opening up the trunk of his car.

"Archie will take them up to your room." Bernie tells me, "Archie is my butler. More of a friend than an employee though. Been with me for years. Since Liam was a boy."

"It'll take me a minute to bring them in," Liam tells his grandpa.

We're already through the double front doors and moving through the biggest entrance hall I've ever seen in my life. I bet, if I spoke, my voice would echo.

"Well, do as you must," he calls to Liam.

I was right. Bernie's voice echoes around the hall.

"Taylor and I will be in the orangery, getting to know one another. Come to us when you're done."

Orangery? What the hell is that?

Turns out that an orangery is basically a huge conservatory.

The glass doors leading to the garden are wide open, letting in the warm breeze. It's a beautiful view. The lake at the far back—further back than I expected—is surrounded by trees. The stone patio has a fire pit and garden furniture and a lot of grass around it. There's an area filled with beautiful flowers and bushes. I remember Liam saying his grandpa liked to garden. I think of the flower Liam gave me, which is now safe in my bag.

"You have a beautiful home," I say to Bernie from my seat opposite him.

"Thank you." He smiles. "So, Liam says you're here on holiday."

"I am." I don't know what Liam's told him and whether he knows about my list, so I don't mention it.

"And he says you met on the flight over."

I smile at the memory. "We did. Liam sat next to me on the plane. We got to talking." Well, kissing and then talking, and afterward, going back to his place for wild monkey sex.

I can't believe I just thought about wild monkey sex while sitting here with his grandpa.

"He hasn't been able to get rid of me since," I joke.

Bernie laughs. His laugh is very similar to Liam's. The kind of laugh that, even if you're feeling at your lowest, it would make you smile.

"Well, I'm just glad he met you and is taking some time off work. That boy works too hard. This is the first time since he set up that company that he's taken a holiday."

Really? I know he said he didn't vacation much, but I didn't realize it was never at all. *But then again, is it a vacation if you're not away from home?*

"Is it classed as a vacation if you're still at home?" I ask Bernie the question in my head.

"I have no clue." He shrugs. "But he's not working. He looks more relaxed than I've seen him in years, so I'm happy."

"He looks more relaxed than I've seen him in years."

That sets me aglow.

Still, I won't burst Bernie's bubble and tell him that Liam has worked a few days in our time together.

An older gentleman in a white suit jacket and black pants comes into the room, carrying a tray.

"Ah, Archie, meet Taylor. Taylor is a friend of Liam's. She's staying with us for a few days."

Archie puts the tray down on the table. It's filled with cups, a small jug of milk, a sugar bowl, a plate of cookies, a coffee decanter, and a tea pot.

"It's nice to meet you, Taylor." He smiles at me. "Where's Liam?" he asks Bernie.

"Putting their bags away."

Archie shakes his head and laughs.

"You staying for tea with us?" Bernie asks Archie.

He shakes his head again. "I need to get the computer in the office working. It's driving me crazy. But enjoy your drinks." Archie leaves the room.

Bernie chuckles. "I've told him to call someone out to fix it, but the man won't have it. Thinks he can fix it himself." He reaches over and gets the three cups from the tray, setting them on the table. "I wasn't sure what you would like to drink, Taylor, so I had Archie make both tea and coffee. Or would you like a cold drink? I can go get you one."

"Coffee is great." I smile.

Bernie pours out three coffees. I'm guessing one is for Liam, who appears the moment I think his name.

"All sorted?" Bernie asks him as he passes me my black coffee.

"Yeah, I just ran our bags up to my room," Liam says, taking the seat next to me.

He reaches over and squeezes my hand. I smile at him.

Bernie hands Liam his coffee.

I pour milk in mine and then pass it to Liam. I drop a sugar cube in mine. Knowing Liam takes his coffee the same, I drop one in for him.

"Thanks." He smiles at me.

I move my eyes from Liam and see Bernie watching us with a smile on his face. I don't know why, but it makes my face heat.

Ducking my face, I pick up a spoon and stir my coffee.

"Biscuit?" Bernie offers me the plate.

I guess cookies are called biscuits here.

Thanking him, I take the plainest-looking cookie, which is apparently called a digestive, according to the word etched into it.

I take a bite. It's actually quite good.

"So, Taylor, is this your first visit to England?" Bernie asks.

"Yes." *And my last.*

"What do you think so far?"

"London is amazing. And from what I've seen of Oxford, it's equally as wonderful."

"I do love London," Bernie says. "But I could never live there. Too busy for my liking. I like to be able to visit and then leave when I've had enough. I don't know how Liam lives there."

"Twenty-four-hour supermarkets and endless amounts of takeaways, for starters," Liam says to him.

Bernie shakes his head. "And that's why I could never live there."

Archie appears in the doorway. He smiles when he sees Liam. "Liam, you good, my boy?"

"Yeah, I'm good. You?"

"Keeping well as always." His eyes move to Bernie. "Sorry to interrupt, but Tate is on the phone, insisting he needs to speak to you."

Bernie sighs.

"Everything okay?" Liam asks. He sounds concerned.

"Yeah, everything's fine. It's just a few hiccups with the Watertown project. Nothing major, but you know how Tate gets."

Liam nods in agreement.

"Why don't you take Taylor on a tour of the house while I take this call? You know what Tate's like once he gets talking."

Liam looks at me. "Do you want a tour?"

"A tour would be great." I smile.

Bernie gets to his feet and comes over to me. "Sorry to run out on you before we barely got to talking. But we'll all have dinner together later and get to know each other better."

"Sounds great to me."

Bernie leaves the room with Archie.

"You want to finish your coffee first or go on the tour now?" Liam asks me.

I take a quick sip of my coffee and then get to my feet, hanging my handbag on my shoulder. "Go now."

Liam pushes his chair out and stands. He holds a hand out to me. I take it, and he leads me out of the orangery.

This place is frigging ginormous.

I've lost count of how many rooms and bedrooms and bathrooms there are. I've seen the library and the kitchen that looks like it belongs in a restaurant.

Now, we're heading for Liam's bedroom. His room is at the other side of the castle from his grandpa's, as he told me, so we can have noisy sex, no problem.

But I don't think so. These hallways echo. Echoes carry sound.

Liam pushes open the door to his bedroom and walks inside.

It's huge.

Large windows overlook the garden and lake. The bed is one of those huge wooden sleigh beds. The mattress looks like I could sink into it and never get back up.

Trophies fill the shelves lining the walls. Framed certificates and photos hang on the walls and sit on the chest of drawers.

"Bathroom is there." Liam points to a closed door at the far side of the room. "And your bag is over there with mine."

I see our bags sitting side by side near a huge oak closet. I go over and put my handbag with our bags.

Then, I walk over to the window, staring out at the view. "It's beautiful here. Thank you for bringing me."

I turn from the view to face Liam, leaning my ass against the windowsill. He's standing in the middle of the room, watching me, his hands in his pockets. The view before me now is so much more appealing than anything the outside has to offer.

Liam is beautiful. I've never seen anything like him in my life.

I meet his stare. The look in his eyes makes my body heat and my spine shiver.

I curl my fingers around the edge of the windowsill. "Your grandpa is really awesome."

"He is. And he likes you a lot."

"You think?"

"I know."

"How old is your grandpa?" I push off the windowsill and take a step toward him.

His eyes darken with interest, sweeping down my body and back up to my face. "Seventy-seven," he answers with a distinct rasp in his voice that I'm getting used to hearing. It's the rasp he gets when his cock is getting hard for me.

I'm tempted to look down, but I force my eyes to stay on his.

"Wow," I say. "He looks good for seventy-seven."

Liam pulls his hands from his pockets and takes a large step toward me, making the gap between us significantly smaller.

"I know you like older men, Boston, but a fifty-five-year age gap is pushing it a bit."

The smile teasing the corners of his lips affects me in all the right ways and all the right places.

So, I decide to tease back, knowing I'll get the result I want, which is me beneath him. Or me on top of him. Either way, I don't mind.

I just want him.

Screw the echoey hallways. I'll just have to bite my lip to keep quiet.

I scrape my teeth over my lower lip, loving the way his eyes follow the movement, getting that lusty, drugged look he gets when he's turned on.

"I don't know, Hunter. Fifty-five years screams experience to me."

His brow lifts. The look in his eyes turns predatory. "I'll fucking show you experience," he growls.

Then, he lunges for me, making me squeal. He picks me up and throws me down on his bed, climbing on top of me.

And Liam spends the next few hours showing me just how awesome that experience of his truly is.

chapter 21

Bernie has taken us out for dinner to this really fancy restaurant called Belmond Le Manoir aux Quat'saisons. See? Even the name is fancy.

Thank God I had the foresight to bring a dress with me just in case we went out. It's a fitted black dress, which flares out at the knee. The capped sleeves and back are lace. It's pretty but sexy.

I'm wearing my silver ballet flats with it. Heels would have been preferable, but I forgot to pack the one pair I had brought to England with me. But the flats look just as nice.

Bernie drove us here in his Range Rover, as Liam's car only has two seats.

We're seated in private dining, which is a whole new thing to me.

The service is absolutely amazing. The food is French. Thankfully, I know a little of what to expect because of the French restaurant that Liam took me to the other day.

Bernie insisted that we all have the seven-course meal.

I know, right? Seven courses? They might have to roll me out of here.

But Bernie assures me that each course is small, so I'll be fine.

We're waiting for the first course to come out, which is wild garlic soup. Thank God Liam is eating the same thing, or I wouldn't be kissing him later.

"So, what do you do back home in Boston?" Bernie asks me.

"I recently graduated." Six months ago, and then I was coasting, unsure of what to do—until I got sick, and then I knew what to do.

"What did you graduate in?"

"English literature." I pick my wine glass up and take a sip.

"Book lover?" he asks.

"Yeah."

"Liam, did you show Taylor the library?"

"I did."

"And I've got my eye on moving in there," I joke.

"Well, you'd be more than welcome. You're a much prettier sight than Archie," Bernie says, making us all laugh. He takes a drink of his wine and puts his glass down. "What about your parents, Taylor? What do your parents do?"

I freeze in the middle of lowering my glass to the table. The temperature in the room drops a thousand degrees.

I know Liam is tense beside me. But I can't look at him.

Then, I feel his hand cover mine, the one I am clenching into a fist in my lap.

The moment Liam's hand touches mine, I feel grounded. His touch brings me back to the now.

My eyes go to his. The look in them washes over me like a safety net, catching and holding me carefully in place.

I release the breath I was holding. I put my glass the rest of the way down and moisten my dry lips before speaking, "My parents passed away."

Passed away.

It sounds so calm, so easy, when said that way.

Nothing about how they died was calm or easy.

They died because of me.

But I can't say that out loud because it would make them feel uncomfortable.

And if I'm being true to myself, I don't want Liam to know.

I don't want to change the way he looks at me. And if he knew, it would change. He wouldn't like me or think of me in the same way.

I don't want to lose that in the time I have left with him.

Liam's hand is still covering my fist. Relaxing my fingers, I turn my palm over to meet his. Our fingers slide together, joining that one part of our bodies.

I can feel Liam's eyes on me. But I don't look at him.

Because I'm afraid, if I do, I might just crack and break.

So, I look at Bernie. His expression hasn't changed, and I appreciate that very much. He's not looking at me with sympathy that I don't deserve. He's just looking at me.

"I am sorry to hear about your parents, Taylor."

"Thank you."

I really hate saying thank you, but what else can I say? Don't apologize. It was my fault they died. I killed them. *No, I definitely can't say that.*

"Do you have any siblings?"

I did…but not anymore.

I shake my head in answer. Talking about my parents is bad enough, but I can't talk about Parker and Tess. At least my parents had some life. They went to college. Fell in love. Had jobs. Had children.

Parker's and Tess's lives were just starting when I stole it from them.

"My wife died when she was thirty-five," Bernie tells me.

And even though we're still talking death, I'm relieved not to be talking about my family anymore.

"Cervical cancer. Liam's father was five at the time. It's tough, losing someone you love."

I see his eyes flicker to Liam, and I know that Bernie is thinking of Liam's mother.

I move my gaze to Liam. His eyes are already on me. I feel this swooping sensation in my stomach along with safety. I feel safe in his eyes.

The doors to the room open, and the waiters come in with our soup, putting a halt to any more conversation for now.

"Thank you so much for dinner," I say to Bernie.

We've just arrived back at Hunter Hall, and we are standing in the ginormous hallway.

"You don't have to thank me. The pleasure was all mine, Taylor."

"You fancy a nightcap, Grandpa?" Liam asks Bernie.

"No, I'm going to head to bed. But you two youngsters go ahead."

"You up for a drink, Boston?" Liam turns to me.

I'm feeling a little wiped out after all that food and wine. The seven courses were small, but I'm stuffed.

I still find myself saying yes to Liam though because I'm not ready for the night to be over just yet.

"Good night, Taylor." Bernie kisses me on the cheek.

"Good night," I say.

He hugs Liam. "Night, boy."

"Night, Grandpa."

We both watch Bernie head for the sweeping staircase.

"Oh, and the good brandy's in the decanter in the drawing room," he calls over his shoulder to us.

Liam chuckles, and then he takes ahold of my hand and tugs on it, leading me across the hall, heading for the drawing room.

"The good brandy? Or something else?" Liam asks, walking over to the drink cabinet.

"It'd be rude not to have the good brandy." I smile.

Liam gets two brandy glasses out and then pours in the brandy from the decanter. He carries them over to me and hands me mine.

"Cheers." He holds his glass up to mine.

"Cheers." I clink my glass against his and then take a drink.

It is good brandy but strong.

"That has some kick to it." I blow out a whistling breath.

"Yeah, I guess I'm kind of used to it."

"Seasoned drinker?" I jest.

"Nah, brandy is just Grandpa's answer to everything. Fall over and scrape your knee? Glass of brandy. Girlfriend dumps you? Glass of brandy."

"He gave you brandy when you were young?" I'm guessing he meant young from the scraped knee comment.

He laughs. "Only a toddy."

"He did have you flying planes when you were barely out of diapers, so I shouldn't be surprised at the hard liquor."

"I told you that he was a little unconventional." He grins.

"But it works for him. He's a wonderful man. He loves you a lot."

"I love him a lot, too."

Hearing him say that about his grandpa sets off an ache deep inside my heart. The one that reminds me that I used to have that. I used to have people who loved me in that way.

And, now, I don't.

Liam clears his throat. "Boston, I'm sorry that my grandpa asked about your parents at dinner. I should've thought ahead and told him it was a no-go area."

"It's fine."

And it was. It could have been a lot worse. But I handled it better than I had before.

That's because of Liam. Because he was there beside me. His strength gave me the strength to talk about them.

A bunch of framed photographs on a table over by the window catches my eye. Leaving Liam, I walk over to them. I put my glass on the table by the pictures and start looking at them.

There are pictures of Liam with his grandpa and ones of a young Liam dressed in his school uniform.

"Aw, you were really cute when you were a kid."

"*Hot*, I think is the word you're looking for, Boston."

I glance at him over my shoulder. He's sitting on the arm of the sofa.

"Um, no, I definitely mean cute. Pedophilia isn't my thing."

"Ah, yeah, good point." He chuckles before putting his glass to his lips.

I look back at the pictures. I see one of Liam, Cam, and Eddie. They're dressed in rugby uniforms, standing in a line, and they have their arms around each other.

I spy a picture at the back. It catches my eye because it's a picture of Liam with a girl.

I pick the photo up and stare at it.

Liam and the mystery girl are standing in front of a small airplane. The plane has Liam's company logo on the side.

He looks younger than he does now. I'd say he's in his early twenties in the picture. The girl looks to be about the same age. And she's pretty. Really pretty. Long pale-blonde hair. Eyes so blue they stand out in the photograph. And she looks tall, standing next to Liam.

I turn to him, the picture still in my hand. "An ex-girlfriend?" I say the words calmly, but the jealousy I feel is shocking in its intensity.

The expression on Liam's face freezes when his eyes meet with the photograph.

I feel an uncomfortable twist in my gut.

His eyes darken. "I didn't know that was there." The tone of his voice is hard and unyielding.

I've never heard him sound that way before.

He puts his glass down on a small table by the sofa. Then, he comes over and takes the picture from my hand. He stalks over to a cabinet and opens the drawer in it. Liam puts the frame in the drawer and shuts it so hard that the cabinet shakes. He walks back over and picks his glass up from the table.

My heart is beating hard. I'm not sure what just happened. And I'm not sure what to say.

But I do know that I feel rattled that a picture of his ex-girlfriend could elicit such a strong response from him.

"Who…is she?" I tentatively ask the question.

Liam doesn't say anything. He just stares down at the liquor in his glass.

I figure he isn't going to answer, so I'm surprised when he does.

"Kate." The word comes out coarse and angry, and it's all he says.

Kate? Why does that name sound familiar?

I search around my mind, trying to recall why that name sounds familiar, when Liam quietly says, "She was my fiancée."

Oh.

Oh, wow. That hurts.

There's an actual pain in my chest, and my stomach feels like it's just bottomed out.

For a moment, I feel cheated. Like he's lied to me. He didn't tell me something as important as the fact that he once had a fiancée.

But then again, why would he? It's none of my business. He's just fucking me.

And it's not like I've been truthful with him.

I've told him that my family died, but I haven't told him that the reason they died was because of me. Because of my selfishness.

I haven't told him that I'm dying. That I'm letting this brain tumor kill me, so I can pay penance and be with them.

It's not exactly like I can get up on my high horse about this.

So, I just simply say and do nothing.

Liam seems to break from the trance he was in. In an angry movement, he downs the brandy in one gulp and slams the glass back down on the table.

"Let's go to bed," he speaks to me without looking at me, already moving for the door.

I don't answer. I just quickly finish my own drink.

Liam is already a good way down the hallway, striding in the direction of the staircase. I have to hurry to catch up with him. When I do catch up, he doesn't acknowledge my presence.

The walk to his room is painfully silent and filled with confusion on my part.

I feel like we've had a fight without actually having had the fight.

As soon as we get into his bedroom, I grab my pajamas and toiletry bag, and I head straight for the bathroom, closing the door behind me.

I'm dressed in my pajamas, and I've just finished taking off my makeup when the headache hits.

And it hits bad.

Fuck. No. Not now.

The weight of the pain in my head has me sinking to my knees on the cold tiled floor. Leaning forward, I cradle my head in my hands. The pain is so bad and intense, worse than anything I've felt before. Tears are streaming down my cheeks.

"Look, Boston, I'm sor—Jesus, Taylor, what's wrong?" Liam is by my side in an instant, panic clear in his voice.

Why did he have to come in now?

I don't want him seeing me like this. The last time I had a headache at his place and he saw it, it was bad enough, and this attack is much worse.

The attacks are getting worse and worse, Taylor. You know what that means.

I just need him to go. I need to be alone.

I try to part my dry lips to tell him to go when the wave of nausea hits.

I'm going to be sick.

Pushing away from Liam, I crawl to the toilet. I lift the lid just in time.

Liam's there, beside me, his hands gathering up my hair and holding it out of the way, while I vomit dinner up.

"It's okay, babe. Get it out of your system. You'll feel better for it."

This time, I will.

But it will happen again.

And again.

I feel like crying.

Liam will probably just think I'm sick with a bug.

But I'm not.

I'm sick because I'm dying.

I'm a liar and a fraud.

Liam is holding my hair back for me, caring for me, and he doesn't even know the reason I'm like this.

I hate myself in this moment.

Hating myself isn't a new concept to me. But, somehow, this hatred feels different to the hatred I've felt for myself ever since my family died.

Liam's other hand starts to gently rub my back.

I don't deserve him. I don't deserve to be here with him.

The sickness subsides to light retching. When that calms and I feel ready, I reach for the flusher.

I rest my arm on the toilet seat and lay my still throbbing head on my arm. "Go—now. I'll be okay."

"I'm going nowhere. Have you been feeling ill long?"

I mumble, "No."

Another lie.

"Do you think it was the food from the restaurant? Because I feel okay. But I should probably go check on my grandpa."

"It wasn't the food." *It's the ever-growing tumor in my head.* "It's just one of my headaches. They make me sick sometimes. I'll be fine."

Lie. Lie. Lie.

Another pain hits out of nowhere, like lightning striking through my head, splitting it open. I cry out in agony as my arms cradle around my head, trying to cushion the pain.

Stop. Please stop.

"This isn't just a headache. Jesus, Taylor...you're scaring me. I'm going to call a doctor."

I feel him start to move, and that forces a quick response from me. I release an arm from my head, and I grab his arm, stopping him. "No," I whisper. "No doctor. Just need my pills. It's just...a headache. My pills always fix it. It's just like the one before, remember?"

"No, it isn't. This is worse, Taylor. Way worse. You're throwing up and crying from the pain—"

"Please, Liam." I lift my head a little, squinting at the brightness. I try to look at his face. "I just need my pills."

He stares at me for a long moment, indecision written all over his face.

I let go of his arm and lift my hand to his face. I press my palm to his cheek. "I'll be okay. I just need my pills. Please, Liam."

He presses his hand to mine that's still against his face. "Okay," he exhales.

When he moves his hand from mine, I let mine drop, and Liam gets to his feet.

I think he's going to get my pills, but he comes back with a toothbrush with toothpaste on it and hands it to me.

"I thought you'd want to brush them now because I'm carrying you to bed. Then, I'm getting you your pills, and you're not moving for the rest of tonight and probably not tomorrow either."

I don't argue. I just put the toothbrush in my mouth and brush my teeth the best I can.

When I'm done, Liam takes the toothbrush from me, rinsing it and putting it on the sink.

He comes back to me. Bending down, he slips one arm under my knees and his other arm around my back. "Put your arm around my neck, and hold on," he says softly.

I lift my arm and hold on to him.

Liam stands with me in his arms. I rest my head against his chest.

The smell and warmth and strength of him soothe me in ways I can't even begin to describe.

"I'm sorry," I mumble against his shirt as he walks.

"Don't be." He reaches the bed and gently lays me on it. "You're sick, babe. You can't help that."

He brushes my hair off my forehead right as another wave of pain hits me. It's not as bad as the last time, but it still hurts. I close my eyes against the torment, my face contorting.

"I'll get your pills," Liam says. I can hear the concern still in his voice. "Are they in your handbag?"

"Yes," I whisper.

I hear him moving around. Then, I hear running water in the bathroom.

He sits on the edge of the bed beside me. "Here."

He puts the pills to my lips. I open up, letting him drop them into my mouth. He slides a careful hand under my head, lifting it a little, and presses the glass to my lips. I take in some water, swallowing the pills down, and then my head is lowered back to the pillow.

Liam puts the glass on the nightstand next to me and stands. He crosses the room and turns off the light switch.

The only light in the room is the glow from the bathroom light that's been left on, the door slightly ajar.

I hear him undressing. Then, he gets in bed next to me, lying on his side.

"How are you doing?" he asks softly.

I turn my head on the pillow, half-opening my eyes to look at him. "Better now that you're beside me."

He smiles and then presses a kiss to my bare shoulder. "Close your eyes, Boston. Get some rest. I'll be here if you need me."

With those words in my mind, I close my eyes.

Liam lies there with me, his hand stroking the skin on my arm, relaxing me.

And I silently pray for the tumor to give me a little more time with him before it takes me.

chapter 22

I wake to warmth and strength and stability wrapped around me.

Liam.

We're still lying in the same positions we fell asleep in. Liam is on his side beside me, his body pressed up against mine. His long leg is bent and lying on top of mine. His foot is tucked in between my legs. His arm is stretched out over my stomach. His hold on me is tight, and I like it. It makes me feel safe.

It's like neither of us has moved all night.

But I don't feel stiff. I feel well rested, and the headache is long gone.

For the time being.

I know Liam is awake because his fingers are stroking the bare skin on my waist from where my pajama top has ridden up.

I open my eyes and turn my head on the pillow. His eyes are open and staring back at me.

There's never been a more beautiful sight than the one I'm looking at right now.

Liam in the morning is my heaven on earth. His wavy dark hair is all tousled up, a few strands teasing his forehead. The shadow of his stubble, which grew throughout the night, covers his chin. And, of course, the naked chest is always a bonus.

I think Liam looks younger than his thirty-two years first thing in the morning. Not that he looks old normally. He just seems more carefree and relaxed in these early moments.

Seeing him at ease and here with me makes me happy in a way I can't explain. There is just something utterly perfect about opening my eyes and seeing Liam beside me.

And knowing it's not forever, that my time with him is limited, makes me appreciate it all the more.

I smile. "Hey." My voice sounds croaky.

"How are you feeling?" The deep scratch of his morning voice tickles my skin, making me tingle.

"Better."

"You sure?"

"I'm sure." I smile again to reassure him.

Then, my stomach rumbles loudly. Liam chuckles.

"And, apparently, I'm hungry," I say.

"I'll have breakfast brought up."

"No, we'll go down and eat with your grandpa."

"He'll have eaten by now."

"What time is it?" I look around for a clock.

"Quarter to eleven."

"Quarter to eleven!" I exclaim. "I can't believe how late I slept."

"You clearly needed it." He's looking at me with concern in his eyes.

"Yeah, I guess. How long have you been awake?" I ask, turning on my side to face him. I put my hands under my cheek.

"A while."

"How long's a while?"

"Since nine."

"That's late for you." Liam's an early riser.

"Guess I needed the sleep, too." His lips lift into a smile.

"So, did you go down and have breakfast and then come back to bed?"

"No. I stayed here with you. I didn't want to leave in case you needed me."

My heart leaps out of my chest and Saran Wraps herself to Liam.

"You stayed here? For all that time?" My words come out a whisper.

He lifts the hand from my stomach and brushes my hair off my forehead with his fingers. "It wasn't that long."

"Nearly two hours."

"Like I said, not that long. And I did catch up with some work emails on my phone, so it wasn't like I just lay here and stared at you the whole time."

"Just some of the time." I tease.

His lips curve up. "Well, you're pretty to look at."

"Right back at ya, handsome."

That earns me another smile.

Liam never looks more beautiful than when he's smiling. Those smiles are all the more special when he's doing so because of me.

In my head, I try to snapshot as many of Liam's smiles as I can because I want to take them with me when I go.

"I need to pee," I tell him.

"Thanks for sharing."

"Sharing is caring."

He chuckles, shaking his head at me. "You need a hand to the bathroom?"

"Thanks, but no, thanks. You seeing me puking last night was bad enough. And, anyway, I feel fine now. I can walk to the bathroom all by myself." I slip out of bed and head to the bathroom.

When I come back, Liam is still in the same place I left him.

I climb back into bed, snuggling into his warmth. His arm comes around me, holding me tight.

"What are we doing today?" I ask him. I know today is clear, as the Grand Prix is tomorrow.

"We're staying in bed."

"Does that plan involve having sex? Because I'm all for having sex, lots of it, but it would seem a shame to spend the whole day in bed. We could go out as well and have sex outdoors." I let a grin out on my face.

He doesn't even crack a smile. "I didn't mean, stay in bed to have sex, Boston. You need to rest."

"I've had all the rest I need. I've slept for almost half a day. I want to go out and do something."

"I don't think it's a good idea."

"Why?" I frown.

"Because I don't want what happened last night to happen again today."

"Hunter"—I touch my fingertips to his face, tracing them up over his cheekbone and around the line of his brow—"I'm fine."

He's staring at me, and I can see from the look in his eyes that he doesn't believe me.

"I'm fine," I reiterate, pressing the words home. "You know I get headaches from time to time."

"That wasn't your run-of-the-mill headache, Taylor. That was a full-fledged fucking migraine that made you puke your guts up. Does your doctor know that you still have headaches and that they affect you in this way?"

No.

"Yes." I swallow past the lie. "Where do you think the headache pills come from? She prescribes them."

A lie.

Well, sort of.

THE *Ending* I WANT

The pills are what were leftover from an old prescription I had when I had the first tumor. I just hope Liam doesn't check the date on the pill bottle because it dates back years.

The pills were in the cabinet in the bathroom on the upper floor of my home where my bedroom was. I found them when I was let in the house after the fire department had deemed it safe to go inside.

The pills managed to survive the fire. My family didn't, but a bottle of fucking pills and a bunch of other pointless things did.

Except for the picture of my family that used to sit on the nightstand in my bedroom. That survived, and that wasn't pointless. It's all I've had of them for the last four years.

But going in my home, seeing it covered in black and soot and knowing they'd died in there…it was one of the hardest things I'd ever had to do.

Except for burying them. That was horrific, watching their caskets being lowered into the ground…and Tess's was so small. Knowing they were all in there because of me…it was an unimaginable kind of pain.

All I wanted to do was climb in with them and have dirt thrown on top of me.

And, very soon, that wish will come true.

But not today.

Because, today, I'm spending with Liam.

"Tell me about it," Liam says softly.

I turn my eyes to him. "Tell you about what?"

"Being sick…the tumor."

I don't want to tell him too many details because I don't want to tip him off that I'm back in the same position now. Liam's smart. One wrong word from me, and he'll figure out what caused last night's headache.

I exhale a breath, lifting my shoulder in a half-shrug. "I got sick. My mom took me to the doctor. The doctor knew something wasn't right, so a scan was done on my brain. There was a shadow, which turned out to be a tumor. It was malignant. The tumor was operated on, but it couldn't all be removed with surgery. So, I had to have radiation therapy to get rid of what was left."

"And that worked?"

"Yes. I got the all-clear six months later."

"Do you still have regular checkups to make sure everything is okay?"

"Yes. They were every month at first. But, now, they're every six months." And I missed the last appointment I was supposed to attend because I know it's back.

"When was the last appointment?"

He's starting to piece things together. I need to get his mind off this train of thought. I need to lie as much as necessary, so he doesn't discover the truth.

"Two weeks before I got on the plane to come here." *Lie.*

"And the results were fine?"

"All clear." I smile. It hurts like a bitch, smiling through that lie.

But he's still staring at me, like he's not sure.

I need to make him sure.

So, I put a wall around that pain I feel from lying to him, and I tell him what he needs to hear to stop him from figuring out the truth.

"Hunter…are you worried that the tumor is back?"

Being so close to the truth like this…I feel like I'm treading land mines. But it's the only way to halt this line of questioning. Tackle it head-on, and then lie my way back out.

He lifts a shoulder in a half-shrug. "It's just…that headache last night…it wasn't right, Boston. It's not normal to suffer that much pain."

"Maybe not to you. But it is to me. I had a brain tumor, Hunter. A *cancerous* growth on my *brain*. I managed to

248

survive it. I'm lucky to be alive. The occasional headache is a small price to pay when it could have been so much worse."

I could have died. I should have died back then. If I had, my family would still be alive right now.

I stare into Liam's eyes, willing him to believe my lies.

He blows out a breath. "I guess when you put it like that…you're right. It's a small price to pay. But I still don't like seeing you in pain, babe."

He presses his fingertips to my lips. The tenderness of his touch and the care in his eyes…it takes everything in me not to cry.

I'm sorry, Hunter. I'm so very sorry.

"Going forward, just let me know when a headache is coming on, so I can help you."

"I will," I say through the thickness in my throat. Then, I force the best smile I can manage.

Liam replaces his fingers with his lips, softly brushing them over mine. He slides his fingers up into my hair as his tongue touches mine. As he runs his fingers over my scalp, I get the impression that he's feeling for my scar.

"Right side, above my ear. Runs the full side and just a little around the back." I take ahold of his fingers, pressing them to the spot.

He doesn't move his hand.

"I'm sorry," he whispers. Pressing his forehead to mine, he stares into my eyes. "I shouldn't have felt for it. I just haven't felt it before when I've had my hands in your hair, and I guess I was just…"

"Curious. It's fine, Hunter." I smile.

And it is fine. I'm just relieved it's the scar he's searching for and not the tumor.

Thank God he can't feel what's growing beneath the skin and skull because that's what I want to hide from him. Not my old scar.

His fingertips trace the line of the scar. It's not a thick scar. Surprisingly thin. But it's long.

His finger follows it around to the back of my head. Cupping the back of my head with his hand, his other hand against my cheek, he tilts my head back, so I'm staring into his eyes.

"You're the bravest person I've ever known, Boston," he whispers. "I feel in awe…and so fucking lucky to know you."

I'm not brave, Liam. I'm weak and a coward. You're the brave one. You're amazing and kind and generous. You are all the things I wish I could have been.

I want to say all those things to him. But I can't.

So, I close my eyes and bring my mouth to his, kissing him, trying to tell him with this kiss what I can't say in words.

The kiss has just started to deepen when my stomach rumbles again, spoiling the moment.

Liam chuckles into my mouth. "Guess that's our cue to get up and get some food."

I release a sigh. "I guess so."

Liam kisses me once last time and then gets out of bed.

I climb out of bed. "Should I get dressed for breakfast?" I ask him, staring down at my pajamas.

"No, you're fine. We'll eat, and then we'll come back up, dress, and go out."

"So, we are going out." I brighten up.

He moves around the bed toward me. "I had planned for us to do something today." He wraps his arms around my waist and bites his lip. A look of uncertainty spreads across his face.

"Why the look?" I ask.

"Well…I'm just not sure if you'll like what I have planned."

"So, tell me what it is, and then I'll decide if I like it or not."

chapter 23

" Nope. No way. I'm not going on that thing. You
know I don't like flying, Hunter. No fucking way
am I getting on that plane."

I'm standing in front of a small plane, similar to the one
in the picture of Liam and Kate—the fiancée. Yep, not
going there again.

Except this one doesn't have his company logo on the
side, and it's white with a black underbelly and a black-and-
bronze tail. And I can see a sign that says we're at London
Oxford Airport. Good to know where I am at least.

Back at the house, Liam wouldn't tell me what he had
planned. And then he insisted on blindfolding me.

Blindfolded. I know, right? Sounds awesome. Would
have been awesome and totally kinky if there had been sex
involved. But an airplane? Not remotely sexy at all.

Standing behind me, his hands on my shoulders, Liam
laughs, and I feel it rumble in his chest against my back.

"Boston, you flew on a plane to get to England."

Turning my head, I slide my eyes up to his. "I flew on
that plane—*your* plane—to get me here for my trip.

Necessity. No way in hell am I flying in a plane for the *fun* of it." I fold my arms over my chest.

Liam moves around me to stand in front of me. He closes his hands around my upper arms. "I know you don't like flying, but I thought you wanted to do something that terrified you to the point of pissing your pants?"

"Stop quoting my list to me. And I did do something that scared me—the roller coaster, remember?"

Smiling, he says, "I remember. But you didn't piss your pants, so you couldn't have been that scared."

"Oh, I was scared. Believe me. And how do you know I didn't piss myself?"

"Because I fucked the hell out of you soon after. The only wet patch on your knickers was from me making you come."

Good point. My mind immediately slips back to that moment in the Hook a Duck tent, making my insides coil. *Awesome memory.*

"So, I didn't piss myself. But I was definitely afraid."

Liam slides his hands down my arms, forcing me to loosen and release them from my chest. He takes my hands in his, holding them between us. "I know you were scared. But after the fear left, do you remember how you felt?"

"Relieved that I'd done it and that I'd never have to do it again."

He laughs a rich deep sound, shaking his head. "You were happy. I could see it in your eyes. You had this look…you looked free, Boston."

Maybe, in that moment, I was. But I'm not free. I won't be free until I see them again. Until I pay my penance.

Liam steps closer. So close that I have to tilt my face to look up at him. His scent washes over me, easing the fear inside.

"*He who has overcome his fears will truly be free.*"

"And you can stop fucking quoting Aristotle to me as well." I frown, but it's not as deep as it should be, and that's because of him and his infectious laugh and his smiling face and his sparkling autumn eyes.

Damn him.

Liam's laughter fades. His expression deepens, his eyes turning serious. "You've faced a brain tumor and survived. Not many people can say that."

"Quite a few can. I can quote statistics, if you'd like?"

It's his turn to frown. "I don't care about other people. I care about you."

He cares about me?

His hands leave mine, and he cups my face with them. "I thought I knew the meaning of the word *bravery*—until I met you. You'd stared death in the face, and you won. Nothing is more terrifying than that."

If only you knew.

Facing death is terrifying when you don't want to die. But when you do want to die…staring it in the face is freeing.

I'm staring at it right now.

Some see death as the Devil trying to take them.

I see death like an angel. Offering me the peace that nothing on earth would ever be able to give me.

Closing my eyes, I take a deep breath.

I know I'm being stupid, not wanting to get on this plane. But that's always been my problem—letting my fears get the better of me.

Knowing death is coming for me is liberating, and I should use that liberation to take risks.

I want to live *before I die.*

I think of the story that Liam told me on the roller coaster. What his grandpa had said to him…

"There's nothing wrong with being afraid. Everyone feels fear. But the day you let your fear control you is the day you stop living."

Very soon, my lungs won't breathe anymore. My heart won't beat. My mind will stop thinking. I'll be no more. Just a memory that will eventually blur and fade in the mind of the one person who I do want to remember me as his life moves on.

Doing things you're afraid of makes your breaths come faster. Your heart beats so hard that it feels like it's bursting out of your chest. Your mind races so fast that it's hard to keep up with the thoughts.

And I'm not just a memory to Liam yet. I'm here and real and solid and in his arms.

I feel his breath against my mouth before his lips touch mine.

"You're brave and strong. You can do this, Boston."

I blink open my eyes and stare into his. "You're right. Let's do this."

"Yeah?"

"Yeah. Let's fly the fuck out of this plane."

Liam smile is so bright that it blinds me, coating me like the warmth of the sun.

Taking me by the hand, he leads me to his plane, walking over the tarmac.

A guy climbs out of the plane as we approach. He is short, looks to be about fortyish, and has light-brown hair.

"Liam," he greets him by shaking his hand. "She's all ready for you."

"Thanks, Henry. Henry, this is my friend Taylor."

Henry smiles at me. "Nice to meet you."

"Taylor's going to be my copilot today."

My eyes shoot to Liam as a gasp of shock leaves my mouth. "What?" I squeak.

"I'm kidding." Liam slides me a look and laughs. "Taylor's not so keen on flying," he tells Henry.

"Well, you're in safe hands with Liam. He's an excellent pilot."

I know it's silly because it makes sense that Liam has his pilot's license—considering what his company is—and he told me his grandpa used to take him out flying, but he's never actually told me that he has his pilot's license.

"Have a good flight," Henry says to us before making his exit.

Liam walks over to the plane, and I follow.

"So, she's yours then."

"Yeah, I bought her new last year. I have a couple of other planes. Older ones."

I wonder if he still has the plane in the photo with Kate. But I'm not going to ask. I don't want Moody Liam to return.

"What do you think?" he asks, stopping by the plane.

"As planes go…it's nice, I guess."

His eyes narrow, a touch of humor in them. "As far as compliments go, I'll take that as a big one from you."

Liam gestures to the door of the cockpit that Henry left open for us. "Ladies first."

I stand and stare at it, seeing the inside of the airplane.

It's high up to get in. That's not what's stalling me. There's a little metal fold-down ladder to aid me in. I'm stalling because my heart is beating faster from just looking at the cockpit. It looks small.

I can do this.

"Okay, babe?" Liam's hand touches me on the shoulder.

I blow out a breath and glance back at him. "Yeah."

I climb up the little stepladder and into the plane, shifting over to sit in the second seat, the one on the left, leaving the seat on the right to Liam.

Liam climbs in behind me. He pulls the stepladder in and folds it away. Then, he reaches out, and he pulls the door shut and locks it.

I glance over my shoulder.

It's really nice inside.

There are four seats behind me, cream leather, as are the ones we're sitting on. The four seats face each other, and there is a well-fitted table in the middle.

In front of me are screens and buttons, and on each side is a steering wheel–looking thing. I don't know the fancy term for them. I just hope Liam isn't expecting me to control one of them.

"Um…so, you were joking out there, right? I don't have to control one of those things." I gesture at the steering wheel thingy.

"The yoke." Liam laughs. "And, no, babe. But you can, if you want, once we're up in the air."

"No. I'm good, thanks," I cut that down quick, flashing a smile at him, making him chuckle.

Liam puts his seat belt on, so I put mine on.

"Ready?" He turns to look at me.

I press my lips together. "Mmhmm."

He cups my chin with his hand, moving toward me as he pulls me closer. He softly kisses me. "It's gonna be fine, Boston. I'm in control here, and I won't let anything happen to you. Okay?"

"Okay." I sit back into my seat.

Liam puts on a headset and then hands me one to put on.

He starts talking into his headset, using airplane jargon, and I have no clue what he's talking about. Then, he starts pushing buttons and turning dials. Suddenly, the propeller at the front of the plane starts to turn. It's slow at first, but it quickly picks up speed until it's a blur in front of my eyes.

And I'm shitting my pants. My heart is racing, and my palms are sweating.

Liam says a few more things into his headset. Then, he looks at me and smiles. "Ready for your first Hunter flying experience?"

Nope. I wonder if I can make a break for it out of this door beside me and just do a runner?

I swallow back, but my throat is dry, so it's like I'm swallowing gravel. "I thought I'd already had one of those." I give a smile, but it feels awkward on my lips.

"My pilots are good, babe, but they're not as good as me." He winks, totally oblivious to the fact that I'm close to freaking out.

His hand goes on to what looks like a gearshift, and he slowly pushes it forward. The plane starts to move, rolling forward.

Holy fuck, we're moving.

My hands curl around the edge of the seat, gripping.

Liam steers the plane on the tarmac, heading for the actual runway, I'm guessing. All the while, he's talking into his headset and pressing buttons.

He maneuvers the plane around and onto the runway strip, and he brings the plane to a stop.

"Just waiting for the all-clear to go," he tells me. "You still good?"

No.

Every muscle in my body is tense. My insides are knotted up.

"Hey…" Liam's fingers touch my cheek, pulling my attention to him. "You don't have to be scared. This is just you and me, babe. And I'm in control here, and I will never let anything happen to you." He runs his fingertips over my mouth.

I stare at him, wetting my lips, after his touch. My heart is racing as I look into his autumn eyes.

"You can do this," he whispers.

I can do this.

I let a smile onto my face. The smile he gives me in return is worth a million snapshots in my mind. I hold on to it and file it to the front of my picture memories.

He takes ahold of my hand and lifts it to his lips, pressing a kiss to it.

Liam speaks into his headset, seeming to respond to whoever is on the other end.

Then, he looks at me and says, "I've got the go-ahead. You ready, babe?"

I assess myself. My stomach is tight with knots. My hands are clammy. My heart is having a dance in my chest.

But all of those things mean I'm still alive. I'm still here with him. I'm safe with him.

"I'm ready," I tell him.

He gives me one last smile before he looks ahead, and then he moves the gearshift thing forward but not slowly this time. He moves it a lot faster, and then we're moving quickly.

Holy fuck.

We're speeding down the runway, and my stomach is somewhere back there.

And—*fuck*—we're taking off. The plane leaves the ground, and my belly does that weird dropping-out thing it does.

All I can see is blue sky as Liam takes the plane higher.

Blue sky and clouds.

Will this be what it's like when I die, making my way up to heaven to be with my family?

That thought has a calming effect on me.

Liam is talking into the headset again and turning dials with one hand as he steers with the other.

It seems like we've been climbing forever before Liam levels the plane. He presses a few buttons as he continues speaking into his headset.

He moves the mouthpiece away from his mouth and looks over at me. "You doing good there, Boston?"

"Yeah." I quickly glance out the side window, seeing houses below. "How high up are we?"

"Twenty thousand feet. We could go higher, but I thought I'd take it easy with it being your first time out."

"You call twenty thousand easy? One thousand—no, one hundred feet would have been fine with me."

Liam laughs deeply. "If we flew low—which you can't fly at a hundred feet, just so you know—you would have missed out on these views. And they're fucking spectacular. Take a look." He nods at the window.

I force myself to look out the window again. He's right. The views are stunning. We're flying over fields now with green grass and trees everywhere.

"Flying at night is even better. Everything is lit up. I'll bring you out one night, so you can see."

Night flight? I don't think so.

"Sounds hideous. I'm good, thanks."

I give him a tight smile, and he laughs.

I look back out the window, still seeing fields and the odd farmhouse scattered around.

Now that we're up here, my fear doesn't seem as magnified as it did when we were on the ground, waiting to set off. In a weird way, being up here with Liam is serene and peaceful.

We fly in silence for a while. And I know I should be looking at the view, but the one in the plane is so much better. And staring at Liam keeps my mind away from thinking about how high we are off the ground.

I can't stop staring at him. He seems so at ease up here, and he looks beyond hot. So commanding, sitting here, flying his airplane.

There's just something so insanely sexy about seeing the man I'm sleeping with in charge of this huge piece of machinery.

I mean, Liam looks hot when he drives a car. The sight of his hands on the steering wheel does something to me. But, looking at him now, controlling this big metal tin…is crazy hot.

And, now, all I can think about is how it feels to have his hands on me…and to have my hands on him.

I'm starting to feel really hot…and turned on.

Fuck. I want him.

My hands are literally itching to touch him.

I look away from Liam and clench my fists in and out, flexing my fingers.

Easy, tiger, you can't have him right now.

Can I?

I look back to him. He's biting his lower lip as he stares out the window, deep in thought. *He looks beautiful.*

I really need to touch him…

Ah, fuck it.

Reaching my hand over, I slide it over his thigh and to his crotch. I cup his cock through his jeans.

Surprised eyes flash to mine.

"Babe…" There's wariness in his voice but a hint of intrigue, too.

And it's that intrigue that has me saying, "Have you ever been blown at twenty thousand feet?" I whisper.

Holy shit, listen to me, little Miss Seductress.

Eyes on mine, he shakes his head. I know he's not speaking because the radio microphone near his mouth is still on, and the people at the other end might hear him.

I drag my teeth over my lower lip, teasing him. "Well, you're about to be."

I don't know who this chick is that's in my driving seat right now, but she's kind of awesome, and apparently, she gets hot while watching her man fly a plane.

Her man?

The words stutter in my brain.

But I shove it aside, ignoring it, and focus back on Liam, who is staring at me with a heat in his eyes that I've never seen before.

"Is it safe to take off our seat belts, or do I just work around them?"

In answer, Liam unclips his seat belt, moving it aside. I remove mine but keep it close by—you know, just in case.

I reach over and pop open the button on his jeans, and then I slide the zipper down. I pull my headset off, putting it on my seat beside me.

I reach inside his jeans and curl my fingers around him. He's as hard as stone already. Knowing I have this effect on him gives me a crazy amount of confidence to see this through.

I squeeze his dick, and his chest jumps on a breath.

I free his cock from its confines and stare down at it.

Can a cock be beautiful? Because, if one can be, then his truly is.

I lean down and lick the tip, loving the silky feel of it on my tongue.

He reaches over, turns off a switch, and then pulls his own headset off, tossing it on top of the plane's dashboard.

His fingers glide into my hair. He grips the strands and tilts my head to the side, so I'm staring up into his eyes. His eyes look like they're on fire.

"Suck it hard." The commanding rasp in his voice has my panties wet and my mouth watering for him.

Lowering my mouth back to him, I move my hand off his cock. I stick my tongue out and lick a path from root to tip. His hips jerk up, his hand tightening in my hair.

"Fuck," he groans.

There's pre-cum leaking from the tip. I lick it up. The salty taste of him is such a massive turn-on. It reminds me of hot, hard, sweaty sex.

Taking him back in my hand, I swirl my tongue around the head of his cock. I hear a growl come from deep within him.

"Don't fucking tease me, Taylor. Suck it now."

I can't help but smile at his dominance.

The alpha in him turns me on so much. My clit is begging to be touched. But she'll have to wait because this, right now, is about him.

I lick my lips, wetting them. Then, opening my mouth, I slide his cock inside and give him what he wants.

"Taylor," he shudders out my name.

Liam's hand leaves my hair, gripping the yoke, like he needs to hold it for balance. Well, he does need to keep flying the plane, I guess.

As I suck him, his hips start to move up in short little jerks, in time with my mouth.

"You're so fucking hot," he grinds out. "So…fucking…hot."

I lift my eyes to his face, his cock still in my mouth.

The look in his eyes…is dark and needy…and something else is there that I can't quite decipher.

Focusing back on my task at hand, I suck him like I'm the queen of blow jobs.

"Jesus…fuck, Taylor…yeah, that's it." He makes a pained sound, but I know he's far from feeling pain. "Shit, babe, you're gonna make me come hard, and if I come, I'll crash this fucking plane. So, you either stop what you're doing right now, or you fly this plane, and I finish myself off with my hand."

That has my head coming up, his cock leaving my mouth with a wet pop.

"I can't fly this plane!" I exclaim, sounding a little shrill.

I didn't think about what would happen when he needed to come and the problem that could present when it was going to happen.

"Then, sit back in your seat, and don't touch me or look at me or even talk to me for the next few minutes, so I can calm the fuck down. If not, I might just say to hell with it and fuck you right now, letting this plane go down while I do."

Surely, he's not serious.

I look at him.

Yep, he's serious.

I might want to die, but I don't want to die in a plane crash. And I most definitely do not want Liam to die.

So, I do as he asked. I shut my mouth, and I look at the view out the window.

It's been a few minutes, and I'm getting kind of bored, not talking.

"Liam," I say quietly, "have you calmed down yet?"

"Getting there." His voice still sounds a little tight.

I risk a glance at him. "I'm sorry." I bite my lip.

"For?" He looks at me, confused.

"For getting you all worked up and not being able to finish you off."

He laughs, and it instantly puts me at ease.

"Boston, don't ever apologize for giving me a blow job even if it doesn't result in the happy ending. While flying my plane, I just got my dick sucked by the hottest woman I've ever had the good fortune to know. I'm golden, babe. But just to let you know, the second we get back to Hunter Hall, I'm taking you up to my bedroom, and I'm fucking every part of your body available to me."

All the right parts of me tighten up in anticipation of what's to come.

I look out the window at the ground far below, and that fear I first felt is no longer there. Just happiness at being here with him.

"I think I can live with that." I smile.

chapter 24

" Get on the bed. I want you on your hands and knees. *Now.*"

We're in Liam's room back at Hunter Hall. He's naked. I'm naked.

He had me undress him and then strip my own clothes off—his personal striptease. Now, he's ordering me onto the bed.

Bossy Liam is back, and it's so fucking hot.

Doing as he said, I climb up onto his bed and get on my hands and knees, facing away from him.

I feel his hand touch over my ass as he gets onto the bed behind me. He moves his palm down my butt, and his fingers slide between my folds. Finding my pussy, he slides a finger inside me.

I moan, widening my knees more.

"That feel good?" he asks, his voice a dark rasp.

"So good."

He slides another finger inside, making me moan again, and then he starts fucking me with his fingers.

My head drops forward. I love the feel of him doing this to me.

"I shouldn't be this good to you, Boston. It should be you down on your knees, finishing off what you started in the plane. If I didn't want to fuck you so badly, then that's what you'd be doing right now."

His finger is still moving in and out of me.

Then, I feel his mouth on my ass cheek. He places a kiss there, and then he scrapes his teeth over my skin, making me shudder.

"I fucking love your arse, Boston." His finger leaves my pussy and slides over my clit, giving it a flick before moving upward toward my puckered hole.

I tense when he reaches it.

"I want to fuck you here so bad." He rubs his finger around that untouched part of me.

I glance back at him. His eyes are glazed and lusty, staring at where his hand is.

"What is it with you and asses, Hunter?"

His eyes come to mine. The look in them is lethal, and it nearly has me telling him to do whatever the hell he wants to me.

"Not asses, plural. Just your ass. I'm obsessed with fucking it. I'm man enough to admit it. It's just…so perky and sexy…and just *there*." He grabs my ass cheek with his other hand. "It's like a mountain I need to climb. I want to stick my flag in there and conquer the fuck out of it. And it's true what they say, you know." A devilish smile slides onto that sexy mouth of his. "It's more fun up the bum."

Laughter explodes from me.

I fall onto my front, my knees no longer able to hold me up. "Oh my God!" My laugh is muffled in the bed. "I can't believe you just said that! Who says that?" I lift my head, looking back at him.

"People…me." He grins.

That sets me off again. I can't stop laughing. My sides ache from laughing.

"Oh God, it hurts!" I clutch my belly, rolling onto my side. "Liam Hunter, you are fucking priceless!"

When I bring my eyes to his, he's just staring at me, a smile on his face and a soft look in his eyes.

"What?" I chuckle, wiping the tears of laughter from my eyes.

"Nothing. I just really like seeing you laugh." He moves up the bed, coming closer to me. "There's nothing more beautiful than the sight and sound of your laughter. And I like it even more when it's me who's made you laugh."

My heart explodes. In its wake are sparkly, glittery bombs of emotions. All for him. And they are floating around my chest, attaching themselves to every part of me, making me want things I can't have.

Him…forever.

Liam takes my face in his hands. His expression is so tender that I think he's going to say something to push me over the edge.

Then, he parts his lips and says, "So…can I fuck you up the arse?"

And there he is, bumping me right back down to earth. Right to the place he and I belong. In this moment.

Biting my lip, feeling a little nervous at the thought, I say, "I don't know…"

"There's no pressure. I just…really want you in that way. And I want you to know that."

I mull it over in my head.

What harm could it do? Well, it could hurt like hell, for starters. But it's not like I'm not used to pain. And I'm pretty sure, out of this pain, I'll get some pleasure. Well, I'd better.

And I know Liam wouldn't do something to me that would hurt me in any way. Especially sexually. Every time we have sex, he's always taking care of me first. He seems to derive pleasure from mine. Something else to adore about him.

And ass sex…it's something I've never done before…

"Will it hurt?" I ask.

"I'll do my best to make sure it's as painless as possible for you. I brought lube. And I got the good stuff."

"Oh, well, if you got the good lube—hang on. You brought lube with you? To your grandpa's house?" I raise my brow.

"When you put it like that, it sounds kind of seedy."

"Well, you are the one who wants to defile me in your childhood bedroom."

He grins, big. "Boston, I spent many nights in this bedroom, dreaming about defiling a hot babe—"

"Hot babe?" I laugh. "Cheesy."

"Not cheesy. True. You are hot, babe." He leans down and takes my mouth in a delicious kiss. Brushing his nose over mine, he stares into my eyes. "Truth is, I wasn't expecting anything at all…but I also like to be prepared. Like a good Boy Scout. So, I brought lube with me just in case the opportunity arose. And, as it happens, it's arisen."

That makes me laugh. "And that's why you're so successful in business. Always prepared for the unexpected and brilliant at negotiation."

"So, is that a yes?" He bites down on a smile.

"Seeing as though you brought the good lube, then, yes, it's a yes. But if you hurt me with that big cock of yours, I will break it in half."

His brows draw together. "You don't need to worry, Boston. I won't hurt you. Hurting you is the one thing I could never do. The only things I plan on giving you are intense levels of pleasure. Pleasure like nothing you've ever felt before. Now, get back up on your knees, and bend the fuck over."

With nervous and excited butterflies in my stomach, I turn over and get onto my hands and knees again.

I feel Liam leave the bed. I look behind me and see him opening his bag.

Then, he comes back over to the bed, and a bottle of lube hits the mattress beside me. He presses his hand to my back and runs it down until his hand is cupping my ass.

His fingers slide down, between my folds, and he slips a finger in my pussy, slowly moving it in and out. My head drops forward again.

His finger comes out of me and rubs over my clit. He pinches it, making me squirm. He reaches over and picks up the lube while still rubbing my clit.

I hear the cap pop, and then his hand is gone from me. I hear him pump the lube.

He's doing it already? I look back, tensing up.

I see him rubbing the lube onto his fingers.

He catches my eye. "I'm going to use my fingers first, warm you up. Okay?"

"Okay," I exhale, relaxing a little.

I feel his slippery finger slide between my ass cheeks. He starts rubbing the tip of his finger around the outside of my tight puckered hole.

His other hand comes around my front, and his fingers find my clit. He's working me up, rubbing and teasing my clit. The feel of the lube on there makes the friction feel so much more intense, or maybe it's that his finger is slowly making its way inside my ass that's making everything seem intense.

The burn is there as the tip of his finger slips inside me.

Oh my God.

"How's that?" he asks softly, his voice sounding rough.

"Good," I breathe.

I feel him start to work a little more of his finger inside me. He's going in so much easier than the last time we did this, and just having him inside me in this way feels so dirty and hot and sexy.

Liam keeps going until his finger is all the way inside me, and I feel full of him but strangely not full enough.

I need more.

"You okay?" he asks, stilling his finger on my clit and the one inside me.

"Mmhmm."

It takes me a moment to realize that he's not going to start moving.

I glance back at him. His brow is furrowed.

"What's wrong?"

"Are you sure you want this?"

I soften my gaze. "Of course I'm sure. I want you inside me, like this." I push back on his finger.

His eyes light up, like the striking of a match. "God, you look so fucking hot right now," Liam rasps out the words.

He slides his finger out and then slowly slips it back in. He starts fucking my ass with his finger, and I have never felt more sexy and hot than I do right now.

He pinches my clit, making me cry out.

"More," I tell him. "I need…more." My own hand grabbing at my breast, I pinch my nipple.

"I'm gonna put two fingers in, baby. I need to get you ready for my cock."

"Yes. Please." I'm starting to feel mindless from the sensation.

His fingers are doing an amazing number on my clit.

His finger leaves my ass, and I whimper at the loss.

I hear the pumping of lube, and then I feel it running down my ass.

Liam's fingers are back, teasing and probing. The push is firmer this time. Two fingers. I feel him rotating them as the tips of them start to slip inside me.

"Oh God," I moan. My head dropping onto the pillow, I bite into it.

He slowly works his big fingers inside me, rotating and stretching and filling me, preparing me for his cock.

I'm panting into the pillow, my fingers clawing at the bedsheets, my body climbing toward what I just know is going to be an amazing orgasm.

"Jesus, Taylor, I could come just from looking at you like this…you on your hands and knees with my fingers up your ass. I've never seen anything hotter."

His words, the sound of his voice…the feel of him inside me, his fingers teasing my clit…I'm so close to coming. My body is begging for all he can give me.

"I need you inside me," I say urgently, lifting my head to look back at him.

He stills. "Are…you sure?"

"I've never been surer of anything in my life. I need this…I need you, Liam." And, in this moment, I really and truly mean that. I've never needed anyone like I need him right now.

Desire rages in his eyes. His jaw is clenched tight. He looks like he's barely on the edge of restraint.

He slips his fingers out of me, and his other hand moves away from my clit, leaving my body crying for his touch.

He picks up the lube and pumps an obscene amount onto his cock, lubing it up. I guess he wants to make sure he's as slippery as possible to get inside me. He pumps the lube down on my ass again, letting it slide down the crack. His fingers work it down and into my hole.

I'm wet and slippery, and nervous and scared, but I'm so ready to have him inside me in this way.

His eyes meet back with mine. "Ready?"

"Yes…just…go slow."

My eyes meet with his. His eyes look raw, and his expression is tight, like he's just hanging on to his control by the tips of his fingers.

"I wouldn't do it any other way. You want me to stop, tell me." He might be hanging on to his control, but it doesn't show in his voice. It's soft and measured.

"I will."

I look back ahead and close my eyes, focusing on relaxing. I figure, if I tense, it'll hurt more. Like when you have a gyno examination, which is something I really shouldn't be thinking about right now—unsexiest thing ever.

I feel Liam's cock press against my ass, and all my focus goes straight to that one important place. He pushes in the tip, and I gasp.

"You okay?" he rasps out.

"Yeah," I breathe out through the burn. It's much stronger than the one I felt with his finger. "Just keep going."

His hands are gripping my hips, his fingers working restlessly against my skin, as he pushes in a little further. And further until he's soon all the way in, deep inside me.

"Boston…is this still okay?"

"I'm not going to lie; it hurts a little, but…it feels good, too…if that makes sense." I look back at him again.

A smile eases onto his lips. He might be smiling, but his eyes are dark and dangerous and hot as fuck.

"It makes sense." His voice is rough.

Liam moistens his lips with his tongue. Holding my eyes, he pulls his cock out, almost to the tip, and then slowly pushes it back in.

I can't take my eyes off of him. I'm mesmerized.

The moment is so intense, and the pleasure I'm feeling is like nothing I've ever felt before.

Liam slides his hand under my stomach and lifts me upright. We're both up on our knees, my back pressed to his chest, and he's deep inside me.

I reach my arms back, holding on to him to keep my balance.

He cups my breast with one hand and begins kissing my neck, sliding his tongue over my skin, as he starts moving again, fucking me with slow, measured thrusts.

At this angle…him inside me…so deep…it's so fucking good.

The hand on my breast makes its way down my stomach until his fingers are back on my clit, touching and teasing.

His other hand wraps around my throat. His finger and thumb holding my jaw, he turns my head to his and takes my mouth in a kiss.

The feel of him inside my body, his tongue in my mouth, his fingers on my clit…has me climbing toward the edge of madness and feeling like I'm falling at the same time.

He breaks from my mouth but doesn't let me move. He presses his forehead to mine, his eyes fixed on me.

"This…*you*…" His voice is deep and low. "You're amazing, Taylor. I've never wanted anyone the way I want you. You make everything better. I'm better…with you."

Then, he's kissing me again. Deep and intense and meaningful.

His words are swirling around my head, tangling up with my own words and feelings that I have for him.

Confusion and desire and how much I want this man leave me feeling breathless.

This sex isn't how I imagined it would be. I expected it to be rough and urgent, that it would be deep, primal fucking. But it's not.

It's tender and meaningful.

Can you make love while being fucked up the ass?

Well, if you can, then that's what Liam is doing to me right now.

And it's making things feel blurry. The right and wrong of things all mixing up together.

But what is clear is how I feel about him.

A lot.

I feel a lot for Liam.

And it scares me.

I'm panting in his mouth, desperate and needy.

His finger rubbing quickly over my clit, his hand on my breast, his cock up my ass…

The orgasm explodes out of me. My whole body tightens to the point of pleasure and pain. My eyes close. I've never felt anything like this before.

Ecstasy. It feels like pure ecstasy.

Liam's hold on me is firm. His movement slows while I come.

His hand leaves my clit as my orgasm ebbs. He grabs ahold of my hip. His other hand comes across my chest, gripping ahold of my shoulder, and he starts moving. His pace is faster now, harder.

"There's nothing hotter than seeing you come," he rasps into my ear. "You coming makes me come…"

He groans, and then his teeth bite down on my lobe. I feel his body jerk against mine, and then his hips start pumping harder against me. I feel the flood of cum inside me. It's the craziest sensation.

But the most amazing thing I've ever felt.

Something else to add and check off my list.

Ass sex.

I'm trying to keep my thoughts light. Because Liam is wrapped around me and still inside me, his breath warm against my skin, his heart beating into my back, and my feelings for him are trying to cave in on me.

The urge to tell him what he means to me is so close to the tip of my tongue. I can feel it burning the inside of my mouth.

But I also know the damage saying those things would do.

How no good would come from it.

So, I lock those thoughts and feelings up, and I focus on the thought of the sex we just had. And, in my head, I turn it from the deep and meaningful thing that it was into something primal and hot.

Fucking. Just fucking.

"You okay, Boston?" He presses a soft kiss to the skin beneath my ear.

"Yeah." I glance back at him and smile. "I'm more than good."

He smiles, his teeth grazing over his lower lip. "I wish we could just stay like this forever," he says softly.

Forever.

"My legs might go into serious cramp mode if we do." I laugh.

I laugh to turn it into a joke. Something less serious.

Liam laughs, but it doesn't reach his eyes. "I'll get something to clean you up." He kisses me on the lips and then slowly pulls out of me.

I feel the trickle down my thighs. I'm not sure what to do, but I figure, if I lie down, gravity might keep most of it in until Liam returns with some to clean me up with so that I make less of a mess on the bed.

I let myself fall onto my front and relax into the softness of the mattress.

I hear Liam's deep laughter when he reenters the bedroom.

"Comfy?" he asks.

"Very."

And I lie there while Liam cleans me up with a cloth. I feel a little sting when he cleans around my ass, making me hiss.

"Sore?" he asks.

I can hear regret in his voice.

I lift my head from the bed and look back at him. "Just a little. But it was more than worth it."

That earns me another snapshot smile.

"I'll just get rid of this." He holds the cloth up.

I watch him leave the room, and then I move up the bed. Turning onto my back, I shimmy the duvet down and snuggle beneath it.

Liam smiles when he sees me. Then, he dives onto the bed beside me, making me squeal.

He pulls the duvet out from beneath him and gets under the cover.

We're both on our backs, staring up at the ceiling.

Liam lets out a breath. "I feel like I should get a badge or certificate or something. I just conquered Taylor Shaw's arse. A place no man has been before. And, fuck, was it good." He turns his head on the pillow to look at me. "I think I'm gonna have that put on my headstone when I die."

I frown at him. "Don't talk about you dying so flippantly. Someone like you is meant to live forever." The words are out before I can stop them.

The look on his face…it burns through me.

"And, anyway, with the way you're going on, I'd think you'd never fucked a woman up the ass before."

There's a pause before he answers.

Please let it go. Let's get back to jokey and light before I screwed it up.

I almost exhale in relief when he says, "I haven't fucked a woman up the arse before. Well, when I say that, I mean, I haven't bum-fucked a woman like you before."

"Oh, yeah? And what's different about me, compared to those other women you bum-fucked?"

"Well, I didn't have to pay you." He grins. "Kidding."

He holds his hands up when I go to punch him.

"I've never paid for sex—normal or bum fun—I promise."

"Okay." I lower my hand back down to the bed. "So, what's different here with me?" I press.

Why I'm pressing, I don't know.

Well, I do.

It's because I want to hear him tell me why I'm different. Even though I know no good can come of it. But my foolish heart is insisting on hearing him say whatever those words are.

"Aside from the fact that you're American?"

"What does that have to do with anything?"

"Nothing." He laughs. "I just like messing with you."

He slides an arm under my waist, tugging me closer. "Well, for starters, your arse was virgin, so that officially makes it mine. You never forget your first." He tilts his head forward, pressing his forehead to mine. He shuts his eyes and exhales. "You're mine, Boston, in every way that matters," he whispers. "You're different and perfect, and you're mine." He presses a soft kiss to my lips.

Then, he just gets out of bed. Totally unaware that he's just punched his fist into my chest, pulled out what was left of my heart, and carried it off with him.

"I'm gonna take a shower, clean up properly, so I'm ready for round two. You wanna join me?"

I force myself to come around, so I can respond to his words.

I sit up, the duvet pooling around my waist. "Round two? We're not doing ass sex again for at least a few days. I'm a little sore, remember?"

Liam stops by the door. Hand on the frame, he looks back at me. "Of course I remember. I wasn't talking about ass sex when I said round two. No, I was talking about your tits. They're my next mountain to climb. I'm going to fuck the hell out of those beauties and then come all over them, so they look like snow-capped mountains." He grins, and then he slips into the bathroom before I get a chance to respond.

But if I'd had a chance to respond, all that would have come is laughter.

Because that's what Liam does.

He sets my heart on fire, and he makes me laugh.

And I'm pretty sure that I'm falling in love with him.

I am falling in love with him.

I'm falling in love with Liam. Or I'm already in love with him.

Either way, I love him, and that realization sends me into a tailspin.

I spent the rest of yesterday outwardly smiling and laughing while spending time with Liam and Bernie. But, on the inside, I was shredding myself to pieces.

But then, later, while I was lying next to Liam in bed, wide awake and unable to sleep, I watched him in slumber. He's so beautiful when he sleeps, but that is so not the point.

It was then, watching him, that I came to the realization that it didn't matter.

I'm in love with Liam. I can't change that. I don't think I would want to even if I had a choice.

But loving him doesn't change anything.

I might love Liam.

But I love my family more.

I owe them more.

My feelings for Liam are mine. He's not aware of them, and he never will be. Liam isn't even on the same page as me in that respect.

He cares about me. I know that.

And to have him care for me…is wonderful.

But feelings like that fade fast.

Love doesn't.

And I'm lucky that I get to love this amazing man in this time I have left, and I get to take those feelings with me when I go.

I got to fall in love before I die.

Falling in love wasn't something I thought I would ever get to experience, even if one-sided, but I have, and it's amazing.

To look at Liam and feel like my heart will burst from the feelings I have for him…is incredible. To have the privilege to love someone like Liam…it's a true gift.

I know it's a gift I shouldn't have. I shouldn't allow myself to feel this way for him. I don't deserve it.

But it's not like he loves me back.

These are my feelings alone, and they're mine to keep, mine to covet.

If that makes me selfish, then selfish is what I am because I won't give up these feelings for anything.

I'm giving my life. I just have to hope that it's enough.

We're at the Silverstone Circuit, attending the Grand Prix, currently seated in the hospitality area of a team called Rybell. Bernie provides sponsorship for them, has done so for years apparently. And, because Bernie is a sponsor, we get to sit in hospitality and meet with the team's drivers. The reigning champion of the Grand Prix is one of Rybell's drivers—Carrick Ryan. I might not follow Formula One, but I know who Carrick Ryan is. Everyone knows who Carrick Ryan is.

Tall, blond, Irish, and ridiculously good-looking—but not as good-looking as Liam.

I know, right? I'm saying Liam is better-looking than Carrick Ryan. I must have it bad. Or it's just the plain truth. Liam is hotter and more handsome.

I'm going with the truth. Because, in my eyes, Liam is better.

He's everything.

Carrick is Formula One's golden boy. Once upon a time, he was Formula One's bad boy, but he's a changed man nowadays. Married to the love of his life.

Yep, I know who Carrick Ryan is.

Bernie, Liam, and I are seated at a table by the window. A few other people are here, too. I have no clue who they are—other sponsors, I'm guessing. I'm staring out the window, watching as people fill up the stands.

To be honest, it's a little boring at the moment because the men are talking business, but overall, I don't mind because I'm here with Liam. Once I get to meet Carrick—*God, I hope I meet Carrick*—and when the racing begins, I know it will be awesome.

We got to Silverstone by helicopter, and, yes, Liam flew the helicopter here. Apparently, he flies those as well as airplanes.

Turns out there is a helipad on his grandpa's estate. They don't travel to the Grand Prix like normal people would—you know, by car. Nope, the Hunter men like to go by air.

Can't say I loved the experience of being in a helicopter, but I am getting used to flying the more I do it, and flying in a helicopter is one more thing to add and check off my list.

The best thing about the flight here was watching Liam control the helicopter. His hand wrapped around that control stick reminded me of our plane ride yesterday and when I blew him at twenty thousand feet.

God, that was hot. And so was the ass sex afterward.

Hottest thing ever.

I hear loud chatter as some people enter the room, and—

Oh my God.

One of them is Carrick Ryan.

He's walking up front, wearing his driver's uniform, and he has his arm around a stunning dark-haired, olive-skinned tall woman. She must be his wife. The one woman that turned his head and changed him.

I think pretty much all the women in the world collectively cried into their wine glasses the day that Carrick Ryan got married. Same as when Jake Wethers got married.

Like how I'll cry from my seat in heaven the day Liam gets married to someone else.

What the hell? Where did that thought come from?

I shake it out of my head when I realize that Carrick and his wife have broken away from the people they entered the room with, and they're walking over to where we are seated.

They might be walking toward us, but they're still looking and talking to one another.

The way Carrick is staring at his wife's face with complete adoration makes me feel a shot of envy.

To be looked at in that way. To have someone adore you so completely. I can't even imagine.

I feel Liam's hand curl around mine. I bring my eyes to him.

"You ready to meet Carrick Ryan?" He grins.

"Yeah." I smile. But I don't really feel it. For some reason, I feel a little sad right now.

"Carrick, Andi," Bernie greets them, already on his feet. He kisses Andi on the cheek and then shakes Carrick's hand. "How are you and the baby doing?" Bernie asks Andi.

My eyes follow down and see a tiny baby bump.

She's having a baby.

Another thing I'll never get to experience. But then, even if I were to have a full life, I wouldn't be able to have a baby because I'm infertile. The radiation therapy from the first tumor saw to that. But I did have some of my eggs frozen. So, if I did live, then I could have a baby…

But I'm not going to live, so I need to stop thinking that way.

God, what the hell is wrong with me?

Stop the pity party, and cheer the hell up. You're about to meet Carrick Ryan.

"Really well. Thanks, Bernie." Andi doesn't have an English accent like Liam's or Bernie's. Andi's sounds different, like there's a hint of something else in there. She smiles at Bernie, pressing her hand to her stomach and lovingly rubbing it.

Carrick's hand covers hers. She smiles up into his face.

She looks radiant. Happy. Baby glow.

Pang of envy hits me again. Harder this time.

Stop it.

"She won't slow down though, no matter how much I tell her to," Carrick says to Bernie, his Irish lilt standing out. "She's still insisting on helping out in the garage."

I've never heard the Irish accent in real life before. Got to say, it's awesome.

"I sit on a stool and watch the guys because he won't let me do anything else," Andi tells Bernie, humor clear in her voice.

"My wife would've worked right up to the day she gave birth if I'd let her," Bernie tells Carrick.

"What did your wife do?" Andi asks.

"She was a veterinarian. Loved animals—more than me sometimes, I think." Bernie chuckles.

I didn't know Bernie's wife was a veterinarian.

Liam gets up from his seat and tugs me up with him by the hand. We make our way around the table to Bernie, Carrick, and Andi.

"Carrick, good to see you again." Liam shakes his hand. "You ready for the race?"

"Ready as I'll ever be," Carrick says.

Liam's voice sounds different.

Is that…a hint of excitement I hear in his voice?

The only time I've ever heard Liam excited is when he's about to fuck me or come.

I know Liam loves the Prix, and I know he's met Carrick before, quite a few times. But I guess if you idolize a sport, you idolize the sportsmen who make it what it is, no matter who you are.

And I know for a fact that, if this were me meeting Jake again, I'd be just as freaked out as I was the first time I met him.

"Andi, lovely to see you again." Liam kisses her on the cheek in greeting.

"You, too." She smiles at him.

I feel another hit of jealousy.

I don't know why.

What the hell is up with me right now?

I need to sort myself out, stat.

"Carrick, Andi, this is Taylor," Liam introduces, putting his arm around my waist.

"Hi." I smile. "It's really nice to meet you both."

"American." Andi smiles.

She really is pretty. Like supermodel pretty.

And she has a husband who clearly adores her, and she's going to have a baby and a long life.

Stop it.

"Guilty as charged." I smile again.

"I love America." Andi tells me. "Whereabouts are you from?"

"Boston."

"Oh, I've never been to Boston. Would love to go though."

"Then, I'll take you," Carrick says to her.

She turns her face to his and smiles at him. He smiles back at her.

It's a secret smile, one filled with love and adoration and memories of time shared that only they know about.

You can feel the love flowing between them. Like a living, breathing entity.

And it's immensely bothering me for some reason.

I have the sudden urge to cry.

"If you'll excuse me, I just need to use the restroom," I say to everyone. But, for some reason, I can't bring myself to look directly at Liam.

I slip out of Liam's hold, but he catches my wrist as I start to move away.

I force my eyes to his face, and pain pierces my chest.

Why is it hurting me to look at him?

"You okay, babe?" he asks softly.

His eyes are burning into mine. And there's concern in his. I can see it clearly.

My discomfort must be obvious.

I force a smile. "I'm fine. Just need to pee."

"You've been quiet. Do you have a headache coming on?"

"No, nothing like that. I'm fine." I give another smile.

He stares at me for a long moment and then finally says, "Okay. I'll be here, waiting for you when you get back."

He releases my arm, and I make my exit, heading straight for the restroom.

I go into a stall and lock the door behind me. I sit down on the toilet.

I don't need to pee. It was just an excuse because I needed to get out of there. I was meeting Carrick Ryan, and all I wanted to do was run away.

Because I felt like I was suffocating in that room.

I was envious. Jealous even. Of the way Carrick looks at Andi. Of their clear and visible love for one another. The baby growing inside her stomach.

Not because I want Carrick. Far from it.

It's because of Liam. And me.

No matter all the pep talks I give myself and all the internal convincing I do that loving Liam is okay, that my one-sided feelings are fucking awesome, it isn't going to change the fact that, deep down inside me, I know it isn't okay.

Loving Liam makes me want him. It makes me want him to feel the same for me as I do for him. Loving him makes me want the things that everyone else gets to have.

Looking at Andi and Carrick together has made me realize that. How much I want that.

I want Liam to look at me like no one else in the world exists, except for me. I want to wear his ring one day. I want to know what it feels like to have his child growing inside me.

I want things that aren't available to me.

And I can't pretend that it doesn't make me sad because it does.

It makes my heart hurt in a way I find hard to explain.

If I were living a different life, I might get to have all those things with Liam.

But I don't get to have that other life.

I don't get to have a life at all.

Soon, I will go, and Liam will do all those things with someone else. He'll love some other woman. He'll marry her. Have a child with her.

And knowing that…it fucking hurts.

I press my hand to my stomach, holding in the pain, and I bite my lip to stop myself from crying, but the stupid tears fall anyway.

I pull some toilet paper off the roll and blot the tears away.

Closing my eyes, I take calming deep breaths in and out.

I need to stop this. A pity party in a restroom stall is not how I should be spending my time.

Standing, I drop the paper in the toilet and flush it. I let myself out of the stall and walk over to the sinks.

I stare at myself in the restroom mirror.

Remember why you're doing this, Taylor.

Mom, Dad, Parker, and Tess.

They're the reason you are choosing to die instead of fighting to live. So you can be with them again.

They are the right choice. It might feel hard now, even confusing because of the way I feel about Liam. But when I'm with them, I will know it was the right thing.

To hear their voices again. To wrap my arms around them and never let go. To tell them how sorry I am for what I did. To be allowed to love them.

That's what matters. That's what's important.

Not how I feel about Liam.

I wash my hands and dry them on a paper towel. Then, I make my way back to Liam.

Carrick and Andi are now seated at our table with us. Bernie is chatting away with them both, and Andi smiles warmly at me as I approach.

I return the smile. I need to get back to feeling like myself and talk to these nice people.

Then, my eyes meet with Liam's. Everything I just said to myself falters and starts to fall away, and I just feel sad again.

I catch sight of worry in Liam's eyes, and it makes me feel shitty.

Fix this, Taylor.

Liam has done so much for you already. He's been kind enough to bring you here with him and have you meet Carrick Ryan, for God's sake. And you still have the chance to chat with him and his lovely wife because they're sitting at your table.

Don't spoil Liam's day because you've got your head up your ass over things you can't change.

I slip into my seat beside him. "Hey." I smile brightly at him.

He reaches over and takes my hand in his. "Okay?" he asks, his voice quiet.

"Fine." I make my bright smile bigger.

But he still doesn't look convinced.

So, I lean over and press a soft kiss to his lips. "I'm fine, Hunter. I promise." I tilt my head back to stare into his eyes, enforcing my words, hiding my multitude of ever-growing lies behind them.

He smiles, and it reaches all the way up to his eyes.

Then, Bernie asks him a question, taking him from me. So, I lean forward, and I start talking to Andi from across the table.

But Liam doesn't let go of my hand while we talk separately.

And he doesn't let go of it for the rest of the day.

chapter 26

I'm in the back of the town car with Liam, and Paul is driving us to a tattoo parlor.

I'm checking another thing off my list. I don't have many left.

After the tattoo, only a few remain—*have something pierced, get totally wasted until I vomit and pass out, dance in the rain,* and *experience a true moment of romance, like they do in the movies.* But I guess I've had a lot of romantic moments with Liam, so any of them could count.

I've had a lot of hot moments with him, too.

Plane blow job definitely tops my list. And sex at the Funfair. And the ass sex. Okay, so all of the sex I've had with Liam tops my list.

After the Grand Prix—which was amazing once the race started—we went back to Hunter Hall and had dinner with Bernie and Archie.

Then, later in bed, Liam did all manner of naughty things to me.

Most of the next day, we stayed with his grandpa, too, and then Liam drove us back to London.

We went straight back to his apartment. I swear, I've barely stayed in my hotel, not that I'm complaining.

Liam and I went out to the supermarket and bought groceries, and then he cooked us dinner. Afterward, we lay on the sofa, wrapped up together while watching a movie.

I fell asleep mid movie. I woke up when Liam picked me up and carried me to bed. I was awake by the time he laid me down on the mattress. So, I pulled him down on me, and that night, I did lots of dirty things to him.

This morning, I woke up before Liam, which was unusual. So, I hauled ass out of bed, made him breakfast, and brought it to bed for him.

That earned me two orgasms.

Then, he told me that he'd booked an appointment for a tattoo today.

I swear, when he gets time to do these things, I'll never know. But then I'm pretty sure he probably just emails his PA and has her do it. I learned that his PA is called Pam, and she's worked for him for eight years. I only found that out because I asked him.

I feel like I should send the woman a bunch of flowers for the appointments he has had her booking for me.

So, we're heading to the tattoo parlor, and I actually have no clue what tattoo I'm going to have done.

Sure, I put it on my list that I wanted one, but I didn't know what tattoo I wanted.

But then I guess it doesn't really matter what I have. It's more about the experience of having the tattoo done, not what it is.

I figure I'll just pick out the first tattoo I see. I just need to decide where on my body to have it done.

I'm thinking, my ass. It's the flabbiest part, so it'll hurt the least.

"So, do you know what tattoo you're going to have?" Liam asks from beside me, almost like he's reading my mind.

"I'm not sure." I lift my shoulder in a half-shrug. "I don't really care what it is."

"You're getting ink permanently etched onto your body, and you don't care what it is?"

"Nope."

He's looking at me like I've lost my mind. I guess, to him, it would seem a little crazy. Because he doesn't know that it's not the tattoo itself that matters but the experience of having it done.

I don't want to die a tattoo virgin.

"You can pick the tattoo for me if you want."

The crazy look leaves his face and is replaced with surprise. "You want me to pick something for you?"

"You don't have to. But I'd like it if you did."

Then, it'll be like I'm getting his mark on me. Something Liam chose to put on my skin.

Yeah, I like that idea.

"I'd love to." He leans over and kisses me.

Paul pulls up outside the tattoo parlor. I let myself out of the car. Paul is out of his door, on his way to open mine. Smiling, he shakes his head in exasperation at me.

"Sorry. I just forget. I'm used to letting myself out of cars."

Liam gets out behind me. "Well, you shouldn't be. You should have spent your whole life being chauffeured around, Boston."

"Aw, you say the nicest things." I grin at him over my shoulder.

Liam shuts the car door, and we walk over to the tattoo parlor.

He gets the door for me. I walk inside. There's a girl behind the counter. Her arms are covered in tattoos. She has a piercing in her lip and another in her nose. Her ears are full of piercings. She has white-blonde hair—shaved at one side, the other side hanging just below her ear.

She's really attractive.

"Hey." She smiles at us.

I see the way her eyes widen at Liam. Can't say I blame her.

He's dressed in jeans and a V-neck gray sweater. His wavy hair is in that just-got-out-of-bed look, which I love so much. He's looking his usual gorgeous self.

"We have an appointment for Taylor Shaw, but I'm hoping you can fit another one in."

"Another one?" I turn to him.

"Yeah. Me."

"You?" My eyes widen in surprise.

"Babe, you're getting a tattoo done, and you're letting me choose the design, so the least I can do is return the favor."

"It's not a favor, Hunter. I want you to pick it."

"I know. And knowing you trust me makes me fucking happy. So, I want to give that feeling back to you."

My heart does that little thumpity-thump in my chest.

"We're pretty clear at the moment." The girl is looking on the computer. "Yeah, we should be able to fit you in, no problem." She smiles at Liam.

"Thanks," he says to her.

"If you'll both just take a seat, we'll be with you soon."

I follow Liam over to the seats, still stunned that he's getting a tattoo. And that I have to choose what he gets.

"So, whereabouts are you going to get the tattoo?" I ask him.

"No fucking clue. I only decided about five minutes ago that I was getting one done." He chuckles. "Where are you getting yours?"

"Ass."

"Are you calling me one? Or is that where you're putting the tattoo?"

That has me laughing. "That's where I'm putting it, silly."

"Then, that's where I'll have mine."

"You're going to get your ass tattooed?" I can't stop smiling and staring at him.

"Yep." He nods, a smile on his lips. Then, he looks at me, catching me still staring at him. "What?"

"Nothing. I'm just surprised, is all."

"That I'm getting a tattoo?"

"Yeah."

"And why does that surprise you?"

"I don't know. I guess it shouldn't. It's not like you're afraid to do anything."

His eyes catch and hold mine, the look in them turning serious. "Boston, there are many things that I'm afraid of."

I don't know why, but his words and the look on his face make my mouth dry.

For a moment, I feel like his words are about me.

That he's afraid of me.

"Which one of you is Taylor?" A huge bear of a man is walking toward us, a smile on his face. He's got long hair tied back, a thick beard, and there isn't an inch of his skin showing that isn't tattooed—aside from his face, that is.

"That would be me," I say, getting to my feet.

"Well, I'm Den, and I'll be tattooing you both today." Then, he says to Liam, "You're welcome to come through and watch while I tattoo your girlfriend if you want. And then I'll do yours right after."

I'm just about to correct him and tell him that I'm not Liam's girlfriend when Liam stands up and says, "Works for me."

"So, what are you thinking of having done?" Den asks me.

"Um…" I'm still trying to come around from the shock of being called Liam's girlfriend.

He's never referred to me as that before. He's always introduced me to people as his friend. But he didn't correct Den.

I don't know why it's bothering me so much. It's not like it's a big deal.

But, for some reason, it feels like it is.

"He's picking my tattoo." I throw my thumb toward Liam.

Den stops by a door and opens it, giving me a look.

"She's picking mine," Liam tells him as we walk into the tattooing room.

"Ah, well, they're your bodies, but I always say, choose wisely 'cause a tattoo is permanent—unless you want to go through the pain of having it removed."

I really don't have to worry about that, Den. But thanks for the concern.

"I've picked a good one for her. She'll like it for sure." Liam grins at me.

"I trust you," I tell him.

His eyes meet mine. "I trust you, too."

"Right. Well, where are we tattooing?" Den asks me.

"My ass," I tell him.

"And do you have a picture of what she's having done?" he asks Liam.

"Yeah." Liam pulls his cell from his pocket and opens up something on the screen. Then, he hands the phone to Den.

Den stares at the screen and then at Liam.

"Trust me. She'll love it." Liam laughs softly, meeting my eyes.

Honestly, I'm not even worried about what he's picked for me. I'm just happy that something he chose is going to be on my body.

"Right. Well, I'll just go draw this up. I'll be back in a few minutes." Den leaves the room.

I sit up on the tattooing bed.

"Are you nervous?" Liam asks, coming over to stand between my legs.

"No. Are you?"

"No."

"You got any idea what you're going to pick for me?"

"I do actually." I smile.

I so have the best idea for what to have tattooed on Liam. I just hope he gets the sentiment.

"Am I going to like it?"

I just smile big at him, and worry flickers in his eyes.

"Don't worry." I pat his arm. "It'll be awesome. I promise."

A few minutes later, Den reappears with a drawing in his hand. I turn away, as I want it to be a surprise.

"Do you want to look at it before I do it?" Den asks me from behind.

"Nope. I want the surprise," I say more to Liam than Den.

Liam smiles down at me.

"I'll take a look," Liam tells Den, leaving me and walking over to him.

They're both quiet for a moment.

Then, Liam says, "It's perfect."

That has me smiling bigger.

"Okay. Well, Taylor, get yourself lying on your front on the bed for me, and lower your leggings. Then, we'll get started," Den tells me.

I do as he asked. Lying on my front, I shimmy my leggings down, exposing my ass. I had the foresight to wear leggings, as they're stretchy and comfy for when I'll have to pull them back up over the tattoo.

Liam pulls up a chair, sitting beside my head.

"Any preference on which side I do the tattoo?" Den asks.

"Left butt cheek." I don't know why I say left. Probably because I'm left-handed.

"I'll go left then, too." Liam grins down at me. "Might as well match."

Den shaves the area on my left ass cheek. Then, I feel him rub something over the area. And the next thing I hear is the sound of the needle turning on.

Liam looks over at the needle and then back to me. "You ready?" he says softly.

"Yeah, I'm ready."

I feel the needle touch my skin, and—

Holy fuck! That hurts!

I reach out and grab Liam's arm, squeezing hard.

And the fucker laughs.

"I don't know what you're laughing at," I grumble at him through gritted teeth. "Because you're next to have this bitch of a needle jabbing you in the ass."

"I can't even begin to tell you how hot it is, seeing my name tattooed on your arse." Liam's deep voice ripples through my body.

We're back at his apartment, and I'm lying on my stomach on his bed. I'm wearing a T-shirt, and my lower half is bare while Liam is applying diaper cream to my tattoo—or nappy cream, as they call it here.

Den said it's the best thing to use on a tattoo to stop the skin from drying out.

"I can't believe you told him to tattoo your company logo on me," I say into the pillow.

Yeah, that's right. I have the Hunter Airways logo tattooed on my butt.

Liam said he could have gone for the Hunter Hotel or Hunter Finance logo, but he thought, as we'd met on the plane, it would be poetic.

I've been complaining, but secretly, I love that he chose this.

It's like he's left a part of himself on me—even though he's already marked me in so many ways…my mind…my heart.

He barks out a laugh. "Says the woman who had a map of Boston—with the word *Boston* and a heart written inside the map—tattooed on my arse."

I snort out a laugh and lift up onto my elbows as I smile back at him. "I thought it would be a nice way for you to remember me."

"I don't need a tattoo to remember you, babe."

His words run through me like hot and cold water in my veins.

Then, he says, "But did you have to put the heart in though?" He's shaking his head with dismay.

Well, the heart was my indirect way of telling him how I feel. That he has Boston's heart…*my* heart.

But, now, I feel bad. I guess I didn't think it through properly.

"I'm sorry." I give him a regretful look.

I might have been trying to give him my heart, but I forgot that he's a guy. Guys don't like hearts.

He stares at me, his expression fiercely strong. "You don't ever have to apologize to me."

I do. I really do.

I bite my lip. "Will you have it removed?" I lay my head on my arm, but I'm still looking back at him.

"The tattoo?" he asks, while he continues to gently smooth the cream over my tattoo.

"Yes."

He frowns, like the thought is absurd to him. "No, because you put it there, theoretically speaking." The frown deepens, forcing lines around his eyes. Then, I see his eyes flicker with a thought. "Will you have yours removed?"

I firmly shake my head.

Never.

Even if I were going to be around for a long time, I still wouldn't get it removed. Because it's him.

He smiles, and it warms my insides.

I lay my head back, brushing my hair off my ear.

Liam chuckles and says, "I can't believe you got your ears pierced as well. Glutton for punishment."

I asked Den if he could pierce my ears after Liam's tattoo was done. He had the time, so he did them.

I know getting my ears pierced isn't crazy or daring, like a nipple piercing would have been. But I never got to have my ears pierced when I was younger. My dad was strict about it and said I could get them done when I turned sixteen. Only the brain tumor happened, and I just never got around to having them pierced.

I've rectified that now.

"It just made sense." I shrug. "I was there. They did piercings."

"Are your ears sore?"

"A little. Not as bad as I expected. My ass, on the other hand…"

"I hear ya. Call me a pussy, but that tattoo fucking hurt. Still does," Liam says with a grumble in his voice.

I look back at him again. "I didn't know the word *pussy* was in your vocab, Hunter."

"Only your pussy." He grins and then tosses the cream beside me on the bed. "My turn."

He moves from behind me and lies on his front on the bed.

He's already naked. Took his clothes off the moment we got back.

Another thing I'm not complaining about. Naked Liam is an awesome sight.

Picking up the cream, I get to my knees and straddle his thighs.

He has the nicest ass. Tight and firm. Makes me want to bite it. But I won't.

I remove the cap, squeeze some cream out onto my fingers, and put the cap back on. I put the tube on the bed beside Liam, and I carefully start to apply it to his tattoo.

He lets out a sound of relief.

"Better?" I ask.

"Much."

"I still can't believe you got a tattoo." I giggle.

"The things I do for you," he says, the words muffled into the pillow.

Did he do this for me? I mean, I never asked him to. But I don't think he means it in that way.

But how does he mean it?

I really don't know how to ask. So, I don't.

I just start to hum a tune, and then I softly sing the words to the song that has been stuck in my head since I heard it in the car on the way back to his apartment after the tattooing was done—Justin Bieber's "Sorry."

When I think about what that song is about, I realize that maybe there is a reason it's stuck in my head.

Because I am sorry. Sorry for every time I've lied to him. And how I still continue to do so.

"Babe, you're rubbing cream onto my arse and singing Bieber's 'Sorry.' Really not sure how to feel about that."

And there he is, making me laugh again.

I let my laughter die, and then I say softly, "Maybe I am sorry."

He looks back at me. I see confusion and a hint of worry in his eyes.

"And what are you sorry for?"

Everything.

"The tattoo. The heart. I should've thought about it."

His brows pull together. "I told you, don't ever be sorry to me. And, yeah, the heart is a little chick-ish, but it's not like many people are going to see it."

Just other women after I'm gone.

Bile rises. I swallow it back.

"The only people I need to be worried about seeing this are Cam and Eddie 'cause those bastards would dine out on this for years. It'd be the new Backstreet Boys. And no way will those fuckers be seeing my arse anytime soon, so nothing to worry about, babe."

He gives me an encouraging smile.

I try to return it.

I finish applying the cream, and then I give his non-tattooed ass cheek a slap. "All done."

I move off of him and lie on the bed beside him with my hands under my head, my face turned his way.

Liam moves his face on the pillow, so he's looking at me.

"What do you want to do for the rest of the day?" he asks. "But, before you answer, I do have a stipulation. I will do whatever you want, so long as it doesn't require me sitting on my arse."

A small laugh escapes me. "I'm happy right here."

His gaze softens. "Yeah, me, too."

We're staring at each other, no words passing between us, and the moment is perfect.

And then I have to go and spoil it by saying, "Hunter…can I ask about…Kate?"

His face immediately closes up, shutting me out.

Why did I have to ask that?

Because it's been bugging me ever since I saw her picture and his reaction to it. And the fact that she was his fiancée.

He had a fiancée. I think that's a big deal. Well, it is to me anyway, and I want to know what happened between them. Because, whatever it was, it wasn't good.

He turns his face into the pillow. I can hear him breathing deeply.

"I'm not trying to upset you," I say gently. "I was just—"

"Curious." He turns his face back to me. His expression is hard.

"Yeah," I exhale.

301

And he does, too. But the breath he lets out is far more pronounced than mine.

"The night you got sick at my grandpa's house, after you had seen the picture, I came into the bathroom to apologize for my behavior. I just didn't get a chance." His eyes focus on mine. "I am sorry. I shouldn't have reacted the way I did."

"I'm sure you had your reasons."

He lifts a shoulder. "Even still, I acted like a prick, and you of all people don't deserve to be treated that way."

But I do, Hunter. I deserve so much more than you acting like a prick. I deserve your anger and your disdain.

He closes his eyes.

I think that's the end of the conversation. He doesn't want to talk about Kate, and that's his right. I'm not exactly forthcoming in things that have to do with me.

I haven't exactly told him about my family's deaths.

And how it was my fault.

I press my hand to his cheek to let him know it's okay that he doesn't want to talk. His growing stubble under my palm is rough and ticklish.

"I met Kate in my first year of university."

He opens his eyes, and I move my hand away.

"We were taking a few of the same classes. We got to talking. She was smart and beautiful and popular."

Liam's Knife, meet Taylor's Heart.

I try to keep my expression straight. Not easy when a blade is being twisted inside my chest.

He doesn't seem to notice though, and he just keeps on talking, "Yeah, I was a Hunter, but all the way through school—after I'd left my old school and started Eton where Grandpa wanted me to go—I wasn't the Hunter my grandpa was—or even my father, for that matter. Instead, I was the bastard child of Charles Hunter, a man who didn't want me. And my mother was a druggie stripper, who was stabbed to death by her boyfriend. To say that school was tough would be putting it mildly. Sure, I had Cam and Eddie…and even Jeremy." He sighs. "But that didn't change who I was.

"Kate didn't seem to care about any of that. She just liked me. And I was dazzled by her. I was never really in love with Kate. Not like I should have been. It took me a long time to realize that." His eyes connect with mine for a time. Then, he looks away. "With Kate, at first, it was lust. I was nineteen, and she was hot. And then, as time went on…I guess I loved the *idea* of Kate more than I did her."

But you asked her to marry you.

I bite my tongue to stop from speaking. I literally bite it, and I get the sharp metallic taste of blood in my mouth.

"We graduated and moved in together. It was what she wanted, and it seemed to be the logical thing to do. So, I went along with it to keep her happy. I was in the process of setting up Hunter Airways and that was taking all of my time. I needed easy at that time." He sighs. "But it wasn't easy. She was always bitching that I was never around, that I never had time for her, that the business was more important to me. To a degree, that was true. I did care more about my business and having it succeed. I didn't want to be like my father, a fucking leech. I wanted to prove that I could make something of myself."

"And you have," I say softly.

"Yeah," he murmurs. "But back then, that was all that mattered. Still does now, to a certain degree."

"There's nothing wrong with having passion for your business."

"I guess not." He blows out a breath. "Kate didn't see it that way though. Right from the beginning of our relationship, she always said that I was distant, that I never let her close. She was right about that, too. I do have a hard time with letting people in."

You've let me in. You're doing it right now.

I don't say those words because making him aware of it won't help things. It won't help me.

"So, one night, after I got back late from a business trip, I went home. I walked in the door, and her suitcases were packed and waiting by it."

"Was this your home with Kate?" My eyes look around his bedroom.

"No." He softly shakes his head. "I couldn't afford a place like this back then. We had a small apartment in West London."

"Oh." I'm glad for that. I guess I would've felt a little weird, spending time here...sleeping in the bed...that was his home with Kate. "Did she leave?" I ask.

I'm guessing she came back if he asked her to marry him.

"No. I didn't see it, but it was a way for her to get what she wanted from me."

"Which was?"

"Marriage. Kate knew that I had abandonment issues. She knew I didn't want her to leave. And she also knew I didn't want to get married. Not to her or anyone. I'd always been clear on that. Still, she was always bringing it up, hinting about it. And I was always avoiding the subject. So, she threatened to leave me to get what she wanted. But I just couldn't see that at the time."

"But you asked her to marry you when you didn't want to. You must have loved her, Liam, to sacrifice your own wants like that."

He shakes his head. "I thought I was losing her. And, back then...I didn't want to lose Kate. Things with her...they were easy. Comfortable. Safe. I guess that was the problem all along. But, back then, I needed the stability she was offering me. So, I knee-jerked and asked her to marry me to make her stay." His gaze lowers as he lets out a soft breath. "I guess...I didn't want to be alone. I didn't want to come home every night after work to an empty apartment."

I can understand that.

"And she stayed?"

He lets out a humorless laugh. "Yeah. And, like the idiot I was, I couldn't see that I'd just been manipulated. If Kate had really wanted to leave me, if I'd made her that unhappy, then she'd have left, no matter what I'd said. But she stayed. Why? I'll never know. Sure, I had money, but no more than her family had back then, and most of mine was invested in the business. I didn't have the money I have now."

How can he think that? That someone would want him only for his money. How can he not see his own worth?

"But after I asked her to marry me, she was the happiest I'd seen her in a long time. Yeah, I guess that made me feel good, like I'd done something right for once. And things were good for a while. Kate was planning the wedding, and I was working hard to grow the business." He rubs his hand over his face. "Deep down, I knew that marrying someone I wasn't in love with wasn't the best idea, but I wasn't ready to lose another person from my life. I might not have been in love with her, but Kate was my friend. I guess, at the time, she was my best friend—or so I'd thought."

"What happened?"

He lets out a laugh. It's not humorous. It's tortured.

"She died."

Then, I remember that night in the pub and Cam saying something about a funeral…Kate's funeral. *Shit, how did I not remember that?*

Oh God.

His fiancée. And his mother.

They both died.

And I'm dying.

He might not love me like he did them. But he does care about me.

What have I done? What am I doing?
I can't hurt him.

"Liam…I'm so sorry." I reach out and wrap my hand around his wrist.

What am I sorry for? My own betrayal? Or their deaths?
Both, I think.

He stares down at my hand on his arm. Then, his eyes flick back to mine. "Don't be. I'm not. I know that sounds harsh, and I am sorry that Kate died, for her and her family. But the Kate I thought I knew wasn't the person she was. The Kate who told me she loved me. The Kate who wanted to marry me. Yeah, I didn't bury that Kate. I buried Kate, the liar. Kate, the cheat." His eyes move from mine. "She'd been having an affair with Jeremy." His eyes come back to mine. "And not just a one-off fling. They'd been sleeping together pretty much from the time she and I'd gotten together."

"Jesus Christ." The breath rushes out of me.

"Six years, I was with her. Six years, she was sleeping with him and lying to me."

"I don't understand."

He lets out a humorless laugh. "I didn't for a long time. But I guess she wanted her cake and to eat it, too."

"No, Liam." I stare into his eyes. "I mean, I don't understand how someone could have *you* and want anything else. *That* doesn't make sense to me."

Something flickers in his eyes, and it has my heart beating faster. But it's gone as quickly as it appeared, and he's no longer looking at me.

"Clearly, I wasn't enough for Kate. Maybe she wanted Jeremy right from the start. Maybe I was a way to get close to him. I don't know. What I do know is, Jeremy wasn't willing to give her the things she could get me to give her—marriage…and kids as well, I'm assuming. She always was good at manipulating me into giving her what she wanted. Apparently, she was in love with both of us—or so she claimed."

"How did you find out?"

"If you're thinking Kate or Jeremy told me, then you'd be wrong. If she were still alive now, I'd probably be the dumb fuck who knew nothing—married to her, giving her half of everything I'd worked hard for. And she'd have still been fucking him. No, I found out after she died. The night before her funeral."

"Jesus, Liam." I can't think of anything else to say.

"It was six months before we were supposed to get married. She'd gone to Switzerland on a skiing trip with her girlfriends. I was in America at the time—Boston, of all places." He looks at me. "I was setting up the office we have there for the airline. I got the call in the early hours of the morning. She was an experienced skier, but she took a hard turn. She fell off a ravine. She broke her neck. They say she died instantly.

"I flew straight there. I packed up her things in her hotel room, but I didn't go through them. I just packed, and then I left. I arranged everything else. I brought her body back home, so her parents could bury her.

"The night before her funeral, I was going through her things. I guess…I was missing her. Her phone was in her bag. She'd left it in her room. The battery was dead, so I plugged in the charger. There was a bunch of text messages. Some were from friends after she'd died, just saying how much they missed her. I scrolled back to see if there were any from before she died.

"There were two texts sent before she died while she must have been out skiing. One was from me, saying that I'd call her when I woke up. The other was from Jeremy. It wasn't odd to me, that they texted, as they were friends, just like she was with Cam and Eddie, too. But this text was different. It said for her to call him when she was back. His dick was hard because he was thinking about her. He missed fucking her.

"I opened the message and then started reading back through their string of messages. There was…a lot of things said, and there were pictures."

I close my eyes, feeling his pain like it's my own.

"I got obsessed with finding out how long it had been going on. I knew, if I asked Jeremy, he'd just fucking lie. He'd been fucking my fiancée and lying to me about that, so I wasn't going to believe shit he might have to say. So, I got into her emails. There was more in there. She had a secret folder, but I found it. And there it all was. Emails between them, dating back years. I read each and every email. They'd started sleeping together not long after she and I started dating. From what the emails said, he wouldn't give her what I would. A few times, they'd called it off. But then, it would start back up again.

"By the time I was done reading the emails, it was morning, and I had to go to her funeral. So, I got showered and dressed. I climbed into the funeral car, sat next to her parents, and rode to the church. And I stood there at the funeral, staring at her coffin, and when the time came, I stood up and read my eulogy. All the while, I knew what she'd done to me. How she'd lied and betrayed me for all those years.

"And he was there. Sitting in the pew, acting the part of the supportive and grieving friend. I couldn't look at him. If I had, I'd have lost it, and I didn't want to do that to her parents. They'd always been good to me.

"And when her funeral was over, I had to go back to her parents' house for the wake. And I was so fucking ready for it to be over. But I went because, if I didn't, I knew it would raise questions. So, I drank and talked to people and avoided Jeremy. Then, the stupid cunt just had to come over and talk to me."

He lets out a hard laugh. "He stood in front of me and told me how he was there for me, no matter what. How sorry he was that I'd lost Kate. How he missed her, too." Liam blows out a breath. "I fucking lost it. I hit him. He went down from the one punch. If he hadn't, I'd have pummeled him to death. Then, I walked out of her parents' house, and I didn't look back."

"What happened after that?"

Liam huffs out a breath through his nose. "He rang me. The stupid fucker would dare face me, so he rang me. He knew. He saw on his phone that the last message he'd sent to Kate had been finally delivered. Maybe he was just hoping her phone had died along with her. But he was smart enough to figure out I was the one who had seen his text message. He even tried to lie to me then. Said it hadn't been going on for long. That they'd only slept together just before she went away to Switzerland.

"I told him that I knew everything. I'd seen the texts and pictures dating back a few months that she had on her phone. She hadn't even felt the need to delete them in fear of me seeing them. She had known I was that fucking trusting and gullible. I told him that I found out it'd been going on the whole time she and I were together. I told him that she'd kept the emails they'd been sending all that time. Guess she was fucking sentimental in that respect. Shame she didn't feel the same way about me.

"He cried. He actually cried. Begged me to forgive him. Said he was sorry. I told him that he was as dead to me as she was. Then, I hung up the phone, and I haven't spoken to him since. Well, not until last week when I saw him at Cam's."

Liam's reaction makes a whole lot more sense to me now. How he was so territorial and possessive over me while Jeremy was there.

"They were both fools. And I don't mean to speak ill of the dead, but Kate was a bitch, and she never deserved a second of your time. You were too good for her, Liam."

Just how I don't deserve you. You're too good for me, Liam Hunter.

I swear, if Kate is in heaven, when I get up there, I'm going to kick her ass all the way to hell.

I rest my palm against his cheek again. He takes my hand and presses a kiss to my palm.

Then, something occurs to me, making me frown. "But Cam and Eddie are still friends with Jeremy?"

Liam brings my hand down, holding it to his chest. I can feel his heart beating strong and well.

"They don't know the truth. I didn't tell them. The only person who knows is my grandpa."

"Why didn't you tell them?" My frown twists into confusion.

"Because…I guess a part of me was embarrassed that it had been happening under my nose for so long, and I didn't know."

"Do you think they knew?"

"No." He vehemently shakes his head. "Jeremy was always a selfish fuck, so his behavior wasn't completely surprising. But not Cam and Eddie. If they'd known, they would have told me."

"I'm glad. But you still should've told them."

"Yeah, I guess."

"I'm glad you had your grandpa to talk to about it."

He gives me a half-smile but doesn't say anything.

He lets go of my hand and strokes my face with his fingers, running my hair behind my ear. "I'm glad you're here," he says softly.

I flatten my palm on his chest, moving my fingers through the soft hair there. "I'm glad I'm here, too."

But I don't deserve to be.

I'm lying to him. Like Kate did. Maybe not in the same way or for the same reasons, but I am deceiving him.

And deceit in any form is just the same at the end of the day.

Lies. They cause the same horrific damage.

Liam doesn't deserve to be lied to anymore. And he doesn't deserve to be hurt—far from it. He deserves everything good that life has to offer.

But how can I tell him that I'm dying? That I want to die.

I can't. Because I'm afraid.

I really am as selfish as I always believed myself to be.

If I were a better person, I would tell him. But I'm not a better person.

I'm Taylor Shaw, the coward. The selfish bitch.

The destroyer of lives.

But I don't have to be that person anymore. I can leave him and clear my conscience, knowing that, while I was still breathing, I didn't fail at the last thing I did here on earth.

I could tell him the truth.

Be worthy of the time and care he's given to me.

But then I fear that he would try to talk me out of my decision.

He could only talk me out of it if I wanted to be talked out of it.

And I don't. I can do this.

I can tell him.

The words are there. Right on the tip of my tongue.

It would be so easy to tell him…well, not easy, but right. And freeing, not having to lie to him anymore.

I can tell him the truth, tell him everything. About my family. What I did to them. How their deaths are on my hands. Tell him that the tumor is back. But that it's okay. Because I want to die. I want to be with them.

That this tumor is setting me free, so I can be with them.

But then he moves closer to me, pressing his body to mine, and he kisses me.

I let him. And then I use that as the excuse to let the truth stay locked in my mind.

And when he breathes against my lips, "I want you," I tell him to take me.

I say nothing when he lifts my leg, placing it over his hip. Tilting me back slightly, he pushes his leg beneath mine on the bed, putting my other leg between his. Keeping us both on our sides, our bodies pressed together, eyes locked on each other, he slowly slides inside me.

"You're so wet already," he whispers.

I shut out the voice in my head that's yelling at me to stop this. Urging me to tell him the truth.

"Because I want you."

And I do want him. That's the problem.

I want him badly. Enough to keep me selfish to hide the truth from him.

Because, deep down inside, I know that, if I tell Liam the truth, I'll let him change my mind. The weak part of me…my heart…she wants him so very badly. She wants to stay here with him, like this, forever.

And if I give her that window of opportunity, she'll take it, and I won't be able to stop her.

But I can't do that.

I can't stay. I have to go.

I owe my family that much. I need their forgiveness. I need to hear them say they forgive me.

So, I'll keep lying to Liam, which means I can be with him during the time I have left.

Selfish Bitch Taylor.

Maybe when I get to heaven and kick Kate's ass to hell, I'll take my own selfish, lying ass there, too.

H *oly God.*
Liam is standing outside my hotel room door, wearing one of his three-piece suits. It's blue, his shirt is white, and his tie is red. Like the colors in his company logo. His hair is all slicked back and parted over to the side. He looks hot and sexy and gorgeous and a million other adjectives that describe how amazing a person can look.

Liam wearing a suit isn't something new to me. But with the way he's wearing his hair, the tender smile in his eyes, the colors of his clothes…the very colors that I have branded on my skin in the form of his name…he just looks different somehow.

I lift my eyes heavenward. *God, you did really good when you made Liam Hunter. Really, really good.*

I bring my eyes to him and smile. "Well, look at you, all handsome and hot."

He catches me around the waist, pulling me to him. "You look beautiful and hot and sexy. I want to lift this dress up and get down on my knees, so I can put my mouth on your pussy and taste you right now," he whispers over my mouth before pressing his lips to mine.

Wow.

I shudder as his tongue curls around mine. He tastes like mint and hot sex and everything Liam.

His fingers skim down the back of my dress, cupping my ass through it. The un-tattooed ass cheek.

I'm wearing the last nice dress I have that I brought with me. It's white and strappy, fitted around the bust and floats off the hips, and it's pretty. Liam told me to wear something pretty. So, pretty, I'm wearing.

His lips slow, and his eyes focus on mine. I'm sure mine are filled with lust right now. Oodles of lust.

"But my Boston tasting will have to wait, as we have to go."

"Oh, okay." Can't say I'm not a little disappointed, but I also know that Liam going down on me would, without a doubt, end up in sex. And I don't want to get all messed up. I look pretty.

"You got everything you need?" he asks, releasing me.

I pat the clutch—holding my lipstick, cell, money, and key card—under my arm, which somehow managed to remain tucked there after his hot kiss. "Ready. So, where are we going?" I ask, taking his offered hand, letting the door close behind me.

He gives me a secret smile. "You'll see."

Liam and his secrets.

Taylor and her secrets.

Except Liam's secrets always have me smiling.

Mine…not so much.

I'm surprised to see that Paul isn't waiting for us, but instead, Liam's Bugatti is parked in front of the hotel.

The doorman tips his hat to me as we leave. I smile at him.

We reach the car, and Liam gets my door for me. I manage to get inside without showing my panties, and he shuts the door with an expensive clunk.

I put my seat belt on and watch him as he makes his way to the driver's seat, loving the way he walks with such confidence and authority. Liam gets in and starts the engine. He puts on his seat belt and then pulls out into the evening traffic.

Liam's not talking. His fingers are tapping on the steering wheel along to the song playing on the stereo— Jason Aldean and Kelly Clarkson's "Don't You Wanna Stay." But it's not a happy tap, not that it's an overly happy song, but…there just seems to be almost an edge to him that wasn't there before. And it's weird.

I kind of want to ask him what's up, but at the same time, I don't as well.

So, instead, I say, "I love this song."

He gives me a smile that doesn't reach all the way to his eyes, and then he just turns the music up.

Okay.

His lack of response and action sets my good mood into unease, so I just stare out the window, looking for a sign of where we might be going, as I hum along with Jason and Kelly.

I'm surprised when I see that we're near where he lives.

I'm even more surprised when he pulls into the underground parking garage at his apartment building.

"Did you forget something at your place?" I ask him.

With ease, he reverse-parks his car into his parking space, turns the engine off, and puts the emergency brake on. His eyes meet mine. "No. This is where we're spending our evening."

"Oh. Okay."

I'm not disappointed that we're at Liam's apartment. I love being at his place. I just thought we were going out somewhere, as he'd told me to dress up and he's wearing a fancy suit.

Liam gets out of the car. I climb out my side, and I meet him at the front of the car.

He takes my hand in his and leads me to the elevator. Calling the elevator, the door opens. We walk in, and he punches in the code to his apartment. The door closes, and we ride up in silence.

When we reach his apartment, he keys in the code and opens the door, letting us in. The lighting is low.

He closes the door behind us. Then, he takes my hand again and leads me through the apartment, heading through the kitchen.

He stops by the door to his roof terrace. He smiles at me and then pushes it open. "Your romantic movie moment, Boston."

I give him a curious look and then step through the door. The air is surprisingly warmer up here than it was downstairs.

In all my time spent at Liam's place, I've never been out here before.

It's gorgeous. There's a seating area to the left of me. To my right is a table with two chairs, all set up with plates and silverware, and champagne is in a bucket standing by the table.

And fairy lights are hanging everywhere—literally everywhere you could put them. They're entwined along the railings that edge the whole area. They're draped over the small shrubs and trees that sit in planters. They're hanging from the trellis.

They're just everywhere, and it looks so pretty.

Music is softly playing in the background. London is receding into dusk. The sky is a soft dusty pink.

And I'm in heaven.

I walk further out, looking around in awe. "This is amazing." I turn to face him. "I can't believe you did this for me."

Well, I can. Because he's done so much already.

His hands are in his pants pockets, his head slightly tilted to the side, his eyes watching me. "There isn't much I wouldn't do for you, Boston."

A smile touches my lips. "Like getting your ass tattooed?"

A heartbreaking smile glides onto his mouth, and I have this feeling of fullness in my chest.

"That would be at the top of the list," he says.

Liam walks toward me. My heart is dancing in my chest. My eyes follow him up until he reaches me.

"Dance with me," he says.

"You dance, too?"

"I do a lot of things, Boston. You just have to let me show you."

I wish I had the time to let you show me everything.

Liam takes ahold of my hand, bringing it up with his, and his other hand goes around my waist. He starts moving me with him in time to the music.

The song playing in the background is the Daniel Bedingfield's "If You're Not the One." It was playing when I stepped through the door.

Has it come on again?

"You're a Daniel Bedingfield fan?" I tease, looking up at him.

"So many things you don't know about me, Boston." He shakes his head. Then, a teasing smile slides onto his lips. "Actually, no. But I don't mind this song. It's the only one of his I know." He chuckles.

"Me, too." I giggle. "But it is a beautiful song."

"You're beautiful."

"So smooth," I tease.

"I do try."

A moment later, he starts softly singing along to the words.

"This another one of your smooth moves, Hunter? I thought you only pulled out the serenading to girls who've dumped you?" I bite down on the smile pushing up my lips.

"Oh, I totally sing to girls whose knickers I want to get into as well," he deadpans.

"Well, you don't have to sing to me to get into my *knickers*." I aim for an English accent on the word *knickers*. It doesn't come off so well.

But it makes Liam laugh.

"Hunter, when will you learn? I'm always a sure thing when it comes to you."

He stops dancing, letting go of my hand. "Well, seeing as though you're a sure thing, guess I didn't need to buy you this then." He puts his hand inside his jacket and pulls out something from his inside pocket.

A jewelry box. One that's exactly the size of a ring box.

Oh, fuck.

My heart stops in my chest.

"Don't worry; it's not a ring."

My heart restarts.

I stare up into his eyes. My lip lifts at the corner, and I bite down on it. "Was I that obvious?"

"You had the fear of God in your eyes." He laughs softly.

Not because I wouldn't marry you, Hunter. I swear, if I could, I would marry you a hundred times over.

"Sorry."

"Don't be." He smiles. "But do open the box."

I take it from his hand. I pop open the lid, and inside is a pair of silver earrings. They're little jet planes. Blue, yellow, and pink make up the colors on the plane.

My heart feels like it's bursting. My eyes fill with tears. I bite my lip to stop them from coming.

"I know you're not the biggest fan of planes. But I just saw them, and I don't know...I saw them and saw you."

"I love them." I blink up at him.

"You do?"

"I really do."

And I love you.

I reach up on my tiptoes and kiss him firmly on the lips. "Thank you, Hunter," I whisper, lowering back down to my feet. "I want to put them in now."

"Will that be okay after just having your ears pierced?"

When Den pierced my ears, he said I was to keep earrings in permanently for four to six weeks. He didn't say anything about not changing those earrings.

"So long as I put them in straightaway, it'll be fine. It's only the holes healing up that I need to worry about."

I hand Liam the earring box and start removing the earrings that I'm wearing, the ones put in when I had them pierced.

It hurts a little, but I brave it.

I have a brain tumor. I can take a little ear pain.

I remove the airplane earrings out of the box and drop the old ones inside.

Liam snaps the box shut and places it on a nearby table.

I fix the last earring in. "How do they look?" I hold my hair back, showing him my ears.

"Perfect."

"If You're Not the One" comes to an end, and then it starts playing again.

Liam glances back at his iPod system. "What the fuck?" he mutters.

"You got this song on repeat?" I giggle. Guess I was right before when I thought it had played again.

"I didn't think so, but apparently, I have. I'll go change it."

"No, leave it playing. I like it."

As soon as the words leave my mouth, I feel a big raindrop hit the top of my head. Then, I see one splash on Liam's forehead.

His eyes go up to the sky. "For fuck's sake." He heaves out a sigh.

Another raindrop hits my nose, and then the heavens open, and rain comes pouring down on us.

I start laughing.

Liam looks at me like I've lost my mind. Then, he starts laughing, too.

"Come on, let's go inside."

"No." I stop him with my hand. "*Dance in the rain.*" I smile. "It's on my list."

Aside from *get totally wasted until I vomit and pass out, dance in the rain* is the last thing left on my list.

Getting drunk can be done at home. I probably should hold on to that one for when I leave Liam. I'm sure I'll want to get hammered to numb the pain of no longer having him.

Dancing with Liam in the rain is the last thing I have left to do with him.

My smile fades, but I still say, "Dance with me in the rain, Liam Hunter."

Rain is trickling from his hair, down his face, catching in his long lashes, dripping off his nose. And he's never looked more beautiful to me than he does right now.

He clears the rain from his face with his hand, and he takes me in his arms again, moving us to the music.

Our clothes are soaked, rain is splashing up my bare legs, my shoes are soggy, my hair is drenched, my mascara is probably running down my face, and I don't care.

Because I want this moment with him.

The last list moment.

Liam's eyes look into mine. There's a raindrop running down his nose. I catch it with my finger. He smiles.

"I totally planned for it to rain," he tells me. "I remembered that *dance in the rain* was on your list, and I thought, *Well, what's more romantic in a romantic movie moment than dancing in the rain?*"

Soft laughter escapes me. "You control the weather now as well, Hunter?"

"Boston," he deadpans, staring me in the eyes, but I see the twinkle in them, "I control everything. When will you realize this?"

I laugh again, shaking my head at him.

Then, I lay my cheek against his wet jacket. The rain has slowed, but it's still coming down around us.

"So…Taylor?"

I lift my head when he says my name. He rarely says it when he's not inside me, so I know what he's about to say is important.

I catch sight of his throat working on a swallow. It makes me nervous for some reason.

"I have something I want to ask you." He's nervous. It's there in the tone of his voice, in his eyes, and in the way he bites his upper lip.

My heart starts to beat faster, but my feet slow to a stop. "Okay. What is it?"

Liam starts moving us again, like he refuses to stop dancing. I go with him, but my feet feel like lead.

"Well…" He exhales softly. "I guess…well, what I want to ask is…"

He's faltering, and I've never seen Liam falter before. He's Mr. Confident. He exudes it in the way he moves, talks, breathes. But, right now, he's Mr. Nervous As Hell, and it's making me more nervous by the second, turning my stomach over.

Liam stops dancing, and he stares down into my eyes. "Taylor…" He blows out a breath. "Well…this is the part in the movie when the guy asks the girl to stay with him."

"Stay?" My voice cracks on the word.

"Yeah." He takes his hands off my body and puts them around my face. "I want you to stay here with me in London—permanently. I want this…I want *you*. I want to keep adding to your list. I want to fill it with new things for us to do together. I want to keep having this adventure with you, babe. The thought of you leaving and me never seeing you again…it's inconceivable to me. I want you, Taylor. Forever."

He wants me. Forever.

You know that moment in life when you're faced with a decision, that crucial moment, that will change everything based on the choice you make?

There's where I *should* find myself right now.

But I'm not there.

Because I don't have a choice.

I never have.

There has only ever been one option for me.

I step out of his hold. His hands fall from my face to his sides.

"I'm sorry. I…I can't stay with you." I'm backing up, away from him, heading for the door.

The look on his face should stop me in my tracks. But it doesn't.

That look on his face is one of the reasons that I have to go.

Stay, my heart whispers.

I can't. I have to leave.

Somehow, I reach the door. I turn for it.

"Don't go." Those softly spoken words hit me with the force of a harsh blow.

If I turn and look at him, this will all be over. My heart will make me stay.

I can't stay.

I'm past options now.

Because, if I do stay, I will die here. And he will have to see that.

I'll hurt him.

I'll be just as bad as his mother and Kate. No, I'll be worse. Because I've known all along that I'm dying, and I chose not to tell him.

"Taylor," he says my name, closer this time.

I place my heart into a steel box, and I force myself to turn to him, but I don't look at his face.

"What's…happening right now?" The words are soft and etched with pain.

That pain hits me hard.

"Two weeks," I whisper, my eyes on the ground, watching the raindrops splashing as they hit the ground. "Two weeks, and that was supposed to be it."

"I changed my mind." His voice is deep, sure. "I fell in love with you, and I changed my mind."

My eyes snap up to his face.

He's in love with me.

I've never felt such a sensation as the one I'm feeling right now. It's like being hugged and slapped across the face at the same time.

"No." I shake my head, glancing at him, still unable to meet his eyes, my fingers curling around the door handle. "You weren't supposed to fall in love."

Anger and pain pull his brows in. "Well, I did. And I think you love me, too."

He takes another step toward me.

I grip the handle tighter.

I'm still shaking my head. I'm not sure at what anymore, but I can't seem to stop.

"I know you love me, Taylor. I see it in your eyes when you look at me. In your voice when you talk to me. In your laughter…" He takes another step closer, his voice lowering. "In your body every time I slide inside you."

My body shivers. My head has stopped moving. I wrap my arm over my stomach. I can't even feel the damp and cold on me anymore. All I can feel is him and his words.

"No," I whisper, my eyes fixed on his chest that's getting closer by the second.

"Tell me I'm wrong," he says like he didn't hear my word. "Tell me that you don't feel the same as I do, and I'll let you walk out that door. I won't try to stop you." Another step. "But I know I'm not wrong, Taylor. I just can't understand why you won't admit it."

Because I'm dying.

Because I don't deserve you.

Because I owe my family…

I might love Liam.

But I love my family more.

"I love you," he whispers. "I'm so fucking in love with you, Taylor."

I close my eyes against the onslaught of pain.

I love you, too, Liam. So much.

But it's not enough.

Then, I shut everything down inside me, putting up steel walls and concealing the truth behind them, because it's all I can do. I pull in a breath and force my eyes up to his, staring straight into them.

"You're wrong." I keep my voice even. "I'm not in love with you. I'm sorry." *And I am sorry. So very sorry.*

The look on his face…I can put as many steel walls around me as I want, but the look on his face and the pain in his eyes right now…breaks through every single one of those walls, tearing them and me apart.

And that's why I can't stay a moment longer.

I turn my eyes from him, yank open the door, and run.

I run through his apartment and out the front door, and I don't look back.

Reaching the elevator, out of breath, tears mixed in with rainwater streaming down my face, I hit the call elevator button. The door opens immediately.

I fall inside, and I press the button for the lobby.

The door closes, and the elevator starts to descend.

I lean against the wall.

Coldplay's "Paradise" is playing in the elevator. Some might call it a coincidence. But, to me, it's a sign from above.

They're calling for me.

I shut my eyes and rest my head back, exhaling out. "I'm coming," I tell them.

My time with Liam is over.

It's time to go home.

LIAM...

chapter 29

I'm sitting on a chair in the middle of my roof terrace.

The place is still lit up like a Christmas tree. The champagne is still sitting in the cooler by the table. The plates and silverware are still in place on the table. The dinner I cooked last night is still on the counter in the kitchen.

Everything is the same as it was last night.

Except *she* isn't here.

I'm alone.

And I'm a good halfway through a fifth of whiskey, which I've been drinking straight from the bottle, 'cause that's how I roll nowadays. I'm just missing the brown paper bag around it.

Also, I'm staring at Squishy and Ducky, who I brought out from the bedroom where Taylor had left them on the nightstand on her side of the bed—she had a side of the bed—and I have set them on the floor in front of me, so I can stare at them and torture myself with thinking about Taylor while getting drunk and listening to Daniel Bedingfield on repeat. It's still playing from last night. I never turned it off.

After Taylor ran out of here and I picked my heart up off the floor, I realized that she'd left her bag. I panicked, knowing that she was out in the city with no money and phone. Her hotel was a good thirty-minute walk from my place.

I could have gone after her, but I was sure she wouldn't want to see me, so I called Paul and had him drive around and look for her.

He found her soaked through and walking in the direction of the hotel.

He got her in the car and drove her the rest of the way. That's what I'd told him to do.

I'd already called ahead to the hotel to make sure they had a new key card ready for her, as that was in her bag, too.

Paul saw her up to the hotel room and made sure she got in safe.

Then, I had him come back here, get her bag, and take it to her.

I wanted to hold on to it, so she would have to come back. But I knew it wouldn't be right because that wasn't the reason I wanted her to come back.

I want her to come...for me.

But she hasn't.

I haven't heard anything from her since last night. And, now, it's today. The night is starting to come in, and I don't know what the fuck to do.

I've just alternated between wandering around my apartment to lying in bed and smelling the pillow because it smells of her.

Yeah, I've turned into *that* guy.

So, now, I'm sitting here like a fucking loser, well on my way to getting drunk, listening to the same sad song because it makes me think of her, and I'm wondering what she's doing right now.

Yeah, I'm wallowing. Fucking sue me.

I do know Taylor is still at the hotel, as I told them to call me if she checked out. Or anytime she left at all.

Stalker-ish, I know, but I don't fucking care.

God, how did I fuck up so monumentally?

I asked her to stay.

She said no.

So, I told her that I loved her. And, like the cocky bastard I am, I said that I knew she loved me, too.

Then, she told me that she didn't love me, and she ran out of here like her arse was on fire.

I laugh out loud at myself. Then, I choke on that laughter 'cause it feels like I might cry. So, I take another slug of whiskey to wash it away.

What a fucking idiot.

Why didn't I just keep my mouth shut?

I was so fucking sure of myself.

Of course, there was a part of me that was worried she'd say no. But I was so sure that she felt the same as I did about her, so either way, we'd work something out. That I wouldn't lose her completely.

How very fucking wrong I was.

I pushed hard, and she ran.

And, now, I don't know what to do.

I just want her to come back. I want to be near her all the time. Have fun with her. I've never laughed as much as I have in the time that I've spent with her.

She lights everything up around her.

She lights me up.

And, now, everything just feels dark.

I put the bottle down on the floor, and then I get up and walk over to the railing. I look out at London. Staring at the city moving beneath me.

She's out there without me.

And, more than anything, I just want her here with me.

I shouldn't have asked her to stay. It was stupid.

And, now, the small amount of time I have with her is gone because I scared her away.

Who could blame her? A week and a half together, and I'm asking her to live here with me. Not go back to her home. To stay and live in mine.

And she's only twenty-two. I forget that sometimes. When I'm with her, the ten years between us seems to evaporate.

When I was twenty-two…well, I was with Kate. But I was setting up my business and seeing the world while I did it.

I was living.

That's what she came here to do. And I tried to clip her wings by asking her to stay with me.

What the fuck was I thinking?

I wasn't. That's the problem. I let my heart get the better of me.

I let my heart go after what he wanted.

Stupid fucking heart.

Fuck, I can't stay here, stuck in my own head, all night. I'll go insane. I need to go out.

Pushing off the railing, I go back inside my apartment.

I grab my wallet, phone, and keys, and then I head out.

Downstairs on the street, I flag a cab to Cam's Bar.

I walk in. Adele is wailing "All I Ask" in the background. Guess I can torture myself with depressing songs here, too.

Cam's behind the bar, serving a customer. Eddie's here, too, sitting at the end of the bar, nursing a pint.

I haven't seen either of them since I lost my temper with them last week.

They've both texted me, but being the wanker that I am, I haven't replied.

Stupid because, aside from my grandpa, they're all I have.

I sit on the stool next to Eddie. His eyes come to me. I see the flicker of surprise in them.

"Hey," I say quietly.

He gives me a nod, and then he picks up his pint and takes a drink of it.

"Look, man, I'm sorry I haven't been in touch. I was being—"

"A prick," Eddie inserts.

I let out a laugh. "Yeah, I was being a prick."

He looks at me again. Then, he turns his eyes to Cam, who's just spotted me and is walking toward us.

The look on Cam's face is contrite. He doesn't look mad at me. He looks...sorry.

"Liam," Cam says, "I'm sorry about last week. What I said—"

"Nothing to be sorry for," I cut him off. "I'm sorry I've been MIA this past week."

His eyes meet mine in a slow understanding. Then, he nods. "It's okay."

"You've probably had Taylor keeping you busy, so we won't take complete offense," Eddie says. His tone is a little lighter, so I know he's forgiven me.

I snort out a laugh through my nose. "Yeah, I've been busy with Taylor."

"Where is she?" Cam asks. "Has she gone back to America?"

"Not yet. A few days to go." I'm pretty sure she won't be spending her remaining time with me after I declared my love and sent her running.

"So, where is she?" Eddie asks. "She saw sense and dumped your sorry arse?"

"Yeah, something like that."

There's a pause, and then Eddie says, "For real?"

I glance at him. "Yeah."

"Shit, I'm sorry, man. I was just kidding when I said that."

"I know." It's nothing I wouldn't have said to him.

"Sucks, man," Cam says. "I know you liked her."

I love her. I don't say that though.

"So, what happened?" Eddie asks me. "You seemed really into each other."

"Apparently, she wasn't as into me as I was her." I take a deep breath, readying myself to tell them what happened. Might as well go all in. "I asked her to stay with me permanently in London. She said no. That was last night, and I haven't heard from her since. Don't reckon I will again, to be honest."

Both of them are staring at me, mouths agape.

I've silenced Cam and Eddie.

It must be bad.

Cam clears his throat. "I'll get you a pint." He reaches for a glass and starts pulling me a beer.

"Wow. Fuck. So…you like her a lot then," Eddie says.

"Yeah." I let out a tragic-sounding laugh. "Unfortunately, the feeling isn't mutual."

"That might not be the case," Eddie goes on. "I mean, you did ask her to leave her home and family and move in with you after knowing her for, like, a week."

A week and a half, but I don't correct him.

"It's a big deal, Hunter, asking someone to leave their home like that. It would definitely take some thinking."

I don't tell him that she has no family back home. That there is no one there for her to go back to…that I know of.

Maybe that's it.

Maybe that's why she won't stay. Because someone is waiting at home for her.

Pain slams into my chest. I grit my teeth, grinding them.

"She's not thinking on it, Eddie. She said no."

"Could've just been a knee-jerk reaction," Eddie suggests.

I know he's trying to make me feel better, but it's not working. Because my mind is now on overtime, wondering if there's someone else. If she has a boyfriend waiting at home for her…

"Why don't you call her?" Cam puts my beer down in front of me. "See where her head's at today."

I could, but the truth is, I'm afraid. Not that I'd tell these two that.

So, I just shake my head.

"You asked her to stay," Eddie says. "That took some balls, Hunter. If you can do that, you can call her. I mean, you put yourself out there. You haven't shown an interest in a woman to that degree since Kate, so that means something."

I slice a look at him.

He holds his hands up. "I know there's that unspoken rule where we don't talk about her in front of you. But it's true, man. Since Kate died…there's been no one of substance for you."

I stare down into my beer and think about Kate…and Jeremy.

I never thought I would trust another woman again after her.

But I trusted Taylor. Still do.

And Taylor means so much more to me, even in the short space of knowing her, than Kate ever did in the six years we were together.

"Kate was having an affair with Jeremy."

Eddie's head snaps around so quick that I hear it click.

"They were having an affair?" Cam steps closer to the bar.

I can see his eyes lighting with anger.

I blow out a tired breath and nod my head. "I found out the night before the funeral. I got her phone out of the stuff I brought back from Switzerland. I was…missing her. I found some texts…from Jeremy." I let his name hang there for a moment before I continue, "They'd been having an affair the whole time I was with her. It'd started just after we got together. There were…emails that I found on her laptop. They told me everything I needed to know."

"Motherfucker," Eddie seethes.

Cam isn't saying anything, but his face is tight with anger.

He feels betrayed for me but for himself, too.

I get that.

I stare back down into my beer. "After finding that out, I had to go to her funeral and pretend like everything was okay—well, not okay, but you know what I mean." I sigh. "And then Jeremy fucking came over, telling me how sorry he was, how he was there for me for whatever I needed. I just…lost it."

"And you punched him," Eddie says. "I'm fucking glad you did. But how you didn't do more, I'll never know. Because I'd have done a lot more than punch him. I'd have beaten the bastard to death. I will beat the bastard to death when I see him next."

"Why didn't you tell us?" That's Cam, and he sounds hurt and disappointed.

I don't meet his eyes. I just shake my head. "I don't know."

I do. I was afraid.

"I guess…I wanted to protect Kate's memory."

"She didn't deserve protecting," Eddie says bitterly.

"Ed…she betrayed me. Not you and Cam. Me. And she was your friend. I didn't want to sully the memory you had of her. And her parents…I didn't want them to be affected by it. They'd always been good to me."

"So, you kept it to yourself and let us think that you were being a shit to Jeremy…Jesus, Liam." Cam shakes his head at me. "I've carried on with being his friend all these years. You should have told us. We wouldn't have told anyone else, but we sure would have kicked the fuck out of him for what he did to you and then kicked him out of our lives."

I lift my eyes but don't look at them. "You've known Jeremy longer than me…since primary school. I guess I…" I trail off because I can't say it.

"You thought we'd have chosen him over you." Eddie sounds even more disappointed in me than Cam did.

Won't lie. It fucking hurts.

"How could you think that? You're our friend," Cam says vehemently. "Our best friend. Yeah, we've known Jeremy a long time, but with him, it's never been like it is with the three of us, and you know that. It's always been me, you, and Eddie. Jeremy just coasted in and out of our friendship. Even now, I see you way more than I see him. He's an occasional friend. You're my best friend."

A lump climbs up my throat. I fight to swallow it down.

"And you have the most money and a private jet, so of course, we'd pick you," Eddie says, a loose smile on his face.

And his words are just what I need to stop myself from crying like the pussy I'm turning into.

Fighting a smile, I shake my head. "Good to know you just want me for my money."

"And your private jet. Don't forget the jet." Eddie's grin gets bigger.

"How could I?" I chuckle.

Cam leans his forearms on the bar and stares me in the eyes. "Liam, we're your mates, your best mates. So, don't you ever fucking keep anything like that from us again. You got me?"

"I got you." I tap two fingers to my head in a salute.

My heart might still feel heavy over Taylor. But it feels lighter from telling them the truth.

Cam straightens up, and as his eyes lift, he freezes. I know he sees something behind me because there's a distinct shift in his expression.

Someone's here, and I have a feeling it's someone I don't want to see.

I swear to God, if it's Jeremy, I'm going to nail the cunt to the wall.

"There's someone here to see you." Cam lifts his chin in the direction of the door behind me.

I look deeper into Cam's expression. He doesn't look angry. He looks…pleased.

And that has me spinning my stool around, my gaze zeroing in on the door.

Taylor.

She's here.

My breath catches as my eyes connect with hers. My heart takes off like a racehorse in my chest.

I slide off my stool, my feet hitting the floor with a thud.

People are moving between us, but I don't lose eye contact with her for a second.

I need to do something. *Go to her.*

I force my feet forward, cutting up the space between us.

My moving seems to set her off, and she slowly walks toward me.

We stop a few feet away from each other in the middle of the pub.

"Hi." Her voice is soft but laced with unease and a hint of sadness.

And it reaches into my chest and curls around me.

I can't speak.

I've wanted to talk to her all day, and now, I can't think of a thing to say.

Everything I want is standing in front of me, and I'm here, acting like a fucking mute.

All I have running through my mind is that I want her to stay.

But, the last time I said that, I sent her running.

I want to take the fact that she's here as a good sign. That she's changed her mind, but I know better than to presume things in life because, sometimes, presumption can come back to smack you in the face with reality. And she hurts like a motherfucker.

"You're here," I finally say because I'm a dumb fuck and because it's all I've got at the moment.

Her eyes move from my face and lower to the floor, her lips pressing together, and my heart sinks.

Because, in that moment, I know she isn't here to stay.

I rub the heel of my hand against the ache in my chest.

"You're not staying, are you?" It's not a question because I already know the answer. I just need to hear her say it.

I need to know why she's here.

Her blue eyes—eyes that always make me think of the sky on a sunny day—lift back to mine.

I can see a world of sadness in them. The sadness she always thinks she's hiding is now clear for me to see.

Taylor shakes her head, and at the same time, she quietly says, "No." Her voice breaks on the word.

And that one single word breaks my fucking heart.

So, I do what I always do when I feel pain. I get angry.

"So, why the fuck did you come here?" I bite out.

Tears instantly shimmer in her eyes, and her lip trembles.

And I feel like a bastard, and that pain in my chest only intensifies.

She bites her lip and closes her eyes, blowing out a breath. Then, her eyes open and focus back on me. "I just...I didn't want to leave things the way we'd left them last night." Her voice is soft, like a whisper, but the blows that come with each word feel like hits in the face. "I didn't want us to end like that."

"I didn't want us to end at all, but we don't always get what we want."

And I've boarded the train to Bitterville.

She exhales a sad sound. "I wish…" She trails off, her eyes looking away from me.

It angers and hurts me that she can't even bring herself to look at me.

"You wish what, Taylor?" I fold my arms over my chest and make my tone sound impatient, like she's a bore on my time. But it couldn't be further from the truth.

She is the *only* way I want to spend my time. Every second of every minute of every day with her.

She is my time.

Or I wanted her to be.

Her eyes come back to me, another soft breath leaving her. "Nothing." She slowly shakes her head. "I wish…nothing."

And, because I'm a bastard, I say, "So, we done here?"

Surprise glitters her eyes. "Yes. I just—"

"What?" I snap. "What the fuck else do you have left to say?"

Probably something else to cut my heart open a bit wider. *Should I get you the knife to do it with?*

Her eyes shimmer with those tears again.

And I fucking hate myself.

She blinks rapidly, clearing her eyes. "I'm sorry," she exhales quickly. "I just wanted to say thank you. For everything."

Blade in the chest.

I stare past her at the door. "Fine. You done?"

There's a long pause before she says, "Yes."

Her word is soft, and it hurts worse than anything I've ever felt before, and I've felt pain.

But, now, we're done, and I don't know what to do.

I called time on this conversation. So, all I can do is walk away.

But I don't want to.

Still, pride has me turning around and walking back over to the bar, taking my seat next to Eddie.

"Okay?" he asks quietly.

I pick my beer up and nod. I don't look at him. I can't. Because, if I do, I'll probably fucking cry.

I take a big mouthful of my beer. It hurts to swallow. Everything hurts. I can't remember a time I felt this bad. Not even after I found out about my mother.

I put the glass down, staring into it.

Taylor's leaving, and I'm never going to see her again.

We're ending on bad words and anger.

But isn't that how everything ends? With pain and sadness.

Is there such a thing as a happy ending? Because, if there is, I've never fucking seen one.

Should I go after her?

But what good would it do?

You want her, and she doesn't want you. End of story.

And she's probably gone by now.

But she might still be here…

If she's changed her mind, then she'll still be here.

I shouldn't look.

But like the masochist I am, I need to know, and I'm turning my head and looking over my shoulder before I can stop myself.

She's still here.

My heart soars for a split second, but then my mind is quickly telling me that something's wrong.

She's standing not far from the exit, faced away from me, her hand tightly gripping the top of a nearby chair. I can see the white of her knuckles from here. Her head lulls forward, and her free hand clutches at it.

She must be having another one of her headaches.

I might be hurting and angry and bitter, but I don't want to see her in pain. I know how bad these headaches can get for her.

"Taylor," I call out, as slip off my stool, taking a few steps toward her. "You okay?"

She doesn't respond.

I think she hasn't heard me, so I part my lips to speak again, but then she turns. It's a slow turn.

Her face is pinched in pain. Her hand is still pressed firmly to her head.

She lifts her eyes to mine. It seems to hurt her to do so.

Something in her expression makes my heart start to race.

"Taylor…what's wrong?" I'm moving toward her.

She winces, lips pinching. Her eyes close. Then, they open, and it's like the light in them has been turned off.

Her lips part and whisper the words, "I'm so sorry, Hunter."

And then she just drops to the floor.

"Taylor!" I run to her, falling to my knees beside her. I pull her into my arms.

She feels limp.

Fuck! No!

Eddie is here in seconds, and he's in doctor mode.

"Taylor, honey." He lifts open one of her eyes by gently pushing her lid up with his thumb, and he shines a light in it. A little torch he got from his pocket. "Taylor? Can you hear me, honey?"

She doesn't respond.

Her eye…it looks…blank.

No.

My heart stops.

Leaning over her, Eddie presses his cheek against her chest.

Cam falls to his knees beside me. "I called an ambulance. One is on its way."

"Is…she…" I stare at Eddie as he lifts his head, the words stuck in my throat.

"She's breathing," he says.

"Thank God," Cam says.

All I can do is exhale as my heart starts back up.

Eddie picks up her wrist and starts checking her pulse.

My mouth is dry. "Ed…what's wrong with her?" My voice sounds small.

Eddie's stare meets mine. "I don't know yet." He looks back at Taylor and puts his hand to her face. "Taylor, honey, open your eyes for me."

Nothing.

"Come on, Taylor. Wake up, honey. You're scaring the shit out of Hunter, and you know what a giant pussy he is." Eddie pats her cheek. "Come on, Taylor. Wake up, and I promise, I'll buy the next round of drinks. Anything you want."

But she's not waking up. She's not responding at all.

"Why isn't she waking up?" My voice is panicked.

I'm scared. I've never been so afraid in all my life.

And helpless, so very fucking helpless.

"I don't know." Eddie slowly shakes his head.

"You don't know?" I yell. "You're a fucking doctor! You're supposed to know! You're supposed to help her!"

Knocking his hand from her face, I cup her cheek and turn her face to mine. "Come on, Taylor. Please open your eyes for me, baby. *Please.*"

I'll beg, do whatever is necessary to get her to look at me again.

Please, Boston, please wake up.

I need you to be okay.

But she's not responding, and I have never felt fear like this before in my life.

Unadulterated fear.

"Has she been ill at all recently?" Eddie asks me.

"No—well, yes. I mean, she gets these headaches from time to time."

"What kind of headaches?"

343

"I don't know! Headaches!" My fear is coming out as anger, and it's directed at Eddie.

"Do the headaches last for long?" Eddie continues, my anger just brushing over him.

"No." I shake my head, frustrated. "Well, yes. I mean, they come out of nowhere. She's fine one minute, and then *bam*. They knock her off her feet—literally. One time, she vomited from the pain. But she takes these pills that her doctor gave her, and she's fine a few minutes later." I look him in the eyes. "That's what I thought was happening just before she collapsed. She was clutching her head, like she always does when a headache is coming on."

"Liam"—he slowly says my name. There's caution in his voice, and it scares the shit out of me—"you say her doctor prescribes her these pills?"

"Yes."

"What kind of pills are they?"

"I don't know." I grit my jaw, frustrated. And she doesn't have her handbag with her so it's not like I can check.

I look back down at her, rubbing my hand over her cheek, patting it.

Please, Taylor, please wake up.

"The headaches—has Taylor ever told you what causes them?" Eddie asks me, that fucking caution back in his voice.

"She had a brain tumor when she was sixteen," I say, staring down at her. "She said the headaches are a lingering result of that." But, as I say those words, as I hear them out loud, coming from my own mouth, it's like I'm slowly slipping underwater.

The headaches.
Her list.
Things to Do Before I Die.
Fuck…no.

I meet Eddie's eyes, and I see it written there. He thinks…

Jesus, Taylor.

No.

"No," I say, my eyes filling with tears. I pull her closer to me, holding her close. "It's not that. It's not—*no*." I firmly shake my head. "If the tumor were back, I would have known. She would have told me."

Wouldn't she?

"You're probably right." He doesn't mean that. I can hear it in his voice. The dip in his tone. The way he flickers a glance at Cam. The concern in his eyes when he looks back down at Taylor.

My Taylor.

I hear the scream of an ambulance siren approaching in the distance.

"She's going to be okay," Cam says to me. His hand touches my shoulder and squeezes.

I stare blankly at him. Then, I take my eyes back down to Taylor's beautiful face.

She looks like she's sleeping.

Pain lances through me. I shut my eyes against the onslaught of emotions.

My mind is running wild with everything she has ever said to me.

"Babe, you're rubbing cream onto my arse and singing Bieber's 'Sorry.' Really not sure how to feel about that."

"Maybe I am sorry."

Sorry. *What was she sorry for?* The tattoo—back then, I thought that was what it was. But, now, I'm not so sure.

"I'm sorry. I…I can't stay with you."

"Two weeks. Two weeks, and that was supposed to be it."

"You weren't supposed to fall in love."

"Don't talk about you dying so flippantly. Someone like you is meant to live forever."

She wrote a list.

A list of things to do before she dies.

Jesus. No.

Why didn't you tell me, Taylor? Why?

She's sick. She's dy—

The thought is like a hole being punched through my chest.

No, I can't—I won't accept this.

I won't lose her. Not my Boston.

Why didn't I see it before now? I should've paid more attention.

I hate myself in this moment. Really and truly hate myself.

The pain I'm feeling is like nothing I have ever felt before. It's unbearable.

Heartbreakingly fucking unbearable.

I can't lose Taylor. I won't survive it if I do.

Then, the paramedics are here, and they're taking her from my arms, laying her flat on the floor. One is checking her over. The other is asking me questions, but I can't speak. Eddie takes over, answering the questions.

And then she's being moved. Put on a stretcher and taken out of the bar.

Away from me.

No!

I try to go with her, but they won't let me.

"We'll follow in my car," Cam says, pulling me back.

Then, he and Eddie are guiding me out of the bar and into Cam's car. We're following the ambulance where the only woman I've ever truly loved lies inside, and she might be dying.

Dying.

I shut my eyes.

Don't die, Taylor.

Please don't die.

chapter 30

"Taylor Shaw's family?"

I'm on my feet and walking over to the doctor who just called out Taylor's name.

She looks young, about the same age as Taylor. I know she isn't though. Because of Eddie, I know how long doctors have to train.

The doctor looks similar to Taylor. Small, petite, blonde hair—well, except Taylor's hair is pink now.

But she could be Taylor.

Only she couldn't be. Because there is no one like Taylor.

She's one of a kind.

My one of a kind.

"How is she?"

"You're Taylor's family?"

"He's her brother." Eddie's voice comes from behind me, his hand pressing down on my shoulder.

Immediately, it clicks in my head why he's said that. They won't tell me anything unless I'm family.

She doesn't have a family anymore.

But she has me…whether she wants me or not.

"I'm her brother," I confirm. "How is she?" The urgency is clear in my voice.

"I'm Dr. March. I've been caring for Taylor since she arrived."

"I don't fucking care what your name is. I want to know how Taylor is."

"Liam…" Eddie's voice is a gentle warning.

I scrub my hands over my face. "I'm sorry." I blow out a breath. "I just need to know that she's okay."

I've been here for hours with no news at all. With the waiting, fear has built up inside me to the point of explosion.

"Let's talk in here." Dr. March gestures to the door.

I follow her through, my heart beating. Cam and Eddie are with me.

She looks at them with unease.

"You can talk in front of them." My tone is impatient. I've waited long enough now.

"I'm a doctor here at the hospital—Dr. Breckon, Cardiology," Eddie tells her.

That seems to ease her mind.

She looks back to me. "Okay, so Taylor is stable at the moment. She did have a seizure in the ambulance on the way here. And then another one when she was taken to get a scan."

The thought of her having seizures, and I wasn't there…pain slices through my chest. I press my hand to it.

"We stabilized Taylor and went ahead with the MRI." Dr. March pauses, taking a breath. "There is no easy way to say this…but the scan shows that there is a definite significant growth on Taylor's brain."

"Significant growth?" Cam says.

"A large tumor," Dr. March clarifies. "Malignant and aggressive in form."

I suck in air, closing my eyes. My heart feels like it's bleeding out in my chest, flooding my lungs.

I feel Cam's hand press against my back.

"I would normally recommend surgery immediately," Dr. March continues, like I'm not dying inside. "And then bouts of radiation therapy shortly afterward to offer a chance of survival."

Would?

I flick open my eyes. "Would?" My word echoes my thought.

"Mr. Shaw—" She thinks my name is Shaw because of Taylor. Because she thinks I'm her brother.

"Liam."

"Liam...there is something I need to ask you." Dr. March shifts on her feet, folding her arms over her chest. "Did you know that Taylor has been aware for some time that she has a tumor and that she hasn't sought medical treatment for it?"

She knew.

Deep down, I knew she knew. But it still hurts like hell to know for sure.

All this time, and she never said a word.
How did I not see it?

I shake my numb head, answering the doctor.

"Well, we're not exactly sure how Taylor knew about the tumor with her not seeing a doctor prior to today—"

"She had a brain tumor when she was sixteen. She knows the symptoms," I tell her, my tone short.

I don't why, but I don't like Dr. March. Maybe it's because she's the one delivering the bad news. Whatever it is, she's irritating the fuck out of me. I can feel my anger level rising.

"That would explain the scar tissue on her brain that also showed up on the MRI." She looks me right in the eyes with an almost accusatory look in her own. "We couldn't seem to locate any medical records for Taylor. She wasn't showing in the system at all. Do you know why that is?"

"Didn't she tell you? Taylor lives in America—Boston. She's here, visiting."

Completing her list.

"Taylor hasn't really been telling us much." Dr. March shifts on her feet again. "Only that she knew about the tumor, and…" She trails off, her eyes sweeping the floor.

My brows draw together. "And what?"

She swallows down, clearly uncomfortable. "Well…Taylor is saying that she doesn't want any…treatment."

"What?" The word comes out on a shocked breath. I feel the blood draining from my face.

She meets my stare. "Taylor is refusing treatment of any kind. She's adamant that she doesn't want surgery. She doesn't want to get better. She wants to…" Her words fall off.

Her eyes sweep the floor again. The place where my heart now is.

"Die." The word comes out of me on an agonized breath.

Her eyes meet mine. "Yes."

God, Taylor, no. Why?

I try to pull in air, but I can't seem to. I feel my body sway. Cam's arm comes around my shoulders, holding me steady.

I feel like the walls are closing in around me.

My eyes shut against the absolute fucking agony the knowledge brings.

She wants to die.

"Taylor…said that?" Eddie says. His disbelief only mirrors a small part of what I'm feeling.

Shock, disbelief, fear, agony, and absolute fucking helplessness.

"Yes. Those were her exact words," Dr. March says softly.

I open my eyes and look at Dr. March. "I don't understand." My voice is barely working.

Why, Taylor? Why?

I need to see her. Now.

"Neither do we." She shifts her stance again. "Liam, are you sure that Taylor hasn't said anything to you?"

She's said everything, except for that.

"If she had, do you think I would be standing here, having this fucking conversation with you?" I yell.

Cam's hand grips my shoulder where it still sits. I know he's trying to calm me, but I don't feel calm.

I feel like tearing this building apart until I find Taylor and force her to explain to me what the fuck she is thinking and then force her to have the surgery.

"I'm sorry. I wasn't trying to—" Dr. March starts.

I cut her off with a wave of my hand. "You said the tumor is operable?"

"Yes. As it is now. But the window of opportunity is narrowing. If the tumor is left any longer, it will go past the point of removal. Then, there will nothing we can do for her."

There's a chance. I just need to make Taylor change her mind.

But she wants to die.

I can't comprehend it in my mind.

Taylor is amazing, so full of life. Her laugh alone is worth living for. She has so much to give the world.

Why would she want to give up on that?

Give up on life.

I have to make her see sense.

But what if you can't? that small voice in the back of my mind says. *What if nothing you say matters, and she dies anyway?*

Someone doesn't just make the decision to die lightly. She decided on this long before she met me.

She's known this whole time.

I can't even feel betrayed because I just feel afraid. So very fucking afraid.

I have to change her mind. Because I can't see a world without her in it.

But I couldn't even get her to stay in London with me. I wasn't enough. *So, how is what I say going to be enough to get her to save her own life?*

Especially when I don't know what's going on in her mind, why she's even doing this.

"Doctor, if Taylor...if I can't get through to her and she continues to refuse treatment, is there any way you can do the surgery without her consent? Force her to have it done?"

I hate that I have to ask this, but I need to know what my options are before I go in and see her.

Because I won't fucking lose Taylor.

I won't just let her die. I will do whatever is necessary to keep her alive.

"Liam..." That's Eddie.

I turn my face to him. The look on his face makes my hope drop to its knees, just like I want to.

"The hospital can only obtain a court order to enforce treatment if we believe someone isn't of sound mind or if it's a child."

"Maybe she isn't of sound mind." I hate that I'm saying this, but I know tumors can affect people, change their personalities. "The tumor could be pressing on her brain, making her think and act differently than how she normally would. Making her think she wants to give up when she really doesn't."

I look at Dr. March. She would know. She's the one treating Taylor.

But the expression on her face takes my hope from its knees and lays it flat on the floor.

"Behavioral changes are always a possibility with brain tumors...but, in Taylor's case, I don't think it is." She

352

shakes her head. "I believe Taylor to be of sound mind. She is lucid and very clear on what she wants. I am sorry."

She sounds like this is already over. Like Taylor is going to die.

Fuck that. Fuck her and everyone.

It's not over.

I won't let it be over.

I won't let Taylor just kill herself.

"I need to see her."

"I'll take you," Dr. March says.

"We'll be in the waiting room," Eddie says to me.

"We're here for you, man." Cam gives my shoulder one last squeeze before letting go.

I follow Dr. March down a corridor and through a set of double doors.

She finally comes to a stop outside a door near the end of the corridor. "Taylor is in here. Now, please try not to upset her. Any stress—"

"I won't upset her."

Dr. March nods and then walks away.

I take a strengthening breath, and then I slowly push the door open. It doesn't make a sound.

The room is dark, except for the light on by the bed. She's lying on her back, pillows propping her up, her face turned away from me, staring out the window at the night sky.

Just the sight of her hurts me.

She looks so small, the bed swallowing her up. Her hair is spread over the pillow, the light highlighting the pink in it. Her skin looks smooth with a golden glow.

She looks beautiful.

She doesn't look sick.

She doesn't look like she's…dying.

Agony crushes its fist into my chest.

353

Letting the door go, I move further into the room on quiet feet. "Taylor…" I gently say her name as I near the bed.

Her body stiffens, and then her head slowly turns on the pillow, her eyes meeting mine.

The look in them terrifies me. She looks closed off. The only other time Taylor has looked at me like this was last night…when she told me that she didn't love me.

Taking a breath, I force myself to speak, "I spoke to the doctor." My words are quiet with meaning.

I stop at the end of the bed, my hands gripping ahold of the footboard where her medical chart hangs.

I stare at her face, willing her to tell me it's not true. That the doctor has got it wrong.

"She told you?" Her voice sounds dry, croaky.

"About the tumor? Or that you're letting yourself die?"

Guilt floods her eyes, and she looks away.

I have my answer.

And, fuck, does it hurt.

I grip the bed harder to keep upright. "I don't understand," I say, my voice broken.

"I don't expect you to." Her voice is soft, but the words incense me, like she just yelled them at me.

"Maybe you don't. But what I expect is a fucking explanation. Hell, I deserve an explanation. Because you don't get to just do this, Taylor. You don't get to just decide that you're going to die, and that's it." My voice is lifting with the desperation I feel inside me.

Her eyes slowly come back to mine. "Yes, I do. It's my life, Liam. My decision."

"But I fucking love you." I slam my hand against my chest. "Doesn't that mean I at least get a say? Or do you have to love me back for that to be the case?"

She closes her eyes, as though the words are painful for her to hear.

Good.

I want emotion from her. I don't want this dead-in-the-eyes look that she has at the moment.

Because she's not dead.

And she never will be if I have anything to do with it.

"I'm sorry," she whispers, her eyes opening back up.

"Don't be sorry!" I cry. "Just don't fucking do this."

She turns her face away from me, like she's dismissing me, and that sets me off again.

"Jesus Christ, Taylor! What is happening here? Why would you do this to yourself?"

She presses her lips together in a tight line, telling me that I'm further losing her.

I need to calm down.

I pull in a few breaths, trying to slow my racing heart. "Please," I say gently. "Please just talk to me."

"There's nothing to talk about." Her voice is stone cold.

"I'll beg if I have to. If that's what you need to change your mind. I'll get down on my fucking knees and beg." I move around the bed, forcing her to look at me. "I'm not asking to be in your life. I'm not asking you to love me. I just want you to live. I could live a life without you, knowing that you were out there, breathing and alive and happy. Just don't ask me to let you die."

She stares down at her hands that are in her lap, fingers curling around the blanket covering her. "Liam…please don't do this. I've made my decision. I made it a long time ago. Long before I met you."

"But you did meet me. And we spent time together. I know you don't love me, but I know you feel something for me. You can't deny that. And it has to count for something."

Her head is shaking, slow and steady. "I'm sorry."

She doesn't say it differently to the other times she's said sorry. But something is there this time that tells me there is no changing her mind.

I've lost her.

Or maybe I never had her at all.

I stand here, numb, just staring at her. My feelings for her and all the confusion and hurt and frustration I feel builds inside me like a monster.

And I let him out.

"I won't watch you die." My voice is as bitter and harsh as my words are meant to be.

She looks up at me. Clear eyes meet mine. "I would never ask you to do that."

I don't recognize her in this moment. Her eyes are completely empty of emotion. Blank and glassy.

Taylor's eyes have always been full of something. Whether it was the sadness she always thought she was hiding. Or those rare moments when she would let that sadness slip away and allow herself to be happy. Or those times when her eyes were filled with so much lust and longing for me that I couldn't breathe while looking at her.

But whether her eyes were filled with sadness or happiness or lust, there was always life in them.

Or maybe there never was. I was just seeing what I wanted to see because I wanted her so badly.

"You need to make me understand, Taylor. Because I don't understand why you are choosing to die."

"You don't need to understand."

"Yes, I do!" I'm yelling now, and I don't care. Because I don't know what else to do, how else to get through to her. "I need to understand why you don't want to live anymore! You're asking me to stand back and let you die. You're asking me to live with that knowledge for the rest of my life. Then, give me the reason."

Her lips come together, her eyes closing on a long blink. "It's complicated."

"Then, uncomplicate it."

"I can't." She shakes her head.

I explode. "You have to! Because I fucking deserve to know the truth!"

"Because I owe them!" she cries, sitting forward. "I have to die because I owe it to them!" The moment the words leave her mouth, she winces in pain. Her brow creases, and her hand comes up to her head, the heel of it pressing against her forehead, as she closes her eyes.

"Taylor…are you okay?" I keep my voice soft, but inside, I'm panicking and afraid and ready to call for the doctor.

"I'm fine," she whispers. She lays her head back on the pillow, her hand falling away to lie on the bed beside her, her eyes opening.

"I'm sorry," I say.

"Don't be. I'm the one who's sorry. I'm sorry for all of this. I didn't ever mean for you to see me this way."

"What you mean is, you didn't ever mean for me to find out."

She exhales a tired-sounding breath, her fingers curling into the bed covers again.

Her silence gives me my answer.

My heart is aching with every hard beat it takes. I wrap my arms around my chest. I back up, leaning against the windowsill. "So, what were you going to do? You were just going to leave here and go back to Boston? And then what?"

Her eyes come to mine, the answer clear in them.

Die.

She was going to leave here, leave me, and go home to die.

I'm not a crying man. It takes a lot. But, right now, I want to cry.

Pinching the bridge of my nose, I close my eyes, taking breaths to hold it in.

All I want to do is beg her to change her mind. Beg her to stay. Beg her to live.

"I'm sorry I've hurt you." Her soft voice is like a thousand knives plunging into my soul.

I drop my hand, opening my eyes. "You haven't hurt me. You *are* hurting me."

Her bottom lip trembles. She bites it. "This isn't what I wanted."

"What did you want?"

She stares into my eyes. I see a flicker of emotion. Real emotion.

And it gives me hope.

Then, her eyes shut down, taking my hope away with it.

"I don't know. But I didn't want this. I didn't want to hurt you. Hurting you was the last thing I ever wanted."

My hands curl around the windowsill, gripping tightly.

I need to get to the root of this. She's talking, but she's telling me nothing. So, I go back to the words she said before. The words she yelled at me.

"You said you owe them. That you have to die because you owe them. Who do you owe, Taylor?"

I'm pretty sure I already know the answer. I just need her to say it.

I need her talking to me.

She pulls in a deep breath. "My family." Her eyes come back to mine. "I owe my family."

"Why?" I ask carefully. Because I know how easily she can shut down when it comes to her family.

I've always known losing them affected her badly. I know how hard it is to lose people you love. That's why I never pushed her to talk. I always figured she'd tell me when she was ready.

I just pray to God that she's ready now. Because I have a feeling that their deaths is why she's doing this.

Her lips tremble again, tears glistening in her eyes. She bites down on her lips, taking in a breath. "They died because of me. I owe them my life because I took theirs."

"Babe...I don't understand." I keep saying that same sentence, and I'll keep saying it until I do understand.

And then, when I do understand why she's doing this, I will change her mind.

"The list...I wrote it when I first found out I had a tumor. My mother knew about the list. She knew what was at the top of it—*go to London*. I had always wanted to visit here. So, she and my dad said we would take the trip when I was better. They expected me to get better. They never for a second believed I would die. Their belief made me fight to live." She lets out a sad-sounding breath. "I should've died when I was sixteen. If I had died then, they would all be alive now.

"When I was eighteen, I recovered from the tumor, and we planned the trip to England. All packed and ready to go, we were due to fly out at five p.m. the next day. I would be starting at Northeastern as soon as we got back, and my best friend, Marie, was leaving for New York. She had a place at NYU. I wasn't going to see her until winter break. I begged my parents to let me stay at her house, so we could have one last girlie night together. They said I could, so long as I was home first thing in the morning.

"When I was getting my stuff to take to Marie's, I realized my lucky hoodie was dirty. My dad had gotten me it from Harvard. I'd had it for years, and good stuff always seemed to happen when I was wearing it. Once, when I was wearing it, Brian Packer asked me to winter formal. Then, I was wearing it when I made the softball team. Stupid, but I was young, and I thought good stuff would always happen when I was wearing it. Before I left to go to Marie's, I asked my mom to wash it for me, so I could wear it on the flight. I was nervous to fly, and I figured nothing could happen if I wore my lucky hoodie.

"But I was wrong. It wasn't lucky at all. My mom must have put it into the wash after I'd gone to Marie's and forgotten to put it in the dryer straight after. She must have realized right before bed. The dryer was on...it was faulty...and it caught fire.

"Taylor..."

"They didn't know the downstairs was on fire because they were all sleeping, and the fire alarm didn't go off.

"A few weeks prior, the fire alarm had kept going off, and it was driving me nuts, so I complained to my dad. He took the batteries out. Said he'd buy another.

"He hadn't gotten around to it...and the smoke got to them first. The fire marshal told me that they didn't suffer..."

"Taylor," I say her name again, moving toward her.

She lifts a hand, stopping me. "I should have died from the first tumor. This is my second chance to get it right."

"That...no, that doesn't make sense to me."

"It does to me." Her eyes lift to mine.

The grief and pain in them almost bring me to my knees.

"I need to see them again," she says softly, agonized. "I need to tell them how sorry I am. I need them to forgive me." Tears run from her eyes and down her cheeks.

I want to go to her, but I know she doesn't want me near her.

So, I stand here, helpless.

"Taylor...your family...they wouldn't want this. They wouldn't want you to die."

With her arm, she brushes the tears away. "You don't know that."

"Yes, I do," I say with certainty. "They loved you. They wouldn't want you to do this to yourself. When you love someone, you only want the best for them. This isn't the best."

"Yes, it is. This is the best for me—paying my penance and being with them. That is what's best for me."

"Taylor...*please*. You need to listen to me. You can't just give up on life like this."

Her eyes come to mine. "I'm not giving up on life. I just want to be free of the pain of missing them…free of hating myself for what I did. I want my family back more than anything. And…I *need* their forgiveness."

Tears are falling again, running down her beautiful face. And I don't care if she wants me close or not. I have to be near her.

I sit on the edge of the bed beside her. "Taylor…what happened…it wasn't your fault. It was a tragic accident. But it wasn't your fault."

She shuts her eyes and dries the tears from her face with her hands. Then, she opens her eyes back up and says, "No." She shakes her head, determined. "It was my fault."

"I don't believe that. And I know your family wouldn't think that either."

"You didn't know them, so you can't make that call," she snaps.

"No, I didn't." I keep my voice gentle. "But I do know you. I know the person they raised you to be—loving, warm, caring, and amazing. So fucking amazing that I couldn't help but fall in love with you."

She closes her eyes again, but I keep talking, "And I might not have met your parents, but I do know those two people you talked about that day at the university, those two people who fell in love and fought to be together, because I saw them through your eyes, babe. I don't believe for one second that they would want you to die. They gave you life. They raised you. Loved you. They sat by your side and fought with you through that first tumor when it threatened to take you away. They would want you to fight now."

"That was before I killed them." She opens her eyes but doesn't look at me.

"It was an accident, babe. A tragic accident. Please…don't do this. Fight to live. If not for yourself, then do it for me. I know you care about me—hold on to that, fight for that. *Please*. I'm begging you."

My heart is beating hard against my chest, fear shaking my body, my mind praying that my words will finally reach her.

She looks at me with a flicker of warmth in her beautiful eyes, and I'm reminded of all the times I've stared into her eyes and seen that warmth and the hope and happiness that it made me feel.

And that tiny bit of hope I have left clings to that warmth in her eyes and silently begs her to live.

She exhales slowly. "You're right. I do care about you, Liam…so much." Her breath catches, and a tear slides down her cheek. She catches it and brushes it away.

"Taylor…"

She brings her eyes to me, and she doesn't need to say anything. I know from the look in them that I've lost her.

She's gone.

That tiny piece of hope I had left is crushed, right along with my heart, and I don't stop the tears that fill my eyes. I let them be. And I let them fall.

She turns her face away from me and stares out the window. "I'm sorry, Liam. It's too late. I want this. I want to die. I want to be with my family. It's the ending I want."

"*It's the ending I want.*"

I couldn't stay at the hospital. Not after hearing her say those words.

Those five words…so final. I knew there was nothing I could say or do to change her mind.

I felt helpless. I still do.

For the first time in my life, I know there is nothing I can do.

There is no arguing. No fighting. No reasoning.

I can't change this.

Even though everything inside me is screaming for me to fight, I know it'd be pointless.

You can't change a person's mind if it's truly what they want.

And Taylor wants to die.

This vibrant, beautiful woman wants to die.

I feel like I don't know her. Maybe I never did.

And I don't know how to deal with that…with any of it. So, I left her there, in that hospital bed, and I walked away.

Now, I just feel lost.

And, when I feel lost, I go to the only place that's ever felt like home.

Well, apart from Taylor.

She felt like home.

From the moment I met her, I knew that she was different. That my life was about to change. I just didn't realize how it would change.

Two weeks, and she's stolen my heart completely.

Every time I touch Taylor, I feel grounded…that safety that only home can give you.

But that's gone now, and there's only one place I can go to get some sense of assurance that everything is going to be okay even though I know beyond a shadow of a doubt that it won't ever be okay again.

Nothing will ever be okay if Taylor isn't here, lighting up the earth.

By the time Cam and Eddie drove me to my apartment, the sun was starting to rise. We'd been at the hospital all night. They had wanted to stay with me, but I told them that I wanted to be alone.

And, at that moment, I did. I wanted to be alone with my pain. I wanted to be alone to think. To try to make sense of all this.

But, when I walked inside my apartment, she was everywhere. On every surface. Every smell and sound…her.

I could hear the echo of her voice and laughter. The feel of her body pressed against mine. Her scent…her *everything*.

In such a small space of time, she had consumed my mind and body. She had become what life should be about.

And I lost it.

Desolation hit me, and I had never felt more alone than I did in that moment.

Still do now.

So, without even showering or changing, I left my apartment.

I walked the streets of London for hours, watching people heading to work, shops opening up. All I could think of was the bus tour of London that we did.

I walked into Hyde Park, the fair long gone. The memory of being there with her is forever embedded in my mind.

I left the park, and all that was in my head was, *She's here, lying in a hospital bed in my city.*

I had left my apartment to get away from the loneliness, from her, and she was everywhere.

So, I went back to my apartment and got my car keys. I climbed in my car and started driving to the only place that'd ever filled that emptiness inside me. To the one person who had never let me down.

When I pull up outside Hunter Hall, I expect to feel a little better, but I don't.

Because all I remember is being here with her.

I was stupid to think I could escape by coming here.

My grandpa is already out the front door and walking over to me, like he knew I was coming.

He probably did. There are security cameras everywhere.

I turn the engine off. Taking a deep breath, I get out of my car.

I don't move. I can't move. So, I just stand there.

"Liam?"

I hear the concern in his voice as he approaches me because I never just turn up like this. I always call to tell him I'm coming. And I must look a fucking mess. I haven't shaved, and my clothes are wrinkled.

"Liam, what's wrong?" His voice takes a stern edge.

I know it's because he's worried, but I don't know how to say this.

He stops before me. "Talk to me."

I can feel those fucking tears fighting to get out again. I take in a deep gulp of air. It even hurts to breathe. I lift my eyes to look at him. "I don't know what to do, Grandpa. I need your help…because I don't know what to do."

Concern flickers over his face. And then he does what he always does. He wraps his arms around me. "I'm here," he says. "Whatever it is, we'll fix it."

I try to feel comfort in his hold. I try to soak up his reassurance, but it doesn't work. Because I know it's not true. No one can fix this.

Only Taylor.

And she doesn't want to be fixed.

"Let's get you inside." His arm is around me, guiding me into the house. "Archie, can you make coffee?" Grandpa calls to him. "Or do you want something stronger?" he asks me.

Only my grandpa would suggest alcohol at ten thirty in the morning.

That actually manages to lift the corners of my lips.

"Coffee's fine," I tell him.

"We'll be in the sitting room," he hollers to Archie.

"I'll bring it through," Archie calls back from somewhere in the house.

Grandpa steers me into the sitting room and down into an armchair, and I let him because I don't have the strength right now to do anything myself. It took everything I had to drive here.

He takes the armchair opposite me. "Tell me what happened."

My grandpa doesn't beat around the bush. He's always been a straight-to-the-point man—just like I am.

So, I tell him everything, only pausing when Archie brings in the coffee. I tell Grandpa about Taylor—her list…what happened to her family. I tell him about asking Taylor to stay in London with me. About her collapsing in Cam's bar, going to the hospital…the tumor…and lastly, the conversation I had with her before I left.

I tell him that she wants to die.

He lets out a long breath. "Liam, if Taylor wanted to die…really and truly die, she would have done it long ago."

"What?" I stare at him.

"Look, this is going to sound harsh, but if a person really wants to kill themselves, they'll do it and make sure it sticks. People throw themselves off of bridges and under trains and swallow a handful of pills to ensure they don't have to live."

"She is killing herself." I grit my teeth.

"She's letting herself suffer because she thinks she deserves it. There is a difference. Taylor might truly believe that she wants to die. But, deep down, if you dig in far enough, there is a part of her that wants to live. The part of her that put her on that plane and brought her here to fulfill that list. The part of her that allowed herself to be with you, to care about you.

"Right now, Taylor is eaten up by guilt, and she's punishing herself in the only way she knows how. She can't make the decision for herself whether she should live or die, so she's letting the tumor do it for her. If you want to reach her, Liam, then you have to reach that part of her that does want to live, remind her of what it's like to truly be alive, what it's like to be happy again."

"That's what I've been doing this last week and a half with her—showing her happiness and helping her to face her fears and showing her what it's like to truly live."

"Then, maybe she's not as far gone as you think she is."

I shake my head. "I saw her in that hospital room, Grandpa. I heard the words she was saying. She's already gone. I've lost her."

"She's fighting an internal battle. I saw the way she looked at you, Liam. She lit up around you—and you, her. I haven't ever seen you look at someone the way you look at her."

It's because I've never loved anyone in the way I do Taylor. It's that comes-out-of-nowhere-and-grabs-ahold-of-you love. The kind where you can't remember how you ever felt anything before her. The all-consuming, nothing-else-matters-but-her love.

That's the love I feel for Taylor.

"I know Taylor has deep feelings for you, and those feelings are provoking the guilt she feels over her family because of what she believes she owes them—her life. But a part of her wants you, too. But, to have you, she has to live. And, if she lives, in her mind, she'll be failing them again."

I ache at the thought of the pain and turmoil she must be feeling. The pain she's been feeling for so long.

"You need to make her see that's not the case," Grandpa continues. "That she doesn't have to die. That she doesn't have to pay for something that wasn't her fault. That she can have a life with you. She deserves to be happy. And then, one day, after she's lived a long life, then she can see her family again."

"I tried, Grandpa. I told her these things, maybe not as eloquently as you just put it, but she wouldn't hear them."

"Then, you make her hear. You keep trying. You don't just give up at the first hurdle, Liam. You're a fighter. You always have been. No matter what life has thrown at you, how many times it's knocked you down, you've always gotten back up, ready to fight. Don't stop now. Fight for Taylor, and fight hard."

My phone starts to ring in my pocket. The first thing I think of is Taylor.

Is it her calling?

I quickly get it out. My heart sags when I see it's not her number calling. I don't recognize the number ringing me. But I answer because I gave the hospital my number and told them to call me if there were any changes with Taylor.

"Hello?"

"Liam, it's Dr. March."

I stand up out of my seat, my heart stopping. "What's happened? Is she okay?"

"We, um…I'm afraid I'm not sure."

"What the hell is that supposed to mean?"

"Taylor's gone."

"She's gone?" I gasp.

My grandpa gets to his feet.

"That's why I'm calling—to tell you that she left the hospital without anyone's knowledge. A short time ago, the nurse went into her room to take her vitals, and her bed was empty. Her clothes and shoes that she had arrived in are gone from the cupboard. We've searched the floor to make sure she hasn't…fallen anywhere and hurt herself, but there are no signs of her. So, I got security to check the cameras, and she was seen leaving through the main entrance over a few hours ago."

She's been gone a few hours.

My heart starts to beat faster.

"I was hoping that she had come to you?" Dr. March says.

No, she wouldn't come to me because I'm not who she wants.

I close my eyes, my insides crushing. "No, she hasn't come to me."

"Do you know where she could have gone?"

I shake my head. "I'm not sure. Maybe her hotel."

Then, it hits me. She's going home.

The last thing Taylor said to me was that she wanted to be with her family.

She was always going to go home. That was her plan all along.

She's going home to die.

Fuck…no.

"Of course, with her condition, I'm worried for her," Dr. March goes on. "But my hands are tied. There isn't a lot I can do, as she isn't deemed a danger to herself—"

"I know where to find her," I cut her off.

She exhales. "Good. When you do find Taylor, please try to get her to see reason and come back to the hospital."

"I'll do everything I can." And I will.

I hang up the phone, and immediately, I dial Taylor's number.

Voicemail.

Fuck!

Frustrated, I hang up.

"Taylor left the hospital?"

I'm guessing Grandpa caught wind of the conversation I just had. After all of his attempts to convince me that this isn't truly what she wants, even he now looks worried.

And it makes me feel sick.

"She walked out a short time ago."

I'm moving to the door and out of the room. He's following me.

"You know where she is?"

"I know where she's heading." I yank open the front door and step through it. I turn back to him. "She's going home. And I'm going to stop her before she does."

chapter 32

I've pulled out of my grandpa's driveway, and I'm speeding down the road when my phone rings again.

The number shows up on my dash; it's one of my hotels in London. The one Taylor's staying at. They were under instructions to call me if she checked out of the hotel.

I connect the call through the Bluetooth.

"Speak now, and make it quick."

There's a slight pause, and then a male voice says, "Um, sir, it's Patrick Squires calling. I'm the day manager at—"

"I know where you're calling from. What I want is for you to tell me if you're calling about Taylor Shaw."

I take a hard turn and then slam my foot back down on the gas.

"Yes, sir, I am. I saw there was an instruction to call you if she checked out—"

"She's checked out?"

A brief pause, and then he says, "Yes, sir."

"When?"

"About an hour ago."

"An hour ago! And you're only calling me now!" My hands white-knuckle the steering wheel.

"I'm sorry, sir. Perrie, the girl who checked her out, is new with us. She must not have seen the notice that was on Miss Shaw's file. I only noticed that she'd gone because I was working through today's departures. I asked Perrie if she had called you—"

"She's fired."

"Yes, sir," he says quietly.

I blow out a breath.

An hour ago. She left a fucking hour ago. It takes about that time to get from the hotel to Heathrow, depending on traffic. She could already be at the airport. And I don't know our fucking flight itineraries to Boston.

Fuck!

I take the exit onto the M40, heading for London. Getting on the motorway, I press my foot down hard, pushing the car as fast as she'll go.

"Sir?" Patrick's voice comes in the car.

I forgot for a moment that I was still on the phone.

"Did Taylor get a cab when she left the hotel?" I ask him, my voice hard.

"Yes, sir. I asked Martin, our porter, before I called you. He said he put her in a cab, but he doesn't know where she was heading. Sir, I am sor—"

I cut the call off. I swear to God, if I hear one more person say they're sorry today, I'll fucking kill them with my bare hands.

Except Taylor.

Taylor can say whatever the hell she wants to me. She can say sorry as many times as she wants, so long as there is something at the end of it…a chance. A chance that she will change her mind.

I search through my contacts, looking for the number for our ticket desk in terminal five at Heathrow Airport. Driving and looking through my phone while I hit close to a hundred miles an hour in the outside lane probably isn't the best idea.

I find the number and hit Call, focusing completely on the road and getting to Taylor.

The phone rings, echoing around my car, and then the call connects. "Hunter Airways Ticket Desk, Amber speaking. How may I help you?"

"Amber, it's Liam Hunter calling."

Silence.

Then, she says, "Liam…Hunter, as in—"

"The guy who pays your salary."

"Oh. Wow. Hello, sir. How can I help you today?"

"I need you to tell me when the next flight to Boston is?" I check the time on the dash—twenty-eight minutes past one.

"Let me just check."

I hear tapping on keys.

"Okay, the next flight with us out to Boston is…at five p.m. Check-in opens in half an hour."

I know Taylor's return flight is tomorrow, but she could have changed that.

"Okay, Amber, I need you to tell me if a Taylor Shaw has tried to change her ticket from tomorrow's flight to today. Or if she's even bought a new ticket. Basically, I just need to know if she's trying to get on that five o'clock flight."

There's a slight pause. "Sir, I can't give out flight information on passengers. Our policy states—"

"I know what the policy states. I fucking wrote the thing. Now, tell me if Taylor is trying to fly out of Heathrow today."

"Sir…it's just…I know you say you're you, but how can I be sure it is actually you? You could be anyone."

I let out a growl of frustration. "What's your surname?"

Another pause. "Crawford."

"Okay, Amber Crawford, when you're getting your final pay slip and being escorted from the premises in about, oh, say, ten minutes, then you'll fucking know it was me. Now, either tell me if she's tried to change her flight, or I can fire you, and then you can put me on the phone with somebody who will do the job I'm fucking paying them to do!"

Another brief pause, and then I hear the clicking of keys.

"Taylor Shaw hasn't changed her flight from tomorrow to today, and she hasn't purchased a ticket for today's flight either, sir."

I feel a beat of relief. But just because she hasn't tried to change her flight doesn't mean she won't. She could be walking in there right now, heading to the desk where Amber is sitting.

"Do you have a pen and paper?"

"Yes."

"Write this number down." I rattle off my phone number to her. "If she turns up at the desk, I want you to call me immediately."

"Yes, sir. Should I put a flag against her name in the system in case she doesn't come to the desk and tries to change the flight by telephone?"

I don't think Taylor would do that. I think she's in the cab on the way to the airport to change her ticket and leave. But I still say, "Yes, and put a note to call me right away."

"Sir, do we let her change the ticket?"

"No."

"And if she wants to purchase another?"

"Tell her the flight is full."

"Won't that only send her to another airline though, sir?"

Fuck, she's right.

I start doing the math in my head. I was going to go straight to my apartment and get my passport. I figured, if I couldn't change her mind, if she chose to get on that flight and go back to Boston, then I was going to go with her, whether she wanted me there or not.

I'm not leaving her side again until I make her see sense. Make her see that the only place she needs to be is here with me.

But, if I do that, I'll have to drive right past the airport and then another thirty minutes to my apartment and back to the airport.

Fuck! Why the hell did I go to Oxford?

I'll have to take my chances and go straight to the airport. Stop Taylor from getting on that flight. Beg her to stay. Beg her to let me take her back to the hospital.

If she gets on that flight, then I'm screwed. I might own an airline, but I'm not God. There's no way I'll be flying into Boston without my passport.

"I'm thirty minutes away," I tell Amber. "When she shows up, keep her there, and don't let her leave, no matter what."

"Yes, sir."

I press the button to disconnect the call, and I put my foot down, speeding down the M40, heading for Heathrow as fast as my car will get me there.

chapter 33

I slam my brakes when I reach the drop-off bay at terminal five, and I jump out of my car, locking it with the fob as I hurry away, heading toward the doors to get inside. I'll get a parking ticket for sure, leaving it here, but like I give a fuck.

I just need to get in there as fast as possible.

Amber hasn't called back to say that Taylor has shown up, but that doesn't mean she isn't there.

I pick up speed, breaking into a fast jog, pushing past people, as I head inside the terminal and straight for the ticket desk.

As I approach, I see a young redhead sitting behind the desk—Amber, I'm guessing—but there's no sign of Taylor. I don't know whether to be happy or worried.

I skid to a stop at the desk, slamming my hands down on the counter.

Amber's eyes come up from the computer she was looking at. Her eyes widen when she sees it's me.

"Mr. Hunter—sir"—she stands up from her chair—"Miss Shaw hasn't shown up or called. I was just checking to make sure she hadn't called to change her ticket." She turns the computer screen to show me.

My brow furrows in confusion.

Taylor should be here by now. She got the cab over an hour ago.

Even if she didn't come to the ticket desk right away, surely, she would be here now, as check-in is now open, as it's past two o'clock.

"Is there anything else I can do to help, sir?"

That's when I realize I haven't actually said anything to Amber.

"No. I'm fine."

I cast my eyes around the airport bustling with people, but there's no Taylor.

Where are you, babe?

"Well, anything you need, just let me know."

I give Amber a brief nod. "I'm just going to wait here until she turns up."

"Do you want a chair?" She gestures to her own chair.

I shake my head. "I'm fine, standing."

I'm too restless to sit. Nervous energy is burning up inside me.

I turn and lean my back against the counter, folding my arms over my chest, and I start watching the people coming in and out, looking for pink hair and a beautiful face.

Where are you, Boston? Come on, baby, throw me a fucking bone here.

Show up. Please.

I need to make you see sense.

I need you…

"Would you like anything to drink while you wait?" Amber asks from behind me.

I shake my head. "No, thanks."

I catch sight of pink hair, but it's too bright.

Where are you, Taylor?

A thought crosses my mind. *What if she was never coming here?*

What if she was—

No. No, she is going back to Boston. I'm sure of it.

She already made her decision. Those were her last words to me. Doing this trip and then going back to Boston to die has always been her plan.

So, I'll wait here until she shows up. And if she doesn't, then I…I honestly don't know.

"Sir…are you sure there isn't anything else I can do? Call through to the other terminals in case she decided to take a different flight to America or maybe a connecting flight?"

"Yeah, sure," I say distractedly, still scanning faces.

I don't think for a minute that Taylor would take a connecting flight. She hates flying, so the idea of her having to get one flight, only to change to another…no, she wouldn't do it.

The thought of her grumbling about it almost makes me smile.

"Okay, I'll start making calls. Sir…Miss Shaw…she's important to you?"

I glance back at Amber over my shoulder. "She's all that's important."

She gives me a gentle, sad kind of smile.

I face back ahead and continue to search every face that comes into the airport, looking for the only face that matters.

She hasn't shown.

Check-in closed thirty minutes ago. The flight to Boston is due to leave in fifteen minutes, and she hasn't arrived.

I walked around the airport, looking for her, having Amber keep guard at the ticket desk, but nothing.

Taylor hasn't shown. Or called.

I've tried calling her multiple times, and all I've gotten is her voicemail.

And, now, I'm scared. Because I have no clue where she is.

I was so sure this was where she was heading.

So, either she's gone somewhere—somewhere I have no fucking clue about—and she's still taking the flight home tomorrow…or she decided not to wait for the tumor to take her, but to take matters into her own hands.

My eyes close painfully on the thought.

No, she wouldn't do that.

But then I didn't think she'd ever slowly kill herself.

What if she's been struck down with another headache or, worse, a seizure, and she's hurt somewhere?

Fuck.

I can't take any more of the not knowing. The waiting.

I don't know what to do.

I get up out of the chair I finally sat in earlier when my legs were aching from standing and walking around. "I'm gonna head out. Thanks for your help, Amber."

She gives me a sad look. "I'm sorry she didn't show up."

Not as sorry as I am.

"I'll leave the flag in the system, and if she does turn up, I'll let you know straightaway."

"Thanks." I push my hands into my pockets and start to walk away.

Then, I stop and turn back. "Amber?"

She looks up from her computer screen. "Yes, sir?"

"I'm sorry I yelled at you on the phone earlier."

She gives me a small smile. "It's okay."

I turn and walk out of the airport, desolation weighing heavily on my shoulders.

I walk up to my car and see a clamp on the wheel.

Pressing my lips together, I shut my eyes and heave a breath out through my nose. "Motherfucker."

I don't even have the will or energy to get pissed about it.

I'll have to leave it. I'll get Pam to sort it.

As I walk to the taxi stand, I fire off a text to Pam, letting her know that my car is clamped at Heathrow.

I get an immediate reply.

Pam: Will sort ASAP.

I reply.

Me: Thanks.

Then, I shove my phone back in my pocket.

Only a few people are ahead of me in the taxi line, so soon, I'm in a cab and giving the driver the address to my apartment building.

Letting out a sigh, I tip my head back on the seat and stare up at the ceiling of the cab, feeling more lost than I ever have in my life.

In the background, on the cab's radio, Oasis's "Don't Go Away" is playing.

I swear, music is set to torture me nowadays.

I let out a laugh, but it's not humorous. It's pained. This fucking hurts more than anything has hurt before.

She's gone.

She came into my life and made it the best it's ever been. She made me fall in love with her, and now, she's disappeared, and I don't know where she is.

I have no clue if she's even still ali—

Pressure quickly builds behind my eyes. Closing them, I press the heels of my hands to my eyes and then push my fingers into my hair as I take a deep breath.

I won't think that way. I refuse to believe that she'd go through with it.

I have to have hope because it's all I've got left.

I'll just go back to the airport again tomorrow when I know she's scheduled to fly, praying to God that she shows up.

In the meantime, I'll keep trying her phone and hope she turns it on.

I drop my hands from my head and force myself to stare out the window, trying to think about anything but what's happening now. Focus on tomorrow when I do find her and make her stay. Make her live.

When the cab finally pulls up outside my building, I pay him the fare and climb out.

I push open the main door to my apartment building. Sid, the building's security manager, is sitting at his desk. He looks almost relieved when he sees me, which is odd.

I lift my chin at him in greeting. I don't feel like talking to anyone right now.

Sid gets to his feet. Tipping his head forward, he says, "Mr. Hunter, there's someone here to see you. Been waiting a long while."

My eyes follow the direction where Sid is looking, and I freeze on the spot.

Taylor.

chapter 34

I watch as Taylor slowly rises to her feet, standing up from the sofa in the building's lobby where she was sitting. Her eyes are fixed on me.

And I can't move. I'm frozen in place, and my heart is trying to kick its way out of my chest and get to her.

She's here. That has to be a good sign, right?

You thought that the last time when she showed up at Cam's Bar.

Look how that turned out.

Taking a deep breath, I force my feet to move, and I start walking toward her.

My insides are trembling. I've never felt as fucking afraid as I do right now.

This tiny, beautiful woman in front of me has reduced me to a mess of emotions and put me on the verge of a fucking nervous breakdown.

But I still want more of her. I will always want her.

I stop a few feet away.

"Hey," she says, her voice soft, small.

She's holding her hands in front of her stomach, wringing them, like she's anxious. My eyes go from her hands to her suitcase sitting by her feet and finally back to her face.

I part my dry lips. "I-I was…I've been at the airport. Looking for you. I thought…" My eyes go to her suitcase again. "The hospital called, said you'd left. And you checked out of the hotel." I meet back with her eyes. "I thought you were leaving. I thought you were going…home."

Her eyes drift away from my face. "I was…I am."

My heart drops, feeling like it's been sucker-punched. "Taylor."

I make a move toward her. She lifts a hand, stopping me in my tracks.

"Let me finish, please," she says.

Her eyes are filled with so much emotion that I can't decipher where her head is at or what she's thinking right now.

And I want to argue. Everything inside me is telling me to argue, to fight for her…but she's asked for the chance to talk. I'll give it to her, and then I'll argue her down on everything she has said. Because I'm not letting her leave here. And I'm not walking away this time.

I will not let her die. I'm fighting for her. And I'll fight dirty if I have to.

So, I say nothing and give a nod of my head in response.

She takes a deep breath, almost like she's preparing to say something, and my insides tighten.

She clasps her hands together in front of her. "I know I've already said I'm sorry to you a million times, but I am." Her eyes come to mine. "I'm so sorry. I need you to know that. And I need you to know that I never intentionally meant to lie to you about being sick. I mean, I did lie, but it was before we were…" She gestures a hand between us. "I didn't know then that you were going to become as important to me as you are, and then when I did realize…I guess I was afraid." She wraps her arms over her stomach.

"Afraid that if you knew the truth about how I felt about you, it would change things, change my mind about what I had to do…" Her eyes lower, her hands dropping by her sides. "And you did—you *have* changed things. You've changed me."

She blows out a breath. I'm holding mine.

"I've kept a lot of things from you, Liam. Things I shouldn't have kept from you. And you know everything now, except for this one thing. The only thing that matters now. And I knew I couldn't go without telling you."

Her impossibly beautiful eyes lift back to mine. "I love you. I'm *in love* with you. I have been for a while now." She exhales softly. "Falling in love might not have been on my list…but I'm so glad I fell with you, Liam."

She's in love with me.

I don't know whether to fall to my knees at her feet or start crying like a fucking baby.

"I needed you to know that," she continues. "From the moment I realized how I felt, I thought that telling you would be the wrong thing to do. Now, I know that keeping it from you was wrong. And I came here to say that and to ask…"

She's wringing her hands again, and I just want to take hold of them. Hold them in mine and never let go. Never let her go again.

What do you need to ask, baby? Anything, and it's yours.

"Well…I came to see if your offer still stands."

She's staring at me, and I know she's waiting for me to speak, but my throat is clogged up with her words.

I clear my throat. "What offer?" *Whatever it is, it's yes, babe.*

So long as she's not asking me to watch her die because, that, I won't do.

"When you asked me to stay here. To live here. With you. I was wondering…if that still stands." She exhales softly. "Before, when I said that I was going home, I meant you, Hunter. Home to me now is where you are. I am coming home to you."

"But I thought…"

"I changed my mind." She smiles, and it slays me. Fucking slays me. "Well, if you still want me, that is…"

I don't let her say any more. She doesn't need to say more.

I clear the distance between us. Then, her face is in my hands, and I'm kissing her.

Kissing her like I've never kissed her before.

Every feeling I have for her is poured into this kiss. I need her to know what I feel for her because words don't seem like enough right now.

Her hands grip ahold of my shirt, her fingers digging into my chest, as I taste her, hold her, feel her.

She's here and she's real and she's mine.

Breaking from her lips, breathing hard, I stare down into her blue eyes.

"So, is that a yes?" she whispers, biting down on her lower lip.

I press my forehead to hers, letting out a low laugh. "What do you think?"

She laughs softly. It's the sweetest fucking sound.

I wrap my arms around her, holding her tight. "I love you, babe. So fucking much."

"I love you, too." She presses her cheek to my chest, her arms coming around my waist.

I just hold her for a long moment, breathing her in, reminding myself that this is real. She's here.

But, as always, reality seeps in. The reality of her situation.

Taylor might be here right now, telling me she loves me and that she wants to stay with me, but she's sick. Really sick. And time isn't on our side.

Releasing her slightly, I stare down at her. "Why did you leave the hospital, babe?"

Her eyes lower. "I needed to see you."

"You could have called me."

She lifts her stare back to me. "The battery on my cell had died. My charger was at the hotel." She lifts her shoulders.

"You could have used a phone at the hospital." I'm not giving up here.

"I don't know your number. It's on my phone—you know, the one that died."

I chuckle, shaking my head. God, I've missed her sass. Okay, I'll give her that. "So, why did you check out of the hotel?"

She lets out a sigh. "Because I needed my stuff, Hunter. And it just made sense. I was due to check out of the hotel tomorrow anyway, and I was coming to see you tonight with the hope that you still wanted me."

"I want you." I cup her cheek in my hand.

She gives me a warm, loving smile. "So, I thought I could leave some of my things here instead of taking everything to the hospital with me."

My heart stills. "So, you are planning on going back to the hospital?"

Her stare catches and holds mine. "Yes."

She says yes, but I can still see that darkness called guilt lining her eyes.

"And the surgery?"

"I'll have it done," she says the words quietly.

And she's saying them, but I can hear the doubt and anguish still in her voice.

But she's saying she'll have it done, so I'll take whatever I can to keep her healthy and alive and with me.

"But, Hunter, you have to know…the surgery isn't a guarantee. I've left it so long now, and—"

"Shh." I press my lips to her forehead. "I'll get you the best doctors, Boston. You'll get through this. You'll be fine. And I'll be with you the whole time."

She blinks up at me. "Holding my hand?"

I smile gently. "If that's what you need."

"I just need you."

"Right back at you, babe." I capture her lips with mine again, kissing her. Moving from her mouth, I kiss her cheek, her forehead, down her nose, and back to her lips. "I love you."

She runs her fingers through my hair. "And I love you."

I kiss her one last time, and then I reluctantly break away. I might want to stay like this with her forever, but in reality, she needs to go back to the hospital.

Taylor might look okay on the outside, but I know the inside is a very different story.

"We need to think about moving. I need to get you back to the hospital."

"Not just yet." She wraps her arms around me, pressing her face into my chest, holding me tight.

"Babe…" I take hold of her arms, pulling them from around me. Then, I bring my hands up to cup her face.

Her eyes are closed.

"Open your eyes," I gently command.

She sighs, and there's a moment of reluctance before she blinks them open.

"You need to go to the hospital."

"I know. And I will go back. I just want a little more time with you before I do."

"Boston…" I don't want to say that time isn't something we have right now. So, instead, I say, "I'll be there with you the whole time. I'm not leaving you. We'll be together at the hospital."

"Not the whole time."

I know she's thinking of the surgery. I'm thinking of the surgery.

I'm afraid for her. I'm afraid for me. But she has to get through this because, for me, there isn't a world where Taylor isn't breathing and alive and with me.

"I'll be with you right until it's time, and then I'll be there when you open your eyes. I need you healthy, babe, and the only way that will happen is if I get you back to the hospital. And, as soon as you're well, I'll take you on a holiday, and we can spend every second of every day together. And, after that, we can spend our lives together."

"You mean that?"

"I never say anything I don't mean. Especially with you."

She's staring into my eyes. Emotions are moving so quickly through them that I can't grab ahold of one.

"Okay," she breathes. "Let's go to the hospital."

"Well, we can either take a cab, or I can call Paul and have him drive us."

"Where's your car?"

"It's currently sitting at Heathrow Airport with a clamp on the wheel."

Her eyes round. "Seriously?"

"Yeah." I chuckle.

But she's not laughing. She looks sad.

"Hey, what's up?"

"It's my fault." Her tone dips along with her eyes.

I place my fingers under her chin and tilt her face up to mine. "What's your fault?"

"Your car getting clamped."

"And why do you say that?"

"Because you went to the airport, looking for me."

"Hush." I kiss her on the lips. "It's just a clamp."

"On a million-dollar car."

One point seven million, but who's counting? "Boston, the car's not damaged. It's fine. And I'll be getting her back tomorrow. Now, are we getting a cab, or am I calling Paul?"

"Call Paul."

"Okay." I lead her back over to the sofa.

She sits down. I get my phone out of my pocket and take the seat beside her.

"I can't believe your car got clamped." Apparently, she's still on that.

I guess it is better than talking about where we're about to go and how difficult these next few days…weeks are going to be.

"Well, I did leave it in a no-parking zone." I shrug. "They probably did me a favor by clamping it. It would probably have gotten stolen, if not."

"I can't believe how blasé you're being about it."

"It's only a car."

"An expensive car."

"And you're worth more."

Her eyes soften on me, and she leans in close, kissing me with a featherlight brush over my lips. "I love you," she says the words like she needs to keep saying them to make it real.

And I'm far from complaining.

For that time, thinking Taylor didn't feel the same as I did about her…it was fucking torture.

To know she loves me…is the best feeling in the world.

"I love you, too, Boston. Now, stop trying to distract me with your hot mouth, and let me call Paul."

"I wasn't trying to distract you."

I lift a brow, and she laughs.

"Okay, maybe I was trying to distract you a little bit." Grinning, she shows an inch with her thumb and forefinger.

Shaking my head, I laugh.

Fuck, it feels good to laugh.

I put my arm around her shoulder, pulling her to me. She lays her head on my shoulder.

I call Paul, and he answers on the first ring. I tell him to come and pick us up from my apartment.

"Paul will be here in fifteen minutes," I tell Taylor as I hang up the phone. I slide it back into my pocket.

She doesn't say anything. And I notice how tense her body is with her fingers curled up in her lap.

"Hey." I lift the shoulder her head is on, gently nudging her.

She slowly lifts her head and looks at me. Her eyes are shimmering with tears.

"Babe?"

She shuts her eyes and lets out a ragged breath. "I'm afraid, Hunter."

A vise clamps itself around my chest and squeezes hard.

Turning to her, I take her face in my hands. "Don't be. There's nothing to be afraid of. I'm here. And I'll be here with you the whole time. I'll keep you safe. I will *always* keep you safe."

But that's a lie.

Not that I won't keep her safe because I will. I'll always do everything in my power to keep Taylor safe.

But this…this is out of my hands, and that scares me.

No, fuck *scared*. It terrifies me.

Part of me is afraid that the surgery won't work. That, after all of this, I will end up losing her anyway.

But I don't vocalize it. I hide it.

And, when she opens her eyes and gives me a weak smile, I return that smile, forcing mine to be stronger. All the while, I conceal my fears as I lean close and kiss her forehead one last time.

chapter 35

The room is dark, except for the soft glow coming from the television across the room.

We're back to where we were last night—Taylor in a hospital bed and me by her side. But I'm sitting this time, not pacing around the room, pleading with her to live.

The same, but everything has changed.

I've arranged for her to have the best brain surgeon in England to come to do her surgery, and it's scheduled for first thing in the morning.

Also, we're in a different hospital room than the one Taylor was in last night. I want her to be comfortable. So, I had them put her in a private room, the best they have.

Donations to the hospital go a long way in getting what you want.

Money brings power, and I have a lot of both, so I will use all of it, if necessary, to ensure Taylor gets better.

Something else that's different now...I know she loves me.

She loves me, and we're together.

And we'll be starting our life together as soon as she's better.

She is going to get better.

I glance back at her face. Her eyes are closed.

I pick up the remote control from the bed and turn off the television. The moon is full and bright, giving some light to the room.

I stare out the window, up at the moon and the stars glittering around it.

I'm not a religious man. I've never been the kind of man who prays, but right now, I'm praying.

Don't take her. Please.

Turning my chair to face Taylor's bed, I lean over, resting my arms on the bed, and I gently press my face into her stomach.

I inhale her scent. She smells of everything I want.

Her. I just want her.

Fingers touch my head, slightly startling me.

"I thought you were sleeping," I say against her stomach.

"Just resting a moment. Talk to me, Hunter." Her voice is a soft whisper.

I turn my head, resting my cheek against her stomach, so I can look at her face. Even in the muted darkness, I can see how beautiful she is. I will never tire of looking at her.

"What do you want me to talk about?"

"Anything…but not about what's going to happen tomorrow. Don't talk about that."

The surgery.

My mind goes blank as I try to think of something to say. Because the surgery is all I can think of.

"Nothing to say?" Her lips lift into a smile. "Not like you, Hunter."

"Your beauty has stolen all my words."

"Did you steal that line from a book?"

"Probably." I grin.

Her fingers start gently sifting through my hair. "Tell me about the time you sang to that girl. The one you were trying to win back."

"I thought Cam and Eddie told you all the gory details?"

"They did, and it made me laugh. I want you to tell me, so I can laugh again."

God, I want to hear her laugh. More than anything, I want to make her happy.

I want her to be healthy and happy.

But I don't have the power to make her healthy. And I hate the way that makes me feel.

Weak and powerless.

But, for her, I shove my feelings aside and decide on the best and quickest way to make her laugh.

I start singing the words to "I Want It That Way."

She laughs, and it's fucking music to my ears.

"You're crazy," she tells me.

"Crazy about you."

My eyes meet with hers. She's smiling, but even in this darkness, I can tell she's not happy. She's afraid. And it hurts to know that there's nothing I can do to eradicate that fear.

"You shouldn't sing that song to me, Hunter. That's your breakup song with another girl. It's not our song."

"We have a song?"

"We do." She smiles. This one seems more genuine. It reaches all the way to her eyes.

That smile makes my heart beat faster.

"Are you going to let me in on what our song is?"

"'If You're Not the One'—that's our song. So, if you're going to sing to me, you sing that to me."

"If You're Not the One" was the song that accidentally playing on repeat when I asked her to stay in London with me. The night when she told me she didn't love me and then ran out of my apartment. The night that was the start of my world spiraling out of control.

Two nights ago.

How was that only two nights ago?

"I don't know if that's our song, babe…"

Her fingers stop moving through my hair. "You told me you loved me for the first time while that song was playing."

"You left me while that song was playing."

Her hand slips from my hair. She goes silent, and I worry that I've upset her.

Fuck. Upsetting her is the last thing I want to do.

I look back at her face. Her eyes are on the ceiling.

"Taylor…"

"You're right. It was a stupid thing to say."

"I'm being stupid. It doesn't matter that you didn't stay then. It matters that you're here now."

That's all I care about.

Her eyes drift back to mine. There are so many emotions in them that I feel them wrap around my chest and clamp down tight, making it hard to breathe.

"I wanted to stay," she whispers. "In that moment, when you asked me to stay with you, I wanted to say yes so very badly. I wanted to tell you I loved you. Because I did love you then and before, and I love you now."

I suck in air. "I know," I say, pressing my face back into her stomach.

I'm such a fucking idiot. Why did I have to say that about the song? It's important to her, so it should be important to me. And it is.

Her hand comes back to my hair, her fingers slipping into the strands. "We'll get our song one day," she says softly.

"No." I turn my cheek back to her stomach. "You're right. It is ours. It might not be perfect…but it's ours. Only

I can't sing it to you because I don't know all the words."
I grin.

Laughter falls from her lips, and my heart feels light
again.

"Play it to me?" she suggests.

Sitting up, I get my phone from my pocket and find the
song in my playlist. I press play and set my phone on the
bed beside her. Then, I lay my cheek back on her stomach,
and I stare up at her face while our song plays.

"What changed your mind?" I ask quietly.

Her eyes come back to mine, and I know I don't need
to elaborate because I see the understanding in them. She
knows I'm asking about having the surgery.

"You. I couldn't stop thinking about you after you left.
The things you said. And my heart…she's kind of weak
when it comes to you." She smiles sadly. "Also…Eddie
came to see me."

"Eddie?" I sit up. "He came to the hospital to
see you?"

"About an hour after you'd left, he turned up. He said
he was due to start his shift. Wanted to check in on me. See
how I was doing."

"And what else did he say?"

Her eyes come to mine. "He told me that he
knew…what I was planning to do."

"I'm sorry." I push a hand through my hair. "I was a
mess. I needed someone to talk to. Cam and Eddie are my
best friends."

"It's fine. I don't mind that you told them. It was the
truth."

Was being the operative word, thankfully.

"So, what did Eddie say?" I ask, laying my head back
down on her stomach.

Her hand comes back down to play with my hair. "He
didn't beat around the bush. He was pretty straight to the
point, but that was okay because I think it was what I

needed." She blows out a breath. "He said that we all die someday, under different circumstances, and he asked me why my day had to be today—figuratively speaking. He knew that I wanted to be with my family, but he said that my family would want me to live, and that...I would be with them one day. It just didn't have to be right now. That I had someone here, who loved me." Her eyes soften on mine. "And he said to be loved by you...that was worth fighting for. Life was worth fighting for."

My throat feels all choked up. "What else did he say?"

"Not much. He left soon after that."

I don't care that Eddie's words were the turning point for her. I just care that she changed her mind. I guess, sometimes, it takes someone on the outside to make you see sense.

Guess I owe Eddie a pint. Or maybe his own private jet.

"After Eddie left, I couldn't get his words out of my head and all the things that you had said to me...knowing that you love me. And knowing that I love you and you didn't know...I just had to see you. Tell you that. I guess..." She bites her lip. "I wasn't a hundred percent convinced that I wasn't still going to go through with it...but then, when you walked in and I saw you standing there, I just knew that I couldn't leave you again. I know that makes me selfish."

I lift my head. "Wanting to live isn't selfish."

Her head tips back, her eyes going to the ceiling.

"Babe, what happened to your family...it wasn't your fault. You have to know that."

She exhales a sad breath. "I want to believe that...and I hear everything that you're saying...but I just don't feel it in here." She touches her hand to her chest, over where her heart lies.

"After you lost your family, did you talk to anyone?"

She brings her eyes to mine. "Like a therapist?"

"Yeah, like a therapist or a grief counselor."

Turning her face to the window, she shakes her head.

She's been struggling through this alone for all this time. The thought of her alone and hurting kills me.

"Boston…I think talking to someone who understands these kinds of things would be a good idea. I saw a grief counselor after my mum died. It helped me a lot."

She blows out a tired-sounding breath. "Yeah, I guess I could talk to someone."

After the surgery and she's better, I'll arrange for her to see a therapist. I will do anything to help her.

She takes a breath, and it sounds shaky.

"I'm sorry," she whispers.

I hear tears in her voice, and it guts me.

"For not telling you I was sick right from the start."

She turns her face back to mine, and I see those tears shimmering in her eyes.

"I know it was wrong of me, not telling you, but…" She nervously bites her lip. "Well, a part of me doesn't regret not telling you, and I know how awful that sounds. But it's because…well, maybe if I had told you from the start, you wouldn't have stayed."

"Boston"—I brush my fingers over her cheek—"I would have stayed." I tell her this with the certainty I know I feel. "I would have stayed because I'm pretty sure I was in love with you from the moment you surprise-kissed me on the plane. You had me instantly. I wasn't going anywhere then…and I'm not going anywhere now."

I run my thumb over her brow, her eyes closing as I do.

The song has long since come to an end. I pick my phone up, moving it to the nightstand by the bed.

"You're tired. You should get some sleep. I'll be here when you wake up."

"Sleep with me." She moves over in the bed, pulling the blanket back.

I don't need a second invitation. I kick my shoes off and climb into bed beside her.

She pulls the covers over us both and lays her head against my chest. I put my arm around her and start playing with her hair.

"Hunter, do you think they'll take my earrings out for surgery?" Her fingers touch the airplane earrings that I bought her.

"I don't know, babe. Maybe."

"I hope not. I don't want the holes to heal over. It kinda hurt when I had them done. I don't want to go through that pain again."

I chuckle. My girl is about to have major surgery, and she's worried about having her ears pierced again. Now, that's the Boston I've come to know and love.

And at least she's talking like she intends to come back. It's a far cry from where we were this time last night.

And her coming back…well, that's all I need to hear from her right now.

She goes quiet, her body relaxing into mine, and then, out of nowhere, she tenses up.

"Hunter…I have to tell you something."

My heart pauses. "What?"

She tilts her head back, staring up into my face, and she bites her lip so hard that I'm worried she's drawn blood.

"I can't have children," she blurts out. "Not in the proper way. The radiation therapy I had because of the first tumor made me infertile. I did have some eggs frozen back then, so I can have children but not in the regular way. Not that I think you and I are going to have kids, but I just thought you should know what you're getting into."

"Babe"—I curl my hand around her cheek—"it doesn't matter to me. All I want is you. Anything that comes after will be a bonus. But it's not a bonus I need."

"You sure?" she whispers.

"I'm sure. Now, sleep."

I'd guessed that she might be infertile, and I was telling the truth when I said it didn't matter. Do I want kids someday? Yeah, I guess so. But I can live without having them.

I can't live without her.

She shuts her eyes and lowers her head back down to my chest. I snuggle down in bed, putting my nose close to her hair. I breathe her scent in.

"I'm going to lose my hair. They'll shave a section off for the surgery, and the rest will fall out with the radiation therapy."

I figured that as well.

"It doesn't matter to me."

"But I like my pink hair."

"When it grows back, you can dye it pink again."

"Hmm. I guess."

Silence.

"Hunter…are you sure it won't bother you if I'm bald?"

"If losing your hair means you get better and I get to have a lifetime with you, then, yeah, babe, I'm sure."

"But I have a weird-shaped head."

"So, I'll buy you a head scarf."

She laughs softly, lightly slapping me on the stomach. "Ass."

"And you love me for it." I chuckle.

"True."

"Now, quit stalling, and get some sleep, Boston."

"So bossy, Hunter."

"You love that about me as well."

She's silent for a long moment. I look down and see her eyes are closed.

She looks so beautiful. She will always be beautiful to me, no matter what.

Closing my own eyes, I rest my head back into the pillow.

"Hunter?" she murmurs, her voice sounding sleepy.

"Mmhmm?"

"I love everything about you. Even your airplanes."

A smile pushes at my lips as tears prick my eyes at the same time. "And I love everything about you, Boston."

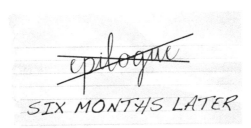

epilogue

SIX MONTHS LATER

"If I should die and leave you

Be not like the others, quick undone

Who keep long vigils by the silent

dust and weep.

"For my sake turn to life and smile

Nerving thy heart and trembling

hand to comfort weaker souls than thee.

Complete these unfinished tasks of mine

And I perchance may therein comfort thee."

Reverend Gray gently closes the sermon book in his hand, looking out over the church.

"Now, let us end the service with the Lord's Prayer." He bows his head and begins praying, "Our Father, who art in heaven…"

I stare at the coffin on its stand behind where Reverend Gray is reciting the prayer.

There's heaviness in my heart. A sadness in my soul.

It hurts.

I let my eyes down, my head bowing, as I join in the prayer.

Then, I feel a hand curl around mine, and it soothes the sadness away.

My eyes lift, meeting with a set of beautiful blue eyes.

The only eyes I ever want to look into.

Taylor smiles softly at me. Her eyes mirror my sadness. Her precious head is covered with a black headscarf to hide the hair loss that bothers her so much. It doesn't bother me because that gone hair means that she's still here. Solid and breathing.

She fought that brain tumor like a motherfucker. *Sorry, God.* But she did, and she won.

We got the all-clear two weeks ago. We're not out of the woods completely. She has another checkup in another six months, but for now, the tumor is gone, and my girl is on the mend.

Months of radiation therapy, watching it wreck her body while healing her brain…was hard. But she did it, and she's here.

I just hate that we're here now. That we've lost someone else whom we love.

Archie suddenly passed away a week to the day after we had gotten the all-clear on Taylor. He'd had a stroke. It had come out of nowhere and taken him with it.

"For thine is the kingdom, the power, and the glory, forever and ever. Amen," Reverend Gray ends the prayer.

I gently squeeze Taylor's hand, and then I turn to my grandpa, who is standing beside me. He's been affected by Archie's passing the most.

Archie might have been his employee for the better part of twenty-five years, but he was my grandpa's friend more.

I press my hand to his shoulder. "You doing okay, Grandpa?" I ask quietly.

He meets my eyes and nods.

The service over, we exit the church. Grandpa is the first to leave. We were the only family Archie had. He was married many years ago, but he lost his wife young, like Grandpa did with my grandma. Archie didn't have any children. So, we were his family.

As I hold Taylor's hand, we follow behind my grandpa, walking down the aisle.

"I'm just going to thank Reverend Gray for the service," Grandpa tells me, stopping by the door.

"We'll wait in the car for you."

Taylor and I walk out into the warm sunshine.

"Thanks for coming with me today," I say to her as we leave the churchyard, heading for the car.

She nudges my arm with her shoulder. "Don't thank me. I loved Archie, too, you know."

I press a kiss to the top of her head. "I know, babe."

After Taylor's surgery and recovery, once she was out of the hospital, we decided it would be best if we moved into Hunter Hall. I still had to work. Owning a company sadly doesn't mean I get to have forever off. I didn't want Taylor at the apartment, alone, during the day, and she needed care after the radiation therapy. We discussed hiring a nurse, but Grandpa said she needed to be with family. So, we moved into Hunter Hall, and Grandpa and Archie took care of her.

Losing Archie has been a shock of the worst kind. I'd known him since I was a kid. His stroke and subsequent passing took us by surprise, and it's been especially hard for Grandpa.

But I'm starting to realize that death is as much a part of life as living is.

So long as I don't lose Taylor or Grandpa anytime soon, I can handle it.

We had planned to move back to my—our—apartment in London once Taylor's radiation therapy had come to an end. But, now, with Archie gone, we've decided to stay at Hunter Hall for the foreseeable future. I don't want Grandpa to be alone, and neither does Taylor. And, honestly, Hunter Hall is the only place that's ever really felt like home for me.

I'll just keep commuting into London when I need to be there for business.

And staying here works well, as Taylor is hoping to be accepted to Oxford for a master's in English literature. She hopes to one day become a lecturer just like her dad was.

She put her application in a few weeks ago, so now, we just have to wait.

I'm confident she'll get in because she's smart.

But, really, all I care about is that she's looking to the future, a future with me.

I open the passenger door for Taylor and wait until she's in before I shut the door behind her. I get in the driver's side, and we wait for my grandpa. He climbs in the backseat a few minutes later.

I turn the engine on, and we head back to Hunter Hall for the wake where we'll celebrate Archie's life with good food and good friends.

It's late in the evening. The wake ended hours ago. Grandpa went up to bed early.

Taylor and I decided to get an early night, too. It's been an emotionally tiring day, and I don't want her overdoing herself. She might have the all-clear, but I still want her to take things easy.

I've just gotten out of the shower, and I'm walking back into the bedroom, a towel around my waist.

I see Taylor sitting in the middle of our bed, legs crossed, a notepad in her lap, and she's scribbling away. Her headscarf is still on. It bothers me that she feels the need to cover her head when it's just her and me.

"What are you doing?" I ask.

She lifts her head, smiling at me. "I'm writing a new list."

"Oh, yeah?"

Pulling the towel from my waist, I see her eyes come straight to my nakedness. Suppressing a grin, I rub the towel over my wet hair and toss it over the back of a chair. I grab some pajama pants and pull them on.

I go and sit down on the bed next to her and look over her shoulder at her list. The title alone makes me smile.

> *Things to Do with Liam (Even If He's Already Done Them)*

"You're cute." I rest my chin on her shoulder.

Smiling, she glances back at me. "You're kinda cute yourself, Hunter." She presses a kiss to the tip of my nose and then turns her eyes back to her list.

I look down at the list. "*Go to France,*" I say, reading the first thing on there.

"I've never been," she tells me.

"I'll take you tomorrow."

Chuckling, she shakes her head.

She thinks I'm kidding. Well, she'll be surprised when she finds herself in Paris tomorrow night, eating dinner on the Champs-Élysées.

Lifting my chin from her shoulder, I slide my hands around her waist, linking my fingers over her stomach. "*Learn to drive, so Liam doesn't have to drive me everywhere,*" I say, reading the next thing on her list. "But I like driving you everywhere."

"I know…but I'd like to get my license, so I can drive you around sometimes."

"Okay, so I'll teach you to drive."

She glances back at me again. "You think that's a good idea? Don't people who know each other intimately end up fighting when they're teaching the other one how to drive?"

"So we fight while I'm teaching you how to drive. Just think of the smoking-hot make-up sex we can have in the backseat afterward."

Her gaze slides back to mine. "You make a good point there, Hunter. Guess you're teaching me how to drive." She winks and starts chewing on the end of the pen.

And, now, I can't stop staring at her lips. I really want them on my cock right now.

And, hello, there he is, hard and ready to play.

I slip my hand upward, cupping one of her tits through her pajama top.

She moans softly, tipping her head back on my shoulder.

I brush my mouth over her ear, loving the way she shudders against me.

Massaging her tit, rolling her nipple between my forefinger and thumb, I continue reading her list, enjoying the gentle moans escaping her, "*Dye my hair pink again once it grows back.* Um, Boston, I hope to fuck that you don't expect me to dye my hair pink."

She giggles. "I think you'd look good with pink hair."

I press a kiss to her ear. "I love you, Boston, a fuck of a lot, but no fucking way am I dyeing my hair pink." I read the next thing on the list, "*Ears re-pierced, and get something else pierced.*"

Taylor had to have her earrings removed for the surgery, and the holes closed up, much to her disappointment.

"Just so you know, babe, I'm not getting my ears pierced." I give her nipple a pinch.

She laughs and squirms against me. "Okay, so no ear-piercing for you."

"So, what else are you thinking of getting pierced?" I ask her.

"I don't know yet." She shrugs.

My hand leaving her tit, I slide it down her stomach and cup her pussy through her pajama bottoms. "Well, if I have a vote in this, I say a clit piercing."

She sits up, turning to me, forcing my hand to drop from my happy place.

"You want me to have my clit pierced?" She's frowning and not looking totally onboard with this suggestion.

"I heard it makes orgasms more intense." I lift a shoulder, smiling.

"And where did you hear that?"

"I do read, Boston."

"What? Porn magazines?"

"Hey! There are some really good pieces of literature in porn magazines."

"Clearly," she deadpans.

I laugh.

And then she just has to throw out, "Oh, and, Hunter, you do realize that if I have my clit pierced, that means no sex for a significant period of time while it heals. Also, if I'm having my clit pierced, I totally expect you to get your dick pierced."

A needle in my dick…

"Okay, so no piercing of the genitalia."

She laughs loudly; it comes from deep within her. And I fucking love the sound. I'll never tire of hearing her laughter.

"Okay, so what's next on the list?" I take the notepad from her hand, scanning down it. I look up at her, surprised. "*Learn to fly a plane.* You want to learn to fly?"

"Well, you love it." She shrugs, the tops of her cheeks turning pink. "And I figured it must be better to be in control of the plane than sitting there in the passenger seat, waiting to plunge to my death."

I chuckle. Gotta love her way of thinking.

"You don't want me to teach you, do you?" I ask her.

"I didn't, but I'm offended that I'm hearing a no in there."

"Boston, again, I love you, but no way am I teaching you how to fly. Teaching you to drive is one thing, but flying…no fucking way. I'll get you a proper instructor."

"I'll try not to be offended by that." She snatches the notepad off me, but I can tell she's not being serious. The smile forcing its way onto her lips is giving her away.

"You shouldn't be. I mean it in the nicest possible way." I chuckle, leaning in to kiss her.

She presses her hand against my chest, but there's no real resistance from her. "You're an ass," she says when my lips are millimeters from hers.

"Yeah, yeah, you love my ass. I already know that." Then, I kiss her, hot and hard.

I release her mouth as quickly as I took it, loving the dazed look in her eyes.

While she's distracted, I take the list back from her hand. There's nothing else on the list after *Learn to fly a plane.*

"That's all you've got?" I say.

She blinks. "Um, yeah, that's all I've got so far. Why? Is there something you've thought of?"

There is. It's something I've been thinking of for quite a while.

Without saying anything, I take the pen from her hand, and I write my thing to do at the top of her list because that's exactly where it belongs.

I hand the notepad back to her, my heart stepping up tempo, as I watch her eyes scan the paper, finding what I've written. I love the way her lips curve up into a beautiful smile.

"Ask Liam to marry me." She laughs, throwing her head back. Her tone is teasing when she says, "Confident much?"

I shrug and then take the notepad back from her. I write something else next to it.

Okay, so this isn't how I planned for this to go, but I'm kind of flying by the seat of my pants here. And fuck if it doesn't feel right. Everything feels right with her.

I turn the notepad back to her.

She reads the words I've just written. "Or say yes when the very-awesome-in-bed and extraordinarily handsome Liam Hunter asks me to marry him." She laughs again, because she thinks I'm winding her up.

I want her to think I'm winding her up. Because I want to see the shock on her face when she realizes that I'm being serious.

Putting the notepad and pen down on the bed, I shift back and open the drawer on my nightstand. Reaching to the back, I curl my fingers around the box that I've been hiding there for quite a while now. Closing the drawer, I take a deep breath, and then I turn back to her and hold the box out in my open palm.

Her eyes widen, and my heart stutters.

"Is…that…" Her wide eyes lift to mine. "Hunter…are earrings in that box?"

I slowly shake my head. "Not this time, babe."

She reaches for it, her fingers trembling. She pops open the top and gasps.

"It was my grandmother's."

"It's beautiful." She's staring down at it.

I wet my dry lips with my tongue. "It's yours, if you want it, but…if you take this ring, it means you're saying yes to me."

"And what would I be saying yes to?" Her eyes lift, her words are careful.

She knows what I'm asking; she just wants me to say the words. And she deserves those words and so much more.

"Marrying me."

"Are you asking or telling?" Her lips tip up at the corners.

"Both." I laugh softly. Then, I turn serious. "Marry me." I take my grandmother's ring from the box and hold it up between us.

Her eyes go back to the ring for what feels like a really fucking long time.

Then, I watch, nervous as hell, as she picks up the notepad and pen. She holds it at an angle, so I can't see what she's writing.

My heart is pounding so hard in my chest that I'm pretty sure I've cracked a rib. But I don't care. All I care about is what she's about to tell me.

Taylor puts the pen down and looks back at me, staring into my eyes.

I see what's in hers. I see her answer.

She turns the notepad around.

"*Yes*," I whisper, my heart soaring, as I read the word she's written…the word I see clear in her eyes.

"Yes." She smiles.

And my world is complete.

I take that notepad from her hand and toss it on the bed. I slip the ring onto her finger, and then I kiss her like there's no tomorrow.

Only there is a tomorrow and a lot of tomorrows to come after it.

Because there is no ending for Taylor and me. Only me and her and a lifetime of possibilities.

And a list.

Our list.

And it's a list that will never end because we'll keep adding to it, and we'll keep living our adventure together.

Forever.

acknowledgments

BEFORE I GET TO GIVING MY THANKS to anyone else, I want to say the biggest thank you to all the bloggers and readers, who help spread the word about my books. I write the books, but it's you guys who make it possible for me to keep doing so. Thank you a million times over.

I may write the books, but it isn't a solo endeavor. There are people behind the scenes who help work and shape my words into the books you read. I'm incredibly lucky to work with people like Sali Benbow-Powers—Queen Beta Reader! Jovana Shirley—Queen Editor! Najla Qamber—Queen Cover Designer! You three make my books become the very best they can be.

Trishy, you're the best long-distance friend a girl could ask for. Thank you for reading my work and for always giving me the honest feedback that I need even if I don't always want to hear it!

Jodi Maliszewski, asking you to read *The Ending I Want* as I was writing it was the best decision ever. Seriously, you can brighten the darkest day, and somehow, you made writing a sad story fun. Don't ever stop being you.

My husband, Craig, who I couldn't do any of this without, and my children, simply for being you. You three truly are the best people I know.

And I just want to put in a note before I go. Writing *The Ending I Want* has been a cathartic and exhausting process for me, but I have loved every second of writing it. I relate to this story more than any of the stories that I've written before. Maybe that's because there's a piece of me in this book. And not in Taylor having a brain tumor because, fortunately, I've never had to endure anything like that. But, for me, it was the need to feel free from something that has crippled me for many years, just like Taylor is crippled by her own pain. Taylor wanted to die to be free. I never wanted to die, but I did want to be free in a way that's hard to explain. But, now, after years of feeling trapped by my demons, by things that have held me back in life, I've found a way to get the freedom I needed. I'm still a work in progress, but I'm working better now than I ever did before. Just saying this cryptic stuff out loud is a big step for me. So, writing Taylor in the way I did was a big deal for me. I really hope that you loved this story and see strength in Taylor's choices rather than weakness.

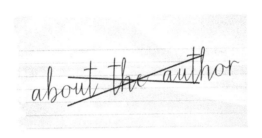

about the author

SAMANTHA TOWLE is a *New York Times*, *USA Today*, and *Wall Street Journal* bestselling author. She began her first novel in 2008 while on maternity leave. She completed the manuscript five months later and hasn't stopped writing since.

She is the author of contemporary romances, The Storm Series, The Revved Series, and standalones, *Trouble* and *When I Was Yours*. She has also written paranormal romances, *The Bringer* and The Alexandra Jones Series, all penned to tunes of The Killers, Kings of Leon, Adele, The Doors, Oasis, Fleetwood Mac, Lana Del Rey, and more of her favorite musicians.

A native of Hull and a graduate of Salford University, she lives with her husband, Craig, in East Yorkshire with their son and daughter.

Made in United States
North Haven, CT
06 April 2022

17985896R00232